LOVERS MEETING

Also by Mollie Hardwick

Beauty's Daughter

The Duchess of Duke Street

Upstairs, Downstairs Three: The Years of Change

The War To End War (Upstairs, Downstairs)

The World of Upstairs, Downstairs

LOVERS MEETING

A novel by

MOLLIE HARDWICK

ST. MARTIN'S PRESS   NEW YORK

C. 1

BL

CONTENTS

BOOK ONE: THE GREEN CURTAIN RISES   7
OVERTURE   9
CHAPTER ONE: *Harlequin Romeo*   11
CHAPTER TWO: *Cat Scene*   26
CHAPTER THREE: *Columbine Loses Her Heart*   42
CHAPTER FOUR: *The Plans of Pantaloon*   61
CHAPTER FIVE: *Enter Dandy Lover*   82
CHAPTER SIX: *The Wooing of Columbine*   101

BOOK TWO: DARK SCENE   117
CHAPTER SEVEN: *The Trap*   119
CHAPTER EIGHT: *The Grave-trap*   134
CHAPTER NINE: *The Love-philtre*   148
CHAPTER TEN: *Columbine Out of Her Element*   162
CHAPTER ELEVEN: *Scene, A Village Green*   176
CHAPTER TWELVE: *Columbine In Castle Dangerous*   191

BOOK THREE: HARLEQUIN BY MOONSHINE   209
CHAPTER THIRTEEN: *Travels and Trials*   211
CHAPTER FOURTEEN: *Crazy Jane*   229
CHAPTER FIFTEEN: *The Isles of Ebony*   244
CHAPTER SIXTEEN: *Harlequin Performs A Transformation*   257
CHAPTER SEVENTEEN: *Harlequin In His Element*   272

To the memory of

TOM ELLAR
Harlequin,
'Prince of our enchanted Islands'

and

JOSEPH GRIMALDI
'King of all the Clowns'

BOOK ONE

THE GREEN CURTAIN RISES

'Harlequin leaps, Columbine dances, and Pantaloon and Clown tumble through as many scrapes as would serve to damp the courage of the most resolute lovers.'

In the London of 1813, the lives of
four actors who meet during the production of an age-old pantomime become,
through their acquaintance with the
great clown Joseph Grimaldi, more
complex and interwoven.

OVERTURE

The night of 26 December 1813.

Tonight Londoners have forgotten the war with America, the war in Europe (and in any case the news is good, Bonaparte beaten by the Allies at Leipzig, his armies chased out of Spain by victorious Wellington). For it is the night when, replete with Christmas food and drink, those who can afford a shilling for the pit, or more for the comfort of a box, crowd into London's theatres for the first night of the most popular entertainment of the year: Pantomime, that strange, age-old mixture of drama and dance, wild farce and acrobatics, played out by characters the old Romans knew, and the Italian and French audiences of centuries ago: young Arlecchino who has become Harlequin, the magic-worker; Colombina, his sweetheart, now Columbine; Pantalone who is Pantaloon, her scheming old father; Capitano, her Lover, a Dandy; and the great grotesque whom the English call Clown, and love best of all.

Outside the Royalty Theatre, whose classic bulk rises majestically among tenements and shops, churches, inns and eating-houses, the air is heavy with fog and the blanket of smoke that lies over London's roofs in all but the finest weather. Round the corner from the theatre, in the fruit and vegetable market of Covent Garden, a great cobbled square that is a hubbub of activity by day, and in the narrow streets that surround it, beggars lurk or sleep uneasily in doorways. It is a good night for pickpockets, among the theatre-going crowds, and for burglars, who can go about their business confident that any house worth robbing will be empty, the family out enjoying itself.

And enjoy themselves they do, these hearty, loud-mouthed Regency audiences, ready to boo, hiss or cheer or blow kisses as the fancy takes them. On the backless benches of the pit lovers cuddle each other, children are dandled or suckled on ample laps,

9

pies and shrimps and ginger-beer and fruit are sold and noisily consumed, regardless of the action on the stage.

But now even the rowdiest are falling quiet, for the moment of magic is near.

CHAPTER ONE

Harlequin Romeo

The audience held its breath as the sounds in the orchestra pit changed from agitated flutterings to a soft, dirge-like melody. The basses and 'cellos mourned, two flutes sang a wistful descant, the powdered heads of their players invisible in the general gloom.

The stage was in blackness, for this was the Cat Scene, before the Transformation Scene which marked the second and most eagerly awaited part of the pantomime. The front-piece, in which a story was told to lead into the Harlequinade, had been *Harlequin Romeo*, a shortened version of *Romeo and Juliet* which owed very little to Shakespeare and a great deal to a hack-writer living in Bow Street. The plot was convenient, for it provided two young lovers, an ambitious old father determined to separate them, a dandified suitor (the unfortunate Count Paris), a clumsy Friar who always managed to do the wrong thing, and a Nurse who would eventually turn into the Benevolent Agent sympathetic to the lovers. Shakespeare really had been most obliging.

Before the dim outline of a cavern (which, of course, was a painted transparency) lay stretched the figures of dead Juliet in white, dead Romeo in black, and dead Paris in blue, while Old Capulet stood by with a dark lantern and the Friar's features and form were completely hidden in a cowled robe. From the shadows came a beautiful female voice, the voice of a tragedy queen.

A gloomy peace this morning with it brings;
The sun, for sorrow, will not show his head.
Here's a sad end to all our playmakings –
Juliet is stabbed, and Romeo poisoned.
Yet why should we make such a sorry end?
Lo! I, Queen Mab, the Fairy Queen, descend,

And bid begone! this place of dim night.
Welcome, thrice welcome, to my Halls of Light!
Hence, Tragic Muse, and snow-haired Father Time:
Hail Joy and Mirth – for this is Pantomime!

Suddenly the darkness was gone, the stage flooded with light, the tomb vanished, the mournful music changed to a merry jig, a whirring and clacking of machinery and a flurry of stage-hands behind scene-flats went unnoticed as the audience gasped with delighted astonishment. For Juliet was changed to Columbine in white satin and spangles, Romeo arisen as a chequer-suited Harlequin, slim as his own magic wand, masqued and mysterious, both poised for dancing, while from the robe and cowl of the Friar leapt the grotesque figure of Clown, in short puffed breeches, a doublet of scarlet dotted with yellow, and a bright blue tufted wig atop his white-and-red painted face, crying, with a screech of eldritch laughter, 'Here we are again! How are you tomorrow?' a familiar gag that was greeted with a roar of welcome by the audience. Paris, Juliet's lover, had been transmogrified into a dandy, ridiculously foppish in a costume flagrantly reminiscent of the Prince Regent at his dressiest, and Old Capulet had grown a stoop, a long pointed beard and a pigtail turned up behind. Above them, on a gilt throne suspended uneasily from the flies and swaying dangerously, sat Queen Mab, a regal lady in purple robes and a starry crown.

And behind them all glowed and glittered a sunscape of gold and jewels, emerald trees and artificial roses, real fountains and bright-coloured birds, backed with a bright blue sky, star-scattered. No one complained that stars and sun were out at the same time, for this was Boxing Night, when anything could happen. An equally blue stream of real water bore four stately swans, drawing, somewhat jerkily, a chariot of gilded basket-work in which a Fairy Personage smiled and nodded a head of bright tight yellow curls. Someone in the pit was heard to say that she was the image of dear Princess Charlotte.

The music was loud and joyous now, Harlequin and Columbine

wreathing and twining in their love-duet, fairies and sprites forming elaborate dancing figures around them. As they turned, leaped, wheeled, one of the ballet-girls stumbled and half-fell, to be caught by the hand and steadied.

She looked up, her large bright green eyes made huge by black outlining, the heart-shaped face glistening with pearl powder, smiling at her rescuer. He was a boy perhaps a few years older than herself, dressed as a moth, all in silver-grey, curling antennae rising from the hood that covered his hair. She had a fleeting impression of eyes that seemed silver-grey as well, the colour of deep water under a cloudy sky, and straight dark brows and a long sensitive mouth.

'Thanks,' she whispered, 'nearly went that time.' Their hands parted and he was lost in the dancing crowd, she in a pose down on one knee, pointing to Columbine, who was kissing her hands to Harlequin from a golden cloud.

And so they were met on stage, five people whose lives were to intermingle and change like the fantastic characters they played: a girl and a boy, a woman past her prime and a man with his pride in rags, a Clown with a heart already cracked, one day to be broken. Fate had chosen her cast for her own Harlequinade. Only one was missing.

The dark green curtain had swished down, its tarnished gold fringe sending up dust from the stage and its loyal blazon of *Geo.III.R.*, set in a crown, dimming as the gas footlights went out one by one. Out into the dark streets poured the crowd, chattering, laughing, singing the Clown's ribald song, shivering as the night air hit them. The empty theatre reeked of beer and shrimps, oranges and onions and unwashed people; attendants went wearily to and fro, collecting rubbish in baskets. On stage there was shouting and banging as the scenery was struck, the Halls of Light reduced to nothing, clouds, trees, and flowery banks no more than pasteboard again.

In the dressing-rooms under the stage the performers were also returning to their normal appearance. Janetta Sorrel, perched on a stool in front of the long high bench that served her and the other girls as a communal dressing-table, nursed her feet, one after the other.

'O Lord! They're killing me. I'll never be able to get home.'

The girl next to her laughed. 'Hark who's grumbling! You be thankful you don't live where I do. It's a wonder me feet ain't worn right off by now.'

Jannie nodded. She was fortunate in living only two streets away, over a coachmaker's in Long Acre. London cobble-stones were murder, when you'd been up on your toes, *sur la pointe*, for the best part of two hours. She eased her feet painfully into her outdoor slippers, and peered at her wavering reflection in the cracked mirror; the management was stingy with its candles. Yes, there was still eye-black above and below her lashes. She began to wipe it off, to be pushed aside by another young lady, just as her mother appeared from Wardrobe where she worked as a sewing-woman.

'You ready, Jannie? Look sharp, or we'll get locked in.'

There was not the least danger of this happening, as a night-watchman patrolled the theatre hourly because of the ever-present danger of fire. But Mrs Sorrel said it every night before she escorted her daughter home, her sharp eyes darting here and there in jealous search of something to complain about. She was a short, spare-built woman, who had been a dancer herself until the bone-ache had struck her. Jannie, who now stood up and wrapped herself in her cloak, was shorter still – hardly more than child-size, ideal for the ballet, but fortunately she had developed a womanly figure that saved her from a lifetime of playing imps. Altogether she was a ballet-master's ideal, with a delicate oval face and a flower-stem neck, great eyes, and a pert nose, brown hair that was straight by nature but twined obediently into ringlets under the influence of curl-papers, those instruments of torture dreaded by all young ladies, but accepted as inevitable in the cause of beauty.

Mrs Sorrel peered closely at her daughter.

'You haven't got half the powder off, and there's red on your mouth. Don't want to be taken for no better than you should be, do you?' This was another of her nightly sayings. Jannie submitted patiently as her mother scrubbed at her face with a very scratchy linen handkerchief, and restored her mouth to its natural soft rose-bloom.

'There. Good thing you've got me to look after you. Too many drunks about to take chances, 'specially of a Boxing Night . . .' She picked up the muslin stage dress Jannie had discarded, noted with disfavour that another chain of sequins had been torn off, folded the garment with professional skill and draped it over her arm to mend at home.

'Come on. If the Captain gets back first he'll be locking us out again, sure as eggs.'

Mr Sorrel was always known among his family as the Captain, though exactly where he had earned that rank was not clear. His accounts of his military service varied: sometimes he had conducted himself valiantly in the American War, sometimes distinguished himself against the French at Toulon in '93, slaying in single combat one of Napoleon's Marshals. One of his favourite campaigns had been the Irish Rebellion in '98, when, as he liked to recount to his comrades at the Nag's Head in Drury Lane, he had dealt the death-blow to the notorious Wolfe Tone. He told the tale so vividly that his hearers were quite content to ignore the fact that Tone had died in prison; just as the Captain's wife never bothered to remind him that he had spent most of the year '98 in and out of spunging-houses in the neighbourhood of the Old Kent Road.

'After all, he don't beat us,' she reminded Jannie, 'or get disgusting drunk, only a bit merry and there's many a time he's brought a good few guineas home, what he's won from his fine friends.'

For the Captain was a gentleman born, from a landed family in Shropshire, he said, and there was no reason to doubt it, so naturally easy and elegant were his manners. In fact, he had been one of the youngest of the ten children of Sir Charles Sorrel, squire of a modest manor near Shrewsbury; an amiable boy without sufficient combative instincts to out-rival his older brothers. Somehow, in the race for position, power, heiresses, and legacies, he had got left behind, and had not unwillingly taken to living by his wits, more happy to do so in London than in Shropshire. It was from his example that Jannie had learned to speak with a better accent than her mother's Cockney, and from his line came the grace of her body and the delicacy of her features. One day, perhaps, she would land a character part at the Theatre, he told her, if she minded her h's and g's. When times were good with him, in Jannie's fourteenth year, he had paid for her to have lessons, from an actress, in speech and deportment. They had only lasted a few months, but the effect had been excellent. The time might come, her proud papa boasted at the Nag's Head, when his lovely daughter would play Belvidera or Mrs Haller in straight drama before the Prince Regent himself, God bless him. With education, who knew how high she might aspire?

Meanwhile the subject of his hopes walked meekly home, on burning feet, at her watchful mother's side.

'And don't think I didn't notice tonight,' said Mrs Sorrel with a sharp jog of her elbow, 'when you went and tripped, and I thought you was goin' to be flat on your face in the middle of the stage. Had me heart in me mouth, I had.'

'I couldn't help it, Ma. It was my ankle. It's never been the same since I turned it. Anyway, that nice boy caught hold of me in time.'

'You watch out for nice boys catching hold of you,' said her mother darkly, and, thought Jannie, very ungratefully.

The boy who had been a silver moth in Queen Mab's retinue was now changed into everyday clothes. He considered himself a man now, for he was twenty-one this year, and to his immense relief he had stopped growing. Too much height was a curse to a dancer, and dancing seemed to be the only thing he did well. In the wildly beautiful Welsh valley where Dafydd Ifor Bryn had been born, the valley of the Dovey in Montgomeryshire, it had been accepted that one might sing – indeed that one *should* sing, either the praises of the Lord in the *capel* or with a view to competing in an Eisteddfod; but dancing of any kind was quite unheard of.

Not that Dafydd Ifor had the least idea that he could dance, or even wanted to dance, though he was so graceful and slender and moved so lightly that the village girls began to regard him speculatively at an early age, and to woo him with offers of ripe apples or ginger-toffee, to be bestowed in the bluebell woods or in the rambling graveyard behind the *capel*. When he kept one of these appointments, and was caught, though innocently enough, by the girl's father, he was soundly beaten.

He was beaten at school, too, for gazing out of the window when he should have been minding his lessons, and at home for general unsatisfactoriness, being a dreamer in a large family of practical folk who were either farmers already or would be when they were old enough. A fine farmer our Ifor would make, said his father contemptuously (there were so many Dafydds in the family already that they had stopped using his first name), leaving the cattle to starve and the crops unharvested while he mooned about idling his time with poetry and such trash – and much of it English, more was the shame. No use, from the time he began to grow up.

'What ails you, Ifor bach?' asked his mother despairingly. 'You can walk and run, and there is no more to you, it seems. What is it you want to do in your life?'

'I don't know, Mam,' Ifor had answered, truthfully enough. And, being harassed by many children, she turned away impatient of this one. If he had but shown any sign of being a preacher, as these dreaming ones sometimes were. But in *capel* his mind wandered, though the music would sometimes take hold of him and bring tears to his eyes. When he got home he was soundly beaten and sent to the room he shared with his brothers Trevor, Hywel, Emrys, and Vaughan, with no dinner and promise of further punishment if he could not recite in Welsh, by supper-time, a large portion of the Scripture laid down for that day.

One wild Spring day he had set off after a breakfast of thin porridge and begun to walk eastwards, aimlessly yet with a dim unformed wish to lose himself among the little rivers and the mountains, to fall down at last in dry bracken, nudged by grazing sheep, then neglected even by them, until his bones merged with the grey hill stones, and he was forgotten. There was no wish in him but to be far from home, so that he walked quickly always, sometimes ran, and with his lithe legs covered miles in a time that another would have taken to cover furlongs.

Some time in the afternoon a mist began to come down. He knew what such mountain mists could mean, and for all his broodings he did not truly wish to die. Down in a valley lights had sprung up, there were cottages and farms, he knew, that would take him in. He went towards them, stumbling, aching, and half-starved, seeing the sky blacken and feeling the wet mist clinging to his face, soaking his clothes; desperate now to live.

So it was that he found himself, dazed, but certainly alive, with his head on a beautiful lady's lap and her sweet scent all around him, in a lighted room crammed with strange faces, handsome and puzzled, and a soft hand stroking back his wet hair from his brow.

'What a love!'

'I swear the boy would have died in an hour more. If you hadn't gone to see to the horses, Charles . . .'

'Yes, indeed, a providence. There he lay, his silver skin laced with . . . Gad, no, mustn't quote the Scotch Play. Ha, thought I, dead or drunken? So I . . .'

'And a sweeter face I never saw.' The soft hand had touched his lips, opened his shirt at the neck and caressed his throat. Ifor opened his eyes and smiled, causing a ripple of pleasurable excitement among those around him. Somebody lifted him from the lady's satin lap, propped him up, gave him a drink which was certainly not the flat ale he was used to.

These people were all so wonderful, as unlike the villagers he had grown up with as if they had been the Fairy Folk themselves. They all seemed to have grey hair surrounding young faces (he had never seen hair-powder before) and their clothes were of beautiful bright colours, not greys, blacks, and browns. He could only just understand what they said, though he knew English well enough, and they laughed and cooed over his halting words. Before long he was quite drunk and communicating perfectly well with them, even understanding that he was at an inn in a little town not far away from the Border where Wales met England.

Somebody undressed him, calling him names like laddie and m'buck, and put him to bed between sheets made warm and delicious by a brass pan on the end of a long handle. When he woke next morning, after the best sleep he ever remembered, he was perfectly refreshed, in his right mind, and for the first time aware of who he was and where he was going.

In this way he joined Mr Faucit's Company of Comedians, and became Ivor Bryn.

These strange, foreign people were much more his own kin and kind than the folk in the Vale of Dovey. They were astonished to find he could read English, shared their own sense of humour, and fitted so well with them that he might have been born in the wings and cradled in a dress-basket. Yet, said Mr Faucit, his speech was too Welsh for him to speak lines convincingly. He must learn, and while learning he might play dumb parts, carry crowns on cushions or cardboard goblets for stage kings to drink from; even take part in the frolic that followed the drama, a piece of nonsense to please the rustics. Ivor had no idea what it was all about, but it always involved a Clown, Columbine (who was the prettiest and youngest of the ladies), a Pantaloon, Mr Faucit leaning heavily on a stick and wearing blue woollen whiskers, and a Harlequin – Ivor himself, in a jacket and breeches of patchwork, made from scraps of the actresses' garments.

'Patchy,' they called Harlequin familiarly. He was the magic one, the person at the touch of whose baton things turned themselves into other things. When it was stolen from him his power was gone. Patchy had wings for feet, Patchy could leap from floor to ceiling as a bird flies, Patchy could dance, like a flower in the wind or a wave of the sea. Ivor had never danced, but he soon learned. Learned, too, to mock and cheat Clown, the comedian with the painted face, eccentric tufts of hair springing out of a bald pate, baggy breeches and a string of sausages. Not real sausages, for the places the company passed through in their travels were often poor, and there would have been an outcry against such misuse of good food. So the sausages were made of stuffed cotton, just as Clown's comic duck was a creature of rags and feathers and his pig a skin-bladder with features painted on it, and a little curly tail which, alas, had once belonged to a real pig.

Ivor learned more than dancing, or the proper pronunciation of English. He learned, as two and then three years passed, that he was what the player-folk called a Charmer. He learned that a tilt of his dark straight brows, or a smile from his faun's mouth could bring women to their knees or to his arms, depending on circumstances. A look that was sweetly beckoning, or proudly contemptuous, or wickedly mocking, was his at will, and had he been other than he was he could have wrought mischief with it. But there was no ill in Ivor; not even enough to take advantage of the plump rosy-faced little girl who sometimes danced Columbine or played serving-wenches, and adored him so dreadfully.

He lost his virginity to Miss Susannah De Vaux, late of the King's Theatre, Haymarket, who would never see thirty again but was uncommonly handsome in a high-nosed way, and had been determined to have him from the outset. From her he learned the romantic aspect of what he already knew from his father's farmyard, and was agreeably surprised by it; and learned also a great deal of Shakespeare, for Miss De Vaux was in the habit of addressing him in the words of the Bard.

> Art thou god to shepherd turn'd,
> That a maiden's heart hath burn'd?

she would enquire of him, on the most prosaic occasions, such as his handing her the butter. 'O, ominous! he comes to kill my heart,' would greet him, with a roll of her fine eyes and a flirt of her fan, if he so much as turned a corner and met with her. He became so familiar with Juliet's lines in the Balcony Scene that he cherished hopes of one day playing Romeo, if he could only get rid of his Welsh accent. Every day, when he remembered, he was glad and thankful to his God, as he had never been in *capel*, that he had run away to the hills one morning and found his own people.

Now walking home to the lodgings he shared just off Covent Garden with two other boys in the pantomime, he thought of the break-up of Mr Faucit's company, and of how he had been recommended to stick to dancing, and had come to London, and to the great Theatre; then, irrelevantly, of the little coryphée he had saved that night from falling, and of her upward glance, the glance of a young doe in the woods at home, lured to feed from one's hand before bounding back to the shelter of the thicket.

Stuff and nonsense, he told himself. It was all in the eye make-up, and he was in any case too tired to think about girls.

Sara Dell was tired, too. There was nothing particularly exacting about the part of Queen Mab, which involved little beyond sitting in state on her uneasy throne, looking regal, and declaiming loudly enough to be heard above the gallery's orange-sucking and the pit's cracking of nuts. But when one was thirty-five and of a nervous disposition, a first night could be a serious strain, not to mention the heat from the house-candles and the new gas floats, which also gave off a peculiar and unpleasant odour.

Because she was the senior lady, a screened-off corner of the women's dressing-room was hers alone, away from the chattering, giggling, squealing young dancers. They thought her a bit uppish, fancying herself. Few gave her more than the time of day, though one or two of the girls were sorry for her and smiled or greeted her as they whirled past the rickety little table she had all to herself: the price of isolation.

Sara had brought her own mirror, rather than use the theatre's cracked, fly-spotted piece of glass. It was a pretty thing that she had toured with for years, an oval set in a brass frame on which were moulded the figures of small animals, a squirrel, a fox, a cat, a frog, with two snails acting as feet for it, and looking upwards. Sara loved her mirror. Every night she wrapped it up carefully and took it away with her. It didn't do to trust anybody.

She took off her make-up as she always did, only half-glancing at her reflection, because it depressed her so much to see herself as she was now, lines coming on her brow and cheeks, the throat beginning to slacken. In fact, what the mirror saw was a face still appealingly pretty. Her skin was wonderfully white and clear, the deceptive result of under-nourishment over the years, making her anaemic. A slightly weak chin and large wistful eyes gave her a helpless air. The imposing gold wig and glittering crown she had taken off were all too necessary to turn her into a Queen Mab.

How she would have liked to resemble her idol, Mrs Siddons! That lady's Roman nose and prowlike jaw, not to mention her heroic form and stately bearing, were all an actress could desire.

But, reflected Sara sadly, *she* was not an actress in the true sense any more. Only a pantomime-player, for her few lines in the garbled mockery of *Romeo* that went before the Harlequinade counted not at all. Still, she comforted herself, she was lucky to have got the part, at her age, and with no management influence. It had been so tiring, travelling with touring companies year in, year out, and now she was comfortably settled for the next few weeks at least. And, most important of all, so was Miranda.

Changed into her street-clothes, her mirror wrapped, she hurried through the long dressing-room, anxious to get out before she was engulfed in a crowd of the younger women.

'Goodnight, ma'am,' one was civil enough to call to her. Then she thought she heard a derisive laugh, and blushed to the roots of her hair. She hurried out into the stone corridor, where she tried not to see the black beetles already emerging from the wainscots, and up the dark wooden stairs that led to the stage-door.

Outside in the street, under the light from the flickering lamp beneath which a knot of idlers were gathered for the excitement of seeing their stage favourites emerging, Sara paused, struck by a sudden thought. What if she had forgotten . . . but no, she had certainly bought the meat-scraps before coming to the theatre. Of course she had. But she might as well make sure. Curiously the little crowd watched, as she opened the large reticule she carried, and began to rummage in it. Nobody recognized the tall woman in the plain hooded cloak as the recently dazzling Fairy Queen, they were merely interested to see what she was doing.

'Lorst the rent-money, 'ave yer, missis?' enquired somebody, causing a general laugh, as she scrabbled ever more frantically in the bag. The mirror was safe, and the clean handkerchief she always carried, and her smelling-salts and cologne, but Miranda's supper was gone.

It was the last straw, after an evening of strained nerves. To the watchers' gratification, Sara burst into tears.

Humiliated, wretched, she stood under the lamp, hands over her face, the rifled bag at her feet. One of the onlookers, a professional pickpocket on the watch for opportunities, crept from behind her and advanced a hand towards it, unnoticed by the crowd who were now gathered round, bombarding her with questions. He had barely touched the handle of it when his arm was seized in a firm grasp, and he was rocked off his balance.

''Ere! Wot the . . . you keep orf o' me!'

A tall figure was looming above him, a slight stoop to its shoulders but none the less menacing for that, in a swirling black cloak with a silver-buckled black beaver hat atop white hair. The pickpocket squirmed away from the imprisoning hand and ran, while his captor majestically pushed aside the crowd.

'Give way, good people. This lady is distressed. Give her air.'

Obediently they melted. Suddenly the light caught the aristocratic features below the beaver hat; he was recognized.

'Pantaloon! It's Pantaloon! 'Ow are yer, old codger?' They were round him, crying out, laughing, jeering, for some of them were too ignorant to know fairytale from fact, and thought him in truth the silly old father of Columbine, foiled in his efforts to sell her to a richer suitor than Harlequin. Half-smiling, all haughty, he pushed them aside, and, one arm round Sara's shoulders, steered her away from them and down the street.

Her sobs died away. 'Oh, you are kind, sir.' She knew him, of course: Raymond Otway, Pantaloon and Old Capulet. They had been introduced before rehearsals, had spoken stiffly and politely, had exchanged lines as Juliet's father and the Nurse. Neither had taken much notice of the other, both reserved, shy persons in an alien company. Now, by a strange trick of Fate, they were walking down the street together, his arm still protectively round her. At the street-corner she halted and detached herself.

'You must think me quite crazy, Mr Otway. To give way so, how shameful. But' – again she scrubbed her little gloved hand across her eyes – 'it was so shocking, to know one had been robbed. I never expected – Mrs Sorrel warned me, but it seems so ridiculous, for so little . . .'

Gently he asked, 'Of what were you robbed, ma'am?'

'It seems so silly. But – it was my cat's supper. Miranda's supper. She – she's been alone all day, and she knows I always feed her when I come home. Somebody took it, though it was only scraps. I suppose some of those girls are hungry, poor things. One must try to be charitable.'

Mr Otway's handsome mouth was set in anything but charitable lines. 'Quite unforgivable. It's uncommonly Christian of you, Miss, er, Dell.'

'No, it isn't. I'm really quite angry. You see, it's so late – where can I buy her anything now, poor Miranda? She gets so hungry. I can't feed her properly when we're touring, and now I'm back in London, I thought . . . I thought . . .'

Mr Otway was deeply touched by the pretty voice, and the pretty sad face turned up to his, like a young hare's before the keeper broke its neck, as he remembered with horrid vividness from his country childhood. He had not been in the theatre thirty years for nothing, and instinct told him that not only the cat Miranda, but her mistress, was rather short of food.

'My dear young lady,' he said, 'there is no problem in this, no problem at all. As it happens I usually repair about this time to a chop-house not many yards from where we stand – an excellent place where one may have something warming and sustaining. I know the people, they will undoubtedly supply you with something from the kitchen for Miranda. And we ourselves – will you do me the honour to take supper with me?'

Sara was taken aback. 'A chop-house? But I thought . . . ladies . . .'

'Not usual, no. This, however, is a most respectable place, believe me. I would take my own daughter there.'

So he had daughters. The most ridiculous pang of disappointment went through her, and she banished it without a second thought.

'Very well, sir. Thank you. If you are quite sure. Only I must not be long, because of Miranda.'

'We will not keep Miranda waiting, I can assure you. If I may . . .?'

He offered her his arm, with his most gallant gesture, and she took it with her brightest smile. Off they went, both suddenly much happier than they had been earlier that evening.

The crowd still hung about the stage-door. It was gone midnight, the streets quietening down as the watchmen made their rounds. The stage-door-keeper, anxious for his bed, came out and addressed them fretfully.

'Get off to your homes, can't you, if you've got homes to go to. There's nobody left here.'

'Yes, there is, yes, there is!'

And there he stood, in the doorway, the slight, stocky man they had been waiting for, his greatcoat collar turned up but no hat on the short-cropped dark hair, and the light full on his face, a swarthy Italianate face with a comical curly mouth but a lurking sadness in the fine brown eyes.

'Joey!' they yelled, throwing up their hats and stamping their feet in ecstasy. 'Joey Grimaldi! How are you tomorrow, then? Here we are again! Sing us a song, do, Joey. Show us some tricks!'

25

The Clown smiled. 'It's a bit late for tricks, friends. Even clowns got to go home sometimes.'

There was a general groan. He raised a hand, quietening them.

'But I'll give you a bit of a song. All right?'

'All right!' they roared.

He struck an attitude, arms akimbo, knees bent. His voice was soft and sweet, used at low pitch, as he used it now. Even without the grotesquerie of red and white paint, and the tufts of hair, he was all mischief, all suggestiveness.

> A little old woman her living she got
> By selling codlins, hot, hot, hot;
> And this little old woman, who codlins sold,
> Though her codlins were hot, she felt herself cold.
> So to keep herself warm, she thought it no sin
> To fetch for herself a quartern of . . .

'GIN!' they roared in concert, at which Grimaldi wagged a finger, crying, 'Oh for shame!' and then burst into the chorus with them.

> Ri tol iddy, iddy, Ri tol iddy, iddy, Ri tol iddy, iddy, Ri
> tol lay!

Before they could cheer him he had swept them a deep bow, and was off, lost in the misty night.

CHAPTER TWO
Cat Scene

Sara's apprehension at the thought of entering a chop-house was soon banished. Brassey's was a highly respectable establishment just round the corner from Covent Garden Market, owned and run by a brother and sister. Miss Brassey was young but formidable, permitting no larks, as she termed anything in the way of riotous behaviour. Covent Garden porters, who were notoriously given to larks and colourful language, were not encouraged to enter Brassey's, nor were the Cyprians, gaudily gowned and painted, who offered themselves for sale alongside the vegetables. Let such riff-raff patronize the taverns that stayed open all night, or opened at dawn, or the stalls where they could buy tea, coffee, or soup, ladled steaming from a cauldron; Brassey's was not for them.

Miss Brassey eyed the couple who entered her doors, then permitted herself a smile. Female customers were not at all to her liking, but this one was clearly a lady, and her respectability guaranteed by her escort. An actor Mr Otway might be, but a more civil-spoken gentleman could not be found. She advanced.

'Your usual, sir?'

'If you please, ma'am. And for Miss Dell . . .?'

'Whatever you think,' Sara said timidly.

'The beef, then. Beef is Brassey's speciality, you must know. Oh, such beef, as pink as a rose, as tender as a lady's heart! It does one good even to think of it – not to mention the subtle fragrance exuding from yon kitchens.' He rubbed his hands and surveyed Miss Brassey benevolently.

'Law,' said she, bridling agreeably, 'I declare you're quite the poet. Shank or er, rump? Or a plate of both?'

'For me, both, with the smallest of roasted potatoes, wrinkled amber, and your delicious greens.'

'Buttered.'

'Buttered, of course. And for Miss Dell?'

'Oh, only one plate, if you please,' Sara said hurriedly. 'Of – of either.' She knew no difference between shank or rump, having seldom eaten anything richer than boiled mutton in her life.

'And to drink,' said Raymond, 'Miss Brassey's particular nectar. In pint pots.'

Miss Brassey bobbed the merest sketch of a curtsey, and disappeared, to return with two mugs of the Particular. It proved to be a full-bodied red wine heated to boiling point and flavoured with ground cloves and cinnamon. Sara drank a mouthful, recoiled at its heat and strength, then tried another, and smiled. Raymond watched with interest a faint pink glow, like a crimson light behind alabaster, creep into the white of her cheeks.

'There, that's better, isn't it, my . . .' He had been going to say my dear, as he would have done to any other actress; but something told him that she would take it as a familiarity. 'My dear lady,' he finished.

'Yes, oh yes, it's excellent. So good on a cold night.' She looked sharply round, like a bird alert for enemies, he thought, at the booth into which Miss Brassey had shown them – private enough, with its two small benches facing each other across a table, but not so discreet as to be concealed by a curtain from the other customers.

Sara was weighing up these others, too, unalarming as they were: a couple of elderly actors from one of the other theatres, a man who looked like a prosperous shopkeeper, and Mr Brassey himself, a balding young man eating his belated supper with a copy of the *Gazette* propped up in front of his plate. Nothing there to make her nervous, yet Raymond could sense fear in the turn of her head and the quick movements of her eyes. Here, he told himself, was a woman who had at some time been badly frightened or betrayed, and he was astonished to find how much he wanted to reassure her.

With satisfaction he saw her begin on the plate of beef and vegetables (a real picture, as Miss Brassey commented in a rare moment of poetic fancy). She ate, not like a starving animal, but like one that was unused to seeing much food on its plate. Raymond, not stinting himself, glanced unobtrusively at her, and wondered why he had never taken particular notice of her before in the weeks they had rehearsed together. He was not indifferent to women; several had shared his life since he and his wife had parted. Sara was quite a beauty, in her delicate way. Her complexion was no less than dazzling, and in her soft fair hair, damp now from the night-mist outside, the grey strands mingled unnoticed. She ate like a lady, he saw with pleasure, and her hands were elegant, with polished filbert nails that would have graced a duchess. He must be very gentle with her.

'Tell me about Miranda,' he said.

'Oh, dearest Miranda! Well, I say very little about her, as a rule, because people seem to think it so eccentric to travel with a cat. I cannot imagine why. They are such company and so fond of one. Besides, Miranda is not an ordinary cat, a – a . . .'

'Moggy?' he suggested.

'Exactly. No, she is most unusual. Her mother was from some Eastern place, Burma, I think, and it seems these cats have not the same aversion to travel as our own. From a kitten, Miranda would follow me everywhere, even into the street, so I was forced to try her with a ribbon collar and lead. And, do you know, she was *proud* of them! So I began to take her for walks, and never mind the laughter.'

'Were dogs not a menace?'

'Oh, she swears at them so dreadfully that they turn tail at once. There *are* people who say I am cruel because I take her with me on tour. But if they could only see how she jumps into her basket when I put my travelling-clothes on! Dear little creature, she is so wise. I have even had offers to buy her, but of course I would never part with her.'

' "Admired Miranda . . ." ' Raymond murmured. Sara's face glowed.

'How clever of you! I'm always quoting that to her and I'm sure she understands.' Sara had finished her wine. Her flush had deepened and she was almost chattering, to Raymond's amusement. 'Don't you think it very odd that Shakespeare hardly mentions cats? He seems to have been so kind to animals, for those barbarous times. Even snails.'

'There's Tybalt – "good king of cats, nothing but one of your nine lives." '

'Tybalt is *not* an agreeable character. No, I fear the good William disliked them. Don't you think it very unfair that even today a cat-loving female should be branded Old M —' She stopped in mid-word, looked away from him, and began to eat again. After a moment she said in quite a different, calm tone, 'Dear me, how I have been rattling on. Tell me something of yourself. Have you a home in London?'

After a little pause, he said, 'My family live near Weybridge, in Surrey. I lodge in Henrietta Street.'

'Oh. Then you cannot see them very often.'

Wondering why he was telling her, he answered, 'My wife and I ceased to share a home some years ago.'

Sara bit her lip. 'I'm sorry. I should not have pried.'

'Pray think no more of it. These things go into the mists, and vanish from one's mind.' He began to talk of the performance that night, of the company and the management, the circuits they had toured, their favourite towns.

'Bath of all places, for me,' Sara said. 'The climate is so temperate and the place so pretty. I had the most charming lodging in Milsom Street, so much superior to some of the dreadful places one finds oneself in.'

'Bath is my choice, too, though the audience tends to be so genteel that the Bard is a *leetle* strong for them. I recall, once . . .' but he remembered that the story might be somewhat too much for Miss Dell's ladylike ears. He had finished his wine, and another tankard of the same, and was beginning to feel an agreeable and familiar glow spreading through his veins. Sara refused a refill, but the lure was too powerful for him; he beckoned Miss Brassey over.

'They rose to my Richard in Bath,' he told Sara. 'Never had such a house, and none of it paper. '02, that was. And I gave them a Hamlet there – or was it Bristol? – that raised the roof. Curiously enough we played Edinburgh that same summer, and they sat through it like stockfish. But then they're notoriously cold, Scotch audiences. I think my greatest Shylock was in Manchester. They know about money-lending and such commerce up there. Lear . . . it should have been my greatest role. "Who would have daughters?" Did you ever play Cordelia?' he asked suddenly.

'Yes. Often.'

'And Desdemona, and Portia, Brutus's Portia, and Ophelia?'

She opened her eyes wide. 'Yes. Why?'

He nodded portentously. 'I thought so. The suffering ones, the victims of men . . .'

Sara threw a tremulous, pleading smile across the room to Miss Brassey, who was yawning, and who thankfully came across to their booth.

'Your lady looks tired, sir,' she told Raymond, 'and we're about to close up. If you'd be so kind as to settle, I'd be obliged. We get what sleep we can here, with that row starting up at first light' – she nodded towards the Garden – 'shouting and cursing and rattling their carts over the stones, not to mention donkeys and the Jew-hawkers. Terrible, isn't it, Jack?'

Her brother, noisily stacking plates, nodded. 'Shockin'.'

Raymond was meekly laying out coins on the table. ' "A great reckoning in a little room." Or rather, a little reckoning in a great room. That's said to refer to the murder of Marlowe, Miss Dell, as I'm sure you know. Goodnight, sweet Miss Brassey, and flights of angels sing thee to thy rest.'

'Get along with you,' said Miss Brassey, affectionately. He took Sara's arm and guided her out, into the night of foggy cold, flickering lights, and random shouts from wandering foot-passengers. She knew he was not drunk, only a little elated, and knew too that he could easily be drunk, disastrously drunk. As they started off down the street she gave a sudden squeak. 'Miranda!'

'Oh God, Miranda.' Raymond darted back into the chop-house, colliding with Mr Brassey and a formidable bunch of keys. A few moments later he was back, bearing a steaming, fragrant parcel.

'A Boxing Night present for Miranda, with the firm's compliments, and hope she may be lent to catch rats if the occasion arises.'

Sara stuffed it into her reticule. 'Thank you, thank you. What would I have done? Without her supper, I mean, or . . . or mine. You've been so kind, so very kind.'

'The pleasure has been entirely mine. Let me take you to your door.'

The streets smelt not unpleasantly of yesterday's vegetables and fruit. Cats less fortunate than Miranda prowled and yowled behind crates in the Market. The pointed roof of St Paul's church towered over the Market. Great wagons of cabbages, turnips, potatoes, brought up in the evening to be ready for first light, stood guard over the growers' men and their boys, asleep on sacks beneath them, their horses, well blanketed against the cold, sleeping too; and beside each wagon a guardian dog, lying head on paws, but ready to open wall-eyes and bellow out a warning should any strange hand approach his load.

Among the columns of the Piazza, and the wagons, and the empty stalls, things slunk near the ground, furtive, grasping anything that might be eaten or serve for clothing. They were the ragged children who haunted the Garden; night-birds, scavengers, creatures from the Rookery slums, knowing neither their own names nor much else but the need for survival. To Sara they were terrifying. She clung to Raymond's arm, glad of a man's company, so strange to her.

At the once-elegant, now shabby, portico of the house where she lodged, they paused. Raymond glanced at the dark fanlight above the door.

'They seem to have gone to bed. Can you see your way upstairs?'

'Yes, I've some lucifers, and it's only the first pair back. Goodnight. And thank you, again.'

'Goodnight.' Gallantly he brushed the back of her hand with a token kiss, raised his hat, and left her fitting her key into the door.

He walked down the street humming a tune from the pantomime. For the first time in many months he had given more thought to another than to himself. She was not young, yet she had a curious innocence. Why had she recoiled from saying 'Old Maid'? He could swear that at some time she had loved and been loved. He was oddly touched at the thought.

And, most strange and commendable of all, she had not asked him why he, an actor of the legitimate theatre who had played

Shakespeare's great ones, was fooling about as Pantaloon in a Harlequinade.

He hoped he would never have to tell her about the years of drinking, the humiliation, the terrible moments on stage when lines he knew as well as his own name deserted him, the night when his memory had utterly failed him towards the end of a scene played with, of all people, Mrs Siddons herself, and ruined her exit. It was, of course, the Scotch Play, and its evil reputation was borne out, for the incident had ended his serious career.

He hoped very much that he would be spared from telling Sara that.

Crouched on the threadbare carpet of her little room, Sara spread out the contents of Miss Brassey's parcel before a purring, wreathing young black cat.

'Such a feast, Miranda! The very best beef, all beautifully cut up for you, and look, there's a bit of kidney too. Wasn't that a kind lady, to send Miranda such a treat?'

But her mind was on the kind gentleman who had given her, Sara, a fine meal and talked to her in a way that did not make her feel in the least uncomfortable, as so much conversation did. She had guessed his secret, of course; by the wine so quickly swallowed and so soon reflected in his looks and speech, by the occasional word fumbled for. It was so sad, especially in a man with such a noble countenance and with so well-bred a manner.

She would rather perish than tell him, or anyone, of her own secret. Of the dreams from which she woke weeping in the dark hours of the morning. Of the memories, the secret courtship in the lanes farthest away from her father's rectory, the young man with the dark blue eyes, who had gone away to join his ship when the French Wars broke out. The tawdry ring she had bought, the letter to her father returned torn up, inside another folded sheet of paper.

And the baby. George.

*

33

To the intense annoyance of everybody concerned, an extra rehearsal was called before the second night of *Harlequin Romeo*.

'It was terrible, quite terrible,' said Mr Tayleur, the manager, having summoned the entire cast on to the stage. 'Don't you agree, Fasoli?'

The ballet-master shook his head. 'I would have laughed if I had not been crying. I thought it was dancers I train – now I see it is elephants.'

A murmur of indignation from the *corps de ballet*. 'They *liked* us,' piped up one of the young girl dancers, for whom Fasoli was known to have a certain *tendresse*. 'They clapped like anythink.'

'They always clap on Boxing Night, that is what they come for. Wait till you see the *Dramatic Censor* this week, that will shame you, miss,' retorted Tayleur. The young lady was heard to mutter something uncomplimentary about the *Dramatic Censor*, but only by those nearest to her. Tayleur and Signor Fasoli then proceeded, in the form of a duet, to anatomize the performances, singing, dancing, and miming. It had been amateur, awkward, slow, and clumsy. Even those who might be supposed to know better had made fools of themselves – 'and that includes you, Miss Dell. Any minute I expected to see Queen Mab's throne topple like Bonaparte's, ha ha!'

There was a sycophantic laugh from some quarters as poor Sara said, flushing, 'It *would* lurch about so. I couldn't keep it steady.'

'So we noticed, so we all noticed. And you, Mr Bologna, call yourself a Harlequin, do you?'

Jack Bologna, tall and sinuously graceful even in his everyday clothes, raised dark Italian eyes to the manager's, uncrossed his ankles from the fourth position *croisée*, recrossed them, left ankle before right, admired the result, and said equably in the accents of North London, 'Best in the business, sir.'

Signor Fasoli shook his long oily locks in denial. 'You only as good as I make you, with practice, practice, practice, and I tell you that you dance very poor last night, like a great dustman. And you, ma'am,' nodding fiercely towards Columbine, 'I see you eating pie too much before you go on, and that is why you jump about so 'eavy. You not eat pie or drink porter, I tell you, before you dance for Fasoli.'

Mrs Parker, a plump young woman whose baby-faced charms certainly threatened to grow out of hand, burst into tears. Bologna, beside her, patted her well-covered shoulders and, looking Fasoli in the eye, directed at him a tirade of rapid idiomatic Italian. He had lived in England with his acrobatic family since the age of five, but round the table they spoke their native language still. Whatever he was saying, Fasoli visibly wilted, and when Bologna chose to stop, the ballet-master gave a swift surly answer and turned away to harangue some of the young ladies. Bologna, hands on hips, exchanged glances with his lifelong friend Grimaldi, another dyed-in-the-wool Londoner whose family roots were in Italy. Joey responded with a wink; not an ordinary man's wink, but the wink of a Clown, the droop of his eyelid emphasizing the brilliant twinkling of the other eye, his chin falling in sympathy with it to an alarming extent, as though it proposed to cover the second button down on his waistcoat. At the same time he uttered his peculiar, bubbling, high-pitched chuckle.

It was irresistibly infectious. Those around him began to laugh helplessly, one setting off another, until Fasoli's words were lost. He threw up his hands, muttering imprecations, and strode off. Bologna watched him go with satisfaction.

'He ain't bad, you know, Joey,' he said to Grimaldi, 'not when it's a matter of setting the little fairies to rights. But let him leave us to our own business, eh?'

'That's right, Jack. Leave the indiwiddle to hisself.'

The rehearsal got under way, when the laughter had died. Fasoli took his temper out on the dancers, who were in no position to answer him back. Jannie stood meekly enough to take the criticisms he hurled at her, bending her head as he mentioned the slip. She was thankful when he passed on to Dolly Grace, next to her.

'Dretful old fusspot, ain't he,' whispered Dolly, when he had moved down the line. 'It'll be all right tonight, don't you fret.

Look at Joey, he's all on edge even if he do seem cock-a-hoop. Come on, let's try a few steps.'

Mr Tayleur's eye was on them as they went into *enchaînements*, posing, twirling, taking hands, and appearing to go into flight, though their muslin wings were missing and their shabby cotton practice dresses no help in appearing ethereal. Fasoli insisted they do the whole sequence of dances from the moment of the Transformation, ignoring their sighs and groans. Jannie, poised to change rhythms as the music changed, thrummed out by a tired accompanist on a tired pianoforte, felt a warm strong grip on her outstretched hand, and looked up into the bright grey eyes of Ivor Bryn.

'Well, there,' he said, 'if it isn't the young person of the *Twlwyth Teg*.'

'The *what*?' Automatically she executed a *ronde de jambe*, holding lightly on to his hand.

'The Fair Family, we Welsh call them. They are very small, and remarkable dancers. No, now I look closer, the hair is too brown.'

Jannie twirled, rested, and panted. 'Who're you calling too brown?' she demanded. 'If you want to talk Italian, go and talk it to Mr Bologna. I'm English.'

Ivor laughed. 'Too brown to be one of our Fair Folk, that's all I meant. Your hair is very pretty.'

She was mollified. 'Well, I had gold dust on it last night. Look out, Fasoli's watching. You'll be for it if he finds you out of place for the Finale.'

But when the entire company, in attitudes, surrounded Harlequin and Columbine embracing on top of a column, Clown and Pantaloon variously defeated on each side of them, and Queen Mab smiling benevolently on all, Jannie found herself still partnered by the Welsh boy, his arm round her shoulders, frozen in a statue's pose. As soon as the music ended and the grouping dissolved she shook him off angrily.

'I told you before, you'll get us both the bag if you keep changing places.'

36

'This *is* my place,' Ivor replied sweetly.

'That it's not. It's Tommy Lee's. What's he doing over the other side?'

'I persuaded him he would look better there.'

'Oh! You . . .' Words failed Jannie, and she flounced away from him and down the dark stairs like an angry bird. It was too bad, to be pestered just now, when the routines had all been carefully worked out and rehearsed. Fasoli would be sure to notice and perhaps hand her the key of the street, and what would she do then? Nobody was going to engage a dismissed dancer at this time of year. And whether he noticed or not Ma would be sure to, and go on at her day and night about how easy it was for a young girl to get into trouble on the stage.

Sure enough, Mrs Sorrel had been hovering in the wings to keep an eye on her daughter, and was waiting with a lecture.

'All very well, saying it wasn't your fault and he spoke polite enough. *I* know when a young man means well, and when he don't, and if you want my opinion that one don't.'

'But I didn't encourage him at all, Ma, I tell you. I spoke as sharp as you'd have done yourself.'

'*Then* you did,' replied her mother darkly. 'But what about the next time, and the next? First it's a please and thank you, then it's Madam, will you walk? And the time after that it's Asking the Favour.'

Jannie flushed up to her eyes. Her mother's homilies had always irritated her, for she fancied herself to be as sensible, not to say as virtuous, as any girl in London. This particular homily struck at her more deeply; she could not have said why.

'All right, all right, no need to keep on at me. I can take care of myself.'

'If it was Mr Bologna I wouldn't say so much about it,' went on Mrs Sorrel remorselessly. 'He's an older man, and well up in the profession, and single, too. Now he might make you an offer . . .' In her mind's eye she saw her daughter promoted to Columbine opposite the great Harlequin, his respected partner in private life, Mrs Jack Bologna with her own carriage, perhaps, and an invitation to Carlton House. Jannie broke in on her visions.

'Mr Bologna don't so much as know I'm on this earth, Ma. I mean no more to him than . . . than Grimaldi's rabbit.' (This was the animal Grimaldi had trained to take part in his clowning; it was heartily disliked by all who were obliged to handle it, so unpredictable were its habits.) 'D'you suppose he's nothing better to do than make eyes at the girls? Besides, he's courting Louisa Bristow, Joey's sister-in-law.'

'Louisa Bristow? Her at the Garden? She's a singer, ain't she? He don't want a singer, he wants a dancer with a future before her.'

'I don't know what he wants and I don't care,' Jannie burst out, 'but I do know I'm going home to put my feet up if it's only for an hour, and curl my hair at my own mirror without Flo Wilkins breathing down my neck. And don't you say you'll come with me, because you're wanted here.' With which she flung on her cloak and fled.

'How very charming, my love,' said the Captain wistfully, surveying his daughter as she put the last touches to her make-up in the dressing-room. She had dressed in comfort at home, and been escorted back to the theatre on her father's arm. Now, as she applied powder to her neck with a rabbit's foot, peering anxiously, to make sure it was not too thick, he thought she looked the sylph she was to represent in the Pantomime. Her high-waisted muslin dress was of faint coral-pink, clinging to her figure and daringly short, barely touching her ankles. Over it was an upper robe reaching from waist to knees, of filmy silver with sequin embroideries catching the light as she moved. Her bodice was hardly there at all, a mere twin corselet that barely enclosed her young breasts, and its sleeves were tiny caps just covering her shoulders. Her hair tumbled round her neck in careful ringlets, a tiny circle of artificial white roses crowning it. The dress was enshrouded now with a plain white overdress, for she began as one of Juliet's attendants, first in the Bridal Dance, then in the Funeral Celebrations.

The Captain stooped and kissed her. 'You look lovely enough for Columbine,' he said.

'Don't I wish I may be, that's all,' said Jannie. 'Now get along, Pa, and don't disarrange me. You shouldn't be here by rights. I'm sure the other girls won't like it.' But, as the Captain perceived by their ogling, they liked it very much.

' "Nods and becks and wreathed smiles," ' he murmured, ' "such as hang on Hebe's cheek, and love to live in dimple sleek." ' He returned the nods graciously, and bestowed a parting pat to Jannie's shoulder.

'Beautiful, beautiful. We'll make a good match for you yet, trust me.'

Jannie frowned. 'Have done, Pa, will you! First Ma and then you. I don't want any kind of match, I want to dance, and if I don't finish getting ready I won't be on stage this side of Shrove Tuesday. You coming in tonight?'

'I – ah – no, I rather think not. Some fellows I want to see . . . a little transaction . . .' He drifted out, encountering in the passage Raymond Otway, solemn in the black doublet and hose he would have precisely two minutes to change from in his transformation from Old Capulet to Pantaloon. They apologized simultaneously, and the actor bowed instinctively.

'A gent, by George,' said the Captain to himself. 'Or not quite, perhaps. Still, a near thing.' He eyed with polite curiosity a lady who was making her way to the stairs that led to the stage. She was gaudily dressed in mock-Elizabethan fashion as Juliet's Nurse. Handsome woman, but too thin, he decided, even with the padding.

Raymond caught up with Sara in the wings, and saw that she was trembling violently.

'Now,' he said softly, under cover of the overture's clashing sounds, 'now, now, now. You've not taken a chill, I hope, ma'am?'

'N-no,' she said between chattering teeth. 'I'm frightened, Mr

Otway, if you must know. You heard how he spoke to me at rehearsal, about my balance? If it should happen again – if they should let me drop! I don't trust those stage-hands, they drink.' She twisted and untwisted her hands painfully. 'I just wish I could run away. Oh, why must I be such a coward?'

He took the icy hands between his own and rubbed them vigorously. 'We're all cowards, dear lady, it's the sign of a sensitive artiste. I'm terrified, myself' (which was untrue) 'until I've taken a drop of my special cordial.' He produced a small flask from an enormous pocket in his baggy breeches, and offered it to her. 'Just a mouthful. It will do you the world of good.'

Sara glanced at it suspiciously, then took it from him and drank with the desperate gesture of Juliet draining the phial. Its fieriness made her choke and cough. Raymond patted her vigorously between the shoulders until she got back her breath and smiled at him.

'I feel better already. Thank you so very much.'

There was no time to say more, for the overture had ended in a highly dramatic flourish, and the curtain swished up to reveal an extremely pretty chorine, one of Signor Fasoli's fancies, improbably dressed as a Tudor page in a costume which revealed most of her legs and brought cheers and whistles from the audience. She raised a very small toy trumpet to her lips and appeared to blow a fanfare which the trumpeter in the orchestra pit got slightly out of synchronization, so that it was still going on after she had taken her own instrument from her mouth, to the audience's noisy delight. Then, with great *savoir faire*, she struck an attitude and began the Prologue:

> Good people all, I pray you lend an ear:
> A grave and solemn tale we bring you here –

Groans from the pit and gallery.

> Two famous lovers were there, you must know,
> In fair Verona – one was Romeo,

A gallant youth and tall, whose heart was set
On a fair maiden, Juliet Capulet.
This pretty lass no sooner caught a glim
Of Romeo, than *her* heart was set on *him*.
But oh, alas, was never such a truth
As this – the course of true love ne'er runs smooth!
For Juliet's Ma and Pa were most unwilling,
And vowed they'd sooner cut off with a shilling
Their daughter dear, than see her wed a Montague –
But here she comes! our actors never want a cue.

Enter a bevy of charming dancers, some in pink, like Jannie, some in blues or yellows, all veiled in the white overgown they would cast off later. And enter Sara, upright and dignified, much strengthened by the draught she had swallowed, leading by the hand Mrs Parker, maidenly in white, her other hand in Raymond's. The piece had begun well. Mr Tayleur, in a private box, sighed with relief. It would have a good run.

When the Transformation Scene came, and they all crouched in the shadows waiting to be transformed, Jannie felt a gentle touch on her cheek, like a moth's wing. Peering through the gloom, she saw the moth's antennae, the grey hood, elfish pointed face and mischievous crooked smile.

'You again!' she whispered. 'Such impudence.'

But that night she evaded her mother for the first time, and let Ivor escort her home.

CHAPTER THREE
Columbine Loses Her Heart

The moon was full that night, dancing behind clouds and out again, then constant against a dark blue sky, star-studded. London's acrid smoke-pall was blown away on a fresh wind, so that the air seemed, for once, fresh, even heady, after the heat and stuffiness of the theatre.

Jannie felt an uncommon lightness of spirits. It was no doubt wicked of her to have jettisoned Ma, and she would get a scolding for it later on, but just now it was extremely pleasant to be on the arm of a young man. He was not in the least impudent, after all, but very civil and somewhat innocent in his manner, after the knowing Cockney boys. She was intrigued by his curiously light voice, and the way it went up at the end of a sentence as if he were always asking a question. As he told her how he had joined the touring company in Wales, travelled with them, and left when they broke up, she hardly took in what he was saying for looking up at him, so much taller than her.

What was so strange and charming about his face? Jannie was not given to staring at men's faces, which were as a rule not worth it. But this one was different, broad in the brow and pointed of chin, and there was something compelling and familiar in his look.

Suddenly she said, 'You make me think of Harlequin.'

'Of Bologna? *Duw*! He's old enough to be my father, look you.'

'I don't mean *him*, I mean when he's masked and in his patches.'

Ivor said nothing for a moment. Then, 'I was Harlequin, when our company put on pantomime. I promise you I shall be Harlequin again, here, where London people will see me. Anything Bologna can do I can. Or will do, one day.'

Jannie stared. 'Go on! You Welsh boys like yourselves, don't you?'

'Oh, I'm not proud, don't think it. I just know what I can do, and one should do it, if the world lets one, don't you think? Do *you* always want to dance fairies and dandizettes?'

'I intend to be an actress,' said Jannie importantly. 'I've had my voice trained by Madame Clare, of the Olympic Theatre.'

'Yes, I noticed you speak handsome.' Perhaps it was that that had drawn him to her, he thought; that and her being so small and dainty. Ivor was deeply superstitious by nature, the more so now for having mixed so long with theatre folk. Sometimes he saw things in his mind that afterwards happened, or was seized with a strong conviction which, however unlikely at the time, turned out to be true.

Now he said, suddenly stopping, 'I think you will bring me luck.'

Jannie stared. 'What do you mean?'

'Only that some people bring fortune, others misfortune. The fortune-bringers are like charms, you know, hares' feet, that kind of thing, and one should always keep them near.'

Jannie laughed sharply, an echo of her mother. 'If you think I'm going to turn into a hare's foot and hang round your neck for ever and ever, you can think twice. The idea! I'll be my own luck and nobody else's, thank you kindly.' Then she was sorry she had spoken so, particularly because she could not help noticing that he had a beautiful neck, long and slender and strongly muscled, lending a kind of classic richness to the folds of his cheap neckcloth. She felt a strange desire to reach up and touch the curve of his throat, the point of the jawbone and the smooth, hollowed cheek. It had never occurred to her before that men could be beautiful. She shook off the discovery – who could tell where such thoughts might lead? And besides, they were standing only a few yards away from the coachmaker's, and there was a light in the living-room window above. The Captain was in, Ma, no doubt still at the theatre breathing fire and fury; any moment now she would catch up with them.

'This is where I live,' she said, 'third door along. Come on, or I'll be in dreadful trouble.' When they reached it she stood on the first of the three steps that led up to the door. Now she was almost as tall as he. They faced each other for a moment, alone in a charmed circle of silence, though noisy footsteps passed them, shouts and cries and the rumbling wheels came from the streets around. Ivor took off his hat, a much-brushed shabby beaver. She saw, as if for the first time, the way that his hair sprang up from a peak on his brow, and went backwards like a wave's crest; black hair against a white skin, ebony on ivory, the black cap of Harlequin.

'Goodnight,' he said. 'I won't ask you to hang round my neck, but I still think you are my luck, meant to stay with me.'

'Stay with you! Much chance of doing anything else, since you was so obliging as to do Tommy Lee out of his place. I suppose this panto'll run for weeks and weeks, so I'll just have to put up with you, shan't I. Go along now, I think I see Ma turning the corner. I'll catch it hot enough without her finding you as well.'

'Tomorrow, then,' he said, smiling, and turned away. She watched him go, only just aware of the avenging figure of her mother drawing nearer. Somewhere in the region of her bodice there was a curious sensation of pain, mixed with pleasure. She had never felt anything like it before; she hoped she was not sickening for something.

Mrs Sorrel very much feared she was. Her tirade that night was the most violent she had ever launched at her imperilled daughter, who had not only given her the slip but had been walked home by a man. 'Oh yes, you thought I wouldn't find out, gel, but there's eyes that sees all, and I don't mean Him Above. Did you think what might happen to you, just in a few yards' walk, let alone two streets and no lamps in one of 'em? It only needs a dark doorway to ruin a young woman, whatever fancy ideas you may have got about gold beds with satin sheets, or the back of the Regent's coach.'

'Oh, dem it, Lucy,' protested the Captain, who was an unwilling listener. 'That's all stuff, y'know. Prinny would never . . . I have it on the best authority, you know who I mean, that no harm would ever come to a defenceless woman from his High-ness.'

'Oh, indeed? And what was poor Mrs Mary Robinson but a defenceless woman, *and* an actress, and where did she end up?'

'In Windsor churchyard, I believe,' murmured the Captain, but his wife was addressing Jannie once more. Yawning, he carried off to bed the bottle of rum a very drunken sailor had obligingly given him, and a steaming kettle of hot water. A comfortable glass, or preferably several, of rum shrub helped him to sleep whatever noise might be going on in the next room, and there was plenty tonight.

Not that he didn't sympathize with his wife in striving so hard to protect Jannie's virtue. His little girl was worth more than seduction, or even marriage, with some down-at-heels actor. He had plans for her, connections that might lead to something. Men of wealth and rank had been known to marry actresses, dancers, before now. There was Lavinia Fenton, the first Polly Peachum, who became Duchess of Bolton. Miss Farren was now Countess of Derby. Dolly Jordan . . . well, marriage wasn't everything, when a Royal was concerned. He began mentally to arrange the wedding reception, for in Jannie's case it should be legal, if he had anything to do with it. An orchestra, oysters, game, un-limited candles, and the bride's father in a purple coat with gold buttons. He slept.

Pantaloon was planning the marriage of Columbine.

Lucy Sorrel regarded her daughter with perplexity. The harangue she had just delivered had not produced the usual sharp replies. Jannie leaned back in her chair, lolling, as her mother thought of it. Her protests had been no more than an occasional 'Oh, Ma,' or 'There was nothing in it.' She even smiled faintly at some extravagant phrase. It was most unlike her.

'What's the matter with you? Aren't you well?'

Jannie came back from some distant place where her thoughts had been. 'I'm tired, that's all. We've been through the piece twice today. Isn't that enough to tire a person out?'

'You're young and strong. No need to come home drooping like a dying duck. Wait till you get to my age, on your feet all day if you're not crawling round the floor pinning up hemlines. Go on then, go to bed if you're as fagged out as all that. But you'll not get any supper, mind. Perhaps hunger'll teach you to behave yourself.'

'I'm not hungry,' said Jannie airily. But when she was in the cold little bed in the sitting-room, which by day turned up flat against the wall and pretended, unconvincingly, to be a cupboard, she discovered that she was hungry, after all; a yawning chasm seemed to have opened up inside her, gaping for food. Yet the next moment she felt faintly sick.

It had been so once before, the night she danced on stage for the first time. Then it had been worse because she was frightened, but the other feeling had been the same. It was excitement, of course, and she was excited now, first cold, then hot, and too restless to lie in one position for more than a few minutes at a time.

And before her eyes, whether she opened them or kept them tight shut, was Ivor's face, Harlequin's glittering smile, in the moonlight and shadow.

When the winter day dawned she knew that she was in love, for the first time in her seventeen years of life.

She was not an innocent, as a creature protected from life would have been. She had grown up in the London of George III, a London teeming like an anthill with open commerce between the sexes, vice unchecked by laws mainly interested in the protection of property. It was impossible to move, in the high narrow streets of Covent Garden, without seeing sights unmistakably shameless and ugly, prostitutes politely known as Cyprians parading in short flimsy dresses with their bosoms propped up like apples on a dish, children sold off to any gentleman who fancied that sort of thing, encounters taking place in doorways

(Ma had no need to warn about that) or in twilight alleys, should one be so rash as to venture down one when the day died.

Whatever the parson might say in church (and the Sorrels dutifully sat in St Paul's, Covent Garden, on a Sunday morning when the Captain was feeling bobbish), nobody could live in the region of Long Acre and retain the idea that humanity's nature at all resembled that of the angels, who, if these Georgians visualized them at all, were lightly-draped creatures of stone bearing stone souls aloft to Heaven with a simper and a flourish of stone trumpets. Westminster Abbey was full of them. Humanity as it flourished or perished in the streets was dirty, ragged, rotten of tooth, diseased in face and limb by venery or maimed in Nelson's and Wellington's wars. It stank, it hobbled, begging and stealing, it hung, horribly dead, from gibbets, it performed functions in public which the better-off reserved for comparative privacy. It did all those things which the general Confession of the Established Church deplored so strongly, it regularly erred and strayed from God's ways, and there appeared to be no health in it.

Yet there was. Wholesome, self-respecting folk, these were its health, young girls such as Jannie, accustomed to the sight of bad ways and able to look without seeing. Such sights were a part of town ways nothing to do with her own life at home or her work in the theatre. They touched neither her, Jannie herself, nor the make-believe world of the stage, where life was all laughter and jokes and songs, tinsel and spangles and blown kisses and happy endings. Cruelty and crudity alike were make-believe there. Now, amazingly, she was awake to real life, all because of a boy's looks and grace. She said his name to herself, again and again: 'Ivor, Ivor, Ivor.' So the pantomime was true after all – there was a Transformation Scene, Jack the peasant turned to Harlequin and Jill the milkmaid to Columbine.

For she was surely to play Columbine in life to Ivor's Harlequin.

She would never forget, as long as she lived, waking up from a happy drowse on that morning of late December to see snow

47

everywhere, thick on the opposite roofs like white velvet, thick on the pavements below though stained with footprints and wheel-tracks, powdery on the tops of carts and carriages and the shoulders of pedestrians. She forced open the stiff hasp of the window and leaned out, inhaling pure cold air that was like a breath of the country. Never again would she breathe the cold freshness of new-fallen snow without the ecstasy of that moment coming back, like a summoned spirit. 'Whiter than new snow on a raven's back': that was Juliet, dreaming of Romeo. Jannie had seen young Miss Eliza O'Neill play the part not long before, and been much impressed. Yet why had she not remembered the lines till now? The gallery had oh'd and ah'd and sighed at them, had gone home chanting 'Romeo, Romeo, wherefore art thou Romeo?' and so had come Tayleur's inspiration for the pantomime that had brought her and Ivor together.

There was a rehearsal call for dancers and supers two hours before the rising of the curtain. Mrs Sorrel was mercifully at the theatre all day, adjusting costumes, sewing and mending, and the Captain absent on his own business, so that Jannie had hours to herself, dreaming and dawdling. Every now and then she looked at herself in the mirror, seeing her face for the first time as a desirable one. She ransacked her very small wardrobe of dresses, finding them all now pitifully unsuitable. The pink was too wishy-washy, the black that had been made for her aunt's funeral quite dreadful. At last she chose the merino, her newest dress (how handy it was to have a dressmaker for a parent), a soft dark-blue with a touch of lilac, very little worn. She held it up in front of her, scanning her reflection critically. Yes, it would do. Of course she would have to change out of it into practice costume, but then he would see her in it when he brought her home.

And he would see what falling in love had done to her looks – the new brightness in her eyes, the clearness of her complexion. She had never looked prettier, she knew, and she was vain of it, not for herself, but for him.

Heads turned as she hurried through the snowy streets, pattens keeping her thin slippers from the slush. Sometimes she slowed

down, because she would be there too soon; sometimes hastened
in case, awful thought, she were late. At last, her colour blazing
and her heart beating fast, she was there, past the stage-door-
keeper, down the steps helter-skelter, for the clock in his little
office had pointed to a minute before the hour, and she must be
changed and on stage exactly on time or pay a fine of two shillings.
The management was severe about such things.

She made it by a hair's breadth, and stood panting in the first
line-up position, Fasoli's eye grimly fixed on her and the fiddler
who played for rehearsals tuning up in the corner. She and the
other girls worked for half an hour, going over and over the
bridal and processional dances ('young ladies, young ladies! how
often I tell you, glide, like swans, not waddle like ducks'). Because
her mind was not on her dancing she got a few cuts round the
ankles from the Signor's stick, but the pain was nothing,
today.

Then she saw Ivor, leaning against a scenery flat, the T-light
behind him putting a halo round the crest of his hair. It seemed
hours before the moment came for him to join her for the
Transformation Scene grouping.

Tremulous, smiling, she looked up at him and down again, and
felt his hand take hers, cool and confident. He said nothing,
though he had returned her smile; his eyes were on the ballet-
master and his mind on the actions as they swung into the dance
of salute to Queen Mab's descending throne, which was absent
from this rehearsal.

Mr Tayleur appeared from the stage box where he had been
watching.

'All right, that'll do. Mr Grimaldi's taking the principals
through the Harlequinade downstairs. Thank you, everybody.'

Ivor followed him to the wings. 'I hope it's not speaking out
of turn, sir. But I'd be very grateful if I might watch Mr Grimaldi's
rehearsal.'

The manager's eyebrows rose. 'Oh, indeed, and why, pray?'

'It would teach me so much,' said Ivor simply.

'Well, well. You want to learn clowning, do you?' He laughed.

49

'I see no reason why not, so long as you don't get in the way. Tell Joey I gave you leave.'

'Thank you, sir.' He ran off into the wings. Jannie stood where he had left her, feeling suddenly cold though a moment ago she had been sweating with exertion. It was hard to put into thoughts just what she had expected; but it was not to be deserted like this, without a word.

At the performance it was just the same. He was friendly, pleasant, her efficient partner, but that was all. Afterwards she changed, very slowly, and went eagerly, hopefully, up to the stage-door. He would be waiting for her, of course.

But he was not there. Her mother appeared, scolding as usual. Jannie, hardly taking in a word, held her mother's frail arm and guided her through the now slippery streets. Where the warm, tingling glow had been, deep in her breast, there now seemed to lodge a cold, heavy weight, like a cannon-ball.

Ivor sat, at leisure, arms folded, watching Joey Grimaldi robbing a property fish-shop. He was perfectly composed and at ease with himself, for he, too, had spent some time in thought since escorting Jannie home.

He had known ever since his schooldays and those rendezvous in the chapel graveyard that he was intensely attractive to women. He had *cyfaredd*, the power to charm. Miss Susannah De Vaux had been no trouble at all, merely a mature and ample lady who liked to boast a young conquest, enjoy him, then turn to another. Since her day there had been several females occupying his spare time, but none, he knew, had thought of him as more than a diversion, any more than he had thought of them.

The little Sorrel was different. In her he recognized a good girl sheltered, yet brought up to protect herself which in this world of wolves and lambs meant nothing at all. The light in her eyes when they had parted the night before had not escaped him. He knew her for one ready to give herself as generously as a country girl would give an armful of wild flowers. And then, ah then, the regrets, the heart-searchings. He was much attracted to her – even had one of his own peculiar instincts about her destiny being written with his own. She was deliciously pretty, charmingly small to one who was not himself tall for a man, only for a dancer.

He might woo her and destroy her, as the wild flowers perished within four walls; it happened often enough. He might woo and wed her, and so find himself a father at twenty-two, with a wife of eighteen, neither able to bear the burden of parenthood and the constant struggle to make the money go round.

There was Joey, dear good Joey, at present upside down juggling with a chain of imitation sausages. At home, Ivor knew, he was a model family man, at home in Islington with his wife Mary and the twelve-year-old Joe; but how he worked for it, for them. Those who knew him saw twinges of pain in his face as he performed Clown's contortions. He was pulled to his limit, yet he must go on, ever more and more energetic and ridiculous, for the sake of wife and child.

Ivor watched Bologna, sauntering through the motions with his own good-humoured grace. He was thirty-three, beginning to be over-muscular. One day he would retire, and so would the other Harlequins, of Sadler's Wells and Drury; and then he, Ivor Bryn, would be their heir. For he knew himself to be touched by the wand, the magic bat, that would transform him into the Prince of Pantomime when the time came. Just twenty-one he was: plenty of years to go. What else was there, indeed? The poverty of London's streets shocked him, as did the devil-may-care attitude of the other male dancers and supers, most of them in the profession for what they could earn at the time, then they would turn butcher's apprentice or go to whatever trade they fancied, or didn't fancy – unless they took to begging outright.

That was not for Ivor. His family would have been surprised to know how hard-headed their dreamer had become. He had a splendid body, a burning ambition, the chance to study the best skills the London stage could offer. And there was something in him, besides, of national pride. He, a boy from the mountains of

Wales, not even brought up to speak their tongue, would show the English what little Gwalia, the Red Dragon, could do against the Great Red Lion. Yet he was humble enough in himself to know how hard he must work for all this.

He whistled very softly to himself, unheard against the banter on the floor, Grimaldi's wild laugh, a thump and a curse from Bologna, Raymond Otway's gentlemanly protests, Mrs Parker's squeal. It was not the Queen Mab music he whistled, but the song of *Caradwg*, king of the Welsh Britons, who had led his people against the invading Romans. There was a rubbishy street version of it, that he had heard the balladeers sing: something about 'Of a noble race was Shenkin, the line of Owen Tudor, But her renown was fled and gone Since cruel love pursu'd her'. There, little Sorrel, that's the lesson for you; take heed of it.

The string of sausages landed at his feet. Deftly he threw them back.

'Thankee,' called Grimaldi. 'Give a hand, will you, cully?' He indicated Bologna, who was sitting on a chair nursing his ankle. 'Mr B. here's done himself a mischief, and we want to get through this next bit of business in double-quick time.'

'I'll live,' Bologna said. 'No call to make a fuss, Joey.'

Mrs Parker broke in. 'Oh, do let's go on, please. My Juliet dress has so many buttons and it takes years to get it on. Let the young man give a hand if he can.'

But Ivor was there already, poised for instructions. Grimaldi threw a giant imitation eel at him. 'You take this here, see, and climb up there and wave it over Pantaloon's nose. He makes a grab at it and you jump on top of that ladder. It's standing in for Columbine's window, you see.'

'I think I know, sir,' Ivor said. Watched by three interested pairs of eyes he dangled the eel enticingly, made a passable spring in the air and landed where he had hoped he would, on the top rung of the ladder in an attitude he had seen Bologna strike.

'Not bad, not bad.' The Harlequin nodded approval. 'You want to get your weight off that other foot, though, when you take off, or you'll come a cropper. I could show you where you went wrong . . .' He was getting to his feet, but Grimaldi pushed him back, to Ivor's disappointment.

'Not now, we ain't the time, and you want to save your ankle for the show. Let's get on. Houp-la, Eliza, chassez across and point at Pantaloon. All right, Mr Whatsyourname, you can get down now.'

Ivor leapt down and went back to his watching-place, with a small polite bow to the others. Had it been a good omen, his spring on to the ladder?

It was hard for Ivor to resist the appeal in Jannie's wistful eyes, but his mind was made up, and now that he had learned how to observe the techniques of the senior dancers, and the art of being at hand when anyone extra was wanted, the pursuit of his art was absorbing enough to keep him from bothering with trifles.

He was only amused when a girl called Bess Ames, who had a ripe rosebud mouth and a headful of natural black ringlets (some said she was the daughter of an Aldgate Jew) sidled up to him and nudged him away from his companion, the boy who played Owl to his Moth.

'There's lovely you talk, then. Won't you say a few of them things to me?'

He stared. 'What things?'

'All them words like singing. *You* know.' She mocked him. 'Inteet, yess, whateffer, isn't it. Ever so pretty, they are.'

'You've a quick ear, mocking me like that.'

She looked slyly sideways, out of big brown eyes. 'I've a quick appetite, too. Fancy a bite and a sup? Oh come on, it's New Year, let's go and drink to Victory.'

Ivor laughed and shrugged. He had just been paid. 'Get your bonnet, then. I'm sharp-set myself.'

Because she turned her nose up at the Garden coffee-stalls with their fragrant smells of coffee and sassafras-tea and soup, he took her to Brassey's, a little out of his class, but he was hungry and the thought of a plate of *à-la-mode* beef was as tempting as Miss

Ames's ripe lips and plump figure. No sense in eating alone. He ordered a tankard of porter for each of them, and they downed it quickly, thirsty and hungry as dancers are after a performance. Her conversation was racy; he had little to do but listen and learn, which he enjoyed, and laugh at her sometimes as she prattled on about the Regent's estranged wife's reputed misconduct in Hamburg.

In the quietest, most secluded booth Brassey's possessed sat Raymond and Sara. They occupied it almost every night now. In only a fortnight or so Sara had calmed down and acquired a quiet steadiness. She no longer feared that the celestial throne would topple to the stage and her with it, or feared Mr Tayleur's tongue should that happen. The apprehension had gone out of her eyes and the skin was no longer strained over her cheek-bones. She looked, Raymond thought, five years or more younger than when he had first taken notice of her, and he knew with a happy certainty that it was because of him.

He too was calmer. It no longer irritated and humiliated him as at first it had done to present himself before the public in the idiotic character of Pantaloon. True, Grimaldi and Bologna were both pleasant, good-humoured creatures, and Mrs Parker an amiable silly; but the real reason was that when the charade was over he could turn to a friend who silently understood his feelings, shared his situation, and treated him as a gentleman and a Thespian, not as a mummer.

It was Raymond who saw Ivor and Bess Ames enter the chop-house. He pointed them out to Sara.

'A remarkable youth, that. I may not be an acrobat, but I saw him stand in for Jack Bologna as to the manner born. I wonder where he learned it.'

'Perhaps he comes from a foreign family; they so often do. He has a look not entirely English.'

'Yet not Italian either. A strange face. He might go far in this precarious world of ours . . . Will you take a little of the pudding, my dear?'

He was not afraid to call her that, now.

It was the first time Ivor took Bess Ames out, but far from the last. Her chatter was tedious and her nature shallow, but she had a sharp turn of wit and a sensual attraction very hard to resist, especially when she wielded her power so relentlessly. Her former beau, Will Shanks, a large-made lad who appeared in the panto-mime as a shambling dancing bear, took jealous note of the time she spent with Ivor, and tackled him one day outside the theatre.

'I want a word with you.'

'Indeed? I don't know that I want one with you.'

'Is that so? Well, I've something to show you, sir.'

'And what might that be, sir?'

'This, sir.' Shanks waved to and fro before Ivor's eyes a large fist. 'You can see it clear, can you?'

'Perfectly.'

'And you think it very fine, I've no doubt. Well, let me tell you it an't only handsome, it's useful.'

Ivor looked bored. 'Oh, indeed?'

' "Oh, inteet"! Yes, it's useful for flattenin' the noses of little Welsh puppies as sneaks other folks' girls, and one of 'em's going to feel it *now* – sir.' With which he made a savage lunge at Ivor, who ducked nimbly aside with a flashing blow which struck his opponent square in the middle of his left cheek, connecting neatly with the bone and causing him to let out a growl of pain. He flung himself upon Ivor, and found himself lying flat on the theatre steps glaring up at his rival.

'That's settled, then?' said Ivor, preparing to leave the pros-trate foe where he lay; but a grab round the ankle brought him down and into Shanks's rough embrace, his ribs crushed and his head banged against a step. A small crowd had gathered, in-cluding Bess, who was squealing in an attempt to get near the combatants. Suddenly Ivor gathered his forces and leapt up, followed more clumsily by Shanks. Determined not to let it become a wrestling match he danced away, lashing out with his fists at whatever portion of the man presented itself. His chance came when he got in a blow straight to Shanks's diaphragm, winding him completely and drawing a cheer from the crowd.

Shanks sat down on a step, bent double and groaning. Ivor made a graceful display of dusting himself down, reclaiming his fallen hat, and languidly inspecting his knuckles.

'There, you see,' he addressed the conquered one, 'Welsh puppies can be a match for bears, isn't that so?'

Bess was clinging to him, all excitement. 'Oh, Ivor, you ain't half a swell! Taking on that great bully, and all for me. Why, you'd be a match for Gentleman Jackson or Cribb hisself. I'm so proud of you, I could kiss you . . .' And she did, to the delight of the crowd, who still lingered to watch the grateful fair reward her hero, and to the annoyance of Ivor. He detached her clinging arms and looked ruefully down at his muddied coat and breeches. Already the knocks he had taken were beginning to hurt; he would be stiff by nightfall and if he couldn't dance it would mean a week's pay lost, the fine for non-appearance.

'There,' he said testily, 'it was nothing. Run along, that's a good girl.' She went, fondly looking backwards.

Somewhere under the stage, filtering up through a grille, Ivor could hear a violin, stopping and starting with dreary patience. A rehearsal was going on, though it was long before Curtain Up. He made his way down and found Grimaldi rehearsing alone, but for the fiddler and a pretty, plump young woman very brightly dressed and wearing a red velvet hat with a turned-up brim and white feathers, in the style of the exiled Princess of Wales. Joey, engaged in a complicated manoeuvre with a vaulting-horse, stopped dramatically in mid-action and swivelled his eyes round to the muddied, limping, dishevelled figure.

'Young Harlequin, so help me!' he cried, reeling back with a hand to the brow, in the gesture common to stage Squires recognizing their long-lost eldest sons. 'What has befallen thee, pray tell?'

'I didn't mean to trouble you, sir. I only came looking for someone who would advise me what to do about . . . about a few bangs I've taken.'

The young woman darted forward, all bright eyes and sympathy.

'Dear life, Joey, the boy's been run over by a chaise, that's for sure. Do look at him!'

Joey looked, and said in quite a different, ordinary, kind tone: 'What is it, lad?'

'Nothing, sir,' Ivor answered, embarrassed, 'only a scuffle. I won it,' he added proudly. 'I am just afraid I might make a poor showing tonight. I feel I may stiffen, or come up in bruises, and I wondered . . .'

The clown gently examined his face, touched his arms and legs. 'No harm done that shows. You're lucky not to have got a couple of shiners out of it. Nothing broken – only a bit sore,' as Ivor winced. 'Mary, my love, the Good Old Remedy, if you please. Young Mr Whatsyourname, this is my dear wife, the comfort of my days.'

Mary Grimaldi dipped a curtsey, highly professional, Ivor noted. He found out later that she was an ex-actress now in the *corps de ballet* at Sadler's Wells, her husband's habitual theatre. It was closed for a season because of the disastrous overflowing of the water tanks which provided the playhouse with its nautical dramas and aquatic pantomimes. She got briskly to work on a large canvas bag on the floor, which, when opened, proved to contain medicine bottles, cloths, pots of ointment, and other bottles of a less medicinal appearance. To this bag were attached strong woven handles, long enough to go over a person's shoulder.

'Which do you want, Joe, dear?'

'The Infallible Embrocation, the Elixir, of course, my love. But first . . .' He went to the door and shouted in a curious, hollow yet piercing voice, like one summoning demons from an underground cave, '*MRS NOAKES*!'

A very small, bent woman appeared on shuffling feet, her head cocked like a worming bird's. Grimaldi met her with a stage embrace, all-enveloping yet hardly touching.

'Mrs Noakes, my enchanting fairy belle, how about a bath? Can you manage one?'

'Oh, deary, deary me. You ain't had another tumble, have you?'

'Not me, my angel. This young man. Just a slight . . .' He mimed a violent prize-fight, ending with the apparent death of one combatant. 'You *know*. Lovely 'ealing 'ot water. Come on, just for Joey.'

'Oh, well. You aren't 'alf a bother. Just you keep out o' trouble yourself, that's all. This way, young feller.' With a jerk of her head she motioned Ivor to follow her, grumbling under her breath as she led him to a small, dungeon-like apartment a few steps down from the dressing-room floor. It had rough-cast walls and a window remarkably reminiscent of a prison cell. But on a primitive fireplace hob stood a huge fish-kettle, a faint wisp of steam coming from it. This, with imprecations, Mrs Noakes jammed on top of the low fire and began to blow up the flames with a gigantic pair of bellows. Ivor watched fascinated. The wisp grew to a cloud, then to a great volume of white vapour filling the tiny room.

Mrs Noakes stepped outside into what was evidently an area, and with heavy clankings returned with a tin hip bath almost as big as herself. This she slammed down on the floor, seized the kettle before Ivor could help her, and poured the steaming contents into it.

'There y'are, get yer clothes orf.'

Ivor stared. Certainly, he had taken his clothes off in a lady's presence before now, but in rather different circumstances. His Mam would have thought it downright immoral, *digywilydd*. If any of his family had taken a bath (and he could not remember such an occasion, for a clear young river ran near his home, and the children took a dip in that when they felt like it) they would have done so in the strictest privacy. Whatever would the Minister have said, otherwise?

Then he laughed at his own prudishness. In the world of the theatre one must do as others do. He stripped off his clothes and stepped into the water, uncomfortably hot at first, then wonderfully relaxing to strained muscles and bruised flesh. Mrs Noakes, completely oblivious to his nudity, occupied herself in hanging out garments on a washing-line in the area, for she was among other functions laundress to the players. When he had lain soaking blissfully for ten minutes or so she returned.

'Right, that's enough. Out yer get.'

Obediently he stepped out, to find himself swiftly wrapped in a rough and none too clean towel and rubbed briskly until he felt as raw as a skinned rabbit. He reached for his clothes, but Mrs Noakes forestalled him.

'You stay still. You got to 'ave the Elixir rubbed in like I does it for Grim.' From a large brown bottle she filled the palms of her hands with a liquid that smelt acrid and medicinal. Then she massaged Ivor from head to foot with her small, gnarled hands, hurting a good deal in the process, and humming tunelessly under her breath. Ivor felt so very like a horse being groomed that he was quite unable to stop himself laughing. Mrs Noakes glared at him.

'You'll laugh the other side of yer face, me laddo, if yer tries to do tricks like Grim and Patchy wivout the Elixir to ease you up arterwards. Show me a acrobat and I'll show you a cripple at forty, that's what. There ain't a quack in London as could give you a better rub than this. *She* makes it up for him, Mary that is. Comes from a tribe of acrobats and such, so knows all about it. I reckon,' went on Mrs Noakes, causing Ivor acute agony in the region of his left shoulder-blade, 'I reckon as she saved his life when he was down with the melancholics arter Maria went.'

'Maria?'

'Mrs Grim the First. Mad with love for 'er, 'e was, poor Grim. Only been married a bit over a year when she died in childbed. It broke 'is 'eart, if ever I see an 'eart broke. They said as 'e'd 'ave been found with 'is throat cut if friends 'adn't watched by 'im, night and day, and Mary – Mary Bristow she was then – was one that was kindest to 'im. She was a nice, pretty young thing, and when they got married arter 'is mourning year was out we was all as pleased as Punch. I wouldn't say as it was in 'im to be *'appy*, azacktly, but Mary keeps 'im as cheerful as can be expected. For a clown, that is. There, that's you finished. Get yer things on.'

For a clown, she had said. A man whose mere appearance on

the stage was enough to set the audience in a roar, whose most casual utterances were regarded as screamingly funny, who must never show any but a grinning face to those who came to forget their own troubles at the sight of his antics, and all the time, in his heart, carrying a black mourning garland for his young dead bride. It made one think. Ivor, so confident and wrapped in his own ambitions, had grown up just a little during Mrs Noakes's revelations.

He strolled one day to the pleasant village of Islington, inspected the pretty theatre of Sadler's Wells by the New River Head, and wondered whether he would ever play there; then crossed the fields towards Clerkenwell, and found the church of St James, driven by what impulse he could not tell. Perhaps it was a morbid curiosity, or an act of sympathy for the sad, funny man he had come to admire so much.

Yes, there was her grave, her epitaph.

Earth walks on gold like glittering gold;
Earth says to Earth, we are but mould;
Earth builds on Earth castles and towers;
Earth says to Earth, all shall be ours.

Ivor stood gazing at the stone. He was thinking of life, and the Stage, and women, and what would become of him, and all of them who pranced and capered nightly in motley to make people laugh and dream. A black Welsh melancholy settled upon him; he walked swiftly back to the Shakespeare's Head beside the Wells, and drank a pint or two of porter to raise his spirits.

CHAPTER FOUR

The Plans of Pantaloon

Though Ivor was not conscious of it, the story of Grimaldi's tragic first marriage strengthened his resolution to keep away from Jannie and the lure she held for him. It was so easy to fall in love, to make oneself vulnerable. Secure now in the knowledge that Will Shanks would leave him alone, he began to flirt with Bess Ames, walked her home after the curtain and sometimes dallied with her in the dark lobby of the house where she lived, strongly redolent of onions and tomcats, and all the less conducive to romance. The one thing he would never risk was to get her with child. In his own village there had been many bastards, in spite of the Minister's tirades from the pulpit, and Ivor could not for his life see why their parents had been so silly. Everybody knew what happened when a man and a woman lay together; why should they risk the degradation and suffering that followed? He would go so far and no further, with Bess or any other girl. Best for her, best for him.

Jannie came to know about his carryings-on with Bess. The other girls had been quick to notice her attraction to Ivor and even quicker to tell her that her beau had found another sweetheart.

'Took her out to Islington on Sunday,' remarked Lettie Mullins to Sophy Cran, as they slapped wet-white on their shoulders and arms in the dressing-room. 'Gave her a shrimp tea at the Gardens, and there was dancing afterwards under the trees, she told me. Ever so well they got on. Mind you, *I* think he's too good for her, though he's not what I'd call a swell.'

'Lovely figure, though.' Sophy fixed a wreath of artificial roses across the top of her head. 'Like one of them statues – *you* know,' and she dug her friend in the ribs with a sharp elbow. 'Only with clothes on. Wouldn't mind him meself.' Then, cruelly, for Jannie was within hearing distance, 'I tell you, someone's had her nose put out of joint, and no mistake.'

Jannie danced on the night she heard of this like a puppet, her hand cold when it touched Ivor's. She neither looked at him nor spoke to him, but she saw Bess's wide smile at him from the other side of the stage, and the answering quirk of his mouth. Bess was wearing pink fleshings that showed off her plump calves; Jannie would like to have torn them off, ripped up Bess's muslin dress, and sat her heavily in a bed of nettles, after which she would tip a bucket of whitewash over her head and kick her into a pond full of tadpoles. Fantasies of revenge on Bess filled her mind, so that she missed a step, and this time Ivor was not there to save her. But Fasoli was in the wings, and she knew a telling-off and a fine would be hers next day.

She left the theatre enclosed in a cocoon of angry misery, defiantly throwing back the hood of her cloak as the cold air hit her outside the stage-door. Let her catch a chill and die of a consumption. *That* would serve Ivor right, and perhaps then he would be sorry, and she would come back and haunt Bess like the Ghostly Nun in the book one of the girls had lent her and her mother had snatched away and hidden.

Her broodings were interrupted by a man's voice.

'Good evening, miss.'

She saw a well-dressed man, in his thirties or thereabouts, hat raised, bowing to her with a pointed toe, a silver-topped cane in his hand. Quite the dandy.

'Good evening,' she said mechanically, though all her training had been to ignore any overtures made at the stage-door. She knew that gentlemen approached girls there, sometimes penetrated into the Green Room and took wine with them, and after that . . . well, it could lead to anything. Tonight she told herself, she didn't care.

'I so much admired your performance tonight, miss. Would it be asking too much of a favour to request you to take a little supper with me? John Doe, at your service.'

Jannie looked hastily behind her. No, Ma was not there, because an entire breadth had by accident been ripped from Miss Dell's Queen Mab costume which had got caught up with the machinery of the chariot, and it must be repaired as soon as possible. She smiled graciously at the stranger.

'You're very kind. I'd be delighted.'

His face brightened. 'Then my life is transformed to Paradise, confound it. Shall we walk?' Firmly he tucked her arm into his, and off they went at a spanking pace, the gentleman chattering on about his Club and a sensational bet he had won on a horse, and Princess Charlotte's coming-of-age and the remarkably cold weather which prophets said would lead to the worst frost in history. Jannie made a few polite replies, nothing else being apparently expected of her. The gentleman, who had introduced himself as Mr John Doe, held her arm very close to his side, so close as to make walking somewhat uncomfortable; she wished he would not, but her efforts to separate herself from him only met with a closer grip.

They seemed to be at the far side of Covent Garden, towards the end of King Street.

'Where are we going, if you please, sir?' she asked nervously.

'Going? Why, to a nice tidy little place I know. They do a very pretty dish of dressed tripe. You girls need feeding up, eh? All that prancing and cavorting with your charming legs ... no wonder you keep your shape so neat, hey, hey?' And he gave her waist an alarming squeeze. She began to wish heartily that she had never come with him. He smelt of Scotch ale and somehow she suspected he knew more about horse-racing than about the Court affairs of which he gossiped so freely. Suddenly he propelled her sharply to the left and round a corner. The alley was dark, only one street-lamp flickering at the end of it.

'Just down here,' he said. 'Little supper-rooms. Nothing showy, but very fashionable with the *ton*, can assure you. Put sparkles in your eyes, little fairy.'

Then he stopped. 'What about a kiss first, though – hey?' And before she knew it she was pressed against the wall, struggling, trying to push him away with all her strength, his face always coming down on hers and his hard body flattening her against the bricks. Panic seized her. Most nights there would have been other couples huddled in the court, all kinds of nocturnal activities taking advantage of its darkness, but tonight the bitter cold had sent them to more sheltered places. She had only herself to rely on. With a flood of relief, even as they struggled, he muttering a mixture of endearments and obscenities, she realized that the advantage was with her, for she was very young and very strong, and had a dancer's muscles, and he a middle-aged man who had been drinking. With a violent heave and push against his chest she writhed out of his clutches and was off like the wind, leaving him staggering and calling her a foul name.

She ran and ran, gasping, aware that she was among people again, people going home from theatres or taverns, who stared at her flying figure. She prayed that one of them might be the Captain, so that she could go home safely on her father's arm, but he would still be at the Nag's Head. All she could think of was to get home, and be damned, she said to herself, to what Ma might say – she would make up a story.

The theatre loomed up before her, darkened, the candles out, the night-watchman on his rounds. She looked up at it, relieved to see its familiar bulk, the sturdy Corinthian columns. Then, at the same moment, her breath gave out and she leaned against a wall, panting like a hunted animal. Out of the darkness a familiar figure came.

'My dear child!' said Sara. 'What can have happened to you? Are you injured?'

Jannie, who had hardly before that moment exchanged a word with the pantomime's leading lady, threw herself into her arms and burst into noisy, uncontrollable tears. The tall Sara looked down compassionately at the bare head, the tangled curls, the dishevelled dress. One of the child's sandals had come untied and the string was dangling on the ground. Sara held her, murmuring reassurance. She vaguely knew this to be one of the dancers, the little one, who had sometimes smiled at her and always looked cheerful and self-assured. Sorrel, that was her name, the daughter of the formidable wardrobe-lady.

Sara's voice, which could without effort reach the back of the gallery, was remarkably soft and soothing in private life. Before long it penetrated Jannie's agitated ears.

'What a fortunate thing I left late tonight. There was an accident to my dress, and your mother most kindly offered to mend it. I fear you've fallen upon some mishap, my dear. Won't you tell me about it?'

Jannie collected herself, ashamed to be blubbering like a baby in front of Miss Dell – indeed, on her shoulder. Sniffing and dragging her arm across her eyes she said, 'It was – a man. I ought to have known better . . . I didn't expect . . . oh, ma'am, I must go home, or Ma will kill me!'

'I doubt that you should go home like that,' Sara said gently. 'I think it might alarm your Mama very much to see you so – so distressed. Won't you come to my lodgings for a little while, and we can spruce you up and make you quite yourself again? I generally make a pot of tea when I come home; now that would do you the world of good, I'm sure.'

Jannie was sure, too. The very thought made her feel better. And the sight of Sara's neat little room, at the back of the tall house, improved her state even more. The candles were soon lit, the fire in the duck's-nest grate had been kept glowing steadily by the judicious application of tea-leaves before Sara had left for the theatre. On the hob a copper kettle sat, beautifully polished; the place was welcome itself.

As they entered, a loud, clear cry greeted them, so clear that Jannie could almost hear words in it, but it came from a cat. Long, slender, black as jet, with the pointed face and long ears of a bat, Miranda leapt from the patchwork cushion that was hers and projected herself at Sara, who picked her up and held her to her breast, where Miranda turned over and lay like a babe, feet upwards, unmistakably smiling. Mistress and cat greeted each other in a language both understood perfectly, then Sara put her gently on the ground and set about making the tea.

'What a . . .' Jannie was lost for words. 'What a strange cat. Charming, I mean. I mean, one sees so many in the streets, but I never saw one quite like it . . . her. I thought they were, well, wild.'

Sara shook her head. 'Most of our Covent Garden cats are, poor dears. They live on the scraps they can pick up from the shops and barrows. Some are lucky and have homes, of course. But even they are despised, more often than not, and kept as mere rat-catchers. If only people knew the wisdom of cats, the sensibility and sweetness of their natures! The old Egyptians knew, of course, and worshipped them. Then they came over to the Western world, and were wickedly abused. Yes, abused, and by people calling themselves Christians.'

Her face troubled and stern, she heated the teapot. Jannie thought she looked very like a picture of Mrs Siddons in a tragic role, only with a prettier nose.

'But Miranda don't look like the cats in the Market,' Jannie said.

'Her mother was Burmese, my dear, from the East, where cats are understood. That is why she is so wise and kindly. She is my friend – aren't you, my black angel?'

Miranda purred and smiled, her eyes firmly fixed on the milk-jug. Jannie thought that some people would have concluded Miss Dell was a mad old maid, but she did not think so at all, herself. She had a strong suspicion that Miranda was her mistress's only friend, and it was quite natural she should feel like that towards her. Anyway, she reflected bitterly, when *people* behaved like . . . she shut out the thought of Ivor, and substituted the man who had solicited her tonight. As they drank their tea, she told Sara about him.

'And he called himself John Doe!' Sara threw her head back in the first hearty laugh Jannie had heard from her. 'My poor girl, John Doe is a fictitious character in some law-suit or other – the other one is Richard Roe, and they are either plaintiff and defendant or the other way round, I forget which. The wretched man was bent on deceiving you. Thank Heaven you escaped as you did.'

'I'm very strong, though I don't look it.' Jannie sat up straight, slender and bird-boned, and flexed one ankle.

'That may be. But why, child, were you so simple as to go with

66

him in the first place? You must know how dangerous such encounters are. You might have come to . . . I shudder to think
what.'

'Oh . . .' Jannie regarded her outstretched foot. 'Some of the
girls do it to better themselves. And besides . . .'

'Besides what? Come now, there's something else. A girl like
you does not "better herself" in such a low way.'

Miranda had wriggled sideways and put her head on Jannie's
feet, looking at her confidently out of up-tilted eyes. Suddenly
Jannie found herself telling Sara about Ivor, the stumble from
which he had rescued her, the night he had taken her home, his
curious remark about her being his luck, the odd feeling he gave
her.

'It's like a pain – like being ill. I don't know. I never felt anything like it. It all means nothing, I daresay. But now, seeing him
with that common, vulgar Bess, not giving me a glance . . . oh,
I could run down Drury Lane and jump off Surrey Stairs into the
river, that I could.'

Sara looked at her with compassion. 'I trust you'll do nothing
of the kind. My dear child, you are in the throes of first love, and
very painful it can be. I should recommend leaving the young
man to go his own way, and go your own. These violent delights
have violent ends, as our Great William put it. Young Mr Bryn
will think none the worse of you for keeping your distance.'

Jannie nodded. 'I know. I have a bit of common sense, if I did
but use it. Ma always told me . . .' And she was off on stories of
her childhood, of the Captain and his fine friends, of her first
dancing-class and the first time she saw the curtain rise on a real
pantomime, while Sara studied her, nodded and smiled. At last
she said: 'How old are you?'

'Seventeen.'

As though a thought had flashed between them, the girl turned
her face, like a white flower in the light of the poor single candle,
up towards the older woman's.

'If you'd been my Ma I think I'd have more sense than do what
I did tonight. We – you and I – seem to be able to talk. Only – I

don't know. Oh, there's so much I don't know, ma'am.'

Sara turned away from the light. Seventeen, a daughter's age. Oh George, oh my baby. She was very much afraid she might disgrace herself by weeping, but Miranda, who had been lying with her chin on the fender staring hypnotically into the dying fire, rose to her feet, said, very plainly, 'Yik,' and strode to the window. Sara opened it for her to jump out onto the little flat roof a foot or so below, planted out with flower-pots, a pathetic London apology for a garden.

'It's her little exercise-ground,' Sara said. 'And now, oh dear me, you must be going, or your mother will be calling out the Watch.'

Jannie stared at the mantelpiece clock, appalled. Nearly midnight. She was terrified at the thought of her mother's reception. To spend the night in the Watch-house would be comparative comfort. Her hair had been straightened, her rumpled dress put to rights, her heartbeat slowed: but now she felt as agitated as when she had broken from the fellow's clutches. Miserably she made her way downstairs, lit by Sara's candle. At the door Sara put down the candlestick and moved out with her into the cold night air. A light came towards them through the blackness, a link-man carrying the lit torch with which he had been escorting home a late theatre-goer.

'Boy!' Sara hailed him in her clear, authoritative voice. 'A lady here requires your conduct. This will serve, I think,' and with Shakespearean grandeur she put into his grimy hand a shilling, one-tenth of her rent for the lodgings. It was as though Lady Macbeth had had occasion to tip the Porter. He ducked his head to her, repeated Jannie's directions, and beckoned her to follow him.

'Goodnight.'

'Goodnight, ma'am, and . . . thank you for the tea,' Jannie said lamely.

It was far worse, even, than she had expected. The first thing she saw near their door was the figure of the Captain, striding to and fro with a dark-lantern. As she flung herself upon him he grasped her fiercely, held her to him for a moment, in a cloud of gin-fumes, then released her, demanding, 'Where the devil have you been? Your poor mother's half out of her mind.'

It was no understatement. Never had Jannie heard such a tirade. Mrs Sorrel was furious, frightened, convinced that the Worst had happened to her only child, unprepared to listen to explanations or excuses. Red-faced, wild-haired, in a formidable ruff-edged bedgown, she knocked down Jannie's defences one by one.

'With Miss Dell! A likely story, when I left the place with her meself. As for you taking a stroll to cool off, when did you ever do such a thing, or when would any respectable girl do such? As to going home with her, what would a lady like her want with you? You was with a man, don't tell me anything else.'

Trembling, Jannie summoned up all her recollections of Miss Dell's room. It was a first-pair back, half of a drawing-room. She tried to describe the remains of ceiling mouldings, of cornices of plaster fruit and flowers, a little marble fireplace with an inset carving of a nymph and a satyr (only Ma would misunderstand that one, so she passed it over quickly), the pretty things that belonged to Miss Dell, not to the landlady – a white bust of Garrick, a figure of Britannia with her lion in colours and gilding, the delicate transparent cups they had drunk from. And Miranda, the cat who was not like a cat, unless it was the white Cat of the pantomime who turned into a lady in the Transformation Scene of *Puss in Boots*.

Circumstantial evidence can be convincing, even to the prejudiced ear. Mrs Sorrel knew that she had only to ask Miss Dell next day, and she would get the truth.

'Well, it sounds like you'd been there – some time. Who's to say when? I'll find out, never you mind, and then perhaps we'll know where you was in the meantime.'

'I told you,' Jannie said sulkily.

'Won't do, yer know,' the Captain put in. 'Out half the night, searching the streets for you.' The redness of his face owed less to drink than to agitation, great corded veins standing out on his temples, a nervous twitch at the corner of his mouth. Jannie felt ridiculously like the Baby with Punch and Judy both glaring at her, painted images fighting with croaking words. She was terribly tired, ashamed of herself, longing only for them to go to bed and leave her. In the despair of her untried youth she longed for everything to change. This was the Dark Scene, the Cat Scene, when everything goes wrong: soon the stage must lighten.

Lucy Sorrel, sitting up in bed with a warm flannel nightcap tied firmly under her chin, pulled the Captain's great-coat over her knees and his as an additional bed-covering, for a sharp frost was in the air. Then she snuffed out their bedside candle.

Her husband had turned over, his back to her. She gave him a sharp dig between the shoulders.

'Don't go off yet.'

He turned over with a sigh. 'I doubt if I could, m'dear. Too much on the mind. Don't like Janetta coming in at all hours, wherever she may have been. All very well to say Miss Dell entertained her – don't doubt it – but who will it be next time? Fasoli? Tayleur? Or even that young Welsh whipper-snapper you thought she had an eye for.'

'Exackly,' said his wife triumphantly. 'Ain't that what I've been saying, all along? All right her being a dancer when she was a child. Now she's a young woman, and it seems like I can't keep her at my apron-strings for ever. What *are* we to do with her, Captain?'

'Wish I knew. She an't up to the legitimate drama yet, or I'd get in a word with Kemble somehow. I don't know, though. She could start off with something on the quiet side – just a few words, ladies' attendants, that sort of thing . . .' He brightened. 'I'll take advice. Know just the fellow to ask.'

'That's right, you do.' Lucy gave him a little approbatory pat. For all his faults, she had a curious trust in him to solve their problems. Perhaps it was because when her early prettiness had faded and rheumatics had bent her body and swollen her hands, he had not turned from her to other women, but had treated her with the same fondness and courtliness as before. For such things a woman is more grateful than for much fine gold.

The fellow whose advice the Captain had decided to ask was Raymond Otway. Dropping into the Nag's Head one day for his customary refreshment, he had noticed him at the bar. With his usual bonhomie, he had made himself known, and Raymond, a somewhat friendless man, for reasons of his own, responded graciously. Over drinks paid for by Raymond they had discussed many things, including the Captain's admiration for his daughter's talents; and Raymond had managed to remember which one of the dancers she was, and had made the right complimentary remarks.

On the morning after the Captain's midnight pillow talk with his wife, he was glad to see his quarry already seated close to the roaring fire the Nag's Head snug provided for its customers. Raymond always did his drinking early in the day. That way, there was less danger of the old menace of forgetfulness during the performance. The pocket-flask counted only as medicine, he assured himself.

'Delighted to see you, my dear fellow,' exclaimed the Captain, rubbing his icy hands and loosening the caped great-coat which had kept him and Lucy warm the night before. 'What'll you take? Same as yesterday? Let's have it mulled, eh?' And with two steaming tankards before him he began earnestly to set his problems before Raymond.

'Would be enormously grateful for your professional advice, sir.'

'Any help I can give . . .'

'My little Janetta. Now, her mother and I are seriously concerned about the . . . how shall I put it? The risks to her reputation. Showing her limbs, letting partners, er . . . embrace her. A

71

pretty young gel has much to lose, sir, as I needn't tell you, and of late she's been, er, spreadin' her wings a bit. Dodges her mother's chaperonage, that sort of thing, gives pert back-answers when spoken to. All part of her age, perhaps, Sweet Seventeen and so forth, but it troubles us, I won't conceal from you. Now, sir, you're a man of the theatre, you know the real thing, I mean, not this pantomime airy-fairy stuff. Do you think my little daughter could make her name in it – with a word from you, perhaps to someone of influence – Mr Kemble – Miss Fanny Kelly? You know better than I.'

Raymond shook his head. 'How can I say, Captain Sorrel? I doubt if I have even heard your daughter's voice; that would weigh much.'

'Oh, I have had her trained,' said the Captain eagerly. 'She speaks very well for – for a ballet-girl. And any little faults can easily be cured.'

'Can she project her voice? Throw it to the back of the theatre, so that even when the play calls for her to whisper every syllable can be heard? That, sir, must be taught too. The head, the throat, the lungs, the muscles, are as important as the voice itself.'

The Captain looked dashed. 'I believe it was merely elocution Madame Clare taught; though of course she herself performed with great *réclame* at the Olympic. Perhaps Janetta could return to her for further lessons, though the cost, alas . . .'

'Madame Clare is old and frail now, Captain. I doubt that she would be prepared to teach the production of the voice. There are other teachers, of course . . .' He meditated, gazing into the fire from the steam that rose from his half-emptied tankard. The thought flashed into his mind that the perfect teacher for the girl would be Sara, who was a professional to her finger-tips, who spoke clearly and beautifully, and had, he knew from instinct, infinite patience.

'There *is* a lady,' he said, 'of my acquaintance, who might be prepared to take on such a pupil. Will you leave it to me to consult her, and to ask what the cost might be, if she consented?'

The Captain clapped him joyfully on the back. 'Done! Forever your debtor. Let's call Sam again and drink to it in a fresh bumper.'

They drank to it, and to several other good causes before the Captain confidentially tapped Raymond's knee.

'Another thing, dear old friend. The matter of marriage.'

'Marriage?'

'You who know this Thespian domain so well: tell me what are my child's chances of a good, sound match, whether she continues to dance or turns to higher things? Some substantial, worthy fellow with plenty of chinkers in the Bank and a name for honesty? These little female hearts, sir, ah, how easily are they broken! Now I, though her father, have been much away from Town, on – on campaigns, missions, other military affairs. I have not the slightest knowledge of a young lady's matrimonial prospects in the Profession.'

A sardonic smile crossed Raymond's face. 'Marriage in the theatre is much as anywhere else – a lottery.'

The Captain noticed the smile and its quality. 'Something tells me you drew a poor prize yourself, sir.'

'You might say that and not be wrong.'

'Married into the Profession, perhaps?'

'No.' Raymond's tone was discouraging. He took pity on the other man's fallen face. 'Some stage marriages have been successful. Mr Grimaldi has married twice, very happily. The Kemble families have conducted very respectable unions. But you must understand that temptations are many, and poverty a constant pitfall. We are not as other men, sir. Your daughter would be better off with a respectable chandler.'

'We had hoped for better than that,' said the Captain wistfully. 'Now – you mentioned the Kembles, Mr John Philip and Mr Charles. Perhaps a hint from you to either, as I suggested before . . .? Influence in high places, you know.'

Raymond put down his tankard. He was feeling the effects of the heated ale, and the all too familiar disposition to talk too freely. The very thought of the Kembles, aristocrats of the stage,

73

chilled his blood, for they knew too well from their sister, Mrs Siddons, of the never-to-be-forgotten occasion when he had dried in the Sleep-walking Scene, and the Divine Sarah had had to ramble on by herself until the end of her lines and then exit, watched by himself, the Doctor, a gaping dumbstruck fish, and the horrified Gentlewoman. Never, as long as he lived, would the memory fade of his encounter with the affronted Siddons, backstage: the Juno-flash of the fine eyes, the flaring of the Roman nostrils, the pointed finger: 'Go from my presence, sirrah!' She even talked like someone in Shakespeare.

No, he would not approach the Kembles. But he would be pleased to speak to the accomplished lady who might be prepared to coach Miss Sorrel in the dramatic art.

To Jannie the lessons, so modestly charged for by Sara, were the only brightness in those icy winter days. It was the coldest time anybody remembered, or their grandfathers either, with coal as much as seven shillings a sack, more than any but the rich could pay, the streets slippery hazards that daily claimed their due of broken limbs, coaches unable to get into or out of London. In the theatre the fireplaces thoughtfully installed in the dressing-rooms in Garrick's day were now filled with kindling, rubbish, anything that would burn, and kept smouldering, to the constant terror of the management. Tayleur saw himself with yet another burned-down theatre on his hands; scarcely a year passed without such a holocaust.

Jannie felt her heart as cold as the weather. A young man called Phil Isaacs was making advances to her; he was not ill-looking, with tight black curly hair and a fresh face, but she treated him like a dog that followed her unasked in the street, and then was peevishly cross with herself. Ivor was still seen about with Bess Ames, then she was back in the company of Shanks, as though they had never been apart, raising Jannie's hopes to the skies. But in no time Ivor was escorting one of the statelier young ladies, Emma Brice, well-known for keeping herself to herself, but now whispered to have taken Ivor home to meet her parents in Bethnal Green.

'I hate her,' Jannie said viciously to Sara. 'Wretch! She's old enough to be his mother.'

'Nonsense, dear. Well on in her 'twenties, I dare say, but no more. And I'm sure you need have no fear that he is serious in his intentions. Don't you remember the gallant Macheath and his ladies?

> I sipp'd every flower, I chang'd every hour
> Till Polly my passion requited.'

'Well, Polly *has* requited his passion, at least this Polly has,' Jannie snapped, 'and much good it did her. I hate him too, and all men that say one thing and do another.'

Patiently Sara laid down the book, her lesson once again interrupted by her pupil's dark broodings.

'Dear child, all men do so at one time or another, or they would be married before they were properly out of the cradle. It does no good to hate, and I wish you would try to put young Mr Bryn out of your mind. It's all too easy to fall headlong into love at your age, and the consequences may be . . . terrible, should you be tempted to give way. Believe me, I know.'

'You? But you are the pattern of good sense, Miss Dell. You would never make such a noddy of yourself as I have. Oh yes, I *know* how silly I am, no need to tell me. I'm a cross, stupid thing, and I ought to be learning. Let's go on.'

Sara told Raymond of Jannie's troubles. He shrugged. 'Only one cure for that – Romeo's. "Take thou some new infection to thine eye, And the rank poison of the old will die." She'll be on with another love before Spring comes – if it ever does.' He shivered. 'As for the boy, he has talent in him; greatness, perhaps. I'm no judge of mountebanks, but Joey thinks him a lad of parts and Bologna gives him instruction, I know. If he's wise he'll keep out of the marriage-trap, or find himself with a wife and brats dragging him down till he's turning cart-wheels in the street for pennies.'

75

Sara was silent. It was unlike him to speak bitterly, and she was afraid to waken whatever private demons might be torturing him. They were walking along Thames Street towards London Bridge, watching the strange sight of the Thames frozen solid, bearing a load of skaters, souvenir-buyers, skittle-players, and spectators at the Great Frost Fair which somebody had been enterprising enough to institute. Swings and roundabouts, coconut shies, skittles and coffee-stalls, abounded for seekers after pleasure. Seen at the end of each street they came to, an ever-unrolling panorama. Sara watched with interest, Raymond hardly saw the pageant, lost in his own thoughts.

Suddenly he caught her arm sharply and pulled her into a shop doorway. Before she could exclaim he said urgently: 'Turn away – look in the window! Point to something – anything.' He stood beside her, his back to the street, and she felt his arm quiver.

She was at a loss to know why he had selected this particular shop, which sold tobacco, pipes and snuff, but she dutifully inspected pipe-bowls carved into the likenesses of dog's heads, Red Indians, negroes and seductive ladies. At her side, he was tense, scarcely breathing. She thought it was like a stage wait in the wings when one must be absolutely silent. Then she felt him relax.

'Thank you,' he said. 'I'm sorry to have been abrupt, but it was necessary.' Turning round, she wondered if he had been shielding her from the sight of some shocking accident, for the streets were a *mêlée* of vehicles of all descriptions, the watermen having lost their trade because of the frost. But there was nothing unusual to be seen, hardly even a pedestrian, only, some twenty yards ahead, two women walking eastwards. In the yellowish foggy atmosphere it was impossible to see any detail of them, only that one was taller than the other. Soon they turned into the street that led to Old Swan Stairs and so to the frozen river.

Raymond linked his arm in hers. 'The other way,' he said, 'we must turn back.'

'But I thought – we were going to the Fair.' Sara could not help showing her disappointment. The Fair was something that might not happen again in anyone's lifetime, and a cheap form of amusement in these dark, miserable winter days when there was little to do until it was time to go to the theatre.

He patted her hand inside the worn little muff of rabbit-fur.

'I'm sorry, my dear. I had truly meant to take you. But another time. I'll tell you why, but not here. Come.' At a brisk walk they set out back towards Blackfriars Bridge, up Bridge Street and left into Fleet Street, where Raymond's striding steps slackened, to Sara's relief. On the south side of the street, close by the Cock Tavern, he said, 'Would you like to see the Waxworks?'

'Oh, above all things! And it will be warm inside.'

He jangled the bell outside Number 17, a small, beautiful house with a Jacobean frontage, ancient diamond-paned windows, and an air of antique dignity not shared by its neighbours. Above the first storey ran an inscription in large painted letters: THE WAX-WORK, and above the door a notice saying that Mrs Salmon's Celebrated Waxworks were now housed within after their removal from across the street.

The door opened by no visible hand, and Sara gave an irrepressible little shriek as they saw in front of them a hideous old woman, bent almost double and leaning on crutches, leering up at them menacingly and holding out a begging-bowl in one claw.

'I think,' said Sara timidly, 'we are meant to put some money in the bowl.'

Raymond produced his purse. 'How much is the admission, ma'am?' he asked the gruesome custodian.

'One shilling for each party,' replied a voice, which came, however, not from the beggar but from a small wizened man sitting behind a table on which were plaster figurines and drawings. He grinned at their discomfiture as they looked closer and saw that the old woman was only a waxwork.

'Oh!' Sara gasped. 'I was quite startled.'

'Very real she looks, don't she.'

'A trifle too real for female susceptibilities,' Raymond observed severely.

'What about that one, then?' The human custodian pointed to

77

another figure on the opposite side of the door. 'Mother Shipton, as in life.'

Whatever Mother Shipton may have been in life, she was singularly unattractive in effigy, having a face of gargoyle-like ugliness with chin and nose almost meeting, a humped back draped in a frowsy shawl, a high conical witch's hat, and a black cat on her shoulder which was far from being a triumph of the taxidermist's art. At the sight of it Sara stepped back and pulled appealingly at Raymond's sleeve.

'I would rather not go in any further,' she said nervously, 'if it is all like this.'

'Oh,' interrupted the custodian hurriedly, for these were his first visitors since morning, 'not by no means, ma'am. This is just by way of being a little joke as customers come in, like. Wait while I lights up another glim or two – though we has to be careful, with the exhibits being waxen and not wery fond of lights.' Indeed, the place was cold and damp, in spite of the extra candles he lit for them. Other figures now appeared, ranged round the room, which he proceeded to explain to them.

'The Hemperor Caractacus. Kindly note the robe of Himperial purple and laurel wreath, signifying wictory.'

'My impression was that Caractacus was a King of Britain, captured by the Romans, if I remember my schoolbooks,' said Raymond mildly. 'In which case he should hardly be wearing imperial purple.'

'Well, be that as it may,' replied their guide irritably. 'And this 'ere is Henery the Eighth, well-known for matrimonial problems and a turn for axing ladies to marry, then axing 'em in order to marry someone else.' He laughed tinnily at his daily joke. 'And now a figure well known to you, no doubt, lady and gentleman – none other than 'is 'Ighness the Duke of York, son of 'is present Majesty, God bless him.' As he pointed out the various details of the Duke's costume, as worn on state occasions, Raymond whispered to Sara, 'I must talk to you.' Aloud he said to the guide, 'Would it be possible for us to inspect the exhibits upstairs by ourselves, without troubling you to conduct us?'

The little man looked dubious, seeing his usual tip vanishing. But Raymond let the glimpse of a sixpence show. 'Well, now,' said the guide, 'there's no lights up there, but if I loans you a candle and you promises to be extra careful with it, I don't see why you shouldn't 'ave a little private view.' His expression conveyed very clearly that he thought they were going up there for what he would have termed a bit of a snuggle, and at Raymond's stern look he laid his forefinger alongside his nose in a highly knowing manner.

Glass eyes stared at them out of the shadows. Tall, ghostly forms, toga'd or robed, in doublet and hose or the dress of the last century, surrounded them like a ring of accusing spectres. Mary Queen of Scots, widely ruffed and ostentatiously fingering her crucifix, stood next to her cousin Queen Elizabeth, red wig glowing in the pale light of the candle which Raymond set down carefully on a wide window-sill.

'Sara,' he said, 'dear Sara, I like this grisly place no more than you do. But at least we are in private.' He sat her down gently on a bench. 'I want to tell you why I behaved as I did this afternoon.'

'You saw someone – you wished not to meet.'

'Yes. My wife and daughter.'

'Oh. Yes, I understand.' Her voice shook a little.

'No, not yet. I told you I was married. But not that my wife pursues me constantly, asks for me at theatres and in places where she thinks I may be known. Not for the pleasure of my company, but for money. I gave her all I had when we parted. The house we lived in was mine, had been my father's – he was dead by then – and I left her living in it. But always she wants to get more, and to . . . to trouble me. As she does, God knows.'

Sara looked up at him, understanding, but not speaking.

' "My gracious silence," ' he quoted smiling. 'The story of my life is not very edifying. I married too early and too young. My father was a solicitor, prosperous enough, who wanted me to follow him in the practice. Well, I was a foolish, wayward, head-in-air young fellow, always in and out of love, knowing as little about myself, I dare say, as I did about the ladies. When I turned twenty I took a fancy to the daughter of a neighbour, Miss Augusta Pryce. Her father had served as a General in the American war, and left a leg behind him; I think it soured his temper, for Miss Augusta was very anxious to escape from him and marry – even a ne'er-do-well like me. Her father thought I would come into money – my father thought she would. She had a fine complexion and a pleasant voice (I always put much store on that) and I told myself she would do very well.

'And so we married in haste. Too much haste, for soon after I got stage-fever and broke my articles, lived as a private gentleman and spent every night up in London acting at one private theatre or another. Augusta thought the stage low and raffish, I thought her a pompous prig. So much for Hymen's torch . . . it went out very swiftly for us. When I found an engagement at a regular theatre Augusta turned her back on me. But by then a child was on the way, Augusta the younger, whom I've seen perhaps a dozen times in her life. It was when I realized how shamefully I had muddled things that I began to drink.'

'Yes,' said Sara, 'I can understand.'

'When her father died my wife was left with a little property, enough to live on from rents. My daughter, Augusta, teaches children. The squire of the place has a brood of eleven, providing her with an endless number of pupils. It's not a splendid life they lead – my wife and Augusta – but better than mine. And I can give them nothing else, not a penny. When I see her waiting for me, or passing me as she did today, I feel my heart turn heavy as a cannon-ball. Perhaps she'll find me tonight, by the playbill. I've tried to reason with her, tell her she has all she'll ever get of me. I changed my name, even – but she found that out.'

'What – is your name?'

He smiled bitterly. 'Nothing so grand as Raymond Otway. Richard Hicks.'

She repeated it, under her breath. 'Richard Hicks. A good name. But I shall forget it if you wish me to.'

'I do. It belongs to an old life. To you I will be Raymond.' He went to the window and stared out through the tiny panes into the gathering fog, then turned back and sat beside her.

'Sara, I am glad to have told you. Because now you know why I can never be free. And for you I would have wished to be free. You know that I love you, don't you?'

She nodded speechlessly. He put his arm round her and drew her to him, her face hidden against his shoulder.

'I'm neither young nor beautiful,' she said, muffled. 'And there are things about me I . . . I have not told you.'

'Nothing you could tell me would make me love you less. And to me you are both young and beautiful. But I can ask nothing of you, my dear, because I can give you nothing.'

She looked up and held his gaze. 'You give me happiness, I think. I've never known it before, if this is it.'

He held her face between his hands. ' "Behold, thou art fair, my love; thou hast doves' eyes." ' And for the first time they kissed.

The room was almost dark, the candle guttering. Its flicker lit up the white face of Bonaparte, a malevolent dwarf in a far corner, and sparkled on the dagger in the hand of Queen Eleanor as she menaced the cowering Rosamond.

'A strange setting for a love scene,' Raymond said. 'I hope these wax creatures wish us well.'

Sara shivered in his arms.

'You're cold, my dear. We must go down.'

The custodian was at the foot of the stairs, having decided they had had their full sixpennyworth of privacy.

'Just about to put up the shutters,' he said. 'Enjoy the exhibits did you? Wery educational, an't they.'

'Very,' Raymond said gravely. 'We leave with our minds much improved.' He slipped the sixpence into the man's hovering hand. As he bowed them out of the door, the leg of Mother Shipton, worked by a string operated from his table, shot out in a power-ful kick aimed at the departing visitors, but to the curator's dis-appointment missed them.

It was another of the establishment's little jokes.

CHAPTER FIVE

Enter Dandy Lover

Fate, with her peculiar fondness for irony, arranged that the theatre's only casualty of the Great Frost should occur on the very day when the sudden onset of a thaw put an end to the pageantry on the frozen Thames, and that the victim should be Jack Bologna. She added an artistic touch in causing the accident to happen not in the street, where it might have been expected, but in the theatre itself; a lump of half-frozen mud, adhering to one of Jack's boots, sent him crashing from top to bottom of the dressing-room stairs.

Not all his athleticism could save him, taken by surprise as he was. Grimaldi, arriving a few minutes later, found him sitting at the foot of the stairs, one leg twisted under him, swearing fluently.

'Well, here's a pretty go,' said Joey, attempting to lift his fallen colleague, and causing him to utter another stream of invective, this time in Italian. 'Let's get you straightened out, for a start.'

White-faced and shocked, the Harlequin sat on the bottom step, the injured leg stretched in front of him; he was surrounded now by people who had heard the crash from the dressing-rooms and others arriving from the stage-door, all exclaiming and enquiring.

'All right, all right.' Jack quelled the sympathetic din. 'Only broke my bloody leg, that's all, or as good as. Get me a swig of brandy, some of you, and send for the quack.'

They carried him, groaning, to the dressing-room he shared with Grimaldi and Raymond, who had been swift to produce his own pocket-flask. The doctor, hurriedly summoned from a near-by street, pronounced the leg not broken but badly strained and quite unfit to dance on.

'Thanks for the information,' replied Jack with heavy sarcasm. 'I could ha' told you as much, and I an't got an M.D. after my name. Well, so what are we going to do?'

The manager and the ballet-master were echoing the question,

Signor Fasoli clutching wildly at his scanty hair until it looked like Clown's wig.

'I knew it, I knew it, I could have tell you this morning, when I see a spotted horse in Haymarket. Ah, *calamita*, ah, *sventura*!'

'Never mind about spotted horses,' said Tayleur. 'We've got to do the show tonight, or give the customers their money back. Trust this to happen when we were having a top-class run. Five weeks, and no sign of business dropping off – could have gone on till Easter.'

The faces round Bologna's couch reflected his gloom. 'Well, *think*, some of you!' Tayleur snapped. 'We haven't got a Harlequin. Ellar's at the Lane and Hartland's at the Surrey.'

'Get one of 'em to gallop round when he's finished, and take over here,' Grimaldi suggested. 'Done it myself, scores of times, between here and the Wells. Nearly killed me, but I done it. Sometimes they sent a cab for me, O Lor, what splendiferousness!'

'And what are we supposed to be doing,' Tayleur enquired coldly, 'while waiting for their shows to end? Put on an equestrian display, perhaps, if Astley's can spare us a few nags?'

'Couldn't we make more of *Romeo*? Drag it out a bit, as it were?' Raymond suggested.

'If you can think of any of our cast who know the lines,' returned Tayleur, 'which seems to me highly unlikely.'

'Miss Dell knows the play well,' said Raymond. 'So do I.'

'But you an't exactly Romeo and Juliet, are you? No disrespect meant.'

'Miss Sorrel would make a Juliet, and she speaks very nicely, for a dancer. But I doubt,' Raymond added despondently, 'that she knows any of the play, and one could hardly expect her to learn much in an hour.'

'Which is all the time we've got,' said Tayleur. 'Sure you can't walk it, Jack, and leave out the jumps?'

The colour had come back to Bologna's face, but he shook his head emphatically. 'Couldn't put my foot to the ground. Look at it.' He extended the elegant leg, now swollen into shapelessness from toes to mid-calf. They looked, and were glummer than ever.

Suddenly Grimaldi gave a wild caper, struck an attitude as of a Clown intensely surprised by some heavenly apparition and flung into grotesque raptures. 'The Leek!' he cried. 'Taffy, Shenkin, Cadwallader, Ap Morgan!'

'What the devil are you babbling about, Joey?' asked Tayleur, in no mood for jesting.

The Clown burst into song.

> In a cottage in Wales, in the sweetest of vales,
> With father and mother lived I.
> Tol liddle, tol liddle, tol liddle . . .

'Damme, you've got it, Joey!' exclaimed Bologna. 'Young Bryn. I'd have thought of it before if I hadn't been knocked half-stupid. He knows a lot of the business and I'd say he was a lad of promise. Fetch him here directly, and I'll give him a quick brush-up on it while Mother Noakes puts a compress on this blasted leg – and I'll thank you for a loan of the Elixir, Joey.'

'It's a risk,' Tayleur said glumly.

'It's one you'll have to take.'

'He will be fright,' prophesied Fasoli. 'His legs they will quiver, he swoon with fear.'

But Ivor, rushed from the male dancers' dressing-room, received the proposal that he should go on as Harlequin with perfect equanimity. His heart beat violently, but no trace of agitation showed in his face. He stood composedly beside the prostrate Bologna. Yes, he had watched Mr Bologna very carefully – out of his great admiration for him. Yes, he had toured in a very humble pantomime and thought he knew the routines.

'Then let's see you do 'em,' Bologna said, and began to drill him in the Attitudes, the tricks with the baton, the abduction of Columbine, the taunting of Pantaloon: all this with the nervous and distressed Mrs Parker acting out her role, and Raymond, almost as nervous, going through his, while Mrs Sorrel, from Wardrobe, hastily sent for, crawled round Ivor on her knees, measuring him for Harlequin's costume, for he was about the same height as Bologna but much slighter – there would have to be tucks and pleats or the garment would hang on him like a sack.

'So, that's all I can do for you,' Bologna said at length. 'Now you're out there on your own. Just one thing, you'll cut the window-dive and the hoop-dive, or you'll break your own neck or someone else's. (Careful, Noakes, or you'll lame me for life.) Tell Fasoli and the others. And if in doubt, stand still and pose and wink at the conductor to slow up for you. My God, there's the overture. No, it ain't, just the fiddles tuning.'

Mrs Sorrel was urgently pulling at Ivor's arm. 'Come on and get *fitted* or you'll never be ready.'

But he was ready, as the call-boy banged on the door and yelled 'Quarter of an hour, please.' He looked at himself in the pier-glass, struck an attitude, and stepped out into the corridor. Jannie, on her way to the wings, spectral in the white drapery and wreath of Juliet's attendant, stopped and gasped. She had avoided him lately, given him a cold smile or no look at all, but tonight was different. She took him in at a glance, looking half a head taller, a glittering creature, spangles sewn in every triangle of his multi-coloured motley, a black skull-cap hiding his black hair and a half-mask making a white mystery of his face. Her heart seemed to turn over and she felt the blood drain from her cheeks, then come back in a hot rush.

'Good luck,' she said lamely.

'If *you* wish me luck I shall have it. I told you.'

She wanted to reply tartly, but the words would not come. Instead she bobbèd her head curtly, and left him standing there, a figure of light in the murky, mist-filled corridor.

Joey in his blue wig tonight, wearing scarlet and white Tudor trunk-hose and a tight red-dotted jacket, the whole muffled in Friar Laurence's cassock, patted Ivor on the back. 'God go with you,' he said gravely. 'Beginner's luck to you.'

Sara, who had heard the news about Jannie's boy, swept up to him in sable robes. The happiness that flooded her overflowed towards him, whatever he might have done to her protégée. Graciously she bent from her height and kissed his powder-whitened cheek, as though blessing a son about to leave for the Crusades.

He remembered nothing else clearly until the swish of the curtain and the final chords of the orchestra. Then, in the dark, listening intently to each cue, to Mrs Parker being wooed beneath her balcony, aware that she was still tremulous with nerves, acutely conscious of the great arena full of eyes keener than its dimmed lamps, of the orange-suckers and ginger-beer drinkers and shrimp-peelers; conscious, even, of the moulded statuary atop the proscenium arch, a lion and unicorn and two flying angels holding up the royal arms.

Then, at last, the Transformation Scene, a great cave-mouth at the back of the stage, waiting to be whipped away and replaced by Queen Mab's throne, himself and Mrs Parker, now uncloaked, side by side in the blackness with stage-hands scurrying round them. He tightened his mask, grasped his baton and poised himself ready to leap up as Sara's voice came from above:

Hence, Tragic Muse, and snow-haired Father Time:
Hail, Joy and Mirth – for this is Pantomime!

And there he was, the most brilliant thing in all the brilliance of the lights, coloured diamonds and swiftness and legerdemain, whirling Columbine to him and away again, magicking them all with his black wand, knowing himself come into his kingdom.

He had never dreamed, for all his ambitions, that such a triumph could be his. Before the first Curtain Mr Tayleur had announced, to the accompaniment of dismal groans from the house, that owing to a slight and temporary injury to Mr Bologna the part of Harlequin would be danced tonight by a Young Gentleman. Now they had seen the Young Gentleman and approved him wildly. He came out in front of the curtain, hand in hand with the beaming Mrs Parker, sharer of his triumph, deafened by the shouts and the clapping. Things were flung on to the stage – not the usual derisory offerings of orange-peel and empty bottles, but fruit, gloves, flowers (in February? where could they have come from?), even a necklace of coloured beads. Time and again he bowed and smiled, gestured, called back Columbine, retreated behind the curtain, and finally, not knowing what more to do, pulled off the mask and gave them the benefit of grey eyes as bright as Harlequin's spangles, slant-outlined in paint.

What was said to him afterwards he would never remember, such were the back-slappings and kissings and kind words. Bologna, who had had himself painfully conveyed to the back of a box, was now carried back again to the Green Room, where, good generous fellow, he gave Ivor the highest praise he could.

'When I step out of my shoes they'll be yours, my boy.'

Grimaldi's soft brown eyes were overflowing with tears of happiness, Signor Fasoli was reduced by excitement to speaking only Italian, Mr Tayleur was confiding to anybody who would listen that he had a very novel idea for the next season, very novel indeed. Somebody sent out to a neighbouring inn for food and drink to be laid out in the Green Room, where it was fallen upon by players, stage-hands, and visitors varying from sprigs of the nobility to Paphian beauties from Covent Garden, heavily decked with feathers, rouge, and false curls, in search of custom.

Mrs Sorrel had firmly got Ivor out of his costume ('Got to press it and go over them stitches again, or you'll bust right out of it tomorrow, because, mark my words, Mr Bologna won't be on his feet for a week or more') and he was once more in his undistinguished dark blue coat and breeches.

A glass of wine in his hand, though he had hardly touched it, he stood leaning thoughtfully against the Green Room's handsome mantelpiece, welcoming the heat of the fire on his back, for it was dangerous to catch cold after the violent exertion of dancing. After the first overwhelming reception they had given him, the company had dispersed into talking, laughing groups. Any excuse for a party, the cause of it soon forgotten. Mrs Parker had been joined by her husband, a cheerful stout man who owned a draper's shop, and their daughter, a twelve-year-old with blonde pigtails whose unfortunate resemblance to her father in build prevented her from following in her mother's dancing footsteps. Mary Grimaldi, dazzling in pink with yellow ribbons, bobbed about on Joey's arm. Sara Dell, gold dust still glinting in her hair from her Queen Mab wig, was in earnest conversation with Raymond Otway. Bess Ames and Emma Brice were exchanging venomous looks across the room because Ivor had returned their enthusiastic embraces in the most casual way, for which each young lady blamed the other.

Jannie had not embraced the hero of the evening, had not even spoken to him, from some strange shyness that she did not understand. What she had felt for him before had been a young girl's first infatuation. Now he was changed, translated from a personable young human being into Harlequin the Enchanter, the maker of magic, someone more potent than the solid middle-aged Bologna had ever seemed. She felt the lure of him as something too strong for her; a power that might destroy her.

The wreath of artificial white roses she had worn on stage was still crowning her head. She had been too bemused to notice it before. She took it off, and with sudden resolution went up to Ivor, and, pulling one of the roses out, gave it to him, wire stalk and all, without a word.

He smiled, and said, 'Thank you. For luck?'

'Why not?' she answered pertly, turning on her heel. He looked after her, his feelings a mixture of pique, surprise, and something like sadness. There had been an attraction between them at first that might have turned to love, if he had let it. But he had gone away from her, for the good of both of them, and on his great night she had not even troubled to congratulate him. He supposed the gift of the jaded cotton flower was derisory. But he remembered that once he had felt her to be his luck-bringer and folding the rose's petals flat, he put it in his breast pocket.

At the Sorrels' supper-table there was talk of nothing but the evening's surprise. Talk, that was, in monologue form, for while Lucy Sorrel praised the new Harlequin to the skies, prophesied that she had always seen something in him, and mentioned the large part she had played in his triumph by altering his costume before one could say Jack Robinson, the Captain, his mouth full of tripe and onions, put in the occasional 'Indeed?' and 'Quite remarkable', while Jannie said nothing.

Her mother mistook the reason for her silence. 'Well,' she said cheerfully, 'you always had quite a fancy for that young chap, hadn't you? Now I'd say that if you was to walk out with him steady you might find yourself quite Somebody one day. Any dancer as can take on Patchy at a minute's notice, when all them Bolognas and Grimaldis and Lupinos has been at it from their cradles, you mark my words, he'll go a long way.'

'Well, he won't be taking me with him.' Jannie banged down her knife and fork. 'I've got other things to think about, and so I'm sure has Mr Bryn. And I'm sick and tired of talking about it, Ma.'

'Funny,' said Lucy to the Captain in bed, 'I could 'a sworn our Jannie was sweet on young Bryn. First she was all of a dream, then as snappy as a weasel, then back from Miss Dell's going on about being an actress . . . and now answering her own mother back at table as if I was no better than a servant. I don't understand girls today, I'm sure.'

'Think no more about it, my dear. Our child has her head screwed on the right way. And there are better things in life, you know, than jumping about on the boards.'

Far better, he thought, drifting towards sleep. Far more suitable for his lovely daughter . . .

Among the convivial haunts frequented by the Captain was a club calling itself The Shiners. Some of its members were gentlemen of uncertain fortune and no particular profession, like himself, others came from the worlds of prize-fighting and horse-racing; while the higher ranks consisted of young bloods and dandies who enjoyed a taste of lowish life, heavy drinking and even heavier gambling. For card-sharping there was little to choose between them and the flash coves they came to meet. Women were strictly excluded from membership, thereby making

the discussion of past and present conquests delightfully unin-
hibited.

The Honourable Frederick FitzNeil was one of the younger and
bluer-blooded members, particularly cultivated by the Captain,
who had a pathetic liking for the company of men whom his own
estranged family would not have considered altogether disgusting.
The younger son of an earl, very unlikely to come into the Irish
title unless some dire tragedy overtook his healthy elder brother
and three nephews, Fred had found nothing particular to do with
his life. The military uniform did not attract him, and he posi-
tively disliked horses at close quarters, though he had no objection to betting on any that were strongly recommended by his
friends. The Church, too, struck him as confoundedly dull, unless
one were given a fashionable parish, but one was far more likely
to be buried in the country.

From an illness in early childhood he was entirely deaf in one
ear. At Eton it earned him ridicule from his school-mates and
punishments from his masters, who thought him a mere scrim-
shanker and beat him for not being able to hear the lessons they
shouted at him. He left, a sixteen-year-old dunce, to return to the
shabby castle in County Cork where his father spent the days out
with the guns or the rods, and his mother only had time for his
brother and the family of grandchildren arriving with gratifying
regularity at the smart Nash-style colonnaded house where the
future Earl and Countess lived.

Frederick was very lonely. The stable-boys were good-natured
enough, shouting obligingly into his sound ear and teaching him
tricks they picked up from gipsies at fairs. He learnt to hunt the
otter, to lay bets on terriers at rat-hunts, to calculate the odds on a
prize-fight, and to play a pretty good hand at whist, ombre, loo,
or picquet, once the rules had been slowly and loudly explained to
him by members of his brother's circle.

Of women he was terrified. His mother disliked him, his sister-
in-law looked straight through him with eyes as bright blue and
prominent as the Royal Family's, and such young ladies as attended balls and parties at the Castle or the Hall merely giggled at

him. Once, leafing through some stuffy book at school, he had come across the mocking epitaph on Frederick, Prince of Wales, King George's father:

> . . . since 'tis only Fred
> Who was alive and is dead –
> There's no more to be said.

It fitted his own case exactly, he thought, and sometimes he wished he *were* dead, except that he was even more terrified of ghosts than of girls, and would walk a mile out of his way in order not to pass the family mausoleum.

Then, as so often at the darkest hour of a life, help came. His uncle, Sir Patrick FitzNeil, on a visit to Ireland for the hunting, took an inexplicable fancy to the shy boy, the Gossoon, as his father facetiously called him.

'Gossoon? The lad's twenty-two and a man grown,' growled Sir Patrick. 'Time he got his passport out of this damned hole. Let him come back to London with me and have his fling. Only young once, isn't he? Well, then, give him a box of guineas and a hunter and let him loose.'

Fred was very happy with the guineas but declined the hunter, and his family saw him depart with the greatest relief. It was, as his mother unfeelingly said, like packing a poor relation off after Christmas.

Sir Patrick's house in Hanover Square, London, was like a vision of Paradise to Fred. In fact, it was nothing particular to look at, and furnished in the fashion of George II's days, for Sir Patrick was elderly and his dead wife had brought her own belongings with her. Old Chinese-patterned designs of tropical birds and pagodas faded on the walls, dust lay on the bedcanopies, the marble nymph in the hall had lost one outstretched finger and, regrettably, the tip of a breast. But to Fred it was the Regent's own palace, Carlton House itself.

Sir Patrick's two sons had both gone into naval service. Kevin was killed at the Nile and Dennis died of wounds after Trafalgar.

His only daughter, Kathleen, had married an English squire and lived in Northumberland. There were no giggling girls about to laugh at Fred, no crawling, messy, fussed-over babies held up for him to admire. He was virtually the son of the house, company of a sort for the tough old man.

Fred's uncle had two excellent points of recommendation to a nephew: he was rich and he was generous. His money had come by way of the East India Company, now declining, and he had nobody to spend it on but himself. He looked long and hard at Fred, a shabby, drooping figure at whom, he knew quite well, the servants sneered.

'Stand up straight, boy. You an't hump-backed, are you? Where d'jer get that coat, off a tinker's barrow? As for the britches, they an't even decent.' He strode to the tapestry bell-pull and yelled at the servant who answered: 'Humphreys! I want the carriage round. Now.'

Fred found himself in the fitting-salon of one of London's most exclusive tailors, in Jermyn Street. Gradually, from the first humiliation of seeing himself in the too-revealing cheval-glass, a shivering figure in a patched shirt, he watched, with amazement, his own transformation to a Fashionable. Not at the first fitting (though they found him something to go home in) but after a week of measurings, assessments of cloths, fatherly addresses by Mr Lampson the head tailor, he stood before that same cheval-glass in a glory he could not have believed. His legs were encased in tight white trousers, ending at the ankle with a ribbon bow and leading the eye to white silk stockings and black leather pumps. His long-tailed coat was as richly ornamented with braid as a military man's, his starched and ruffled shirt and cravat stuck out like a pouter pigeon's, gold fobs and seals swung from his waistcoat. A large, black, cockaded hat, as worn by Bonaparte, was tucked under his arm.

Mr Lampson stood back and surveyed him.

'Elegant, most elegant. Perhaps a lorgnette . . .?'

Fred looked vacant. 'An eyeglass on a stick!' bellowed his uncle. 'No, leave that, he don't need it. Tell yer what, though,

Lampson, a touch of whisker wouldn't come amiss, hey?'

'The very thing, Sir Patrick. Just the suspicion of a moustachio – carried on along the chin-line, perhaps?'

It took a fortnight to grow, but Fred was pleased with the result. It improved his long, pallid face, and took away attention from the dark lank hair which grew so high up on his brow as to suggest premature balding. Now that he felt well-dressed and well-heeled his spirits began to improve. He began to go out and about with this or that friend of his uncle, to Newmarket, Ascot, even riding in Rotten Row (though he was in constant terror that his meek old mount would take fright and bolt with him), and to the theatre.

It was a new world to him, as new and delightful as his own changed appearance. In Ireland he had seen companies of strolling players perform in barns, and once he had been to the theatre in Smock Alley, Dublin; but none of it had been like this glowing paradise of gilt and carvings and crimson drapes and chandeliers like bunches of diamonds; and then the players! His ears, used to the Irish tongue, were enraptured by this pure, clear speech of England, every syllable audible even to him with his half-deafness. The beauty and grace of the actresses and dancers took his breath away. The fine ladies he saw riding in the Row and in Bond Street were handsome enough, but these nymphs of the Opera were perfection itself, to be sure! He leaned on the red velvet edge of his box and stared at them, hardly blinking, throughout what his amused companion, Sir Piers Compton, thought a dashed long and dashed dull piece. The Irish colt was stage-struck.

So, when introduced by an acquaintance to The Shiners, whose premises were in a little old tavern down an alley off Pall Mall, Fred came by a process of elimination into the company of the man who most interested him there: the Captain.

Fred was exactly to the Captain's taste. A genuine slap-up aristocrat, yet not the sort of snob who would jeer at a shabby-genteel gentleman whose only proof of good birth was a fine silver snuff-box with his family crest upon it; a civil young fellow, in fact, and one whose clothes, if a trifle too modern and foppish for one of old-fashioned tastes, proclaimed money. It took only a few games of chance, two of which the Captain graciously let Fred win, and a few bumpers of rum punch, for the whole of Fred's life-story to be unfolded to his new friend.

'I tell you, though,' said Fred, 'folk here think there must be something mighty grand about living in a Castle, but there an't nothing to it. Give me London and the theatre, any time. Bless me, sir! I never set eyes on anything so fine as the Opera House. And the young ladies, oh what sweet creatures! London for beauty, believe me.'

'Oh,' said the Captain interestedly, 'I always heard that the fair colleens of the Emerald Isle were noted for their fine complexions.'

Fred snorted. 'If you call faces as red as fire fine complexions, why then, 'tis quite true, for they're either in the saddle in confounded bad weather or dancing 'emselves silly in the ballroom.'

The Captain surveyed his young friend with an air of patriarchal wisdom blended with benevolence. He now knew more about Fred than did Fred himself. No amorous entanglements – no experience of women, most likely – and certainly not what a popular ballad referred to as a 'heart for falsehood fram'd'. He leaned back in his chair, thoughtfully lit his pipe, and spoke.

'By an uncommon chance – and it's very odd you should have brought the subject up, sir – I myself am the parent of one of the theatrical goddesses you so greatly admire.'

Fred opened his droopy-lidded eyes as wide as they would go.

'You mean an actress, a real actress?'

'More than that, sir, more. A dancer, at present displaying her talents in one of our metropolis's greatest theatres. But she is young, very young. Her Mamma and I have been advised that she may yet rival the greatest ladies of the legitimate stage, if she fulfils her present promise.' It was totally untrue, for Sara, consulted about Jannie's prospects, had admitted that she had a pretty voice and a quick ear but very little turn for drama, and was unlikely to prove a serious rival to anyone. It had made up her father's mind. But his version, given to Fred, sounded impressive and could do no harm.

Fred sighed. 'Oh, how I should like to see her perform! Or . . . or even to be so happy as to meet her, if – if you had no objection, sir . . .' He felt himself to have been too forward, and blushed.

The Captain was thinking very hard. Jannie's part in the Pantomime was by no standards a large one, nor did she shine conspicuously among the other pretty dancers; in fact her small size made her difficult to follow except with a quizzing-glass, as someone had wittily said about another pocket Venus. Would the Honourable Fred be disappointed, even take a fancy to some other lady? He dwelt wistfully on the miracle that had happened in young Bryn's case; if only the Gods would arrange for something awkward (but, of course, not fatal) to overtake Mrs Parker, and for Jannie to replace her as Columbine!

Well, one mustn't expect too many miracles. Meeting Fred had been a gratuitous hand-out by Fate. He must take a chance on Fred's susceptibility, and put in some smart work of his own.

'I will be most happy to procure an order for you, sir.'

The Tayleur management were less than open-handed in giving away complimentary seats, but the Captain's charm was more than equal to that. What he saved on the price of the seat he spent to good purpose, for before the performance he took Fred to Brassey's and entertained him to its best fare, tipping off Miss Brassey that his guest was a young nobleman just lately come to England. Duly impressed, she fed the under-nourished young man and waited upon him with a certain softening of her usual brusque manner. The Captain saw to it that he had enough, but not too much, to drink.

The National Anthem and the rising of the curtain began the working of the spell on Fred. Raptly he leant forward, his good ear bent attentively towards the stage. The pretty page-girl who spoke the Prologue charmed him – not too much, hoped his host,

95

watching the reaction out of the corner of his eye. He thought Fred took in very little of the action of the front-piece, though he had explained it very carefully before in words suited to his simple-minded hearer.

'The whole entertainment is called *Harlequin Romeo, or Queen Mab*. And that, you see, is because every Harlequinade or Pantomime must have the same . . . dear me, my daughter would describe this to you more lucidly . . . the same characters in its frontpiece, so that they may be changed to those in the Harlequinade itself.'

'But you said, sir, that the what-you-call-it, the front-piece, was called *Romeo and Juliet*, and I'm sure I've heard William Shakespeare wrote that.' He beamed triumphantly.

'So he did, very true, but the personae of the play fit very neatly those of the Harlequinade: thus, Juliet is to become Columbine, Romeo is to turn to Harlequin, Juliet's father is Pantaloon who wishes his daughter to marry Paris, that is the Lover, in the afterpiece, and the Friar who mis-handles everybody's affairs is to turn into Clown.'

'Then where does Queen Mab fit in?'

'Queen Mab? Oh – she is the – the Benevolent Agent who causes all to come right at the end. I'm sure you'll understand it perfectly,' he added kindly.

But it really mattered very little how much Fred understood. The important thing was to direct his attention to Jannie.

He pointed, whispering, at the little figure at the end of the row of Juliet's attendants. 'That's my girl. Moves prettily, don't you think?'

It was not easy for an unpractised observer to follow one figure through the mazes of the dance and the formation of gracefully-poised groups as the leading characters took the centre of the stage, but Fred did his best, persuading himself that she was the one who tripped most lightly and looked most charming, even with that veil-thing over her face. He was well-fed, pleasantly wined, warm and comfortably seated, in the reassuring presence of the man he liked more than anyone he had met in his life before.

How much he appreciated Captain Sorrel's kindness, bringing him here and promising him an introduction to his own accomplished child! To be sure, Fred could have asked Piers Compton for something of the sort. But Piers was a confoundedly chilly sort of chap, fish-eyed, and one of those who, like the neighbours in Cork, sneered at a fellow who was none too bright and had no title of his own. Better to have waited.

The Dark Scene thrilled him, and the Harlequinade woke him to amazement and laughter. Mrs Parker in her white spotted muslin, agile yet alluring, Queen Mab stately in her gold throne, that highly humorous old fool of a Pantaloon, the incredibly active Harlequin (Bologna restored and not a scrap worse for his accident), and above all the Clown, whose merest mop or mow reduced Fred to helpless mirth. What a man, eh? The like was never seen, what with his rabbit and his sausages and his rolling head over heels like a hoop and giving out with such a comical laugh. Nothing, sure, could equal this chap with the foreigner's name that he had not quite caught from his friend's whisper. And then, the way they all popped up from under the stage and flew into the air quite magically! Sure, there was enchantment in it somewhere.

At the end he clapped and clapped, and people in the pit looked up to point at him, the Dandy who'd never seen a show before, by the sound of it.

Well-pleased, the Captain allowed the applause to subside before attempting to move his companion from his place. Still he stared, as though mesmerized, at the fallen curtain with its twined royal initials that had cut him off from the visions so lately seen behind it. When the house was mainly cleared, the Captain touched his shoulder gently. 'Come,' he said.

They went down a flight of stairs and through a little door just below the Royal Box. The curious, heady smell of the stage came from that great space, empty now but for scene-shifters hurrying, lifting, and cursing, and blended with the waxy exhalation of many extinguished candles. The Captain pushed open a handsome double door. 'The Green Room,' he said.

Green Room it was indeed, in traditional manner decorated in pale *eau de nil*, with a grass-green carpet. A large stove sent out heat from a corner, a small fire burnt in a grate too big for it. Every wall sported a long mirror illuminated by wall-candles, and on scattered small tables other small swing-mirrors stood, together with wig-stands, candle-snuffers, and glasses and bottles.

There were few people here tonight. The usual number of beaux had come to greet their girls; gentlemen in military or civil costume, some of them husbands arrived to see wives safe home. None of the 'stars' was present. Grimaldi was by now half-way back to his little house in Islington. Sara and Raymond had gone to eat their modest supper.

The Captain helped Fred to a glass of the house wine, and took one himself. Then, through the door that led down to the dressing-rooms, she came, his own Jannie, in the charming dress her mother had made up for her from a bolt of silk on which he had spent every penny he could win at cards or on the gees. It was in her favourite colour, a deep strawberries-and-cream pink, with an effect of shot silver woven into it. In style it was much like the dresses worn by Columbine and the dancers: straight and clinging, high-waisted with a ribbon confining it below the breasts, short in skirt and sleeve to show off dainty ankles and white rounded arms. Round her slender neck was the prettiest of necklaces, a confection of Venetian glass, pink flowers, and silver leaves. Her father had given it to her the day before, and she had wondered why, for it was not her birthday until May.

But it was at her face that Fred stared. To him she looked like a creature of another race; he was too much of an Irishman to define which one, for it was notoriously unlucky to mention them. The huge green eyes were still exotically outlined, the merest trace of rouge on the soft cheeks high-lighting them; and her mouth was like a rose at morning. She was just a girl, after all, but ah, how different!

'My daughter, Janetta,' said the Captain. 'May I present the Honourable Frederick FitzNeil, my love?'

Jannie curtsied. She was used enough to the young dandies who haunted the Green Room, though she had never been in it without her mother's chaperonage before. Tonight the Captain had wilily persuaded Lucy to go home early from Wardrobe. Fondly though he regarded her, she was not quite the Mamma he would have wished to present to Fred.

Fred stammered something, he did not know what, and Jannie responded politely, with a stage smile. What an odd, over-dressed cartoon of a young man, and how quaintly he spoke, like Paddy straight from the bogs but in a sort of toneless shout. They exchanged what she considered a perfectly idiotic conversation, with Papa putting in remarks now and then. Once she suppressed a yawn behind her hand. It had been a long evening. They were all getting rather tired of the show, even Joey had snapped at somebody, Sara and Raymond had seemed in a strange state, as though they were not quite quarrelling, and Bess Ames had stolen Jannie's comb, and returned it 'accidentally' broken. And now she had to talk to this curious protégé of Papa's. She guessed him to be a source of the guineas that were brought sometimes; perhaps her beautiful necklet had come to her by way of his pocket.

Because she was particularly bored, she talked and laughed more than usual. Ivor was not there. He seldom came to the Green Room, considering it a waste of time when he might be resting. She wondered where he was, with whom, what his lodging was like, whether Bess or Emma had ever been to it. *She* never would, that was for sure. The silver moth touched her hand every night but Sunday, then was flown, and that was all she would ever know of him.

She gave Fred her brightest, most artificial smile with a little laugh thrown in, at something perfectly inane he had said. They had a glass of wine or two, and his courage rose to previously unknown heights.

'Would you . . . that is, I'd be most uncommonly honoured . . . consider dining . . . taking supper with me . . . in company, your Papa and Mamma . . .'

Jannie looked at the Captain, and received an undeniable if unspoken Yes.

*

99

And after all, the supper was quite a success. It was held at the Crown, a highly superior place in Conduit Street, not far from Hanover Square. Jannie was a little over-awed by the servility with which their host was treated. Lucy had been on the stage long enough in her youth to remember how to behave like a lady and the Captain was at his most suave and elevated. The food was very fancy, not at all what they were used to, French sauces and all sorts of kickshaws, and because Fred was by now accustomed to such things at his uncle's table he was for once in a position of knowing better than his company what mayonnaise went with, and what soy and cayenne did not.

He was not in the least put out by finding that his charmer's mother worked in the Theatre Wardrobe. Where he came from, ostlers, stable-boys, and servants were more often his familiars than the nobility. And Mrs Sorrel for her part was gratified to find how easy and pleasant the gentry could be. In her youth she remembered great gentlemen in search of a bit of female flesh who could be mocking and hurtful in their manners towards a poor dancing-girl.

As for the Captain, he was completely satisfied and content with the way things were going.

In the weeks that followed Fred courted Jannie sedulously. She lay awake at nights, tossing and turning, wondering what would come of it all. She was not simple enough to think that whatever her charms might be, they had nothing to do with the Honourable Fred's pursuit of her. But he seemed so unlike the blades who chased after her fellow-dancers with bouquets and presents; why, he had no more elegance than Bess Ames's Shanks. If it came to that, the other girls laughed at him when time and again he reappeared in the Green Room, calling him Fumbling Fred and Porker Pat and other rude names. Surely he meant nothing but politeness to her, stranger that he was in town. She began to feel like a mouse being irresistibly urged towards a trap; yet what trap could any fellow as countrified and dull as Fred possibly be setting for her?

And her heart, against all likelihood and hope, was still set on Ivor.

CHAPTER SIX

The Wooing of Columbine

Bologna's accident had put into Tayleur's mind the thought that he would do well to have a reserve Harlequin on hand. It was not a highly original thought, for the first great English Harlequin, John Rich, had trained the young Henry Woodward, who appeared with him in a scene showing a baby Harlequin being hatched from a great egg by the heat of the sun, and since his day, half a century before, many pantomimes had contained tricks in which Harlequin disappeared and reappeared instantly in an impossibly different place: the secret being that there were two of him.

But it was Tayleur's first season as a pantomime manager, and he had chosen to keep the traditional 'business' simple as much for economic reasons as anything else. Now that the cold March weather and the consequent high prices of food were keeping people away from the theatre, it seemed to him the moment to introduce some novelties into his entertainment. Grimaldi's twelve-year-old son, Joseph Samuel, known as J.S. and the pride of his father's heart, was at last allowed to come to the theatre out of school hours and study his father's tricks and routines, so that he might appear as a miniature Clown, made up exactly like Joey, and delight the ladies.

And reluctantly, for it meant paying a higher salary, Tayleur appointed Ivor as Bologna's assistant, 'double', and pupil; an arrangement which enraptured Ivor and which Bologna accepted good-naturedly.

'There's a deal more to it than prancing about,' he warned his junior, 'and as many risks as a steeplejack takes. Joey here's hurt himself bad twice, coming up through the grave-trap.'

'Twice it was,' Grimaldi said lugubriously. 'Manchester and Liverpool. First time the rope broke was an accident, all right, but the second I fear was meant. Bad feeling, you know.'

'And that's another thing,' said Bologna. 'You want to keep on the right side of the stage-hands, or you're in for trouble. I gives 'em enough to keep a pig for a fortnight in catching-money.'

'Catching-money?'

'Catching-money, my innocent. You don't suppose when I jumps through the "moon" or the "window" I floats down on the other side like a fairy?'

'No, they hold out a carpet to catch you, I know that, sir. But isn't that what they're paid for?'

'Not enough, to their thinking,' Bologna said darkly. 'Any night you've got a Vanishing Leap, or a Trap-rise, and one of the men as holds that carpet or manages that rope happens to mention as it's a dry night for the time of year, you put your hand in your pocket, quick, or you might be sorry, for it's the price of a drink he expects.'

'Oh.' Ivor saw his extra salary dwindling away.

'Mind you,' said Joey, 'people are good-hearted on the whole, I can't think it's any other than the sick of mind who'd do such a thing to one. That affair at Liverpool, well, I did hear the man had had a disappointment and took it out on me. You mustn't believe the worst of anyone, young Taffy.'

Bologna took his friend by the shoulder. 'Joey,' he said, 'if your heart was a turnip, they'd chuck it in the Market gutter, for it'd be too soft to sell. Now go and look after your youngster, or he'll be in mischief.'

Grimaldi was off like a shot. Ivor wondered whether his extreme concern for his son was justified. J.S. looked like his father, mimed very prettily, spoke better than anyone in the Theatre because Joey and Mary had seen that he had proper schooling and kept him mostly tucked away in a cottage in rural Finchley, away from Islington and the corruptions of the wicked stage. Yet there was something about the boy which was not likeable. Was it the melancholy which peeped out of his father's spaniel eyes, when he was not being professionally funny, or was there a hint of slyness in his manner, or was he merely spoiled? Ivor had a brother just a little like J.S.: neighbours had said he would come to a bad end.

But Bologna was still talking. 'You'll see a lot more now than you've been seeing, dancing out there in front of the floats.'

'What, sir?'

'The trickwork. The Falling Flap, the Rise and Sink, what makes a Windmill into a Giant or a post-chaise into a wheelbarrow. And the magic in Patchy's wand. That's secrets. Don't you go a-telling 'em to other managements or outside folk.'

'I wouldn't dream of it,' Ivor said. But his own rise in the world was another thing. Full of it, and sparkling over with happiness, he met Jannie in the cold dark corridor that ran between the men's and the women's dressing-rooms. She wore a blue cape and a little blue bonnet, and he very much wanted to kiss her, partly from the joy that was his and partly from her own prettiness. As it was, he caught her at arms' length and told her his news.

She took it coolly. 'Yes, I thought you looked like a branch of the Gaslight and Coke Company.'

He took out of his pocket a crushed, disintegrating artificial flower. 'It brought me luck, you see. I told you.'

'H'm. Luck comes easy to some.' Seeing his disappointed face, 'I didn't mean that. You deserve it, every bit. You'll be celebrating, I suppose.'

'If you'll join me. We could do the grand and have a bang-up supper, or take a boat to Greenwich after the rag comes down . . . oh do, Jannie, please!'

She avoided his eyes and the bright allure of them, and said pettishly, 'You an't half as Welsh as you used to be. Just like any other super you talk. Oh, pardon me, of course, you're a star now. My mistake.'

'Never mind that. Will you come out with me?'

'Thanks, but I've a previous engagement.'

'With that lah-di-dah fellow in the man-millinery?'

'If you mean Mr FitzNeil, yes. Not that it's anything to do with you. Time I was changed.' Her nose in the air, she marched away, longing to run back to him, hating herself for her pettishness, seeing his puzzled reproachful face. Then she made herself remember Bess Ames and Emma Brice, and how he had stopped holding her hand in the Transformation Scene; and she hardened her heart.

He watched her vanish into the dressing-room, and for a moment hesitated, wondering whether to follow her. Had she turned back, or he gone forward, their whole lives would have been transformed utterly.

'The little Sorrel is not to have any more lessons,' Sara told Raymond. They were walking with Miranda on her lead in the comparative peace of Gray's Inn Garden, where the native cats eyed the pampered one with suspicion, and were in return stared out of countenance by her confident gold glance.

'Why is that? Poverty?'

'No, in fact they seem better off than they were. It is simply that Captain Sorrel asked me whether I thought his daughter would ever make a Siddons, and I had to say no. So he answered that my time was obviously being wasted, and that she must work hard at her dancing instead. But I think – do come along, Miranda – there is another reason.'

'The aristocratic escort?'

'Yes.' She sighed. 'I do feel it such a pity, that pretty child going the way of so many girls on the stage. For a year or two she will be in keeping, then pensioned off – if she's lucky. How can her mother allow it?'

Raymond shrugged. 'What else is there for her? A dancer is old at thirty. Then it will be marriage to some player, and a brood of children in lodgings, and debts and brokers' men. I've seen plenty of it.'

'She had a great passion for Ivor Bryn, but he cooled towards her. I told her to take no notice when he flirted with other girls, then he might come back. Perhaps I was wrong. Oh dear!'

'Think no more about it. People will do what they will, whatever advice one gives them.'

'You're very cynical today. Look, the sun's coming out – shall we sit down?'

When they were seated, and Miranda at their feet luxuriously nibbling grass, he turned to Sara and said weightily: 'We must talk.'

She opened her eyes, her face tilted up to the sunshine. 'We're always talking.'

'Yes. And where? In the streets, by the river, here or in the Temple Gardens. We might as well be vagrants. Sara, *why* will you not let me into your home?'

She hesitated. 'It is not my home, only a lodging. I have to be careful of my reputation. It would not do for me to be seen entertaining men.'

'And what do you suppose reputations count for, in such lodgings as we inhabit? Sara, my dear girl, can we not stop this farce and live together, as any other two people would, in our circumstances? We're getting no younger. No, put that cat down and listen to me. You said just now that it grieved you to think of the little Sorrel going to the bad. But it would not be like that with you and me, I swear to you. I would never desert you.'

'I know, I know.'

'And though I'll never be rich I live carefully. We'd have a better life together than we have apart. Come now, won't you see reason?'

'I do see it,' she said wearily. 'I know what you say is true. Believe me, it would make me very happy to live with you, only . . .'

'Only what? Are you afraid I shall take to the bottle again? I'm far more likely to do that living on my own.'

'No, no. It . . . I told you when we first said we loved each other that there were things you didn't know about me.'

'Yes. And I said that nothing I could know about you would alter my feelings.' He smiled and took her hand. 'Come, what is it? Have you stolen the Crown Jewels, taken a shot at the Prince Regent, forged a Bank of England note? If so I forgive you unconditionally.'

'Be serious! I don't wish to talk about it; believe me, it's best not.'

He said shortly, 'Then I think it's best we don't see each other again, for I'm tired of this pretence of friendship.' He got to his feet, but she pulled him down.

'Very well, I *will* tell you, though I've spoken to no living soul about it before, because I could not bear the distress of going over the story again.' Her look was so sorrowful that he felt remorse, and would have stopped her, but she went on.

'I was brought up in the country – in Wiltshire. My father was rector of a large parish, and I was his only daughter. My mother died when my youngest brother was born, and I kept house for my father and helped him with the parish duties. Oh, I was a model daughter! Then, when I was twenty-four, and quite resigned to spinsterhood, my eldest brother, who had gone into sea-service, brought home a friend, a naval lieutenant. They were waiting for a ship, because we were expecting war with the French any time.'

'Go on, my dear,' Raymond said gently.

'You must have guessed the end of it by now. He – Edward – was very handsome, very dashing. I knew no young men but farmers' and squires' sons, and curates, and I lost my heart completely, and my sense too, for I . . . he begged me to . . .'

'Yes, yes. Don't go on if it distresses you so.'

'I was alone in the rectory one night. My father had gone to visit a dying parishioner. The servants were in bed, in the old part of the house. And I let Edward in.' She was remembering her own pretty bedroom, the rose-sprigged wallpaper, the dressing-stand that had belonged to her mother, the mirror that she now carried with her everywhere, the old doll, Caroline, that always sat in the baby-chair that had been Sara's; and Edward's face, Edward's eyes and the ecstasy of passionate lips on hers. The room that would never be the same to her again, or she the same to it.

'He promised we should be married as soon as he became a captain, as he was sure to be, but he never spoke to my father for my hand. I think he was afraid of him; most people were. So many parsons live only for hunting and care little about morality, but Papa was not like that. He would have made a splendid Puritan. Well, war was declared, and Edward and my brother were off to Portsmouth. It was weeks before we heard from Thomas – my brother – but there was no word of Edward, and by then I knew . . . the situation I was in. My father put me out of the house.'

'God, not possible!'

'With him, yes. He let me pack a few necessities, then walked with me to the garden gate and locked it behind me. I tried to beg him to let me stay, but he said, "I am as the deaf adder that stoppeth her ears." I could see the servants watching from the windows. Then I think I walked and walked . . . I came to Chippenham, and sold a gold chain that had been my mother's. The jeweller thought I had stolen it and called the Watch, and I went to prison. At least it saved me the price of lodgings. They let me go at last, I don't know why; I remember hardly anything about that time, except how hot it was and my feet being blistered. Somehow I got to Bristol, and found work in a low house where sailors were entertained. They left me alone because my – my condition showed very much. I called myself Mrs, and bought a cheap ring, saying my husband was at sea. Then when . . .' She stopped, picked up Miranda, and stroked the cat rhythmically from head to tail, until it stretched out sleepily on her lap.

'My baby was born in that place, and they were kind to me. I was not strong and he, he was too small because I had not eaten properly. I wrote to my father begging him for help, but the letter came back torn up. And then my little George died. I'd called him George after the king, but it brought him no luck. I woke one morning and he was quite dead.

'They put him in a pauper's grave because I had no money for a proper one. And after that I went a little out of my mind, and they took me to a madhouse.'

Raymond could not speak, but took her hand and held it tightly.

'Isn't it merciful,' she said, 'that one cannot remember the worst times of one's life? I recall nothing about it, nothing at all, except being beaten. At last they thought me cured, and turned me out.' She put her hand to her brow. 'I forget where it was. But

I know I came to Bath after that, and by God's mercy met with an actress playing at the Theatre Royal, and she took pity on me, and gave me an introduction to the manager who tried me out in a small part. And so I came into the profession.'

She looked him full in the face, almost defiantly. 'And now you know why I will not live with a man, or bear another child.' Then she fell into a passion of weeping, and Raymond took her in his arms and held her.

When she had calmed a little he said, 'We're attracting some attention, my dear. Let us walk under the trees a little where we shall not be noticed.' He scooped up the affronted Miranda, and, one arm round Sara's shoulders, led her towards South Square. Before long she had controlled herself completely, and he talked to her quietly.

'Your story is a terrible one, Sara my love. But there have been many sadly like it, and you must not feel yourself alone. For you are not alone – you have me. And I swear to you now that I will never press my attentions on you, or ask you to do anything in the least against your conscience. I am content with your friend-ship, if you are with mine. And now I am going to take you home.'

The sun was out again, a scent of spring in the air. People in the streets looked cheerful, a boy was shouting something about a French victory. When they reached Sara's door she looked up at Raymond, her eyes quite dry now and a brightness in her face he had not seen before.

'You are to come in,' she said. 'I see now I have been most re-markably foolish.'

The Sorrel family read with mixed emotions a very curiously ill-spelt, ill-phrased letter which arrived addressed to the Captain. It stated that the writer would be more than obliged by the favour of a meeting with Captain Sorrel at his residence on the following Sunday morning, at the hour of noon, to discuss a matter of the greatest importance. The signature was Frederick FitzNeil.

'Well!' exclaimed Lucy, arms akimbo. 'What's the meaning of this, then?'

Her husband rubbed his hands. 'Fairly clear, I should say, Mrs S. The noble gentleman wishes to make a formal proposition . . .' At that moment Susan, the small servant who lived in the coach-maker's premises and 'obliged' for the Sorrels, made her appearance with the breakfast, and the Captain hastily stopped in mid-sentence. When Susan had gone Lucy said: 'I don't half like it, Captain.'

'What don't you like, my dear?'

'That our girl should come to be the toy, the plaything of a gentleman as may turn her out when he's tired of her, and who knows when that might be? Miss Dell was saying . . .'

'It's none of Miss Dell's business, and I trust you'll leave me to decide what's best for my daughter,' he said, with unaccustomed asperity. 'Bad times always follow the end of a war, and the theatre's going to be no better off than any other institution. To my mind, Jannie . . .'

Jannie, who had been washing at the bowl kept in her parents' room, came in with a scrubbed and glowing face. 'Yes, Pa?'

'This communication may interest you, my love.'

She took the letter, read it, then read it again, and the beautiful colour left her face. So it had come, what she had feared. She sat down suddenly at the table. Her mother, understanding, put her hand over her daughter's.

'We've got to see Mr FitzNeil, Jan. But I'm not having any "at the hour of noon" nonsense. This is a God-fearing house, and we go to church like we always do, and as the service don't end till half-past twelve or so you may bid Mr FitzNeil for one o'clock, Captain, and if he cares to take a saddle of mutton with us he'll be welcome, whatever the . . . whatever 'tis he wants to discuss.'

Jannie hardly slept on the Saturday night before the appointment. In the morning she rose pale and yawning, dark rings round her eyes. Her father noted it with disapproval.

'Touch of rouge would do no harm, young lady.'

Lucy bridled. 'No daughter of mine attends church wearing

rouge, Captain. And what's more I don't hold with it, not on a young girl. Turns the face yellow in time and rots the skin. But she may wear her best walking-dress to church, and I shall wear mine.'

Jannie's Sunday best was of a sensible but pretty damson-colour, knots of dark blue holding it together down the front and a small ruffled collar bone framing her neck. Her bonnet was a modest grey, trimmed with damson ribbons and a posy. She looked charming, and felt like Mary, Queen of Scots, going to execution, but without that poor lady's pious fortitude.

The service seemed to last for months. The Captain repeated the Responses and prayers in a loud, confident voice, and sang the hymns in equally stentorian tones. Jannie could not bring herself to sing, but here and there in the service lines penetrated her consciousness and made her shiver.

> Thou, Whose almighty word
> Chaos and Darkness heard,
> And took their flight,
> Hear us, we humbly pray,
> And where the Gospel day
> Sheds not its glorious ray –
> Let there be light!

Let there, indeed! prayed Jannie. She looked round what had been Inigo Jones's pride, 'the handsomest barn in London', burnt down and rebuilt in elegant imitation by Thomas Hardwick only a few years before; and wondered whether when she was in keeping and therefore regarded by polite Society as a variety of whore, she would be supposed to stay at home on Sunday mornings because her appearance among a respectable congregation would be an affront?

The sermon seemed interminable, but at last it was over, and they were wending their way across the corner of Covent Garden, quiet today, up James Street to Long Acre and home.

At one o'clock to the minute the front door bell jangled.

Unpunctuality was, oddly enough for an Irishman, not one of Fred's failings. Shown into their sitting-room by Susan, he looked like a peacock strayed into a farmyard, Jannie thought unkindly, but he seemed not to notice the humbleness of his surroundings.

The Captain stage-managed the proceedings. Offering a glass of wine and a cheap segar, he said, 'Very honoured to entertain you, sir. Perhaps you and I may have a word alone – if you don't mind, my dears?' with a nod of dismissal to the two women. Lucy led the way to the room she shared with the Captain, and they stood by the window, looking out unseeing at the familiar prospect of the tall houses opposite, with their medley of window-curtains, no curtains at all, shabby front-doors and new-painted ones, spear-headed railings and gold-painted trade-signs. Jannie had her hands to her ears, though the voices from the other room were not loud enough for words to be audible. Lucy sat down, took up a piece of sewing and began to work at it, snarling the cotton into a tangled knot which had to be broken off. 'Drat,' she said.

The door opened, and the Captain stood there, his face unusually flushed.

'If you'll step inside, my loves?'

They stepped inside. Fred was standing, very stiff and uncomfortable-looking, by the chair he had been occupying.

The Captain gulped. 'Mr FitzNeil has just made me a formal request for your hand in marriage, Janetta.'

'*Marriage*? You an't offered the wench *marriage*? A ballet-gel? 'Pon rep, Fred, I knew you wanted brains, but not this far.' Sir Patrick FitzNeil kicked up his booted heels on the fender and roared with laughter at the gracefully-moulded ceiling of his library; so it was called because it contained a great many calf-bound volumes, none of which he ever opened. His nephew stared back at him glassily.

'What else did you expect, Uncle?'

'What else? Why . . . there's no need for it. They don't expect it, these little fairies. Just a few years' keeping, and a brat or two, then you can find 'em a footman or a shopkeeper and marry one of your own choice.'

'She *is* my choice.' Fred's father would have been astounded at the firmness of his speech. Even his uncle was halted in mid-merriment.

'Rubbish. Mummer to mummer, that's the way of it. You may not be in the line for the title, 'less Augustus and his brood perish at one stroke. Three boys, now, or is it four. Still, blood's blood. Her father don't have two farthings to rub together, an't that so, so there's no tradesman's profits to be had. You've got yourself a beggar to support.'

Fred went an unlovely, high-flushed red, which threw his spots into relief. 'Miss Sorrel is no beggar. She's an artist of the stage, and brilliant. I'm privileged to have her.'

His uncle roared again. 'But not the first, I warrant. Now, the next minute you'll be telling me she's a virgin, and the Aldgate Pump is to walk behind you in procession to your wedding, with Queen Bess from St Dunstan-in-the-West behind, and Gog and Magog bringing up the bridal train.'

'I don't follow you, sir,' said his nephew truthfully. 'But I've no reason to suppose Miss Sorrel otherwise than – pure.'

'H'mph! Pigs have flown before now. And what's your father going to say when you ask his leave?'

'No need. I'm turned twenty-one and my own master. If you'll keep me with you, Uncle, which I'd take very kindly.'

Sir Patrick, a well-meaning man, got up from his wing-chair and stretched out a ham-like hand. 'D'you doubt that, when I've seen the hell and all you lived in across the water? This place is big enough for a regiment. Bring your little heel-kicker here, and we'll all be merry and drink fine sherry, till all the cows in Cork come home, and bad cess to them. Here's to the nuptials, and may the marriage-night never end.'

*

The nuptials took place in the bride's church, St Paul's, Covent Garden. Anywhere else would be unthinkable, just as it would have been unthinkable for Jannie to refuse an honourable offer of marriage from a member of the nobility. What she had feared was one thing, this was quite another. Love, Cupid, the little god of the pink-tipped wings and silver bow who spent so much time flitting about the pantomime stage, had no place in this union. There was no question of her loving Fred. But at least he was amiable and could support her, thereby taking the burden from her parents' shoulders and banishing the spectre of a future like her mother's, stitching, stitching away with bowed back and crippled hands.

She was taken for a formal visit to Hanover Square, her parents in attendance. Sir Patrick concealed his mirth at the commonness of the mother and the pretensions of the father (good family there, a long way back, though), but stared his blue stare at the bride-to-be. Actresses, dancers, what you pleased to call them, were to him all flaunting little whisk-tails, painted and powdered and ready to lift their indecently short skirts to any gent with a guinea in his hand. Fred's Janetta confounded him by appearing to be an uncommonly pretty, unpainted, refined young lady (just a touch of Bow Bells in the speech, perhaps) who moved more gracefully than any of the daughters of his own friends, and seemed not only quiet but a shade melancholy. He admired her, behaved more politely to her than a Georgian gentleman considered it necessary to behave to a player, and privately wished Fred joy of a very tame dove.

Her father gave her away, as full of pride as John Bull himself in that April when Bonaparte's throne had fallen, the Allies were triumphant, Peace reigned. Easter Monday dawned in a yellow blaze of daffodils and bridal-white blossom, the Pulteney Hotel announced *Thanks Be To God* across its frontage, the Percy lion atop Northumberland House wore a laurel-wreath round his ears (what intrepid person had climbed up to put it there?) and the pillars of the Regent's Carlton House were entwined with lamps, blazing stars of gaslight, the arms of Russia and Austria, Prussia and England. While illuminations and transparencies adorned every shop-window in London's highways and every private one that could afford something celebrating the downfall of Revolutionary France and the restoration of poor, fat, Bourbon Louis.

The wedding took place on St George's Day, by a happy coincidence the birthday of Shakespeare, a splendid excuse for the entire cast and staff of the theatre to turn up wearing red roses. Two days later Bonaparte was to take farewell of his Old Guard at the palace of Fontainebleau on his way to exile in Elba; a circumstance nobody at the theatre would mark particularly, for they were still talking of Jannie's wedding.

She looked extremely pale and lovely in white lace, like her appearance in the *Romeo* front-piece, except that no pink underlay the gauzy drapes of her gown; and the wreath on her head was made of real white roses, procured at who could guess what cost from some hothouse, and intertwined with tiny feathers. Her face would have been as white as they, had not her mother stained her cheeks with the petals of early geraniums, giving them a hectic flush that stood out painfully. But she smiled and bowed, and walked very straight, first at her father's side on the way to the altar, then at her husband's on the return from it.

The congregation contained a great many fashionable people, and the music a great deal of Handel. The theatre guests, from Tayleur and Signor Fasoli down to the property man and his boy Lewis, all were afterwards invited back to Hanover Square by sporting old Sir Patrick, who hadn't enjoyed such a party for years. Worth every penny he had stood for the ceremony and the entertainment. The tables at Hanover Square (manned by hired staff, for his own old buffers could never have coped with it) groaned with boars' heads, cold game from an aristocratic ice-house, oysters, lamb chops dressed up with frills, pork, veal, rabbits, and delicious salama-gundy, a collation of anchovies, chicken, eggs, and lettuce, garnished with grapes, not to mention endless sweetmeats and puddings. There was red wine, white wine, champagne, beer and porter, lemonade for the squeamish, coffee and chocolate, and segars for the gentlemen, though they were requested to smoke them in the ante-room.

Sara, sitting away from the thickest of the throng, with Raymond at her side, had eaten very little; but in her reticule was a napkin full of the choicest bits of meat, fowl and fish for Miranda.

'Cheer up, my dearest,' said Raymond. 'It is, after all, a wedding.'

'And what sort of a wedding? Don't you see, Columbine has married the Lover, not Harlequin. Ivor is not even here.'

'Are you sure – among so many?'

'Quite sure.'

But the other principals were: Jack Bologna with the ravishingly pretty Louisa Bristow, Joey's sister-in-law, on his arm, giggly and triumphant because they had taken this opportunity of announcing their own engagement; and Joey, likewise escorting the gorgeously-apparelled Mary and J.S. in a sort of Eton suit with a large neck-frill. Joey, at this moment, was standing on a chair, his face decked out in its Clown's livery of scarlet-triangled cheeks, great grinning scarlet mouth, and huge arched black eyebrows, hastily applied. He was singing, to somebody's not very accomplished strumming of a guitar.

> Sing and quaff,
> Dance and laugh,
> A fig for care or sorrow.
> Kiss and drink
> But never think:
> 'Tis all the same tomorrow.

Sara reached for the wine-glass beside her. It was her fourth. 'Some years ago,' she said in her deepest and most Siddonian voice, 'I played the Benevolent Agent in *Harlequin Highflyer*.'

'Did you, my dear lady?' Raymond had never seen her slightly foxed before.

'I did.' She turned portentous eyes upon him, reproaching the gentle amusement in his. 'I remember quite well what I said to

Pantaloon at the end of the piece when he attempted to wed her to Lover.

> 'And *you*,' I said, 'for wealth who'd tie her to a fool,
> Must feel the rod in disappointment's school.
> But now, whate'er the future may prepare,
> Let not the wedding-day be cross'd with care.'

'Amen,' said Raymond.

But Columbine, the white bride, sat with untouched plate and empty glass, smiling like a mechanical doll at her *corps de ballet*.

BOOK TWO

DARK SCENE

'Harlequin being tempted, stakes
his Magic Sword, which he loses.'

CHAPTER SEVEN
The Trap

The Honourable Mrs Frederick FitzNeil jerked impatiently at a fold of the heavy curtain behind her, releasing a cloud of dust and revealing a few inches more of the parlour window. Even so, there was not sufficient light for her to paint by. She rose and lit a candle-branch on the high marble mantelpiece, and brought it back to a table beside her.

By its rays she surveyed her work. Painting flowers on velvet. Of all the stupid, tedious occupations, even if it *was* the newest fashionable craze. The silly things didn't even look like flowers; more like great bulbous insects, and the paint was getting all over her hands and the apron she wore to protect her frock.

With a heavy sigh she threw down her brush and went to stare out of the window at the garden of the house in Hanover Square. It was a bleak prospect, on this wet day of late Spring; a few trees with their young leaves covered with smuts, a bed of half-hearted tulips which had provided her with the models for her painting, a bevy of sparrows pecking among the daisies on the grass. An old man looked after the garden; everybody who served Sir Patrick seemed to be old, except her own maid, Betty, who had been engaged specially and was pert. Jannie knew there were sniggers behind her back when she made a mistake with the cutlery at dinner, or committed some other social *faux pas*.

She began to wander idly round the room. There was nothing in it to waken her interest. She opened the harpsichord which had belonged to Sir Patrick's long-dead wife, and fingered out a dance-tune on its yellowed keys, sadly out of tune, some of them dumb. If she could play the instrument properly she could amuse herself; but the timid little governess they had appointed for her was making poor progress with her pupil, either in music or the French language.

Jannie picked up a copy of *The Lady's Monthly Museum* and flipped through it. 'Costumes Parisiens. Bonnets of yellow satin, trimmed with black velvet, the front ornamented with a quilling of white blond, are much worn. The materials for full dress are silver striped gauze, and white, or coloured crape, trimmed with Lama work . . .' She turned the pages from an illustration of two simpering females draped about on Grecian-style furniture, and paused at the Drama column.

Mrs Mardyn has attempted the Widow Cheerly in *The Soldier's Daughter*, and Peggy in *The Country Girl*. In the former character she was favourably received; but in the latter, the public appeared to be disappointed. Mrs Jordan's excellence is not forgotten . . .

Jannie shut the magazine. 'Mrs Jordan!' she said aloud, to a large porcelain figure of a tropical parrot surrounded by unlikely tropical foliage. 'All very well for Mrs Jordan, even if the Duke of Clarence *did* throw her over when he thought he'd a chance to be king. At least she could go on acting, and when she wasn't on tour she was having babies. Ten, was it, or eleven?'

The parrot stared back at her with glazed black eyes.

Babies: it would be something to have them, but woman's instinct told Jannie that they were never to be. Poor Fred, kind Fred, who meant so well and adored her still, had in two years of marriage shown only the faintest interest in her as a flesh-and-blood wife, and displayed only the feeblest ability at playing the husband. Perhaps a midwife's examination would now pass her off as no maid – or not quite a maid – or almost a maid? She wondered why he had married her, quite as often as she wondered why she had married him. At least she had had the pressure of her parents to improve her state in life, the temptation to flaunt it over the other girls at the theatre. But Fred – what need had he of a woman, or of her in particular? Perhaps he should have taken a good hearty widow who would have drilled him into manhood. Instead he had picked her, one of the pretty ballet-girls who charmed his eye, and now he had no idea what to do with her, any more than a hunter would have known how to treat a bright bird caught in a tropical forest, thought Jannie, looking at the gloomy porcelain parrot in its gaudy reds and greens, so out of place against the dull, tarnished grey-gold of the wallpaper. On one point he was adamant – she must not go on dancing. So he lost the pleasure of seeing her on the stage, and found himself landed with a pretty girl poorly educated for his rank in life, humble as it was compared with that of the English aristocracy who looked down on him and her. She could read and write, to be sure – thank Heavens for that, when she remembered her mother signing the marriage-register, as witness, with an X. She could dance the quadrille and the new daring waltz, at the dull race-balls to which they were invited. Horses, to her, were things that pulled drays, dogs the wretched scavengers of the market-stalls and butchers' shops, and cards objects of torture that made her yawn on sight.

They went to the theatre often, and that was something between pleasure and pain, for the dancing and the lights and the costumes brought back all the excitement of which she had once been a part. How could she have resented Fasoli's sarcastic comments, the cut of his stick across her ankles, the invasion of her mirror by other painted faces? For then she had been all eagerness and ambition and hopeful youth, and now . . .

She stood on tiptoe to peer at herself in the mirror above the mantel, dark pitted glass which had reflected so many dead faces. She was only nineteen, but already the pointed oval of her face had taken on an unbecoming roundness, the chin had a distinct appearance of doubleness. She put her hands round her waist. They failed to meet. The truth was that she ate too much. The food at Sir Patrick's table was not fine, but it was richer than she had ever had at home and came to table in far greater quantities. There was so much temptation to eat, when one was bored and lonely.

For she was very lonely. The Captain dropped in often, and looked not at all out of place in his daughter's new home, but his conversation was all too conscious of its grandeur and she despaired of his ever being the father she had known.

'Very proud of you, Janetta,' he would say. 'An adornment to your husband's halls, and no more than you deserve.' Then he would take one of the segars which Fred kept in a silver box for visitors, having little stomach for them himself, and pour out a handsome swig from the cut-glass brandy decanter. ''Pon my word, if you don't remind me of your grandmother, my own dear Mamma, as I well remember her.'

'Won't you tell me more about her, Pa? About your family? It might . . .' she fumbled for words, feeling dimly that if she knew herself to belong even tenuously to Fred's world it might help her to feel at home in it. But always the Captain would fob her off with a platitude about least said soonest mended, or some things being unsuitable for delicate ears.

And Ma never came to Hanover Square. Resolutely she insisted on knowing her place. If she had come, it would have been to the servants' entrance. Every second Sunday Fred and Jannie were formally welcomed to dinner in Long Acre, and then they all sat upright on the edges of their chairs and talked about Bonaparte's exile to St Helena, and the coming marriage of Princess Charlotte, and the interesting fact that game had been shipped from Lapland to London in a frozen state, yet perfect for eating, and was now being sold in Covent Garden at an extortionate price. Quails were said to be delicious stewed in cream, with a little butter on it.

Afterwards they would drive back home, if home it could be called, and Fred and she would sleep – in separate rooms. Much later Jannie would awake, and lie, listless, watching the shadow of a tree on the wall, silhouetted there by the light of a street-lamp. She felt her life was ticking away like the great lacquered long-case clock in the hall, and the gloomy clock in the dining-room, supported by two carven Sphinxes and bought by Sir Patrick on an unusual impulse in '98, when he had been fired by Nelson's victory at the Nile. It was possibly the newest thing in the house, except for Jannie herself.

Her thoughts came back to the present time, this April afternoon. Recklessly she went round the room lighting candle after candle, a thing Sir Patrick would have deplored if he had come in, for though he was rich enough he had a parsimonious attitude to the over-use of candles and fires: 'sending money up in smoke' he called it. But he was away at a race-meeting in Yorkshire. The place might as well look cheerful, for once.

She paused by a small writing-desk, a faded old thing that had once been bright with gold ormolu. It was useless to her, who never wrote letters, but in the 'secret' drawer which all such objects contained was a box of sweetmeats. Tempting little confections of sugar and almonds, small biscuits decorated with chopped cherries, delicate twists of angelica woven round creamy centres; walnuts in thin chocolate shells. They were her solace, fulfilling a need for comfort and something to do, if it was only picking them up and eating them, one by one, until the box was empty. She kept it hidden in the hope of making herself forget it, but in moments of extreme boredom it always came out. She pressed the spring that made the drawer shoot open, and contemplated the charming contents, her hand poised to choose.

'Sir Piers Compton, madam.' The voice of the old butler at the door made her jump with surprise. Guiltily she shut the drawer. Sir Piers entered, cane in hand and hat under arm. His natural elegance made Fred look like a potboy when they were together, and gave Jannie the uncomfortable feeling that her back hair was coming down and her petticoat-frill showing. Yet he was pleasant enough in appearance, somewhere in the thirties, dark hair growing becomingly grey at the temples, high-nosed like the great Wellington. Jannie repressed an impulse to curtsey ('only to Royalty, ma'am, in your state of life', her governess had taught her). Instead she went forward and extended her hand. Sir Piers bowed over it.

'I hope I don't intrude, ma'am. I thought to find your husband at home.'

'No. That is, he's gone into the country with his uncle,' Jannie said nervously, her eyes on the bell-pull. Another thing her governess had impressed on her was the unwisdom of ever, ever receiving a gentleman alone.

'Indeed. I'm sorry to have missed him.' Sir Piers' tone was not at all sorrowful, which was not surprising, as he had refused Fred's invitation to accompany him to Yorkshire, so that they could while away the tedium of watching the nags by playing cards for high stakes. Sir Piers was bored with cards and with most other things. The dull wife in the Buckinghamshire manor he hardly ever visited was about to present him with another boring infant to inhabit her boring nursery, and he was avid for new entertainment, if London could offer any. The Honourable Mrs Fred had always intrigued him by her incredible *gaucherie* – Peggy in *The Country Girl* to the life, if she were not obviously as Cockney as Bow Bells – a Bow *belle*, rather good, that, he congratulated himself. Such a simple creature would surely be as easy as a sitting rabbit, and the conquest might be quite a novelty. Besides, she was quite pretty in a big-eyed way, though her figure was going; and not for the same reason as his lady wife's. His sharp eyes had seen the contents of the secret drawer before she hastily shut it.

'I'd thought,' he went on, 'that Fred might care to keep me company at Sadler's Wells tonight – with your permission, of course, ma'am. There's a new piece, some nonsense called *Harlequin April Fool*. Silly enough stuff, I daresay, but a change from the old hacks they trot out at the Wells. I suppose *you* would not enjoy it at all?'

'I?' Jannie looked as startled as when he had come in, and there was a flush of pretty colour on her pale cheeks. 'Why, I hadn't thought . . . I wouldn't . . .'

'Wouldn't wish to accompany me without your husband. Quite understood. The thought merely came into my mind that . . .' No, it would be quite out of place to mention her old profession. But she was looking eager; she was going to agree.

'I should very much like to,' she said, half-stammering, 'if . . . that is . . . it mightn't be proper to be seen . . .'

'But of course, you would wish to bring some female friend,' he said swiftly. 'Your companion, perhaps, or your maid.'

'I have no companion, sir, only a – well, a governess, and she

visits me in the mornings. As to my maid, I – I don't think she
would . . .' What she could not tell him was that she heartily
disliked the waspish Betty, and had no intention of giving that
sarcastic young woman fodder for a good laugh in the servants'
hall next day over the fool her mistress had made of herself in
company with a gentleman.

'Then why not come alone?' Sir Piers' tone was warm and
gallant. 'Beauty can do no wrong, and Innocence is above slander.
I am, after all, your husband's closest friend. My wife would
accompany us, but she is in a delicate situation. Come, say you'll
honour me, ma'am.'

'Yes,' she said, quite loudly and naturally, like Jannie of the old
days. 'I won't half look forward to it.'

Sadler's Wells Theatre, once the site of a flourishing spa distribut-
ing healing waters, was practically in the country. The village of
Islington was the resort of Londoners every weekend, for its
pleasant air, tea-gardens, cream from the cow, pretty lights strung
between trees, and general merry-making. The night-soil col-
lectors of the metropolis had, certainly, a habit of depositing their
nasty stock-in-trade at a dump near the head of the New River,
but the river's water flowed unpolluted beside the theatre, between
willows and poplars, sailed upon by ducks and fished in by hopeful
Islingtonians. The theatre itself was like a rambling country house,
something between a manor and a large barn, with the waters Mr
Sadler had discovered in the seventeenth century still bubbling
away at the back of the pit. Because of its salubrious situation the
theatre attracted great custom during the warmer months of the
fine months of the year, and its boxes were extremely comfortable.

Piers Compton was a shade disappointed that Jannie had not
responded more warmly to his proximity to her in the carriage
travelling northwards. His knee had been meanly pressed
against hers, but her nose had been even more closely pressed to
the window-glass, as she took in the interesting vistas of the road
to Islington, and she seemed unaware that his gloved hand was

almost resting on the sprig muslin draping her lap, the tantalizing blue satin ribands of her high bodice trailing over it. Her Waterloo Hat, with its white feathers coquettishly hiding her face, was as elegant as it was irritating to him, as was the manteau of French silk in delicate pea-green which hid so much of her. Wenches of her type, in his opinion, looked better in undress or no dress at all.

But never mind her coldness. Young parties new to the fashionable world couldn't be expected to know its rules, the flirtatious glance, the accidental-on-purpose press of the fingers. That would come later.

In the best box of the theatre Jannie took a professional look round at the audience. Fairly respectable, no rioting likely, some handsome bonnets even in the pit. She had been there before to see an Aquatic Spectacle, and had been worried about the hazards of swimming horses and a slightly intoxicated Neptune. It was fortunate that the water-display had been abandoned. The curtain was red, a colour that was replacing the old traditional green. The Regent's heraldic arms loomed above the proscenium arch: the orchestra was tuning up for the National Anthem.

For the first time she scanned the programme. The fore-piece looked to be the usual silly hotch-potch of fairy-tale characters, goblins and peasants. Her eyes moved on to the Harlequinade.

'Clown, by Mr Grimaldi. Columbine, by Miss Valauncey, her first appearance. Harlequin, by Mr Bryn.'

Piers Compton, at her side, felt her start and stiffen. There could be nothing in the programme to excite her. It must be some gesture, some word or smile of his own. He congratulated himself on his new conquest.

Even more gratifying was the inattention she paid to the fore-piece. Jack, the hero, was played by an actor. Piers sensed her breathing in short impatient breaths, fidgeting with her fan and handkerchief, glancing round the theatre. Good, she was bored, waiting for the end of the performance and the little supper he had suggested.

At the entr'acte (for the fore-piece was tediously long) he took her down to the foyer, where refreshments were served, and was pleasantly surprised when she accepted a glass of maraschino. Very fast behaviour. Limonade or a fruit cordial would have been more ladylike. It was all very promising.

The drama wound its weary course to the Transformation Scene, and Piers felt his companion stop breathing. He took the opportunity of the general darkness to place his hand firmly in her lap, and was piqued to find it ignored. Her own hands were at her mouth, clenching her fan; he could not see her expression.

Then the gloom splintered into dazzling light, the Benevolent Agent was speaking the transformation speech, Joey Grimaldi was bounding and grimacing, the peasant girl Jill posing in white muslin, a very young and appealing Columbine, and Harlequin dancing lightly, stage centre, touching this and that person with his magic wand, making their rags fall away and their fairy selves emerge like butterflies from a chrysalis.

It was Ivor: but an Ivor changed in stature and power from the boy she had last seen two years and more since. Bologna had been excellent, faultless, but this Harlequin transcended mortality. Bologna had been near to middle age; this Harlequin showed his youth in every line of his lissom body, in the pure, strong line of his throat, the long slim beauty of his darting hands. Enchantment glinted from the eyes behind the black mask, summer lightning seemed to strike from gold and silver and many-coloured spangles that covered his skin-tight costume. In the pit, unknown to any-one there, was a small boy holding tight to his father's hand, who, one day when he was an immortal writer, remembered this Harlequin as 'covered all over with scales of pure gold, twisting and sparkling, like an amazing fish'; such was the magic wielded over the little Charles Dickens.

Jannie had gone cold at first sight of Ivor. Now the blood came back to warm her, to flood her cheeks, so that she had to lift her fan swiftly, hiding all but her eyes. It was as though she had had one of those religious experiences the travelling Methody preachers spoke of to sceptical listeners at street-corners. Her own past jealousy and anger, her attraction to the boy he had been, his avoidance of her, were as clear to her now as if she saw them in a tableau set in the circle of stage fire in which he was darting and diving. He had known what his future was to be. His technique was now far ahead of Bologna's, his confidence supreme. He was more than a dance-acrobat: he was Harlequin, gifted with a more than human power to bewitch. He was genius, she had been only a ballet-girl, a flower he might have carelessly picked and put to his lips (the triangular, enigmatic smile beneath the mask drew her eyes remorselessly) but must not keep lest it turn to poison in his grasp.

Now she saw it all, by the light of a love which had been with her since their hands first touched, if she had only known it. She felt tears trickling from her eyes and down her cheeks, falling on the lace frills at the high neck of her bodice; tears she had not been able to shed for her barren marriage or the loss of her career. If she had waited; only waited, stayed within his circle, within his world, worked at her dancing, striven to match him or at least be near him.

The wild, jolly music soared, but Piers beside her heard her almost silent weeping, and cursed to himself. Damn the silly little dollymop, was she mad, that he should bring her out for an evening's enjoyment of more than one kind, and she should sit beside him blubbering like a baby while all else laughed? He wondered if Fred's near-idiocy were matched by his wife's, and impatiently turned away from her to look for faces that were both pretty and cheerful.

Their carriage was waiting not very far from the stage-door, for there was only one road fit for vehicles running alongside the river. Piers was impatient to reach it, but Jannie hung back, dropping a glove and retrieving it, adjusting her hat.

'Come along,' he said testily, 'or we'll be hemmed in. I don't want to be here all night, whether you do or not.'

Now quite dry-eyed, she said, 'I'm sorry. But the air is so fresh after the theatre, and the river so . . .' There was really nothing complimentary to say about the river, which smelt faintly of sewage, but she leant pensively on the railing that edged it, positioning herself so that the stage-door was never out of her sight, while Piers stood beside her tapping his foot impatiently.

Then she saw Ivor. Cloaked and bare-headed, he was quite unmistakable, the crest of dark hair, the light step. People were gathering round him in an admiring swarm. Rapidly she moved forward to see him more closely. As she did so, the door of a small carriage almost opposite the stage-door was opened from within, and he leapt in. She saw the gaslight shine golden on his uptilted face, and his smile for whomever was in the carriage.

'Will you take me home?' she said with false brightness to Piers. With mocking courtesy, he offered her his arm. On the journey, baffled and annoyed, he took little liberties, toyed with her hand, caressed her curls (but confound the drooping feathers, tickling his face), talked pleasantries, and got in reply vague answers and a face turned away towards the dark streets. At last he fell silent, folding his arms and staring out at the prospect on his side of the carriage.

It would not be the end of his pursuit of his friend's wife, and by God he would make her pay for her poor manners.

Ivor's travelling companion sat severely upright beside him, not touching him. But he knew that her eyes were turned towards him, as they had been for the whole of the performance, never wavering, still as a statue's, and herself as silent, as she was now. Sometimes he wished she would chatter; it was relaxing, after a performance, to be able to talk.

'How was it tonight, then?' he asked at last. His quick light voice had lost much of its Welsh sing-song, yet had not caught any other accent; which was perfectly proper for Harlequin, who came from no particular place.

'It was perfect,' Clara answered. 'You know that.'

'I don't know it at all. How can I, when I'm here, there, and everywhere? How did the little Valauncey acquit herself?'

'Quite well, I suppose,' she said indifferently.

'Glad to hear it. She was as nervous as a witch and as heavy as a sack of flour, but if she looked all right from the front I needn't worry. Joey's taken her home for supper with him and Mary – he'll jolly her up, I daresay.'

Clara made no reply. She was not interested in Miss Valauncey, or in anybody on the stage but the man she had captured for herself and kept as a collector keeps a priceless jewel.

Clara Thurloe had been married for almost ten years to a doctor of medicine nearly twice her age. She had not talked much to him, either. A man absorbed in his practice, and in the study of new methods of surgery and treatment, he had been absent-minded, always with a book in his hand, completely impervious to the fires that smouldered in the girl he had married. Clara had wondered why he had married at all, when a housekeeper would have done just as well; possibly because her own parents, with five daughters on their hands, had pushed her at him and he had been too polite to refuse. All through their wedded life she had been bored, frustrated, revolted by the sick and maimed patients who came to the house, by the medical books with their horrible illustrations that lay about on every chair and even appeared at table until she made a scene and Dr Thurloe meekly laid them aside and ate his meals in silence.

Clara could not have said what she wanted in her life. She knew only that stormy passions raged and beat in her and could not be satisfied by anyone or anything she had so far discovered. She eyed men, from her husband's colleagues to the very tradesmen who came to the back door, with a speculative, searching gaze from her dark eyes, as though one of them, some day, might prove the prize she sought. Yet she saw nothing in any face that promised her reward, slaking the desire that burned in her day and night.

Particularly night. The time came when she began to take a little laudanum from the room where her husband's prescriptions were made up. With that, she could sleep heavily and dream wild dreams, more fulfilling than the experiences of real life. She began to take a little after their midday meal, and sleep away the afternoons.

Then came her release. A road slippery with ice, a stumbling horse, and Dr Thurloe, on a night journey to a patient, lay dead.

He was beyond the help of those who crowded round, recognizing and exclaiming with pity, for he had been liked and respected for his knowledge and skill, and his generosity towards the poor.

After her year of mourning Clara changed her ways. Dr Thurloe had left her comfortably off; she took herself to Bond Street and bought clothes that made the most of her elegant figure and severe good looks. She would never be beautiful, but neither would she be ignored, her slightly sallow face discreetly touched with colour, her almost black hair dressed by the best coiffeur in London.

On a winter night at the Royalty Clara saw the new Harlequin, just returned from two years in Dublin and on tour, and said to be the best in the business. Instantly she knew; she had found her treasure. In the Green Room, she sought him out as arrogantly as a male admirer might have sought out an actress, and invited him to supper.

Ivor was amused. He had made many conquests, deliberately or otherwise, in Dublin, but he had never been approached so boldly before, and by such a well-dressed and obviously wealthy woman. He was not rich – what dancer or player was? The supper was lavish, for Clara kept a good table now, and the house in Colebrooke Row, Islington, imposing by his standards. Not high living, but something better than theatrical lodgings. She gave him wines and spirits to drink that he had never tasted before, and he woke, with a fearful headache and the taste of ashes in his mouth, in her ample mahogany four-poster with rich, sombre curtains.

When he gave himself time to think, he despised himself. A widow's kept man, her lap-dog? Could it be he, the independent, who had escaped from his family, from a whole stifling way of life, who lived thus? Certainly it was something to be away from sordid theatrical lodgings, from the smells and discomforts of the streets, with free bed and board. But the bed he found distasteful in a way he could not understand, a vortex of passion and possession and resistance on his part always overcome by ... by what?

It was not true charm or beauty, for Clara had neither. Uneasily, and with difficulty – for he was a man of action not given to philo-sophical musings or the baring of his own soul – he came to the conclusion that he could not bring himself to reject anything that might better him, after the glittering success of his last two years. He had become a better performer than Jack Bologna, he knew. Whatever had gone to make up his disposition belonged to Harlequin, the magician from times past: he was as a priest pos-sessed by a god, though he was not learned enough to make the comparison. The applause of audiences, the adulation of women, had told him that in his own time he might be great.

Then Clara had come along, offering him the homage of her body, her house, her wealth. It was only his due, and he took it as a god takes offerings. And yet – he was only a man. He acknow-ledged now that his flesh rebelled against her age, her coldness of spirit, her stifling ownership, and he longed for the freedom of his own world, the freedom to take his own chosen woman from it. Jannie. He put away the thought of her. She was married to a man outside that world, was no longer of it herself. And Harlequin, for once in his roving life, was in a cage, a trap. He thought of himself standing under the stage on the square of wood that should lift him gracefully up into the bright scene above. He wished passion-ately that he could break out, reject Clara outright. But then Harlequin never openly defied people, only by trickery. And he, Ivor, was a Welshman given to soft words courteously spoken.

As soon as he was able decently to leave in the mornings, he was off to the theatre, either to rehearse or to walk about, exercising all he could to work off the heavy suppers and the wines Clara served him. He was at his best now, he knew; was he to be spoilt, pulled down, by an obsessed woman's pampering? He tried to talk to Grimaldi about it, in the pleasant, ordinary small house in Baynes Row, Spa-Fields, not far from his Circe's home.

'Confound it, Joey, I don't *like* her.'

'Then don't live with her. Easy as pie.'

'I don't know how to break away. It's like being at the bottom of the grave-trap, with no scene-shifters on duty. I can't tell you *what* it's like.' He shivered. 'Yet I go on, day after day. It's not the money, I swear that. I may not be flush, but I could live on my own.'

The clown's liquid brown eyes surveyed him, through a puff of smoke from the pipe he occasionally allowed himself.

'When I was a nipper,' he said, 'not as old as our J.S., my grandad kept a Fortune Box for me. When I was taken to see him, of a Sunday, dressed all in my best in a green coat with as many flowers on it as you'd see at Kew Gardens, a white weskit and a cocked hat – ah! I can see me now. Well, there was good old Grandad, pleased as Punch, and there was I, key of the Fortune Box tucked in me green small-clothes, as tight as a tick. Out it came, and into the box went a guinea and he'd say, "There, now, you're a gentleman, and something more, you've a guinea in your pocket."'

The fragrant scent of a goose roasting in the kitchen downstairs floated up to them through the cupboards on each side of the fireplace. Joey sniffed it appreciatively.

'Seems to me, young Patchy,' he said, 'as Dame Fortune's been a-handing out guineas to you lately, thick and fast.' Ivor began to speak, but a large hand silenced him. 'I don't mean in the way o' chinks. I means talents, like the Bible says. So, ain't they enough, without this mort that's a-making personal property of you?'

Staring into the fire, Ivor said, 'I may have the guineas, or talents, or whatever. But I don't feel like a gentleman. Nothing like.'

Joey looked up from the stage-trick model he was painstakingly constructing from wood and glue and a coiled spring, and in his eyes, with one of those flashes of intuition that had visited him since his boyhood, Ivor read a warning, as though the clown saw something he did not. Then Mary summoned them to dinner, and the moment was past.

Yet Ivor thought he had read the warning aright, and it meant that he must free himself, as Harlequin always did when things were going badly for him.

CHAPTER EIGHT

The Grave-trap

The night that followed her visit to Sadler's Wells was almost sleepless for Jannie. Some time in the early hours she was broad awake, staring into the darkness, her thoughts full of Ivor, and memories of her old life. Now more than ever she regretted bitterly having let herself be pushed into surroundings quite unfitted to her, shackled to a husband with whom she was barely able to hold a sensible conversation. She had grown up enough now to blame herself, not her parents, for all that had happened. Instead of indulging in childish jealousies of the other girls Ivor had flirted with, she should have kept a calm and smiling face and waited for him to turn to her again, as she now believed he would have done. And when Fred appeared in her life, she should have had the sense to tell him to go away again, for she was a dancer with a living to make.

At last, weary of tossing, she lit a candle and stared round the big shadowy room, hating it. She hated the whole house. The stags' heads and skulls in the hall were things not to be passed without a shudder, the rooms not as clean as her parents' lodgings. How she longed to be back there, in the turn-up bed, with a performance to look forward to next day! Slumped on her heaped pillows, she heard church clocks strike, the watchman's call telling the hour and the state of the weather, the rumble of carriages from Bond Street. Where could people be going at such a time, and why? Her thoughts drifted into fantasy, and so at last into an uneasy doze.

Tired and heavy-headed in the morning, she took her breakfast in bed, to the scarcely-hidden scorn of the pert maid. Downstairs late, she wandered listlessly about, almost wishing Fred and Sir Patrick back for company. There on the sofa lay the copy of the *Lady's Museum* she had been leafing through the day before. She picked it up, and it fell open at the page of drama criticism. Eagerly she looked down it for any mention of Sadler's Wells.

There was none; but she began to read a notice of *Hamlet* at Drury Lane Theatre.

The uncommon and deserved success of Mr Kean's Prince of Denmark has induced the Management to revive yet again this perhaps too-oft performed work of the immortal Bard. Miss Sommerville wrung all hearts in the part of the sorrowful Ophelia, and the Gertrude of Miss Sara Dell exhibited a dignity and depth of sensibility not always to be met with in this character. As Claudius, Mr Raymond Otway appeared somewhat too noble for the villainous King . . .

Jannie dropped the book, overjoyed. It was as though the names of her friends had appeared by magic to comfort her. 'I shall go and see them this very night!' she said aloud, clapping her hands. The porcelain parrot stared at her, sadly, she thought. Perhaps it, too, would like to turn to flesh, blood and feathers again, and fly away.

In the Green Room at Drury Lane she ran into Sara's arms and was warmly embraced.

'My dear child! Let me look at you. No, you haven't grown. But how fine you are – what a charming dress!' Sara held her at arm's length. Still in her mourning gown as Gertrude, feathers waving in her hair, she had acquired a new dignity and, Jannie thought, a serenity of expression.

'You were *so* good!' Jannie said earnestly. 'I thought it was too sad that you had to be poisoned at the end, and Mr Otway too.'

'Our consciences were not enough punishment for us, my dear,' Sara said, laughing. 'The Bard was moral above all things. How pleased he'll be to see you! Mr Otway, that is, not the Bard. He's changing because his costume is so very padded, but he should be up any minute. Look, here's another old friend of yours.' She stretched out a hand, and from one of the best chairs a sinuous black form uncurled itself, gave an immense pink yawn, and blinked at Jannie.

'Oh, it's Miranda! Oh, you dear thing! How often I've thought of you. There's a cat in our kitchens, but it's only kept for mousing and don't like to be picked up.' Graciously Miranda allowed this liberty, arching her neck in its pale blue collar to Jannie's caress. Then Raymond was with them, all pleasure at seeing the little Sorrel again. Only she was no longer the little Sorrel. He addressed her as Mrs FitzNeil, and Jannie made a face.

'Pray don't call me that! My name it may be, but not to you. No, Fred's not with me – he's away.' Sara and Raymond exchanged a quick glance which said, on her part, 'I was right, you see,' and on his, 'Of course. You always are.'

A bottle of wine and some glasses appeared, borne by a small black boy who played pages and who seemed in imminent danger of being trodden underfoot by the larger creatures among whom he darted. Raymond pulled up chairs and poured wine for them all.

'To us – to our reunion.'

'But where have you been?' Jannie asked. 'This morning was the first time I'd seen you billed.'

'Oh – touring. Hither and thither. We were both firmly resolved to get out of pantomime, so we took what offered – some of it pretty rough,' Raymond said cheerfully. 'Had it not been for Sara I might have weakened.'

'Yes, the bugs were dreadful,' Sara put in. 'Lodgings seem to get worse instead of better. But there, it's all the luck of the profession, and we *did* have some very warm audiences, especially in Bath.'

'Ah yes, beloved Bath . . .'

Jannie wondered if the lodgings had been shared. She glanced at Sara's left hand, but it was ringless; yet she sensed that they were very close, these two handsome people, curiously alike in their looks, both tall, distinguished of feature, Raymond's hair grey, Sara's silvering. As husband and wife often grew to resemble each other, so had these two; Jannie wondered what their circumstances might be. She was plucking up her courage to ask a question, and at last she said, feeling a blush rising: 'Did you hear anything of Ivor Bryn on your travels?'

Sara considered. 'Why, we did – where can it have been? Dublin, that was it – the Crow Street Theatre. We heard he had been there for a season and caused riots – those Irish people are so excitable. And somewhere else – Manchester, was it, my dear? I always knew that young man would go far. Bologna is married, had you heard? To Louisa, of course.'

Jannie had been given her cue. 'Is – is Ivor, do you know?'

Sara shook her head. 'I have no idea. Certainly not to any of the young ladies who were with us at the Royalty, because I met one of them the other day – dear me, what was her name? – and she told me the news from there.'

Jannie felt she could ask no more. The wine was almost finished, and the Green Room clearing. She noticed that at the last pouring, Sara had put her hand over Raymond's glass as he was about to fill it, and he had given her a resigned little smile. Before they parted, she had invited them to dine with her at Hanover Square. What matter if Fred were there or not? They were quite as suitable to a nobleman's house as he was. Affectionately Sara bent to kiss her.

'We are so very happy to see you again, Jannie. And to know that all is well with you.'

But they agreed, as they went back to their separate lodgings, that all was not well with her.

The evening of Jannie's first visit to Sadler's Wells had been grey and drizzly. Her next one followed a perfect day of Spring, blossom suddenly appearing where there had only been buds before, a warm sun and a feeling of excitement in the air. She dressed carefully, choosing a simple white gown, and over it a mantle of deep apricot velvet, with a high ruffed neck that framed her face like the calyx of a flower. Critically she peered at her reflection. It seemed that her face looked less plump tonight; which might well be, for she had eaten so little in the last three days. Would he know her? Would he be pleased to see her, or not?

Betty watched her mistress with a beady eye. There might be something in it for gossip, going out of an evening three times in the week, and the master away.

'Sir Piers calling again tonight, madam?' she enquired.

'No,' said Jannie. 'I shall need you to accompany me.' It was not an attractive prospect, but to go to the theatre unattended was really carrying unconventionality too far. 'I daresay they'll find you a place in the pit.'

'Oh, madam! are we going to the play?'

'To Sadler's Wells. There is a new Harlequinade.'

Oho, thought Betty. Back to our old flash companions, are we?

Jannie sat through the performance rapt as a child at a fairy-tale, yet with a fluttering excitement she had not felt the first time. When it was over, with its stage-tricks and rainbow of changing colours and softening of lights on tinsel and spangles to an expectedly romantic finale, Miss Valauncey and Ivor posed within a ring of very small fairies with candles attached to their heads (a nasty risk for the management, Jannie thought), she hurried to meet Betty in the foyer.

'Did you enjoy it? Good. Then go and wait for me in the coach.'

'For long, madam?'

'I don't know . . . I have someone to see. Hurry, now.'

She herself hurried to the stage-door, though there was no need, for he had to change and take off his white make-up. She stood, cold in her short-sleeved dress and light cloak, watching the sky over the river change like stage lighting on a grand scale, from pinks to greys and oranges, all in the shadow of scudding grey clouds. There was a crowd round her, watching the emerging faces, disappointed when the person leaving was of no account. Joey Grimaldi, Mary on his arm, came out, and they mobbed their favourite, crushing Jannie into the back of the crowd. Then, as they ran after him, she saw Ivor, and her heart raced. He looked round cautiously, saw with obvious satisfaction the chase after Joey, and was almost past her with his famous light step, as though his heels scarcely touched the ground. She made herself step in front of him and pull at his cloak.

He stopped and looked down at her, his face pale in the edge of the lamplight. She saw recognition in it, and something else – what? Then he smiled, the sweet triangular mischievous smile that was Harlequin's and his.

'Little Jannie.'

'I had to see you,' was all she could say.

She heard him murmur something in Welsh. Then he said, almost under his breath, 'I can't stop. Where can you be found?'

She shook her head. 'Too difficult. But you?'

'Here, tomorrow, at noon. The dressing-room.'

She nodded, and he was gone, darting towards the carriage that waited, and its occupant who had not missed the encounter.

At supper Clara said to him, 'You're not eating.'

He looked up with a start. 'No? I wasn't aware.' He began, listlessly, to turn over the food on his plate.

'Is anything wrong? I noted the clown did something awkward and put you out.' She would never refer to Grimaldi or any of the other performers by their names.

'That? It was a new gag between Joey and me, a put-up job. It got a laugh, didn't it?'

She made a moue of distaste. 'If you're not hungry, come and sit down.' She moved to the double-ended chaise-longue by the fire, and patted the place at her side. He was expected to move to it, put his arm round her shoulders, and allow her kissing and toying until it became too urgent to resist and they went upstairs, entwined. A sudden coldness came over him, like the onset of physical illness, a rebellion against this quiet prison, its ugly Hogarth engravings, the faint gruesome smell of medicines that came from the locked dispensary, the unseen servants and the rich food provided for him, Clara's kept man.

Against her, more than anything, he rebelled. So cold and yet so hot, his selfish, single-minded protectress. It was as though that moment in the Spring night when a small remembered face looked up at him a spell had been broken, a prison key turned. He despised himself bitterly, but thanks to Jannie and her reappearance in his life, he was free, as he had resolved to be after Joey's homily; or would be free.

Half way to the couch, he said, 'Forgive me, Clara. I think I must be a little unwell. Goodnight.'

She watched him go, knowing him bound for the bedroom that was officially his out of propriety, though he had so far hardly occupied it; and her face was ominous.

At home, the fairy who had freed him was herself deep in enchantment. In the album she kept for agreeable scraps and comments Jannie was laboriously copying a poem. It seemed to say what she could not have put into words.

By the tremulous sounds which unnerve my fond heart,
Now confession first tells me thy choice,
By the lip that was never the herald of art,
And bids my torn bosom rejoice;
    I'll ne'er forget thee!

By the mild moonlight hour, which o'er hears thy pure vow,
Breath'd in accents more grateful to me
Than e'er youthful Philomel's lute could bestow,
Who learn'd Music's language from thee,
    When first she met thee,
    I'll ne'er forget thee!

He was not up from rehearsal, his elderly dresser informed her when she came to the theatre at noon, and his tone implied that she was expected to go away again.

'Then I'll wait,' she said, and perched herself on a small uncomfortable chair, to the old man's silent disapproval. He went out, leaving her to look round at the guise of a Harlequin: the two costumes hanging on a rail, one spare in case of accident, shimmering with colour and light, a stage jewel set in every triangle of red, blue and lilac, the mask, the black cap, and the cocked hat

Harlequin sometimes wore, the magic bat and the black leather belt that held it when it was not in play; two shirts with ruffed necks, a pair of dancing-pumps almost worn through.

The door opened and he came in, still in practice dress, black tights and a shirt open at the neck, a towel draped round his shoulders. The moment Jannie had thought and dreamed about all night and morning had come, and she was suddenly stricken with a terrifying shyness, all the things she had meant to say flown from her head. What was she doing here, like a Cyprian soliciting a customer? What did she hope might come of the meeting?

Then Ivor made it easy for her. Smiling, he took her cold gloved hands and held them in his.

'There's kind of you to come and see an old friend,' he said, exaggerating his native accent and completely ignoring the emotion of their last meeting.

'I had to, when I saw your name,' she said, hoping her voice was not trembling. Then, rushing on, 'You will think it very bold of me to come alone.'

'Why should I? Will you take a glass of wine with me?' He opened a drawer in the mahogany dressing-table, in reality a cupboard for bottles, and filled two glasses. 'I allow myself one glass now, or some porter, nothing else at this time of day.' He patted his slim waist. 'It don't do. Your health, Jannie.'

She raised her glass, thinking that she seemed to make a habit of taking wine in theatres these days. Ivor, leaning against his dressing-table and chatting about how much of an improvement it and his dressing-room quarters were from the old Royalty, watched her with a mixture of feelings. He had seen plenty of bored, desperate young wives on the look-out for amusement (had not his own situation with Clara come about like that?); he detected the dancer of old days under the slightly over-dressed exterior. So pretty, so pale, so unhappy; and he felt the physical pull of her attraction to him, and his to her. Taking her empty glass, he said, 'Old Pratt will put it about that I'm no better than a philanderer if we stay here alone. He probably has his ear against the door. Come and walk in the fields.'

He disappeared behind a screen and emerged, with incredible speed for anyone but a Harlequin, in his ordinary clothes.

They strolled by the margin of the New River Head, a pleasant semi-circular walk, below the regimented line of poplars that fringed it, now in young green leaf. The river's staleness had been blown away by a recurrent little breeze, ducks paddled and up-ended themselves, one followed by a train of tiny brown duck-lings. Here and there boys were fishing. Behind the theatre Jannie's carriage stood; the coachman, walking the horse, gazed curiously after the two strolling figures, his lady's hand on the young man's arm.

They said little at first. Then, abruptly, Jannie asked, 'Why did you not come to my wedding?'

'Why? Well . . . I supposed you would not want me there.'

'You were invited.'

'With the others. Out of politeness, I thought – in view of your opinion of me.'

'I don't remember giving an opinion.'

He smiled quizzically. 'But you do remember giving me a rose from your coronet – a particularly tattered one?'

'Yes. I – it was all I had to give you. I'm sorry it was tattered, but they all were. What did you expect, a bouquet?' she added with a flare of her old spirit.

He was puzzled, not smiling now. 'I thought you meant it as being all I was worth.'

She would not look at him. 'Why should I think of you so badly? We hardly knew each other, after all.'

He pulled her to a halt and made her face him. 'Jannie, let's stop fencing. You know I treated you badly. Don't shake your bonnet at me, it's too true. I led you to think I was courting you, then dropped you for somebody else.'

'Bess Ames!' she flashed back.

'Was that her name? I don't remember it, or her, or any of the other ladies I may have entertained.'

'She was a bold, fast creature, and I don't believe she ever washed her hair in her life,' said Jannie with retrospective malice.

'How *could* you take up with such a person?'

Ivor sighed. 'I won't say because I was foolish, though perhaps I was that too. It was because I had to break away from you to make my way in the world. Jannie, we were too young, you must know that. You were little more than a child, and I was simpler in those days than I am now. I could never have betrayed you, and I was not ready to marry you, or anybody. Can't you understand?'

'It was cruel,' she half-whispered.

'Oh, Jannie!' They were standing beneath a tall weeping willow, its green tresses veiling them like the drops of a fountain. There, in the willow's shade, he kissed her for the first time, tenderly and slowly. In that kiss all was said that they had not been able to say, all vows made that they must not make to each other.

'"Too early seen unknown, and known too late,"' she murmured, against his heart.

'What, my love?'

'Juliet. When she met Romeo. I learned it for Sara when she used to teach me. Ivor – what is the Welsh for sweetheart?'

'*Cariad.*'

She looked up at him, still close in his arms, her face soft and radiant. 'Ivor, *cariad*. What a pretty language Welsh is!'

He broke away from her and the temptation of her lips with a sort of groan. 'What are we to do?'

She was sad again. 'I don't know. Here am I, married to Fred ... oh, poor Fred, I should never have agreed.'

'He doesn't ill-treat you?'

'No, indeed, he's very kind. But we are so unsuited to each other. He never wanted me, only the girl he saw on the stage, and I never wanted him at all. Oh, why don't people stop to think?'

'I stopped to think, and look where it's put me,' Ivor said a shade grimly.

'You're not married too?'

'No.' Damned if he was going to tell her of Clara and his disgraceful situation. 'No, one barrier between us is enough. Jannie, now let us be sensible. I love you, and you love me, and that must be enough for us. How can I ruin you, drag you back to my shabby world?'

'I want to be ruined – I want to be dragged back!' she cried passionately. 'It was *my* world, too, and I want it. I don't care what you say, or what happens. I lost you and now I've found you, and I won't let you go!'

'Oh, *cariad*, you don't know what you're saying. Give me time . . .'

The breeze was stronger and the sun had gone in. A drake with a burnished jade head swam enquiring up to these thoughtless humans who had not provided themselves with even a crumb for deserving birds, seeming only interested in each other. For a moment his bright beady eyes surveyed them, then he swam away, disappointed.

'Will you meet me here,' Ivor said, 'when you can? At this time. Then at least we can talk, and . . . your reputation will not be spoiled. Say you must exercise for your health. Or will your husband think that strange?'

'He'll think nothing at all; he never does. He's hardly at home. And nobody else will take any notice – except my maid, and I'll deal with her somehow. Yes, Ivor, I will meet you, if that's all we're to have.'

She reached up and kissed his mouth. 'Let's go back now, because I might cry and it would look very bad if people saw us like that, so I must get into the carriage first.'

Ivor laughed. 'It would look terrible indeed. I can picture Pratt's face, seeing me with a weeping lady.'

They said goodbye at a discreet distance from the stage-door. Jannie, aching to kiss him again but not daring, saw that the emotion of their little scene had left him white and strained, lines of stress about the long sweet mouth. She ran to the carriage and sat in it, watching him walk slowly back to the stage-door.

' "Methinks I see thee, now thou art below, As one dead in the bottom of a tomb." '

As the carriage started, she began to shiver uncontrollably.

*

'But why must you go to the theatre, when there is no harle-quinade?' demanded Clara.

'Because I must practise.'

'I should have thought you were accomplished enough to need no more practice.'

'My dear Clara, if a dancer failed to keep limbered up he would stiffen like an old man.' Ivor had his hand on the door-knob, his eyes on the sunny prospect outside the window. If only Clara had the slightest idea of what the life of a professional performer was like, he might be able to tolerate his present situation better – even now that there was Jannie. But Clara's face was ominously set.

'You could perfectly well practise here, if you must.'

Ivor sighed in exasperation. 'Where, in a house full of furniture? I need space and proper equipment.'

She looked round the room. 'The table and chairs could be pushed back against the wall – temporarily.'

Ivor felt his temper rising. 'You haven't the remotest notion of what I'm talking about. Now I must go.'

She jumped up. 'In that case I'll go with you. It is a pleasant day for a drive.' She pulled the bell for the maid.

'For God's sake! Is there the slightest need to drive from here to the Wells, when one can walk it in ten minutes or less? For that matter, there's no need for you to drive me back at night – I'm neither a child nor an invalid.'

Clara flushed dark red. 'So now you want to get rid of me! Thank you, thank you so much. I do think gratitude such an admirable quality, don't you, especially in a gentleman?'

As soon as the girl had gone Ivor faced Clara, furious. 'I tell you I won't be dominated like this! Go for a drive if you must, but I shall walk.' He was out of the room and the house in a flash, leaving her to explode into a passion of tearful rage.

Jannie, waiting patiently in her usual place, was relieved to see him, but baffled by his black mood. He would tell her nothing of the cause, and they talked almost like polite strangers. Unwisely, she asked him where he lodged, the thought in her mind that they might meet there instead of in this embarrassingly public place, but he brushed off the question.

'Not far away. Convenient enough. But I intend to leave.'

She glanced at his grim expression and said brightly. 'Fred is home. He seems not to mind my driving out each day. I know Craigie has told him, because he don't like having to come out every day and wait about. It's bad for the horses, he says. Still, I think . . .'

He cut her short. 'Jannie, I can't meet you tomorrow.'

'Oh!' Her face was a picture of disappointment. 'But why not?'

'Because they're putting on an aquatic spectacle, *Neptune's Triumph*. As there's no Harlequinade I'm not wanted. I'll try to get here when I can, but . . . there are reasons why I may not be able. I have some business to settle.' A plausible excuse came into his mind. 'Besides, the rehearsal rooms will be needed – they're getting up new stage effects and the place will be crammed with carpenters and horses too, I shouldn't wonder, as there's to be a Chariot Finale.'

The tale sounded lame to his ears, and he knew it did to hers, true though it was in essence. Grieved at hurting her, he cut the meeting short and parted from her without a kiss.

All that afternoon he wandered aimlessly about, watching the preparations for *Neptune*, the great tank under the stage being uncovered, stage-hands going to and fro; then he took to the streets, stared into shops at objects he had no intention of buying, went into a chop-house and ate an indifferent meal. Reason told him that he must make an end of life with Clara. Yet how would that bring him nearer to Jannie? Impossible to ask her to give up her comfortable station in life, however she might protest, for what he could offer her. But at least he would be his own man again. And untrammelled by Clara, he could soar into the place meant for him, and become the Harlequin of the age.

The meal finished, he wandered westwards, through Soho, across the great new street that was being built between the Regent's residence, Carlton House, and the park named after him, beyond elegant Portland Place. Just across it was Hanover

Square. Ivor knew now where Jannie lived.

There was the house, on the other side of the rail-enclosed gardens in which the public were not allowed to walk. He crossed the square, and stood looking at the imposing town mansion, the porticoed door with its huge brass knocker made in the likeness of a Bacchante's head, the heavily curtained windows. Yet there was a look of gloom and disuse about it. He tried to imagine it ablaze with lights, receiving trains of visitors from their carriages and chairs, music and dancing in the long drawing-room. But the picture would not form; he could only see in his mind Jannie, like an imprisoned princess, a very small figure moving through great melancholy rooms.

If he waited long enough she might appear at a window and see him. Then perhaps she would send a servant to ask him in, and he would have at least a little time with her. But passers-by were beginning to look at him oddly, and he realized that he might well be taken for a thief weighing up the possibilities of breaking and entering. Reluctantly he moved away, depressed in spirit. This might not be Jannie's true setting, but neither was it his. A gulf far wider than the breadth of Hanover Square lay between them.

When he got back to Colebrooke Row, walking all the way, he found Clara sewing at a piece of tapestry intended for a chair-back. As he entered she glanced up, with a smile as artificial as the flower she was embroidering, but he was relieved to see it at all. Relieved, yet curiously uneasy. Their conversation during supper was restrained. He knew that she was still angry with him, and feared an outbreak of temper. It was in his mind to tell her then and there that he was leaving her, but the thought of a scene, tired as he was, daunted him too much. Soon after supper he excused himself, yawning, and retired.

Clara put down her needle and sat gazing at the fire. Though she would not confess it even to herself, she knew that she was useless to him, and he to her, but for the physical passion she could arouse in him, and her pride in his beauty. Ironically, he was as absorbed in his profession as her husband had been in his, wholly a man of the theatre who had no real interest in anything outside it. He would have been happier talking to that common man Grimaldi than to her, she knew, and sooner or later he would tire of her and go back to his own kind. Perhaps the change had already begun.

But she needed him so much. She had always loved to own beautiful things. As a child she had not broken her toys as other children did, but kept them immaculate, to be envied by other little girls less fortunate than herself. There had been one doll, bought for her by her harassed mother after she had seen it in a toyshop window and screamed for it: not an ordinary wooden moppet or a lace-draped baby, but an Indian prince, dark-faced and clad in robes of silk and glittering tissue, a gold turban swathed round his head. She had adored him like an idol, kept him jealously away from her sisters' reach: had indeed slapped and punched little Maria for touching him with jammy fingers. Over the years moths had invaded his splendid robes, the plaster face had chipped, and Clara had cared for him no longer.

In the same way she revelled in her possession of Bryn the Harlequin, her glittering prince come to life; hers, all hers. Suddenly a longing for him swept over her, and she went upstairs. But he was not in her room, and when she tried his own bedroom door it was locked. Slowly, quietly, she went down to her parlour, and sat for a long time by the dying fire.

CHAPTER NINE

The Love-philtre

On a beautiful day in early May the Captain and Lucy Sorrel stood in a huge crowd in Pall Mall watching the very slow progress of a splendid carriage, containing a fair, plump, beaming young woman in a dazzling gown of white and silver tissue, the transparent manteau glimmering with silver thread, her blonde curls crowned with a wreath of brilliants forming rosebuds nestling in leaves. She bowed and smiled to the crowd from each wound-down window in turn. The Princess Charlotte, only daughter of the Prince Regent, was going to her wedding to Prince Leopold of Coburg.

'Bless her, she looks so happy!' Lucy drew her hand across her eyes. Without looking at her husband, she knew that he shared her thoughts. If only our Jannie had looked like this on her wedding-day. All that money spent, and the fine banquet, every bit as fine in its way as this young couple would be having, and yet . . .

Huzzas filled the air, hats and caps waved, children were mounted on shoulders to see the girl who would be their future queen, people who had reviled the Regent for his extravagance and improper goings-on cheered for his daughter. A royal wedding procession was better fun than a hanging, any day.

The Captain felt his wife's weight heavy on his arm, and looked down on her with concern. She had limped all this way, how painfully, he knew. Now the gilded coach was past, the silvery apparition only a white-gloved hand waving.

'Come, my dear,' he said. 'We must get you home. There'll be no more to see here, and we'll never make our way through this mob. Let's work our way to the back and I'll find a chair or a hackney to take you home.'

Lucy's legs ached so much that she protested less than she might have done. After a struggle, in which the Captain's soldierly height and strong right arm were of considerable assistance, they heard the welcome cry of 'By your leave, gentlemen!' from a pair of sedan-chair porters skirting the fringe of the crowd. They were doing badly for passengers, with everybody reluctant to leave the scene for fear of missing anything in the way of spectacle. The Captain stopped them, helped Lucy in, gave her the fare and enough for a tip, and waved her off.

His time was now his own. He had no fancy to make his way to Carlton House or York House, or wherever there might be sights to see, and he had an uncommon thirst, what with the heat and the exercise. Thankfully he reflected that The Shiners' Club was within a stone's throw, and towards it he made his way.

Almost at its doors, he collided with a man walking rapidly in the opposite direction. Instantly they recognized each other, though they had not met since Jannie's wedding.

'Captain Sorrel!'

'Mr Otway, 'pon my word!'

They exchanged felicitations, and the Captain said, 'What a confounded rum thing we should meet only on wedding-days, what? Though this is a showier affair than ours, an't it. Did you see the bride?'

'Charming. And a glimpse of Prince Leopold, on the balcony. A very well-set up and amiable sort of young man, I thought him, not at all like those scurrilous caricatures.'

'Tell you what – my club is just down the street. How would it strike you to drop in there with me and drink their healths?'

Raymond hesitated. It was not his habit to drink so late in the day, and Sara preferred him not to drink at all. But he too was hot and tired, and conscious of the hardness of the pavements. If a gentleman of middle-age might not sit down and drink a toast, on such a day in the annals of England, then it was a pity. Smilingly he agreed.

The dark old snug-room of The Shiners was agreeably cool and quiet. The Captain, who had had a win the previous day, called for champagne – 'the only thing for such an occasion' – and, while it was being submerged in ice, a tot of brandy each.

'To the bride – God bless her.'

'The bride.'

'May all her troubles be little Charlottes and Leopolds.'

They followed the bride's toast with a health to the bridegroom and even to the Regent, and, over the champagne, fell to discussing the last wedding at which they had drunk together.

'I saw Miss Sorrel – Mrs FitzNeil, that is – only a little while ago,' Raymond said, 'when she kindly called on Miss Dell after the play.'

'How did you think she was looking?' enquired the Captain, with deliberation.

'Why – exceedingly pretty, as ever. A little . . . pensive, perhaps. Mr FitzNeil was away, she said. No doubt she was missing him.'

'Ah.' Jannie's father drew circles on the table with his glass and stared at a print of a cock-fight. 'I've sometimes wondered. Don't like to say too much to her mother, but it don't seem all it might be, that marriage. If you say these things to women they start crying, that sort of thing, quite needless for I expect there's no call for alarm. Fred don't seem the straying type. Pity there are no young ones, though. By now you'd have expected . . .'

Raymond thought morosely of his own marriage, that had dragged on so many years: the harpy-wife who still pestered him with letters and sudden visits, the 'young one' who was now a spinster of twenty-five, brought up to hate her father. He drained his glass at one gulp.

'Well, no use repining,' said his host. 'Let's have another bottle.'

Because his spirits had suddenly dropped, Raymond made no objection. Another glass of golden sparkling cheer and forgetfulness was put before him; he drank it and smiled, and began to tell stories which were a little too *risqué* for Sara's ears, but vastly entertaining to the Captain, who replied with some of his own, of a generally military and dashing character. The bottle was almost finished before he noticed Raymond's glazing eyes and slurred speech. Guilt filled him, for he knew what drink could do to a player; Lucy's stories had left him in no doubt of that.

As though casually, he said, 'You on stage tonight, sir?'

'Yes. Yes. *School for Scandal*. Curious choice for royal wedding night, very.'

'Not unfitting to the Regent's, come to think of it. Dead drunk in the fireplace. But look here, sir, you strike me as being just the least thing . . . overcome.' The words 'bottled' and 'lushed' were in his mind, but one could hardly utter them to such a stately gentleman.

'Tired. And not used to . . . this stuff. Thank you kindly, though.' His head drooped.

For the second time that afternoon the Captain went in search of transport. There was a hackney-coach stand nearby, to which he conveyed Raymond, and after a long wait they were able to board a coach that would take them to the Strand, not far from their lodgings. The air seemed to revive Raymond a little. He made no objection to the Captain accompanying him up to his room and deftly preparing for him a pot of strong tea, while he doused his face with cold water.

'Trust you don't feel too poorish, sir. All my fault, letting loyal sentiments get the better of judgment. Should have had more sense.'

Raymond managed to smile. 'Not at all. My fault. Thank you for all your kindness. I shall be better soon.'

Tactfully, the Captain left.

There were still two hours to go before Raymond need be at the theatre. Mercifully, his condition improved in the meantime. He made himself stay awake, even walk round Covent Garden and take a cup of soup at a stall, remembering from the bad old days the curative effect of the hot savoury draught. It still worked; he was himself again. His head was clear, if not his conscience.

He was given a further respite before he had to make his entrance by the playing of the National Anthem and the recitation by Miss Eliza O'Neill, who played Lady Teazle to his Sir Peter, of an Ode in celebration of the royal nuptials. Loud cheers greeted it, and the curtain rose a quarter of an hour later than usual.

In his dressing-room, putting the final touches to his make-up, and noting ruefully that the old-fashioned wig he wore was scarcely greyer than his own hair, he heard bursts of laughter and applause at the witty scandal-mongering of the first scene. That appalling destroyer of reputations, Lady Sneerwell, delighted pit and boxes with her shameless scheming, the arch-hypocrite Joseph Surface oiled and oozed his way into her plot. There was Sara's voice, as the gently malicious Mrs Candour. Yes, she was getting laughs, though comedy was not her strong point.

The call-boy banged on the door. 'Five minutes, please.' He adjusted his lace stock and moved towards the wings, hoping not to meet Sara coming off stage, for she might smell the wine still on his breath.

The curtain fell and the orchestra played while stage-hands rapidly changed the set to Sir Peter Teazle's drawing-room. Then, with Raymond centre-stage, it rose again, and he began his first, querulous soliloquy.

' "When an old bachelor marries a young wife, what is he to expect? 'Tis now six months since Lady Teazle made me the happiest of men – and I have been the most miserable dog ever since!" '

Good, the first laugh, and he was in fine voice. His scene with the Surfaces' servant went well, they left the stage together, the orchestra played an interlude, and Raymond returned in company with Eliza O'Neill, the lovely young Irish girl who had captured the heart of theatregoing London. Though her speciality was romantic emotion, a critic admitted that 'her performance of Lady Teazle filled us with astonishment', so prettily did she pout and scold as the spoilt young wife.

They began their famous quarrel scene.

'Lady Teazle, Lady Teazle, I'll not bear it!'

'Sir Peter, Sir Peter, you may bear it or not, as you please; but I ought to have my own way in everything, and what's more I will too.'

Accusations and retorts sparked between them.

'Am I to blame, Sir Peter, because flowers are dear in cold weather? For my part, I'm sure I wish it was Spring all the year round, and that roses grew under our feet!'

'Oons, madam! if you had been born to this, I shouldn't wonder at your talking thus; but you forget what your situation was when I married you.'

'No, no, I don't – 'twas a very disagreeable one, or I should never have married *you*.'

'Yes, yes, madam, you were then in somewhat a humbler style – the daughter of a plain country squire. Recollect, Lady Teazle, when I saw you first sitting at your tambour, in a pretty figured linen gown, with a bunch of keys at your side, your hair combed smoothly over a roll, and your apartment hung round with . . . with fruits in worsted . . .'

She waited for him to end with ' "of your own working" ', but the words did not come, and she went on with her next speech, which gave him the cue ' ". . . comb my Aunt Deborah's lapdog." ' Again he dried, and hurriedly she carried on. ' "And then, you know, my evening amusements . . ." '

Raymond was cold with panic. The audience were not laughing; they knew she should not be going on uninterrupted. And she, equally alarmed, gave him as clearly and deliberately as she could his next cue: ' ". . . to strum my father to sleep after a fox-chase." '

He stood staring and dumb, then cast a wild glance towards the prompt-corner. Loud and only too audible came the voice of the prompter.

' "I am glad you have so good a memory." '

A spontaneous roar of laughter went up from the house, and a cat-call or two. Shaking, Raymond repeated the line, and tried to go on.

' "Yes, madam, these were the . . . the recreations I took you from; but now you must have . . ." ' Oh God, what must she have? Something about footmen and a pair of white cats, but the speech had gone right out of his head. Even the prompt left him silent. A few boos started up from the pit. Eliza O'Neill's charming face was for an instant a mask of horror, then, completely professional, she began to improvise, altering as best she could the lines he should have spoken and putting the words into Lady Teazle's mouth, while he stood helpless and trembling. Then, as soon as she could, she brought the scene to an end.

' "But Sir Peter, you know you promised to come to Lady Sneerwell's too. You must make haste after me, or you'll be too late to save your reputation. So goodbye to ye." ' She swept off the stage, Raymond stumbling after her, and the curtain fell to hisses and boos for him and cheers for her.

In the wings she turned on him.

'For God's sake, what ails you? Have you gone mad?'

But he rushed past her without answering, back to his dressing-room, and there, before the mirror, ripped off the wig and stared blankly at his own image.

A few weeks later Eliza O'Neill left the stage for ever to marry a wealthy member of Parliament, and ultimately to become Lady Becher. The awful incident on the night of Princess Charlotte's wedding, when her leading man had had to be replaced by another actor hurriedly crammed into his costume and furnished with the book, had done her no damage at all: quite the contrary. But it had ended Raymond Otway's London career once and for all.

And Sara left her comfortable engagement and a part she enjoyed playing to go with him into the wilderness.

Clara wandered about the long-disused dispensary where her late husband had spent so much of his time. Its shelves and cupboards were crammed with medical books, sheaves of notes on patients' case histories, bottles, phials, pill-boxes, pestles and mortars, cases of instruments, bleeding-bowls and a jar in which leeches had been kept. It was an unattractive place, stuffy and strong-smelling. Clara wondered why she had never had it all cleared out and its contents thrown away or given to a hospital. The one object she had insisted on removing was the skeleton which had hung in a corner, a hideous grinning thing held together with wires, that had once been a criminal whose corpse remained unclaimed after execution at Newgate.

But the dispensary itself was so small a room that it was not needed in a house already too large for a widow and her servants, so she had turned the key on it and left it to gather dust. Now impulse and memory had drawn her back to it. As a bride she had been mildly curious about John's treatments and medicines, an interest which had soon worn off. But she remembered certain things he had told her.

From a low shelf she took down a jar. It was of clear glass, with a round gold knob on the lid and a gilt cypher, meaningless to the layman. But she remembered very well the properties of the white powder it contained. The powder was, John had told her, an antidote to low fevers, a modifier of swellings and inflammation in gout and rheumatism, a remedy for syphilis: and an aphrodisiac. 'At once the cause and cure of the disease,' he had remarked, one of his rare jokes. He had also mentioned that taken in excess it was a fatal poison. She had briefly toyed with the idea of administering it to him, when she found out just how little of his energies were to be devoted to her, especially as he said that it was virtually undetectable if given in food or drink of a strong taste. But she feared he was too much of an expert not to find it out.

Twice now Ivor's door had been locked against her, and on the one night he had shared her bed his lovemaking had been perfunctory, even impatient. She remembered very well a young woman had accosted him at the stage-door, and he had seemed abstracted afterwards. It was true, then; she was losing him.

She had a new dress made, of a damson-red which flattered her face and figure, and had her hair re-dressed and faintly coloured with a discreet burnished rinse. Ivor noticed neither. That evening she made one of her rare visits to the kitchen, where the cook was preparing a dish from which savoury steam filled the air.

'What a delicious odour, Mrs Meakins. What is it?'

'Pigeon Allemand, ma'am. It was a special favourite of the Doctor's.'

'I remember.' She surveyed the well-scrubbed table, laden with ingredients which the cook had been about to clear up. 'I hope it's not too strongly flavoured. This warm weather a milder taste is preferable.'

'Try it, ma'am.' Mrs Meakins proffered a wooden spoon, and Clara sipped daintily from the bubbling pan.

'Ah. Do you know, I think it's a little *too* mild. Another dash of sherry, perhaps, and a touch of cayenne . . .' As she spoke she was adding them, and something else. The cook, annoyed at the

156

interference, had turned her back and was noisily putting things away.

Ivor made no remark on the taste of the dish, or on the devilled kidneys he was given for breakfast next day, though the dose in them was stronger. His manner to her was no more affectionate, to her disappointment. Jannie had broken their rendezvous two days together, making him uneasy and anxious; she had found no way of letting him know that she and Fred and Sir Patrick had gone down to stay in Sussex with Lord Friston, a friend of the family.

It was weekend before he brought himself to speak to Clara. She had been particularly irritating, clinging to him, touching him at the slightest opportunity, watching him as though she expected to see some change. What change? He longed for Jannie, longed to be back at work; and he felt as though he were sickening for something. It was very unlike his usual robust health.

Clara joined him on the sofa, where he lounged languidly, wishing he were in bed. She put her arms round his neck and tried to draw him to her. With a sudden resolve, he sat up and put her away from him.

'Don't. I must . . . I've something to say to you.'

She tensed. 'What?'

He had meant to make a fluent, highly reasonable speech, something that would convince her of the wrongness of their situation and would be so eloquently put that she could not be angry, or even argue with him. Instead he blurted out: 'I'm leaving. Going away.'

Her eyebrows arched. 'Indeed? From town?'

'From here. I can't go on living with you.'

'Would you be kind enough to give me a good reason? I have not made you comfortable enough, perhaps? Not fed you or housed you as you're accustomed?' Her tone was only mildly sarcastic, but it made him feel an ungrateful lout, as it was intended to do.

'Of course you have.' He felt himself flushing. 'How could I complain of your kindness? Only . . . this is not a right way of living. It harms your good name, to have me in your house.'

'I think I am the best judge of that.'

'And I don't like to owe you so much, when I can't pay back . . .' he rushed on.

'I was under the impression that you paid me in kind,' she said drily.

'Then – I can't do that any longer.'

She looked at him, a long steady look. 'You have another woman.'

'Not as you mean it,' said the miserable Ivor. 'But I do have – an attachment. This is not the reason . . .'

'And I suppose this young person is of your own age and your own profession? Yes, I see. Very suitable. You may even have intentions of marrying her, since you seem to have become so moral suddenly. Or perhaps your scruples don't apply to ladies of your own rank in life?'

'I love her,' was all Ivor could find to reply.

Clara turned her head away. 'You never once said that to me.'

'Oh, damn it! I'm sorry to swear, but I thought it was under-stood between us that we . . . that this was . . .' He wished he could break into Welsh, since he seemed quite unable to express himself in English. She finished for him.

'Not an affair of the heart, merely of the . . . passions? Oh, quite. I entirely agree. In that case, let us conclude it. You are quite free to make what arrangements you please; pray don't con-sider my feelings. You may stay here until you find other lodgings, of course.' She rose suddenly, with a bright social smile. 'And now let's forget this rather tedious conversation, for supper is almost ready and you must enjoy what remains of your time here.'

Ivor shook his head. 'You're very kind, Clara. I've come off very poorly in this, I know. But I'm not a gentleman, only a dancer. I should never have let you take me into your home. And as to supper – I couldn't eat.'

'Oh, nonsense! You take things too much to heart. I shall send for a bottle of the Doctor's best Madeira to be brought up from the cellar, and *that* will give you an appetite.' She rang the bell.

Ivor, left alone, reflected gloomily that if anything could improve his state of mind, a strong drink might, though the thought of food repelled him. He was in any case very thirsty these days, not so much for wine as for anything liquid at all, and sometimes his throat seemed on fire. When they sat down to table, Clara chatting as composedly as though nothing at all unusual had been said, he drank three glasses of the Madeira, then asked for water. But of the food, sweetbreads in a rich sauce, he could eat only a few mouthfuls before pushing away the plate.

'I'm sorry, Clara. It's very good, but I can't eat. I have a sort of . . . please forgive me.' He rushed out of the room.

Clara looked after him with a curiously satisfied expression. She applied herself heartily to the sweetbreads, and the course that followed, but touched none of the creamy trifle. If the servants ate it, it would probably do them very little harm. It was the regular doses that counted – or would in the future. Perhaps the powder had lost its aphrodisiac power. If she could not keep Ivor then at least she could make him very, very sorry for slighting her and destroying all she really cared for in herself: her pride in her attraction for men. Then, when he was sufficiently humbled and broken, she would turn him out, to go back to his mummer friends and his new fancy, or do what he pleased, while she found herself another lover.

Or, perhaps, a husband. She was young enough still, and rich enough, to catch a beau with honourable intentions. But first she would have her revenge. What was the use of being a doctor's widow if one might not make use of his knowledge – for one's own purposes?

Ivor was too ill next day to leave his bed, and the next. He could eat nothing, so Clara made him broth and possets, in which she weakened or left out the white powder. Not that she minded seeing him suffer, for all warmth for him had left her: but if his illness became too acute she would have to call a doctor, who might suspect.

On the third day, Monday, *Harlequin April Fool* was to resume. Ivor woke feeling better, though still weak and nauseated. The walk to Sadler's Wells, on a balmy Spring morning, helped to restore him, and the very sight of the theatre raised his spirits. Work and companionship, absence from the house where he had just spent a nightmare weekend; and perhaps, a sight of Jannie.

Grimaldi was in one of the rehearsal rooms, going through a routine with Barnes, his Pantaloon. He greeted Ivor enthusiastically, then the huge brown eyes widened and the famous jaw dropped in consternation.

'Law! what you been and gone and done to yourself, young Bryn? You looks like Monday's washing a-left out till Friday.'

'Oh, it's nothing, I daresay, Joey. A colic or something that made me as sick as a dog. I never was so ill in my life before, indeed I never was ill, that I remember.'

Joey studied his young friend's pale face, and the figure even slighter than it had been. He disliked what he saw, he who had seen his young wife sicken and die, and two of her sisters, not to mention friends and neighbours, so many of them from complaints that were a mystery to the doctors. Satisfied with his own work-through of the night's performance, he watched Ivor give a sketchy impression of Harlequin's leaps and tricks, until, panting and exhausted, he sank down on a dress-basket, his head in his hands.

'I say, young feller,' observed Joey, 'what you need's a good pot of porter inside you. You stay there and I'll send out for one.' This he did, watching with gratification the strong dark drink bring a little colour back to Ivor's face and more strength to his voice.

'It's my legs, mostly,' Ivor said. 'My calves ache most devilishly, as if I'd the rheumatism in them. Can I have the loan of some of your embrocation, Joey? That ought to cure them, if anything can.'

'Of course, and no question. You can have the loan of Mother Noakes, too – she'll give you a going-over in that tub of hers as'll make a new man of you.'

Ivor finished the porter. 'If I must, I must. Or . . . I would, but I doubt I could get myself to the Royalty and back today. No, I'll dispense with Mother Noakes. Joey, I wanted to ask you – do you know any good lodgings? For myself, I mean. The . . . place where I am . . .'

'Don't suit. I've not forgotten what you said. I'll set about it at once, Mary can ask round the neighbours. There's one or two respectable folk wouldn't mind a good theatrical let, and look after you a sight better than it seems your *friend*'s been doing. Some friends is better than others.'

'And you're the best I have, I know that, Joey. But I want to get away from this part – Islington. Can you think of somewhere near the Royalty – Bow Street or St Martin's Lane, something like that?'

Grimaldi shook his head. 'I'd look round for you myself, but I shan't be in town after this week. My contract's up, they won't give me a raise in salary nor a second benefit. So I wrote Dibdin a nice letter as he never answered, and the next I hear is young Paulo's been engaged, and I may go and whistle, far as the Wells is concerned. As from next Monday.'

'Oh, Joey! Things won't be the same without you. I . . .' He realized that he had unconsciously been counting on the older, wiser man to help him out of this pit of weakness and moodiness that he had fallen into; but it sounded unmanly to say so. Instead he asked: 'Then what will you do? Go to the Garden or Drury?'

'Not me. I've got an offer to tour, with J.S.' He nodded towards his son, juggling with plates at the other side of the room: the fourteen-year-old who was everything to him, after Mary – his hope, his joy, his youthful reflection, for the boy copied his father in dress and mannerisms and promised to be yet another great clown. He had been properly educated, could speak well, and had a sharp mind. Ivor was not sure why he could not entirely like the boy.

But J.S. could do no wrong in Joey's eyes. Ivor wished them luck; and Joey returned the compliment. He felt that his young friend was going to need it.

CHAPTER TEN

Columbine Out Of Her Element

In the Green Drawing-room of Friston Place four German musicians were playing a quartet by Mozart. Or had they said Haydn, or possibly somebody else? Jannie looked round the assembled company and wondered if they were all as bored as she was; they certainly looked it. Lady Friston, once a county belle and now a thin faded lady with too many ringlets obviously not her own, was wearing the fixed rapt expression of a hostess who has provided a treat for her guests and expects them to revel in it as much as she is doing. Her husband, a gentle amiable man in his sixties, with a long face very like that of one of his own sheep, who roamed the Marshes in large quantities, was looked fixedly up at the painted ceiling, working out the price of feeding stuffs by the bushel.

An old gentleman with artificial teeth was struggling with the remains of the toughish beef they had eaten for dinner an hour or two ago. Jannie wished he would simply take them out and stop making such tormented faces. Fred, beside her, was on the edge of sleep. Every now and then his head drooped and he gave a strangled snore and jerked upright again. As a good wife she should have kicked him gently to keep him awake. But let him snore, she thought. What does it matter? We'd all like to. She envied those guests who had frankly admitted their bad ear for music, and gone off to play faro. Piers Compton was one of them, to her relief. He had done nothing but ogle her and try to take her hand or press close to her since they arrived. Her bored her as much as the music.

She wondered what would happen if she suddenly stripped off her clothes, kicked off her shoes and jumped up on a table to perform a solo dance, as the late Lady Hamilton had been whispered to have done in her wild youth, in a great house here in Sussex. Well done, thought Jannie. But this was not even music for dancing, with a good thumping measure to it, but weary grinding stuff all trills and dying falls, that would have had an audience throwing orange-peel before you could say knife.

The music had mercifully stopped. There was a ripple of genteel applause from the circle of uncomfortable chairs, and then, oh Heavens, the musicians' place was taken by a lady in white satin, seated at a large gilt harp, who proceeded to sing in a high off-pitch soprano a series of Moore's Irish Melodies, to her own accompaniment.

'Charming, sweetly pretty,' said the ladies, and someone requested a Scottish song, for they were even prettier than the Irish, if possible. The singer appeared modestly reluctant to perform further, but yielded to their urgings and struck her harp again, announcing that the words of her next ballad were by the Author of Waverley. The song was pitched a little lower, so that Jannie could hear the words.

> O, Brignal banks are wild and fair,
>   And Greta woods are green,
> And you may gather garlands there
>   Would grace a summer queen.
> And as I rode by Dalton-hall,
>   Beneath the turrets high,
> A maiden on the castle wall
>   Was singing merrily:
> 'O, Brignal banks are fresh and fair,
>   And Greta woods are green;
> I'd rather rove with Edmund there
>   Than reign our English queen.'

Jannie sighed, and sighed again. It was bad enough to have one's ears punished by squalling cats of singers, but to have one's heart wrung by sad romantic words that made one long for an absent love was a little too much.

She allowed herself a short bout of artificial coughing, then with a murmured apology slipped out of the room by a door fortunately near to her, and so through the hall to the garden door, and outside.

The night was so warm that she hardly needed the light shawl that covered her almost bare shoulders and the short sleeves of her yellow dress. She stood and breathed the evening scents, fresh after that room which managed to be both stuffy and draughty: the sweet damp of the earth, the breath of flowers and closed buds, the air that blew from farms and fields. The Downs were high smooth shapes against a dark blue sky, with here and there a star prickling or a constant planet burning whitely. A lamb bleated, and was answered by its mother. Far off a shot cracked; a poacher, or a gamekeeper after rabbits.

The country was a new world to Jannie, who had never been further into it than Hampstead. It was beautiful, but it frightened her with its space and silence; she felt very small and alone, a tiny figure on an enormous stage on which anything might be hiding in wait behind the scenery.

If Ivor had been there she would not have been afraid, for he was a country boy, from the wild mountains of Wales, beside which the Downs were molehills. She knew that much about him, at least, but how little else! There had been no time to talk, to find out; he was as mysterious to her as Harlequin himself.

She wondered what he thought of her for vanishing from London without a word to him. But their departure had been so sudden, Sir Patrick opening the letter from Lord Friston and flying up from the breakfast-table, saying that they must all go to Sussex that very day, for the sport was good and the weather fine, and the place a deal nearer than Ireland. How was she to know that such country-house visits could go on and on, for weeks and months? She ventured to ask Sir Patrick, when they had been there for three weeks and there was no sign of their bags being packed, if they were not overstaying their welcome.

'Why, what's it to Lady F. how long we stay?' he boomed. 'She don't have to look after us, there's a regiment of servants to do that. Just so long as we make room for others with fresh news from town for her.'

'And when will that be?'

'Good Gad, how do *I* know?' Sometimes he thought his niecein-law was a kind of idiot – a different kind from his nephew, but certainly a trifle wanting. Came of poor stock, of course; nothing else was to be expected.

Fred's voice from the shadows startled her.

'Jannie? What's the matter?'

'Matter? Nothing. I came out for air, that's all.'

'Thought you might have been took faint. Lady F. looked down her nose when you went out so sudden.'

'Let her,' Jannie snapped. 'It's long enough. I don't seem able to do right for her or anybody. Like a fish out of water, I am, and I wish we could go back to town.'

'You always do right for me, Jan,' said Fred gently. 'They look down their noses at me, too, but you never snub me and make me feel a fool.'

She put her arm through his. 'You're not a fool, Fred dear. And you're much more part of Them than I am. You ought never to have married me. What you wanted really was some lady with good connections, that could have taken you up in the world, instead of down.'

This was so true, even to Fred's slow mind, that he did not answer, but only pressed her hand and held it as they went back into the house.

As they lay in bed that night (for Lady Friston's housekeeper had put them in the same room, most inconveniently) Jannie stared into the darkness, dimly aware of the prison-like four-poster, its curtains closed round them, its canopy lowering above. She wanted to twist and turn, to get comfortable, even to light a candle and read one of the dusty books on the escritoire. But it would disturb Fred.

He spoke suddenly. 'You can't sleep, can you. What's the matter? For I know there's something.'

She almost told him then. But he went on, 'It's not Compton, is it? I've seen him making sheep's eyes at you. If he's annoying you I'll put a stop to it.'

'No, no. He's tiresome, but I take no notice of him. Nothing's worrying me. Go to sleep.'

The next morning, when he had gone down to breakfast, which went on for most of the morning, she sat down at the escritoire and on a piece of expensive notepaper headed with the Friston arms she wrote a letter to Ivor, addressing it to the Wells. It was ill-spelt and childlike.

I axpect you will wonder why I have not been to the Theater, I could not let you know as we was coming hear and now it semms we arnt to get away for too more weeks. I thout I would let you know. I hope you are very well. I wish you was hear. Let me have a line by the Mail.

Your Jannie.

It did not look quite right when she read it over, but as she sanded and sealed it she felt happier that it was written. Before putting it in the bag kept in the hall for letters to be collected by the mail-coach, she kissed it.

A week passed, and no reply came; a week of desultory walks in the garden and the lanes, yawn-provoking card-parties and more musical recitals. Jannie committed one social error after another, sometimes purposely – if she made herself sufficiently unbearable perhaps Lady Friston would ask her to pack and go. Even the mild Lord Friston was provoked by her, when, meeting him at the head of a company of jolly gentlemen returning from hare-coursing, Fred among them, she broke into their loud conversation.

'How can you say you had a great chase, and Puss was killed after a good run, and all that? All those great dogs and one poor little hare – how could it have got away? I don't call that sport. You don't even *eat* the hare, because the dogs tear it to pieces. I think you're very cruel.'

'I don't think I quite follow you, my dear.' His Lordship's tone was unusually icy. 'You may not be used to our country ways, but I can assure you the hare or any other beast enjoys a good chase.'

'I'll believe that when I hear one say so,' Jannie snapped, and turned on her heel.

Piers Compton, who had been at the hunt, watched her with a gleam of admiration. Spirited little thing, she was worth the chasing herself; she had got away from him the first time, but he would get her in the end, and whether she enjoyed it did not concern him at all.

By chance, as she thought, but actually by his contrivance, she found herself alone with him, in one of the oldest rooms in the house, a Jacobean panelled chamber with recessed window-seats. She had taken to sitting in one of them, watching for the mail-coach to round the corner of the lane, just within sight. Sir Piers was well aware of it. He chose the right moment to join her, and sat down beside her without waiting for an invitation.

'A deucedly pretty sight,' he said, his eyes on her. She looked round the room, which appeared to her much as usual, a dark, brooding place very well suited for pining in. Surely he couldn't mean the enormous chimneypiece, with its half-human monsters flanking the cavernous recess now empty of logs. She thought it perfectly hideous.

'This ancient room,' said Sir Piers dreamily, 'and such youth and beauty lighting it up like . . . like a sunbeam.'

'*I* don't think I light it up. I don't think anything could, unless it was a gas chandelier. How is your infant?'

He was utterly taken aback. 'My – infant?'

'I understood Lady Compton was brought to bed recently. Is she well, and the baby?'

'Why – she was well enough, last time I saw her. But what makes you enquire?'

'I thought it might have done her good, to be brought down here, and the little one too. What is it, girl or boy?'

Visibly he had to think before he answered, 'A girl,' and visibly he was very vexed at having the conversation turned to such mundane matters. 'It has been christened Lavinia, in case you were thinking of asking.'

'Oh, what a pretty name. Now if you'll forgive me I must go and write some letters.' She rose swiftly before he could detain her, and swept out of the room. He set his lips very tightly as the door slammed. A reprieve for the hare, but the hunter was very close after.

Her letters were in fact only one: to Grimaldi.

My dear Mr Grimaldi, I hop you will not mind me riting, but I am concerned to know if Mr Bryn is well or not as he as not replied to an inquiry of mine. I shall be hear for another week if you will be so kind as drop me a line.

Yr. obdt. servant, J. FitzNeil.

And this letter, too, went unanswered.

Piers Compton was getting tired of a pursuit which became increasingly difficult, as the quarry took care to keep out of any situation which might lead to their being alone together. She gave up sitting in the window-alcove – after all, it was useless, since the mail never brought her any news. She cultivated the company of the ladies, to her hostess's surprise and very modified gratification, and when she walked in the gardens or beyond the boundaries of the estate she took care to be in company with Betty. Betty spent all the time not devoted to her mistress's toilette in servants'-hall gossip and flirtation with the footmen.

So Betty sullenly trailed behind her on this fine day of June, plucking heads off flowers and pulling them to pieces as she walked. They were in the Wild Garden, far away from the elegant landscaping that surrounded the house, Capability Brown's symphony of lake, ornamental bridge, and serpentine walks. Here, on a little eminence, stood the mock-Gothic temple placed there by Lord Friston's father, in what he thought of as shady groves. Gardeners tended this part of the grounds discreetly, but wild creatures from the wood behind could not be kept out; it was impossible to leave traps set in case wandering guests stumbled into them.

Jannie turned at a sharp cry from Betty, to see her on the ground, clutching at her leg.

'Whatever is it?'

'Oh, my ankle!' Betty moaned. 'I stepped in one of them dratted rabbit-holes. Oh, I'm sure it's broken, ma'am!'

'Let me feel.' Jannie, who had had plenty of experience of broken, sprained, and otherwise injured ankles in the ballet, felt the leg from knee to foot, and Betty gingerly stretched it out.

'No, it's not broken, only strained. It will mend.'

'But how am I to walk on it, ma'am?' Betty began to blubber. 'And us so far away from the house.'

'Sit there till you feel better, and I'll fetch one of the gardeners or someone to carry you back – or give you an arm, at least,' Jannie added, for Betty was of a lumpish build. 'Or perhaps he could pop you into a wheelbarrow.'

'I don't want to go in no wheelbarrows!' Betty cried. 'I'll get back as best I may.'

Jannie looked round and saw a stout branch, fallen from a tree in the autumn, lying among the grass. 'Here, the very thing. You can lean on this like a walking-stick.' She gave the maid a hand to get up. 'I'll walk back with you if you like.'

'You wouldn't be much help, thank you all the same, ma'am,' Betty answered with barely hidden contempt for her mistress's child-like stature. 'You stay here and enjoy yourself.' Martyred, she hobbled off, leaving Jannie thankful to be alone for once. She wandered up to the mock-ruin, which looked cool and inviting, then realized that she would be dangerously isolated there.

'Betty!' she called after the limping figure, 'find out Mr FitzNeil and ask him to come and walk with me. I believe he's in the smoking-room.' Then, relieved at having solved the problem, she went into the ruin and sat down on one of the stone seats that were fixed against the walls, looking round the curious little building, with its pointed windows filled with leaded panes, saintly statues in niches, and birds' nests in the timbered roof. What very odd ideas of decoration some people did have, to be sure.

Piers Compton was standing in the doorway, smiling dangerously.

'Again, a charming setting for a charming creature,' he said lightly. 'The nymph, tired from Bacchic revels, seeks seclusion among rustic shades, dreaming of her shepherd, who is doubtless piping to some other fair one.'

Jannie's heart was fluttering, but she said sharply, 'I don't know what you're talking about. Do go away, Sir Piers, and let me have a bit of peace. I wish you wouldn't follow me about like this, I didn't ask for it and I don't like it.'

'Oh, but I believe you *did* ask for it,' he answered, 'if in a somewhat different sense.' He sat down beside her, moving nearer as she edged away. 'I've not forgotten that expedition of ours to the theatre. Now why, I wonder, did you behave in that extraordinary fashion, when you had led me to believe my devotion to you would be rewarded? Was it some girlish mood – a phase of the moon, perhaps?'

'Don't be personal!' Jannie retorted angrily. 'How I behave is my business, and I didn't lead you on to believe anything – I was just glad to be going out to the play, for once.'

'And afterwards you were not so glad, or you had some kind of disturbing experience: saw some gentleman, perhaps, whose presence reminded you of – happier days? Oh, don't tell me that little heart is fixed on your nincompoop of a spouse, Droopy Fred from the Irish bogs? No, I'll never believe that. So why, my adored one, shouldn't it be fixed on me?'

Backing into the corner, but still more furious than frightened, Jannie said, 'Don't you call my husband names. He's a better man than you any time, and you needn't despise him as you do. I've seen the way you look at him.'

Sir Piers forced his arm round her waist. 'But not quite the mate for a pretty little hot-blooded vixen like you? Come, what ails me? Am I so absolutely ill-looking?'

She surveyed him, the superficially handsome face with the bags of dissipation under the eyes, the grey-streaked hair worn in artificial curls, like the Regent's wig.

'I've seen worse, I suppose. But you're so *old*.'

'Bitch!' It was the one thing she should not have said, for under his airy manner lay a deep fear of ageing and death, and a raw vanity. He pulled her against him and began to kiss her savagely, biting and bruising, at the same time dragging up her muslin skirts. With a violent effort she wrenched away and gave a piercing scream, and another.

'That will do no good.' He pulled down her bodice, baring her breasts, and getting a hand free she scratched his face from temple to chin. It was thus that Fred, heated from hurrying, found them. Deaf as he was the screams had reached him.

As he appeared at the door the struggling group dissolved and faced him, Jannie panting too much with fear and effort to get out a word, Sir Piers fumbling for a handkerchief to staunch the blood from his cheek.

'What the devil's going on?' Fred said. 'Though I daresay I needn't ask. Did you invite this behaviour, Jannie?' His tone was sad as well as angry, for he had known for a long time that she was preoccupied with some man not himself, despite her denials.

'No!' she cried. 'Do I look as if I invited it?' at the same time that Sir Piers shouted, 'Of course she did, the trollop. A nice wife you've got, Fred.'

Fred surveyed them both. His knees trembling with shock, but he sounded calm and firm as he said, 'I believe you, Jannie. Pull your bodice up, there's a good girl. As for you, Compton, you'll give me satisfaction for that last remark.'

'Satisfaction! I don't know what you mean.' He was mopping his left cheek, the handkerchief now bright red. Fred stepped forward and gave the other cheek a resounding slap.

'That's what I mean. Insults given and taken – there's only one solution to that.'

Sir Piers stared, the unwounded cheek scarlet from the blow.

'You mean you're calling me out? God damn me, that's rich. You!'

Jannie, on her feet, caught Fred's arm. 'Don't be silly, Fred. There's no harm done. You can't go fighting . . .'

'Can't I?' She did not know this new Fred. 'Choose your weapons, Compton.'

'Swords would be rather antique, don't you think. I hope you're a good shot.'

'I don't carry pistols. There's plenty in the gun-room.'

'Good. Care to choose your seconds?'

'Be damned to seconds. Man to man.'

'As you like. At two o'clock, then; there's a clearing in the woods behind this place.'

On the way back to the house Jannie clung to Fred as she had never done before. 'Please don't carry on with this farce. Nothing happened – and if it had, what's a rape beside somebody's life? That man's a pest, and somebody will kill him some day. Why don't you let it be? Oh Fred, do be sensible!'

'Just for once,' he said, 'I want to do what's expected of a gentleman.' He stopped and turned to her. 'Only one thing, Jannie. There was – nothing in it, was there? Between him and you?'

'How can you ask that? No, of course not. I hate him, but that's no reason for you to fight. Fred, please.'

Two o'clock was the dinner-hour at Friston Place. Sir Piers had named it with the sardonic notion of coming to table late when he had winged his man, who would by then have very little appetite. As the rest of the party sat down to their meal, the two men met in the little clearing, a broad space where trees had been chopped and logs were piled ready for the winter. They stood armed, coats off, in their shirt-sleeves.

'No surgeons, no seconds,' said Piers Compton. 'A very unorthodox meeting. Are you sure you wouldn't like to change for bare fists? I don't mind in the least. But perhaps madam here is squeamish about blacked eyes and flattened noses.'

Jannie had come with Fred, trying to argue down his objections. The whole wretched business had started with her, even though she had discouraged Piers Compton's attentions so firmly. She put their discarded coats down on a log and said, 'I don't know anything about fighting, or boxing either. You're both being fools. I've a good mind to go back and call Lord Friston.'

'You do that,' Sir Piers said pleasantly, 'and I'll shoot your petticoats full of holes. Since you must be here, stand still and see fair play. Now. On three, when I turn round, we fire.'

Back to back, they moved the required number of paces in

opposite directions, then turned to face each other.

'One. Two. Three.'

Fred's hand was slower than his opponent's, and his pistol cracked a few seconds later. As the other's shot rang out Fred dropped, without a cry. Jannie ran to his side, calling out incoherently, and knelt by him. His waistcoat and breeches were already saturated with blood, and blood was trickling from his mouth. She shrieked and sobbed, lifting his heavy head, trying to undo the waistcoat buttons, watching his eyes glaze and his jaw drop.

'You're wasting your time,' said Piers Compton, white-faced and grim. 'I've seen hits like that before. He's done for. I didn't mean it to strike so low, but the fool moved. Well, you can take care of the rest of it yourself. Think up a good story.' He put on his coat, turned his back on her and flung his pistol away, high above his head, as far as it would go, to land somewhere in the woods.

'You're not *going*?'

'What do you think, m'dear? I've been suddenly called away, haven't I. My man will pack within minutes, and when I re-emerge in Society I shall of course know nothing of this idiotic business. Good-day.'

Still on her knees, she stared after his retreating form, shocked beyond action or tears. Somehow she must go back to the house, tell them truthfully what had happened, have the murderer stopped and brought to trial. But she was sickened and dazed, and her knees seemed to have lost their strength. She bent over Fred and closed his eyes. The sun was still shining; how odd. Overhead a blackbird was pouring out its liquid song.

'Oh Fred, forgive me,' she said; but could not touch him again.

At Friston Place it was made perfectly clear to her that the whole affair was to be treated as an unfortunate accident. To her protests and tears Lord and Lady Friston returned stony looks of apparent incomprehension. She was not, they implied, in her right mind, or if she was, there must be some disgraceful story behind it all which certainly must not involve any friends of theirs.

'But he's gone!' she cried. 'Piers Compton's run away. He said he would. He said he'd deny everything. How can you let him escape like that! He ought to be hung.'

Lord Friston cleared his throat. 'Sir Piers was called away, yes. Not entirely unexpected. He will not be questioned further. It is unfortunate about Mr FitzNeil, but one had always noticed his aim was erratic. No doubt he was potting at pigeons, and accidentally turned the weapon on himself. That is what the coroner will conclude. No point in dragging cock-and-bull stories into it. These things happen . . . townsmen dabbling in sport.'

Lady Friston broke in. 'We do understand your grief and shock, Mrs FitzNeil. You will wish, I'm sure, to take meals in your room – until your departure.'

She was not present at the hurried inquest, because she was not told about it. Lord Friston, with aristocratic efficiency, took over the funeral arrangements, Sir Patrick being too stricken to deal with them. A short service was held in the family chapel on the estate, Sir Patrick, who looked twenty years older overnight, weeping continuously. Then Fred's body, enclosed in lead and wooden caskets, was dispatched in the undertaker's coach to be shipped to Ireland, for burial among his ancestors.

Sir Patrick's collapse was followed by a stroke. When he partially recovered his power of speech he seemed not to recall the recent tragedy, only the loss of his sons. He took to telling rambling, confused stories about Nelson and Howe, Jervis and Collingwood, topmasts shot away and men cut in half by cannon-fire, men floundering in a sea of blood. His daughter, up from Northumberland, paid him one impatient visit, then declared that her household was not suited to the care of an elderly invalid and departed. In the gloomy house in Hanover Square he sat hour by hour, mumbling while Jannie crouched by his side, trying to make him understand who she was and where they were. But the girl in her black dress and widow's cap was a stranger to him now;

merely someone who held his hand and was kind, unlike the doctors who looked at him contemptuously because he would put no more money into their pockets.

'Bedlam!' Jannie cried furiously. 'You shan't send him to that place!' Everybody knew about poor King George and the awful treatment meted out for his supposed lunacy, strait-jackets and blisterings, emetics and purges and hard words. 'I won't have him put in a madhouse – no, not even a private one. I daresay they're no better than the others. He has plenty of money, and he shall have nurses here, in his own home, and I'll see to it that they're kind ones.'

And so she did, by searching London for two clean, honest and reliable women able to deal patiently with the old man. They were as rare as gold on a rubbish-heap, among so many drunken sluts. In their care she left him, with a kiss on his brow.

'Nice girl,' he mumbled. 'Dunno who you are, though. When's Fred coming home? Too late to be out. He's simple, you know, simple. But where is he? Damn lonely without him . . .'

Jannie found, to her surprise, that a certain amount of money was due to her by the will Fred had somewhat unexpectedly made. Not a fortune, but more than she had ever dreamed of having. With that, and her clothes and modest jewellery, she was a rich woman compared to most. She could have taken handsome lodgings in a fashionable part of town; instead, she went back to the old rooms in Long Acre, and her parents.

They thought her much changed, and suspected there was more to her husband's death than she told them. If there was no bringing the criminal to justice, why trouble the innocent, was her reasoning. With gratitude they accepted the luxuries she could give them, new clothes, good food, even an extra room, plenty of coal for the fire. Once again she slept in the turn-up bedstead and shared their nightcap of toddy.

'But what will you do now, Jannie?' asked her mother.

Jannie flung her arms wide. 'Dance!' she said. 'Dance, dance, dance!'

But first she must find Ivor.

CHAPTER ELEVEN

Scene, A Village Green

As Jannie's coach, on its way to London, had passed through mid-Sussex, she was too far lost in an uneasy doze between thought and sleep to be aware of the village of Hallsfield. It was a thriving place, for those parts, a long high street with a substantial church and rectory, many shops, an inn to every few houses and those houses varying from respectable cottages with vegetable gardens in front to handsome new villas wedged in between lop-sided ancient buildings. Their lath-and-plaster walls seemed about to crumble into dust as fragile as that of their original owners, who lay in the churchyard.

Pigs and hens wandered in the unmade roadway, and children played at hoop and top, skipping out of reach of coach and rider with dexterity. It was, in fact, like many other Sussex villages, but for one distinction. It had a theatre.

The theatre might very well have been mistaken for a small Presbyterian chapel, so modest were its proportions, a mere single-storey affair with a few long windows and a rough driveway round the side to the scene-dock. Raymond and Sara and Miranda, hot and yowling in her basket, stopped before it and wondered how one got in, for the front door looked firmly locked, and there was no sign of life.

Sara, who hated change and journeyings, wished they had never left London. But what other way had there been for them, when it had been put round the theatre world that Raymond Otway was utterly unemployable? He had been unable to play the week out, and his salary had been accordingly docked. There was nothing saved: a recent raid by his wife had seen to that.

Because he was so wretched, Sara took him into her own lodgings with what few possessions he had. They had never slept together before; now they did, as naturally as though they had been married for twenty years. If her landlady had held liberal views, there they might have stayed; but only a day or two passed before there was hammering at the door, and a peremptory demand that Miss Dell leave as soon as she could get her things together, and take her fancy friend with her, because word got round about these things, and there was other things too, like empty bottles, which one didn't wish to find a-stinking the place out.

Fate led them, and their pitiful belongings, to an eating-house where they met with a broken-down, purple-faced, cheerful man called Henry Faucit. Raymond vaguely remembered him as an actor-manager who had once had his own touring company; it must have fallen on bad days.

'Poor houses, soaring expenses, couldn't make ends meet – aye, there's the rub,' said Faucit. 'So I gave it all up, settled for the management side – little place over the river, not much class but the saloon does well.' He was an excellent advertisement for it. 'But if you want to tour, I know the very man for you. Young, oh yes, I grant you, but full of ideas, promise, enterprise. Got his own little playhouse down in Sussex, charming place, Drury in miniature. All he needs are actors, actors! My dear friends, you must go there at once, lose no time.'

Raymond looked eager, but Sara drooped her head and prayed silently for help. She could have tried harder – stayed in her own part, found other lodgings, kept both herself and Raymond, or got him an engagement as a clerk, for his copperplate handwriting was beautiful. And here they were, because of a shrew's scoldings, out on the street and bound for who knew where? And oh, Miranda, what will become of you?

'Thaddeus Porter, that's the name,' Faucit was saying. 'And the village is – it will come to me in a minute – yes, I recall it, Hallsfield. Delightful hamlet, village green, rustic arbours, all that sort of thing. You'll like it. Now pray lose no time – the Lewes coach stops there.'

'Should we not write first?' Sara timidly suggested. 'He may have a full company.'

'Full? Not he. Always glad of change, and names from the top London theatres. Mr Otway of the Royalty . . . and that reminds me, did you ever know a Welsh boy name of . . . bless me, I think my memory's going, it's all these accounts I have to deal with. Gwyn? No – Bryn, Ivor Bryn? Come out very strong at the Royalty as a Harlequin, then went round the circuits and made quite a name, I hear. Did you ever work with him?'

'Yes,' said Raymond, omitting reference to his own role of Pantaloon. 'A brilliant young man. I heard he was at the Wells lately.'

'Give him my felicitations if you see him. It was I who brought him out, you know, picked him up half-dead in Wild Wales and made a performer out of him. Cocky young sprig, but full of promise. Like Thad Porter.'

Mr Porter himself might be a miracle of enterprise and power, but his playhouse appeared singularly lifeless. The gate to the side path was locked. There was no knocker on the double door of the building itself, and knuckles made no impact.

'Try the cottage next door,' Sara suggested. 'The caretaker may live in it.'

Their knocking produced signs of life from the cottage in the form of infant howls, so loud that it seemed improbable anything could be heard through the din. But at last the door opened, to reveal a buxom young woman with her cap askew and her hair coming down, bearing in her arms a baby of perhaps a year old, the source of the howls. Quite scarlet in the face with passion, it continued to shriek, while Sara, Raymond and the young mother looked at each other, unable to exchange a word. She turned to shout to someone in the cottage what sounded like 'Psyche!' and an older child appeared, a girl who might be six or seven, as untidy as her mother. With the deftness of experience she seized the baby and removed it to inner regions, where its yells continued.

'Yes, sir, madam?' said the young woman, in a prettier and more refined voice than they expected from her looks. 'Can I direct you anywhere?'

'If you please, ma'am,' Raymond said, with a sweeping bow. 'We were looking for Mr Thaddeus Porter, with an introduction from a mutual friend.'

She smiled. 'Oh, then you've come to the right place. I'm Mrs Porter, and Thaddeus is out at the back in the workshop. Pray come in.'

The living-room into which the front door opened was shabby. The one small window was bare of curtains, the walls plain rough-cast. A deal table, two upright chairs and a spinning-wheel were all the furnishings, except for a chair by the primitive grate over which hung an iron cooking-pot, evidently containing stew, by the savoury smell; the chair was occupied by a middle-aged female in dress as plain as the younger woman's, if rather tidier. She was sewing at a length of material which trailed on the floor, but looked up and smiled at the visitors.

'This is Mr Porter's mamma,' said his wife. 'Both the gentlemen are working on the scenery, that is Mr Porter and his papa, but I'll call them in.' A bang from upstairs, and a fresh outburst of yelling from the baby, caused her to look up anxiously.

'Oh dear me, I hope Psyche hasn't dropped Clio again, the child's growing into such a great girl. I don't know who she takes after, I'm sure.'

Nor did Raymond and Sara, when Mr Porter and his father had been summoned from their work. Thaddeus Porter was a slight young man with an expression as harassed as his wife's, his father thin and gnome-like; both wore leather aprons and rolled-up shirt sleeves, and both were liberally daubed with paint and powdered with sawdust. Thaddeus executed a neat bow, and said, 'Mortified to receive company like this, but there's more work to do than time to do it in. Pray sit down, and Matilda, put on the kettle, my dear, for I'm sure our visitors will take a cup of tea. Unless ale would be preferable?'

Sara hastily said that tea would be the most refreshing thing in the world. She had a horror of anything stronger being put before Raymond. They introduced themselves, and Thaddeus Porter's face became a battle-ground of emotions: one was wistful covetousness of the presence of two London players in his company – and what was more real ones, not the unknowns who often applied to him, allegedly 'of Drury Lane' or 'of the Haymarket'. The other emotion, and, alas, the dominating one, was the knowledge of his finances.

As the visitors drank their tea, he said nervously, 'I'd be most honoured to engage you. What could I wish for better? Only . . . we have very few resources here, you see, and the smallest audiences on the circuit. My father and I are stagehands, scene-painters, carpenters, everything, and my wife and mother make the costumes.'

The lady by the fire lifted and complacently surveyed the stuff on which she was embroidering a pattern in gaudy colours, purple and yellow, strident pink and green. They would look well from the front.

'We perform, too,' said Matilda Porter proudly. 'Even baby. She comes in very handy sometimes, and Psyche is really quite accomplished. We put on *A Winter's Tale* lately, with baby as the infant Perdita and Psyche coming out quite remarkable in Mamillius.'

Psyche, who had reappeared without the burden of the baby, said in a surprisingly deep and sinister voice. ' "There was a man dwelt by a church-yard." '

Raymond smiled approvingly. 'Very nice, my dear.' She returned a cool professional look; it was obvious that nobody in this family needed patronizing.

'Mamma here does the heavy matrons,' Thaddeus said, indicating the frail form of his mother, 'and papa the comic men and so forth.' Mr Porter Senior, who had a cast of countenance rather melancholy than otherwise, murmured an excuse and disappeared, a sound of violent hammering following his departure.

'But surely,' Raymond said, 'you can hardly perform all the parts yourselves.'

'Oh, no, we hire guest artists as well,' replied Thaddeus, 'ladies and gentlemen touring the circuit. That is, when . . . when we can afford it. You see, our salaries are not very high, and even for Names, well . . .'

'What, in fact, would you be prepared to pay?' Raymond asked. Both he and Sara were taken aback at the answer.

'I could allow you twelve shillings a week – each, that is.'

They said nothing, only exchanged a quick sidelong glance. In London they had earned £15 a week. It was a shocking come-down: hardly enough to subsist on. Sara was ashamed to feel tears coming into her eyes. To have travelled all this way, with high hopes and an introduction, and instead of the brilliant manager Faucit had described to find a humble family man who might as well have been running a grocery business. She had seen Raymond's face fall. Another blow for him, another temptation to look for comfort at the alehouse. It was bitterly disappointing. And if they were to refuse and move on, what would the next country theatre be like, in this sparsely-populated country area?

Tactfully, Thaddeus said, 'You will no doubt wish to consider it. Matilda, my love . . .' The Porters retreated to the room at the back of the cottage, firmly shutting the door.

Raymond and Sara turned to each other, with no need to ask what the other was thinking. He put his hand on hers.

'The Fates seem to have a spite against us.'

'We couldn't live on it,' she said tearfully. 'What shall we do? I thought . . . they're strange people, but very pleasant. I thought we might settle, even though it's not what we're accustomed to. But oh, twelve shillings!'

In the little parlour at the back Matilda was saying, 'They're stars, Thadd. Better than any we've ever had before. You can tell she's a lady at a glance. And Mr Otway would be superb as kings and dukes and things. You can see they've fallen on hard times. Oh, Thadd, they'd do wonders for us! Can't you help them – just a little?'

As the Porters re-entered Sara hastily wiped her eyes. They had decided to refuse. Then Thaddeus said, 'Mrs P. and I have been talking. I *could* make it thirteen, if that would be more acceptable.'

Matilda put in hastily, 'And you could eat with us. Mamma is such a good and economical cook, aren't you, Mamma, and we have a little garden at the back where we grow nearly everything we eat, except butcher's meat of course, and even that we get given sometimes, because the tradespeople pay us in kind for a place in the house. So you see it would not be too costly to live, and there's Mrs Tottle over the way just widowed and would be glad to let you have a room, I'm sure.'

Again there was no need of words between them. Graciously, Raymond told Thaddeus that on consideration they would be pleased to accept a place in the company.

Gallantly, Thaddeus kissed Sara's hand, and manfully shook Raymond's. 'Welcome to Hallsfield Playhouse, Mr and Mrs Otway.' Neither of them gave away by a flicker of expression that he had got their relationship wrong. It was of no consequence now.

Psyche, who had been hustled out when the money discussion began, now reappeared.

'Mamma, baby wants feeding. Oh, look, that basket moved! What can be in it?'

Miranda had stayed in her basket on the floor throughout the interview, silent and motionless. She was not asleep, and she was extremely hot and uncomfortable, but the goddess who rules cats told her that her mistress wanted her to remain quiet until some trouble was solved. She knew that Sara had not forgotten her, that she would be released; and now the hated door of the basket was unlatched, and she came out slowly, lengthening herself and yawning delicately.

Psyche suddenly became a very ordinary and excited little girl.

'Mamma, papa, a pussy-cat! Oh, how pretty it is. Look, Nan. Is it a boy or a girl, and what's it's name?'

'A girl,' said Sara. 'Miranda.'

Thaddeus, looking with approval on the elegant shining form of the cat, assumed his Shakespeare Voice.

> There's nothing ill can dwell in such a temple,
> If the ill spirit have so fair an house,
> Good things will strive to dwell with't.

Suddenly a great wave of contentment swept over Sara, and she gave the Porters her lovely smile. They were accepted, she and Raymond and Miranda too, and they were going to be happy at Hallsfield.

Miranda very gracefully elevated one leg in the air, and began to wash.

Thaddeus showed the Otways, as they were unquestioningly known, the draft of their first playbill under his management.

On this night, Wednesday and Saturday only,
by popular request,
the admired and celebrated tragedy
called
VENICE PRESERV'D, or
A PLOT DISCOVER'D.
Duke of Venice by Mr Augustus Porter
Priuli, the cruel father of Belvidera, by Mr Thaddeus Porter
Jaffier, husband of Belvidera, by Mr Raymond Otway
of Drury Lane Theatre
Pierre, the cruel rebel, by Mr Timpson
AND
Belvidera, daughter to Priuli, and wife to Jaffier, an unfortunate lady, who will by desire, for these evenings only, Die Mad,
by
Miss Sara Dell of Drury Lane Theatre
Servants, Guards, Conspirators, Rebels, &c., &c., by
the rest of the Company
After which will be presented the admired comic
song *Giles Scroggins' Ghost* sung by Mr Otway.

'Now what's your opinion of that?' asked Thaddeus proudly. Raymond stared in consternation. 'But I can't sing a note!'
'Oh, come now, you're too modest, sir.'

'I assure you, my dear friend, I have no more ear for music than . . .' he glanced round the room '. . . than a warming-pan. Less perhaps, since it may give off a musical note if properly struck. And if I *could* sing, I should find it rather improper to sing a comic song after a tragic piece.'

'Oh, it's always done. The customers like it, you know, and the broader the better. I suppose you couldn't intone, or declaim, or something of the kind, with the fiddler playing the tune?' he asked wistfully.

'Not on any account – even to oblige you,' Raymond said firmly.

Thaddeus sighed. 'Oh, very well. Then we shall have to get up a farce at the end, though I'd hoped to avoid it.'

Sara spoke up. 'I can sing a little – that is, I was taught as a girl, and my Ophelia was quite well thought of in the Singing Mad Scene. If it would help, perhaps I could render something.'

Thaddeus brightened. 'That would be capital. I suppose you couldn't sing *Mrs Waddle was a Widow*, with comic monologue?'

'No,' said Sara, who knew the words. 'And I don't think comedy is quite my style. I might manage something sentimental, perhaps.'

'Well, they do like to laugh, as a relief, after the tragedy, you know. I have it! *Billy Taylor*. Now that's the very thing. Not too near the knuckle. You *must* know it.'

Sara laughed outright. 'Who doesn't? Well, if it was good enough for Mrs Siddons to render in public, I suppose it must be good enough for me. I'll practise it tomorrow if you'll lend me the fiddler. But this bill . . .'

A worried frown creased Thaddeus's brow. 'Not up to snuff, for London taste? It's the usual lay-out. I thought it read uncommonly well.'

'Oh, it does,' Sara said hastily. 'Only – as I remember, there are a great many characters in it, and I don't see them in the bill – Antonio, the Senator, for instance, and Aquilina, the courtesan . . .'

Thaddeus looked shocked. 'Oh, we couldn't have that sort of

thing here, we play strictly to family audiences.' Sara recalled very well the ever-popular *risqué* scene in which the naughty Aquilina scorned the old gentleman with a taste for whips and riding-boots in the boudoir. Perhaps it wouldn't do in Sussex; except possibly Brighton.

'As to the rest of the cast,' Thaddeus went on, 'we can manage that very well. Matilda will double Conspirator and Belvidera's attendant, Psyche will make herself useful as another Conspirator and the Executioner at the end, and we have one or two local gentlemen taking part for the sheer love of the drama. Oh, yes, we shall do very nicely. I suppose your husband is no relation of the poet Otway, ma'am? We chose the play out of compliment.'

'Very kind, but there's no kinship at all,' Raymond said with more truth than Thaddeus knew.

After all, it went beautifully: if one could overlook the great improbability of Psyche in high heels, a cloak and a mask, playing even more parts than her father had suggested, and the rustic accents of the drama-obsessed gentlemen from the countryside around. A mercifully cut version gave all the 'fat' to the Jaffier, Pierre and Belvidera, who knew their parts impeccably. Tears were in every eye at Belvidera's demented death, a reference in Jaffier's lines to 'the dear little infant left behind me' produced Clio in somebody's lace christening-robe, to the accompaniment of cries of 'Little dear!' and 'Quite a Cupid!' from the ladies in the audience. It was with some trepidation that Sara stepped before the tin floats, after the curtain, for her rendering of the dramatic ballad of the faithless Billy Taylor. The author of that artless number may have meant it to be funny, but Sara gave it a dramatic flavour worthy of Siddons's self, as, her eyes flashing, brandishing an invisible pistol, she sang of how the jilted maid had 'shot her true love William, with the bride on his right arm'.

> If young folk in Bath or London
> Were served same as she served he,
> Then young girls would all be undone –
> Very scarce young men would be!

Some laughed, many gawped, but they all cheered and shouted for more; which, graciously she gave then in an encore she had rehearsed, *Crazy Jane the Mad Girl*, one of the sentimental ballads at which they loved to cry.

The evening had been a roaring success, and Mrs Porter senior, doubling the role of money-taker with that of Spinosa, a Conspirator, counted four pounds fifteen shillings as her takings.

As the weeks passed, the Otways' admiration for the Porter family, and particularly Thaddeus, grew exceedingly. There was nothing he would not, or could not do for his theatre. With Matilda he painted the scenery, with his more plodding father he fitted up two new boxes for the reception of prosperous patrons and decorated them with gilt and red lead. After a particularly good week's takings, he paid the local printer for the use of his press, so that the family might be saved the labour of making out the bills by hand, and the elegant results were distributed round the district by everybody concerned, including Psyche, with Clio sucking her thumb in a go-cart made from planks by her father.

Sara envied Matilda, a happy, busy wife, actress, Jill-of-all-trades; and mother. She had lost two, she confided in Sara, between Psyche and Clio, one by convulsions, the other a miscarriage. 'It was a pity,' she said in the most matter-of-fact way in the world, 'because we can do with all the hands we can get.'

'You'll have more, I'm sure you will,' Sara told her, thinking as she so often did of George. But she was glad she had not consented to live with Raymond, until now, when she knew that it was too late for motherhood.

Yet it was a mercy, for Raymond was not fit for the responsibility of being a parent. She must be mother to him, as well as wife, for he needed all the care she could give him. She knew instantly when he was irked by something, or bad on his lines, or brooding on the past; his eyes would stray towards the White Hart, the village's coaching-inn, which had a public bar. If they were in the theatre, she would contrive at such moments to get him some strong tea, or a cup of broth, and if at their lodgings, ask him to hear her lines for the play they were rehearsing – anything to take his mind off the drink he craved for.

He turned to her one night, as they lay in bed, in the low-raftered cottage room, sweet with lavender-scent from the linen and the heady perfume of roses from the garden rising to the latticed window. He had longed very much that evening for a bottle of wine, and then another, to obliterate the memory of his obtuseness over the play in hand, and a slight tiff with the usually amiable Thaddeus. Now she had got the difficult passages into his head, tomorrow he would know them, word-perfect; and he no longer wanted the wine.

'Thank you, Sara,' he said.

'For what?' came her sleepy voice.

'Don't pretend. You remember the dictum? "Nor pen nor pencil can the actor save: The art and artist have one common grave." '

'It sounds very melancholy.'

'It's all too true. Thank you – wife.'

'Go to sleep,' she said.

They were living an idyll; and like all idylls, it could not last.

'For the tenth time, madam,' said Charles Dibdin the younger, 'I have no idea where Mr Bryn is to be found. I wish I knew. It's a shade inconvenient to have a leading artist disappear in the middle of a run, and to be put to the trouble of hiring another. But the fact remains. I – do – not – know.'

Jannie, on the edge of the chair in front of his office desk, sighed impatiently. 'But surely you've a record of where your artists live, so that you can call them if you need to?'

'Where they live an't my concern. The stage-door-keeper should have a list of such things.'

'Don't you think I haven't asked him? And all he does is to stare at me like a fish on a slab and say he was never told about Mr Bryn's address.'

Dibdin was beginning to dislike this young person very much.

Widow of an Honourable she might be, and daughter-in-law to an earl (for she had flourished every credential she could), but he knew a ballet-girl when he saw one; and heard one.

'If you are so anxious to find Mr Bryn, madam,' he said, 'I'm surprised you've no knowledge of his address yourself, as you appear to know him pretty well. He's very attractive to the ladies, I'm told. Perhaps one of the young women in the ballet could tell you.'

Jannie flushed. 'I don't know what you imply, sir. But there's nothing like that about it.' She had not missed the rake of his glance over her figure, and she sat up straighter so that the slender lines of it were defined by her tight-fitting pelisse. 'I'm an old friend of Mr Bryn's. We were in pantomime together at the Royalty, years ago.'

'Then I suggest you go to the Royalty and enquire there.' Dibdin ostentatiously consulted his handsome fob-watch, a legacy from his famous father. 'Good day, ma'am.'

At the Royalty nobody knew anything about Ivor. The company was largely changed from the one she had known. Emma Brice had gone on the streets. Fasoli was still there, drilling away, but it was as much good to talk to him about an artist not in the company as to a sausage. Other people knew about Ivor's disappearance, who didn't? But not a guess as to what had happened to him. If he'd suddenly vanished, then that was life for you, wasn't it.

Jannie was tired and dispirited. She had spent three days since leaving Hanover Square in pursuing her enquiries. Months had gone by since Ivor and she had parted. Soon the summer season would be over, and the Wells 'dark' again. Perhaps he had gone back to Dublin. Or made an advantageous marriage. Any other possibility she did not care to consider. It would be so easy to shrug off the whole episode. They had met, and taken a great fancy to each other, and now it was over. If he had wanted her to know where he was, he'd have found some means to do it.

'Haven't you got any pride, Jannie?' Her mother, who had known of her visit to the Royalty, sat sewing with gnarled fingers in the shabby room in Long Acre. Jannie had not talked to her; there was no need.

'You could take a passage to Ireland,' Lucy Sorrel suggested, 'and go to the Castle. The Earl might take you up. There's been a lot of young Irishmen killed with Wellington, but plenty's left and come home again. You could make a good second match there, among Mr Fred's brother's friends.'

Jannie shook her head. 'And risk the biggest snub I ever had? No, Ma. Marrying Fred was the silliest thing I ever did, and it brought the poor soul to his death. I'm not leaving my own sort again, after what I've seen, I can tell you that. Please don't nag at me, Ma.'

Her mother glanced across at her, sitting like a tragedy queen with her chin on her hand; so much slimmer than she had been and with an air she had never worn before. She wondered if Jannie had minded about Fred, wept for him, or if there had been some hanky-panky with the other one, the man whose name had crept into Jannie's much-edited account of her time in Sussex. It seemed strange she would say no more. In Lucy's world the death of a husband and the attentions of an aspiring lover would have merited satisfying gossip from morning to night, and again the morning after; yet Jannie said almost nothing, only went haring off in search of this mountebank she had set her heart on. Lucy remembered him all too well. Harlequin, indeed, thought Lucy grimly; Harlequin Don Juan.

'If they don't know anything at the Wells,' she said, biting off a thread, 'then nobody don't, because it's there he was last seen, and I'm sure Mr Dibdin would 'a known if anybody did, so I reckon you're wasting your time.'

Jannie raised her head. Her eyes had brightened and the hopeless look was gone from her face.

'Am I? Am I?'

She was back at Sadler's Wells again by post-chaise, waiting in the Green Room for the rehearsal of the new piece that was to end the season, tapping her foot and tearing a scrap of paper from her pocket into small fragments. There were voices, footsteps on the stairs, a man was bringing in ale and cold meats. She saw the performers enter, half in and half out of their practice costumes, sweating and panting, chattering away to each other. At last she saw the man she wanted; Jim Barnes, only twenty-eight but already the professional old man of Pantomime, king of Panta-loons, nightly stooping his short figure to make an old fright of himself, peering with sharp pig-eyes from beneath beetling artificial grey brows, whacking Clown with his stick and shaking it feebly at Harlequin as Columbine was abducted. She leapt up and ran across the room to him, catching him with ale-mug half-way to his lips.

'Mr Barnes. I don't mean to take up your time, but you were here for *Harlequin April Fool* – weren't you?'

He stared, not knowing what to make of her, all dancer in looks and movement, but dressed like a lady. Had he, he won-dered, collected a Swooner? It seemed unlikely for a Pantaloon, but there was always a chance.

'Yes, my . . . yes, ma'am, I was. I hope you saw the piece?'

'Oh, I did, indeed. You were very fine,' she added, knowing every artist's longing for a word about his own performance. 'But I wanted to ask you about Mr Bryn.'

His hopes faded. 'Young Taffy, we called him. What an artist! And then to fade away like that.'

He saw her eyes widen like a frightened horse's. 'Fade away? What do you mean? What happened? Nobody seems to know.'

'There, sit down, my dear.' Her status was fairly clear to him now. 'I don't know all that much myself. Only that Joey (Joey and I dressed together, you know), Joey said one day that he had come in to rehearsal, very peaky, and said he'd been took ill. He played the show out, though we could see he wasn't up to it, and from then on we never set eyes on him.'

Jannie looked down at her clenched hands, and when Barnes offered her a sip of ale, she took it.

'Did you know where he lived? A carriage used to call for him. Did you ever hear the address?'

'How should I, my dear? He was what you might call just a

colleague. We had a chat once, about the days I spent soldiering –
I was in the 43rd Foot, though you might not think it to see me
in me nightly rig – but apart from that I never exchanged more
than a dozen words with him off-stage. Joey was the one who
knew him best.'

She caught his arm, looking eagerly up, her faint sweet scent
killing the stale miasma of the theatre, and he thought young
Taffy a lucky man. Wife, mistress, sweetheart? He patted the
small gloved hand and wondered if a kiss would be in order, at
some point in the conversation.

'Joey,' she was saying. 'Joe Grimaldi, of course. Oh, where is
he? Not here?'

'Not here, no. He left here in Spring, in a bit of a huff, after
some bother about a benefit. Joey thought he was due for one,
Dibdin didn't agree. Mr D., you know, not the most generous
...' He winked. 'So Joey took J.S. off touring, and a great
success it's been, by all accounts.'

Jannie was thinking quickly. 'Is Mrs Grimaldi with them?'

'Mary? No, she's dancing at the Garden, or was last I heard of
her. No, wait, it's "dark". So she'll be at home, most like. It's
only a bit of a walk, towards Bagnigge Wells, then just over
Coppice Row. Baynes Row's the street. Anybody'll show you
Joey's house.'

She thanked him with a flattering smile, and, much to his
regret, was gone. Sad that the best ones were always for others.
Philosophically, he finished his ale.

CHAPTER TWELVE

Columbine In Castle Dangerous

Mary Grimaldi's sitting-room itself was almost invisible beneath
the number of objects it contained. The rose-papered walls were
plastered with playbills, theatrical prints, Pantomime Attitudes,
portraits of Joey, the mantelpiece obscured by figurines, peacock-

feather fans, paintings of J.S. at various stages from babyhood onwards, and a pair of worn ballet-shoes hanging from a nail. The furniture would have testified to Mary's expensive tastes if it had been visible but it was draped, every piece of it, with costumes belonging to all three Grimaldis, a bonnet Mary was decorating with artificial flowers and feathers (some of which had got themselves on to the floor, where they were providing amusement for two kittens), a large tray piled with apples, and a half-filled showcase of preserved butterflies.

Jannie found herself clasped in a warm embrace and kissed on both cheeks. Mary, a bright robin-like creature almost as small as Jannie herself, beamed with genuine joy.

'Mrs FitzNeil, my dear! After all this time. Why, I remember the wedding as if it was yesterday – *what* a spread! I'm honoured, I really am. Do sit down, pray.' She snatched a pink tarlatan skirt from a chair. 'There. I'm afraid we're in a bit of a pickle, but with Joey and J.S. away I've took the chance of putting our costumes to rights. And is your good husband with you?' She looked round hopefully, as if expecting him to flutter down from the ceiling.

'No, Mrs Grimaldi. I lost him – recently.'

Mary's eyes took in the black pelisse and bonnet with the purple lining.

'Oh, my dear! I *am* so sorry. I ought to have seen . . . was it a long illness?'

'No, very sudden. A shooting accident.'

'Tck, tck. And him so young. Well, the Lord knows best, I suppose, but it does seem cruel. Joey's first wife went the same, you know, not thirty and everything to live for.' She looked up at the late Maria's portrait, a coiled tress of brown hair framed with it. 'Poor dear! How desolated you must be!'

'Well,' said Jannie, 'grief's the most useless thing in the world, to my mind, for it neither brings them back nor does one good. I intend to put all that behind me and come back to the theatre.'

Mary's eyes widened. She had not failed to notice the costliness of Jannie's clothes. 'I don't blame you,' she said. 'Once you're in it, it takes hold of you. I'm sure Joey and me would never quit it, not if we was as rich as Creases. So are you in an engagement already?'

'No.' Jannie hesitated. 'I have – something to do first, and I wondered if Mr Grimaldi might help me.'

'Oh, that I'm sure he would, if he were here, but he's been touring for weeks. Just he and J.S., on the northern and western circuits, and even up to Scotland. Such receptions, my dear! Packed houses, wonderful takings, Grimaldi's name on all lips, so he tells me, and our boy just as popular. Perhaps that'll show Dibdin he can't do without his Clown. Over a thousand pounds they've taken already . . .'

Jannie ventured to break into what promised to be a lengthy monologue.

'Are they touring with a company? I mean, have they taken – anybody with them?'

'Oh, no, that would have been too costly. Of course, where there's a resident company Joey uses it, like to give his Bob Acres in *The Rivals*. But mostly he does favourite scenes, the Mother Goose Jig and so on.'

Another hope gone; Ivor was not with them. Jannie decided on comparative frankness. 'Mrs Grimaldi – you know Ivor Bryn, who was Harlequin to Joey this season?'

'Why, of course I do – such a charming boy, though a bit on the mysterious side. All the girls were mad about him, but Joey said he didn't care a fig for any of them. He seemed to have something else on his mind, and quite right. I don't hold with flirting-games when one's working, nor does Joey. Oh, he used to come here quite often, young Ivor, when they were rehearsing; seemed to think of Joey as a sort of father. Then, just before Joey left the Wells, he said Ivor seemed far from well – taken with some kind of sickness. And then he gave up coming to the theatre, and they engaged someone else.'

'And you don't know where he lived?' Jannie asked desperately. 'Nobody else seems to know.'

Mary shook her curls. 'Never asked him. But Joey would know, if anyone does.'

'Where is he now – Mr Grimaldi? Does he write often?'

'Bless you, every week.' She took a pile of papers from the mantelshelf. 'Now the last was from Worcester, that was second time round, the first having been such a riot. This week . . . let me see . . . yes, Bath.'

Jannie's spirits soared. Not too far to go. It was only Monday – she could be there in time to see Joey on Wednesday. She admired the garden outside and the rosy apples which had come from it, heard a glowing account of Joey's prize pigeons up in the loft, inspected the butterfly collection, and was taken out into the yard to see the famous rabbit, now retired from the stage and resident in a hutch, surrounded by fluffy offspring. Mary was, to say the least, hard to escape from, but at last Jannie was on the doorstep, returning Mary's embrace, and thanking her over and over again.

For what? Mary wondered, closing the door. Perhaps it was not too hard to guess. One never knew what went on in the lives of other people. Money, and a husband to mourn for, and yet chasing after another man; what were girls coming to? Could she be intending to go and see Joey? Mary's bright little face clouded. If only she'd known she could have sent a message – her best love, and to take care of himself.

Jannie had visited Bath before, when Sir Patrick's gout had flared up and he had gone to take the waters. But then it had been in his private carriage, with just the three of them inside, Fred snoring in one corner and his uncle in another, herself in between and the servants outside. Relative comfort compared with the stage-coach, stuffy and cold, one's feet among straw on the floor – was it clean straw? – strangers on each side, fortunately respectable enough and quiet. She was young enough not to mind the bouncing of the vehicle on rough roads, or to feel exhausted from the early start – six o'clock in the morning from the Bull and Mouth Inn, St Martin's-le-Grand. Here they were at Hounslow Heath, famous for highwaymen's attacks on coaches

– now Maidenhead Thicket, big, bustling Reading, and the Thames left behind, Newbury, the deep Savernake Forest, the handsome market town of Marlborough . . .

The day was wearing on, stops and refreshments more and more welcome. Jannie felt as free as air. Nobody thought it strange for a young woman to be travelling alone, for she had left off her mourning – poor Fred, but it hampered her so and caused awkward questions. Now she wore a modest brown walking-dress made by her mother, and a neat, if slightly saucy, bonnet in the Scotch style. After some hesitation, she had left on her wedding-ring: it deterred wolves on the prowl.

Calne, Chippenham – only nine miles now to Bath. The light was going, a rosy autumn sky darkening into opal colours. And here was Bath in its valley, starry lights pointing it all over, the loveliest of stage settings, from the hand of a master designer. Even in the shadows, she could imagine how the golden stone of the houses glowed, how the whole town crystallized the grace and beauty of building, from the Romans to the day of the present George. And here at last it was, the inn near the Pump Room, passengers alighting stiffly, tired steaming horses released from the traces, guards hurrying off to bury their noses in mugs of rum or brandy and water.

And a blessed night's rest in a small clean inn-room, without even a dream to trouble her.

She waited all next morning at the smart newish theatre, next to Beau Nash's house. Mr Grimaldi was rehearsing, nobody knew how long he would be. Sometimes she went out and walked about the streets, revelling in the air fresher than London's, the clear river, the heights clad in wood and meadow. In a shop that sold antiquities she bought a ring, a tiny enamel miniature of Shakespeare set in pinchbeck. It would remind her of a time of release, of hopeful quest. Then she went back to wait.

J.S. was the first to appear from the stage exit, as the sound of voices, music, and shifted scenery died. He was taller than she remembered him, less like his father in the face, and with a kind of restless, discontented air. She recalled stories of his grandfather, the tyrannical old Italian, who had beaten Joey when he was little and made a slave of him.

'Ah,' said J.S. patronizingly, in his superior voice, 'I remember you, don't I?'

It was clear that J.S. considered himself a gentleman.

'I remember you, too. But I came to see your father – is he free?'

J.S. jerked his head casually towards the wings, and Grimaldi was there, beaming with huge astonishment, great brown eyes completely round, hands outstretched to her.

'Little Sorrel!' He gabbled astonishment, welcome, query, tucked her arm through his, and before she could speak they were across the road in the Garrick's Head and he was ordering for her in the little private parlour they proudly kept for him.

'So Mary sent you! Dear creature, how was she?'

There was half an hour of chatting – for Joey was starved of London news. Her own fortunes were mentioned and dismissed briefly before she laid down her knife and faced him.

'Mr Grimaldi, shall I tell you why I came?' And she did tell him, everything, while he listened patiently, understandingly, though the Abbey clock had chimed one, and he should have been back on stage. When he had heard her out he leaned back in his chair, gazing out at the bright street scene.

'Yes, I do know where you can find your lost Patchy. No, don't kiss me, child, keep it for him. Not that I can swear he's still where he was.' And he told her of Ivor's confession to him of his uneasy life with Clara, his longing to escape – 'and if he was walking out with *you*, my dear, I'm not surprised.' He described the ominous look of Ivor the day before he disappeared. 'And that's the last I heard. Or anybody.'

Jannie was still, thinking, taking it in. She felt a sharp pang of desolation and hurt. But it all fitted, his dazzling quality, a starved older woman, the poor way players lived. If it had been herself, with such an offer, ten to one she'd have accepted. Hadn't she thought it was Fred's intention, and been prepared to say yes to it? Uppermost in her mind was fear, and the thought of the long weeks that lay between that day at Sadler's Wells, and this autumn morning.

'Do you know this lady's name, and where she lives?' she asked Joey.

'Mrs Clara Thurloe. Of Colebrooke Row. Don't rec'lect the number, but it was a doctor's house, everybody knows it. He wouldn't 'a told if I'd not made him, for I misliked the look of him, and the performance he gave that night's best forgotten. I thought as I'd go and see how he was, if he didn't turn up. And then I'd to leave town, and damme, begging your pardon, if it hadn't all slipped my mind till now.'

He was watching her set, resolute face. 'If it's not impertinent to ask, what's your intentions?'

'I shall go there. As soon as I get back to town.'

He put his hand over hers, a hand gnarled and calloused with falls and jugglery. The face that had set thousands in a roar was a mask of melancholy.

'Don't expect too much, my girl. You can't always knock on a door and find what you're after on the other side, life an't like that. Shall I tell you a story?'

'You'll be late if you do.'

'They'll send for me if they wants me. This here story goes back a long way, to '03. I was playing the Lane – I well remember the piece for I was just married to Mary. It was *A Bold Stroke for a Wife*. We was between acts, the curtain due to rise, when a message come from the door-keeper as I was wanted down there by two gentlemen. Soon as I'd a long enough wait, I went down. There was the two gents, handsome enough young men with a good tan to their faces, as if they'd been in foreign parts, and well-dressed, much alike. One had a gold-headed cane, and it was he as said to me, "Joe, my lad! How goes it with you, old feller?"

'Well, I didn't know him from Adam, and said so, at which they both laughed very much. Then he said, in a different voice, "Joe, don't you know me now?" and he pulled his cravat and his shirt aside to show me a scar there, just above the ribs. I knew him then, though I couldn't hardly believe it. He was John, my only brother, as had disappeared fourteen years afore, having skipped from an East Indiaman to a King's ship, and never been heard of since.

'We shed a good few tears, I can tell you. Then I took him upstairs to meet the company, for I wanted everyone to know my good news, but before that his friend wished him good night and appointed to meet him at ten in the morning.

'They all crowded round in the Green Room to shake his hand, so that I'd little time to talk to him alone, for I was on again in five minutes, but I did ask him if he'd prospered at sea.

' "Prospered?" says he, a-slapping his breast pocket. "I've six hundred pounds in here."

' "Why," said I, "an't it very dangerous to carry so much about with you, John?"

' "Dangerous? We sailors don't know the meaning of danger. And even if this lot were gone, I shouldn't be penniless." And he gave me a comical wink, like he used to when we was lads. Just then I was called, and had to leave just as he was showing one of my pals a big canvas bag stuffed with coins. I told him very quick where we lived, me and Mary and mother, and that we'd go there and sup as soon as I was changed. After the curtain I made haste, though I was all fingers and thumbs with confusion and pleasure, and ran down from my dressing-room to the stage where he'd promised to wait.'

Joey's voice had sunk almost to a whisper.

'He weren't there. Many had seen him, and spoke to him; he'd gone out of the stage-door. I ran into the street, to the house of an old friend close by, for I was sure I'd find him there. But I didn't, nor at our old landlord's in Wild Street though he'd been at both places, I was told. To cut it short, I ran from house to house before it struck me, of course he'd be at home. So there I hurried, but he wasn't there, and when I told them the news, Mother swooned away. We waited up all night, but he never came. And nobody ever set eyes on him again.'

'But what could have happened to him?' asked Jannie, aghast.

'God above knows. Murdered for his money by thieves, by his

friend (as never showed up again neither) or press-ganged, though the press-gangers didn't hang about Drury Lane, and the Admiralty could find out nothing. Either that,' he said darkly, 'or he was a ghost.'

'In which case he wouldn't have been seen by all the company, would he?'

'Who knows? More things in Heaven and earth, like Hamlet says . . .'

Jannie had gone very pale. 'Are you trying to tell me you think Ivor's – not alive?'

'Bless your heart, child, 'course I'm not! I know no more than you do about it. I'm only warning you that mysteries do happen, and sometimes they never gets solved. And – take care. Don't go a-dancing into anything without a helping hand.'

As she travelled back by the night coach the story came into her mind again and again, frightening her, on its own account and for Ivor's sake. Had he, like John Grimaldi, saved a lot of money during his successful season in Ireland, and if he had, would he be rash enough to carry it about with him, and let the fact be known? It seemed unlikely. But every night in the London streets people were knocked on the head for as little as a silver watch or a cravat-pin. She tried to put the possibility out of her mind, and soon the jolting of the coach acted as a distraction from the haunting picture of the prosperous young sailor hurrying out of the stage-door into nothingness.

Lucy Sorrel did more and more of her wardrobe work at home, so crippled were her limbs. She was completely, uncomfortably, aware of her daughter's restiveness. Nowadays she felt hardly in the same world as Jannie, after the girl's translation to Hanover Square and its imagined glories. The journey to Bath baffled her completely and roused her worst suspicions.

'Going to see a friend? What friend? Well, Mr Grimaldi an't exactly a friend, is he? How can *he* help you to get work, and why do you want to work, in your position, when you could live like a lady? I don't care, it don't make sense. Oh, very well, go, it's your money you're spending.'

To her husband she said, 'It's that Moth, mark my words.'

The Captain started from a reverie. 'What moth, my love?'

'That young shaver what took her hand when she tripped, oh, donkey's years ago. I always knew no good would come of him.'

The Captain said nothing, but pulled on his pipe, and watched his daughter. He had known something of love and its stresses, long ago, before Lucy's day and during it, and he felt deeply and guiltily for the child he had sent to a barren, loveless marriage, for no particular reward. 'What female heart can gold despise? What cat's averse to fish?' some poet or other had asked. Once the Captain would have laughed at that. Through his theatrical connections, he was aware of Raymond Otway's stage breakdown, and he was not so stupid as to fail to connect it with their revel at The Shiners' Club. That was another error on his part.

He felt the burden on his shoulders of his daughter's abstracted air, her jumping at sudden sounds, the dark shadows round her eyes.

He watched her, therefore, on the day after her return from Bath, sleeping off her fatigue in the new room she had rented for them, toying with her food. On that day and the next morning he gave no thought to his tavern companions or the tipsters, but stayed solidly at home, until Lucy scolded him for getting under feet. When, in mid-morning, Jannie said she was going out, he made no comment, only smiled and nodded. But before she had reached the bottom of the stairs that led through the coach-maker's office to the street, he had donned hat and cloak, and was a few paces after her.

She went to the nearest hackney-stand, where he saw her engage a dingy vehicle drawn by a broken-down horse with drooping head, and propelled by a red-nosed coachman. There were three cabs waiting. He saw hers move off, then engaged the second. From her behaviour at present, she would never notice that she was being followed. The cab turned northwards, up Gray's Inn Lane. Was she going to the New Road, or Pentonville? No, for at Battle Bridge, the end of Gray's Inn Lane, the cab turned right, clopped along the road to Islington, past the junction of High Street and St John Street, then stopped. She was going to Colebrooke Row.

Hastily he directed his driver to stop at the other side, and watched her alight before paying his own cab off. From the corner of the Row he watched her walking swiftly up the right-hand side, and he began to follow, many yards behind her, lost among the other pedestrians and tradesmen. A girl with rabbits strung on a pole crossed in front of him, and he cursed mentally, afraid that Jannie would have disappeared; but she was still there, walking determinedly. Abruptly she stopped, surveyed one of the houses, opened its garden gate and vanished from his sight. He memorized the position of the house, counting swiftly, and reached it only a few moments after her. The front door was just closing.

The Captain stood musing. One part of his mind told him that he was a fool, following a young woman perfectly able to look after herself, whose errand was in any case none of his business. Another part warned him quite clearly that his daughter was going into some sort of trouble or danger. He had not taken enough care of her in the past – he would do it now.

He became aware that he would attract attention if he continued to stand there. He began to walk, a few yards in one direction, then a few yards back in the other. There was no plan in his mind, no clear idea of what he was here to do. If he rang the bell and asked for Jannie, to find that she was merely keeping an assignation, he would feel more of a fool than ever, and she would be very angry with him. She might be visiting a female friend: but why, then, dismiss the cab so far away from the house? Doggedly he continued to pace, always keeping the windows of the tall house in view. At least it was a fine autumn morning . . .

Jannie's heart was beating violently as she stood on the step, hearing the jangling of the bell inside the house. Sternly she told herself to be calm and bold. What was there to fear, from a social call on a respectable widow: or not so respectable, according to Joey's story. But he had told her to be careful, too.

The door opened; an elderly maid stood there, very upright and correct. Jannie, well-used to dealing with domestics, asked crisply whether Mrs Thurloe was at home.

'I'm not sure, ma'am.' This was, of course, the formula for going to find out whether her mistress wished to receive. 'What name shall I say?'

'Mrs FitzNeil.' Jannie wished she had worn her very best clothes to appear as impressive as possible. Her mother had been so shocked at her leaving off her mourning that she had taken to wearing a plain jaconet dress of a fawn colour that she felt did not suit her, and a spencer of dark brown velvet. At least her Leghorn bonnet was becoming, and its height made her feel less ridiculously small, facing the tall, grenadier-like maid, who now disappeared, to return with the message that madam would see her.

Her first impression of the woman seated in the parlour was: 'But she's quite old.' Her second was one of coldness, suspicion and – yes, fear. It went with the curiously repellent atmosphere of the house. Was there a strange scent, or a draught . . .

'Mrs FitzNeil,' Clara was saying. 'I don't think I have the pleasure.'

'No, ma'am. I took the liberty of calling without introduction.'

They eyed each other like two cats. Clara noticed the strong ankles and high-arched feet beneath the fashionably short skirt, and the pointed face with the doe-eyes: she knew very well what circles her visitor came from, and the question did not take her altogether by surprise, though the mere uttering of it caused her a momentary shock.

'I was told you might be able to give me some news of a friend of mine – Mr Ivor Bryn. We are – we were in the same theatrical company, and I have – messages for him.'

Clara's thin eyebrows rose. 'Really? And why should you think I know anything of the gentleman, ma'am? As I'm sure you can see, I have no theatrical connections.'

'I was told,' Jannie said, 'on very good authority. By someone who knows him well.'

'Then I'm surprised your informant can't help you.' But Clara was aware now that her visitor knew something; it might be wise to yield a little ground. She pretended to think. 'If you refer to a Mr Bryn who took the Harlequin at Sadler's Wells, I believe I was introduced to him once – at some gathering or other. At least, I think that was the name. One meets so many people when one socializes a good deal.'

Lie number one, thought Jannie. No point in fencing any more. 'I was told he lodged here,' she said bluntly. Now the scent of fear from the other woman was stronger, mingling with that other scent – what was it? Powdered roots and spirits of wine, liquorice and calomel, the nauseous ingredients of pills . . . of course, Grimaldi had said the house had been a doctor's.

Clara drew herself bolt upright and eyed the bell-pull. 'I don't like your tone, ma'am, any more than your words. What you say is preposterous.'

'And I don't like being told lies,' Jannie said. 'Come now, it's true, isn't it? And I wouldn't pull that bell if I was you, ma'am, because I assure you I know for a fact that Mr Bryn was here with you in the summer – and why.'

With an icy stare, Clara said, 'Then you know all you're likely to know.'

'Why didn't you say so in the first place?'

'Because . . . I took the man in out of charity, till he could find other lodgings. One doesn't want to advertise any low connections one may contract out of good nature.' Clara's hands were tightly clenched together, and trembling slightly. Jannie watched them, and the white line round the tight-lipped, unpainted mouth. She was sure now. It was as if the ghostly form of Joey's brother stood behind the woman's chair, warning her, yet she was full of courage and resolve.

'And after Mr Bryn left you, ma'am,' she asked sweetly, 'where did he go? Where were these "other lodgings"?'

'I have no idea. Wherever such people do go, I suppose.'

The Leghorn bonnet was slowly shaken. 'No, ma'am. I've enquired of everyone in the districts where actors lodge, and no one has seen him. It's impossible for a well-known player to disappear, in our small world. So I conclude he's still here.'

A violent flush spread over Clara's face. She leapt to her feet.

'I think you'd better leave at once, since it's clear you're out of your senses.' Before she could reach the bell-rope Jannie was at the door and out of it, dashing into the room opposite, and the half of it that lay behind double doors, Clara after her, shouting: 'Baynes! Agnes! There's a madwoman in the house!' But nobody heard her, and Jannie was half-way up the stairs, round the curve of them, into the first-floor drawing-room and beyond it, Clara panting behind, so many years older and heavier and slower of foot, breathlessly crying: 'Come back! You're mad!'

'Oh no, I'm not. I'll search every corner of this house!' Jannie was in the best bedroom, which looked out on the garden and was meticulously tidy. She wrenched open a wardrobe cupboard; it held only dresses. Clara caught up with her in the opposite bedroom, looking on to the street. It was even more austere than the other, and some instinct made Jannie look round it keenly. Ivor had known it, she was sure. There was no trace of him, not the least, and yet ... Clara was behind her, clutching her, pinioning her arms and gasping out desperate, incoherent words. Jannie struggled against her surprising strength, feeling one arm come round her waist like a steel vice and the other round her throat, bruising it agonizingly. Somehow she lurched towards the window, dragging her enemy after her, half-choking, and got a hand up to beat against the pane.

As they fell to the floor, wrestling, scratching and clawing, neither heard the clang of the front-door bell, two storeys below, or the opening of the door by Agnes. She had been in the kitchen when the foray had been going on, and was too deaf to hear cries through the double doors that separated the servants' quarters from the rest of the house.

'Well!' said the Captain from the bedroom door. 'Great

heavens.' In a second he was beside the two women, wrenching Clara away from Jannie, pushing her away so that she fell heavily. 'Beg your pardon, ma'am,' he said politely, then, 'Jannie, you're not hurt? Yes, by God, you are.'

She sat up, bonnetless, her hair about her scratched face and bruised throat, panting, half-crying with pain, yet managing to smile at him.

'Not hurt a bit, Captain.' Then, like a little girl, she threw herself into his arms. 'Oh, Pa, I'm so glad to see you! How *did* you get here?'

He patted her shoulders. 'Never mind. Here I am. And waiting for an explanation, madam.' He looked towards Clara, also sitting up, her long black hair hanging in snake-like ropes, her face, like Jannie's, bleeding from scratches. She could hardly speak from the shock of the fall, but managed to pant out: 'Get out of my house! How dare you? I'll call the Watch . . . have you put in prison!'

'I'm this young lady's father, ma'am,' he answered politely, 'and I had some reason to suppose she might be – in trouble of a sort, so I followed her. I see I was right.'

'Like father, like daughter – both mad!' She was on her feet, on her way to the bell-rope which in this room hung beside the bed. To the Captain's surprise Jannie said, 'Yes, call the Watch, do. I want to talk to them.' Even more to his surprise Clara turned away and flopped heavily into a chair, where she sat hugging herself, as if she were very cold.

'Come, Pa.' Hobbling slightly from a wrenched ankle, Jannie led him out of the room. On the landing he said mildly, 'I hope it don't seem presumptuous, my love, but may I know what all this is about? One hardly expects to find one's own daughter engaged in a mill with another lady.'

'I haven't time to tell you. Come on.' She was exploring a smaller bedroom, with an old powdering-closet leading off it. Nothing there. He followed her up the last staircase, to a section of the house lower-ceilinged than the rest.

'Servants' attics,' he said, as she opened the door of the first room they came to. It was full of litter – trunks, wig-stands, bundles of old bed-clothes, dusty books.

'No,' said Jannie. 'Store-rooms. You can see nobody comes up here. There must be another staircase at the back that leads to where they sleep. You see I know these sort of houses, Pa.'

'Of course you do. I'd forgotten.' Jannie was rattling at the handle of a door at the end of the small passage, while he peered into another attic, that held broken-down furniture and a few pictures with holes through their canvases. Suddenly she turned, ran past him without a word, down the stairs and back to the bedroom they had left. Clara still sat there, and her hands were over her ears. Jannie wrenched them down.

'Give me the key of the small attic. Oh yes, you know what I'm talking about. Give it me this minute or I'll make you sorry!'

Silently, Clara put her hand in the pocket of her frilled morning apron, and produced an iron key, part-rusted. Jannie snatched it and ran back upstairs. Watched by her father, she struggled with the old key in the stiff lock, until he moved her aside and applied his strength to it.

With a slow creaking the door opened. Inside the room it was very dark, the small window covered by a short, rough curtain. Jannie pulled it to one side; it was only threaded on string, and had not been there long. As the morning light came into the room, they saw the narrow servant's bed, little more than a pallet on legs, the rough blanket, the still form under it.

Jannie gave one shriek and threw herself down by the bed.

'Ivor!'

She clutched the cold hand hanging over the side of the bed, kissing it, calling to him, as her father watched helplessly. He had little doubt that their strange, violent quest had been in vain, if this was the quarry. As Jannie's self-control finally snapped, and she broke into wild sobbing, he gently moved her away from the bed, pulled down the blanket and examined the man who lay there. He looked unlike anyone the Captain had ever seen before, and he lay dreadfully, unnaturally still.

The Captain gently raised one eyelid, then lifted a wrist and bent his head close to the quiet breast. When he straightened himself his face was happier. The person on the bed was emaciated to skeleton thinness, the skin paper-white, a whiteness hardly credible in a living man, the breath and pulse barely perceptible; but he was not dead.

Gently he told Jannie, and as gently held her back from embracing the near-corpse. 'No, my dear. That way you might finish him off altogether, and he's near enough the edge as it is.' He looked round the attic, filthy, its surfaces thick with dust, but for the marks of footprints on the floor. There was no other furniture than the pallet-bed, nothing to be seen in the way of food, drink, or medicine. The air was full of the sickly miasmic stench of untended illness, and old dust, and something else. The Captain sniffed. Could it be, possibly, garlic?

'Come,' he said, 'we must get him out of here, and quickly. That is, if your charming friend downstairs don't stop us.'

'She won't,' Jannie said, half-choked with tears. 'She daren't. She did this.'

'I thought as much. Hold the door open, will you, my love.' Very gently he stooped and gathered the boy up in his arms, skilfully, as he had carried many a comrade from the battlefield, and steadily he moved downstairs with his burden, Jannie at his heels. The door of the front bedroom was shut; as they reached the landing, it opened, and Clara stood there, watching them expressionlessly.

'Murderess!' Jannie cried, but the other neither spoke nor moved, only watched their progress down the main staircase into the hall, past a servant who backed away from them, squealing.

The Captain sat cautiously down on a chair near the front door, holding Ivor closely and firmly. 'Run out and get a hackney, my dear. I noticed a stand at the end of the street.'

She was back in less than five minutes, though they seemed five years to her, a cabman at her side. The Captain nodded to him affably. 'Friend of mine not altogether well,' he said. 'Been overdoing it. So you'll go very carefully, won't you, there's a good fellow.' The man, staring, nodded and went back to his cab. What the gentry got up to was none of his business, and he'd most likely get double fare.

'Where to, Guv?'

'Long Acre. Daniels the coachmaker's.'

'Oh, Captain, Pa! We're going home!' Jannie's eyes filled again.

'Where else? Your mama will have a fit of the megrims, or vapours, or whatever you ladies call 'em, but I daresay she'll soon come round.' As they rode, the cabbie obediently going quietly as he could through the streets, the Captain chatted cheerfully on, though privately he prayed that his charge would still be alive at the end of the journey.

Twenty-four hours or so later, Jannie, heavy-eyed and drawn with sleeplessness, sat by the bed in her own room, where Ivor lay, in clean warm sheets under thick blankets, a fire burning in the grate. Sometimes he stirred slightly, and once he murmured: 'Mam, Mam,' and some Welsh words she could not catch. She watched him anxiously, avid for a sound or movement. Every hour or so she would lift his head gently and urge a spoonful of medicine or broth between his lips. They had cleaned him up, and there was now the faintest tinge of colour in the porcelain whiteness of his face: a pallor caused, said the doctor, by arsenical poisoning, and, of course, starvation. The crest of black hair still rose above his brow; Jannie touched it, and his cheek where the bone almost broke through, as softly as though they would crumble under her fingers.

Poor Harlequin, robbed of his beauty and his magic, his brilliant colours faded and his jewels dimmed, it seemed that the evil Genius of Pantomime had conquered him, this time.

But the doctor, though still solemn and head-shaking, had pronounced that with care his patient would live.

Out of a deep sleep, Ivor opened his eyes and saw who was sitting close by him, holding his hand at her breast. He smiled, and said not 'Mam', but 'Jannie'.

BOOK THREE

HARLEQUIN BY MOONSHINE

'Though claim to Columbine thy conduct lost,
No longer, Harlequin, shalt thou be crost.
Thus, then, I waft ye to more virtuous ground,
Where Truth and Industry are ever crown'd.'

CHAPTER THIRTEEN

Travels and Trials

'It's not of any consequence, Mrs Porter, I assure you. We shall manage very well.'

Sara felt she had said it a hundred times before. But still Matilda Porter's hands were distressfully twisted in the apron which now rose high above her swelling waist, and her eyes were full of tears.

'I wish it didn't have to be, Mrs Otway, my dear. And so does Thaddeus and every one of us. But you see things simply can't go on as they are.'

Sara patted her arm consolingly, but was far from feeling as calm as she seemed. The months of late autumn and winter had been disastrous for Hallsfield Playhouse. The scattered, fickle country public found the Otways no longer a novelty, London-stamped though they might be. 'He's a stick, and she's no chicken, for all that yellow dye and paint,' said fashionable, play-going Sussex, spoiled by the proximity of sophisticated Brighton. Receipts had gone down. Almost three months of hard weather had kept folk by their own firesides. Even the garden behind the Playhouse cottage had failed, winter cabbages limp and rotten, late apples blown down and eaten by slugs, the few scraggy hens refusing to lay, the local rats making free with what eggs there were. Psyche had tramped all over the district collecting firewood to keep them warm, pushing Clio's baby-cart.

There was nothing for it but to close the Playhouse down. The floats were snuffed, the single chandelier which was Thaddeus's pride muffled in a drape, the brave red paint and gilding hidden in shadows; while Thaddeus and his father offered their services to local farmers and builders as carpenters, odd-job men, anything, and their wives volunteered to take in sewing, mind babies, or give an extra hand in the kitchen to any lady who required it. Soon Matilda would not be able to do that, for another little Porter was on the way and she was sickly. A heavy cold had begun with

Psyche, brought home from the village dame-school, and had gone through the family and the company, reaping a harvest of red noses, streaming eyes, sore throats and hoarse voices. For a fortnight they had had to close. Now Thaddeus had taken the final decision, and the Otways must quit Hallsfield, which could not support them any longer.

They had started to talk about it, and stopped. Only one thing was clear: they must leave Sussex.

'There's Brighton and Worthing,' Sara suggested hopefully, thinking of the few miles that separated them from those centres of high life.

'With the choice of London actors? Kean, Kitty Stephens, Pritt Harley . . . even Grimaldi and Bologna, from what they were saying . . .' Raymond's voice tailed off as Sara looked at him sharply.

'*Who* were saying?'

He looked sheepish. 'I forget. Some people at the coach-office, I believe.' They both knew his informants had been at the White Hart.

'Well. You may be right. We can't afford to travel there without an engagement. And such places are expensive. No, we must go back to London.'

Wearily Sara packed up their few belongings. She had grown very fond of the cottage, the nearest thing to a settled home she had had, since her flight long ago, and all the sweeter for her pretence of being married. She had even allowed herself to dream of a time when quiet old Mrs Tottle, who spent her days smiling toothlessly and smoking her clay pipe by the kitchen fire, might die, or take herself to relatives, leaving the cottage to her lodgers, who would by then be prosperous from their savings. It was perfect for Miranda, too. Thaddeus had built her an ingenious cage of wire covering a grass plot in the garden, so that she might have something like freedom, fresh air, green shoots to nibble and shrub-wood to sharpen her claws, yet be safe from the local toms. Now she was to lose it all, be packed into the hated carrying-basket: for what future?

The farewell to the Porter family was emotional. Thaddeus could hardly speak, full of shame that his ambitions should have taken such a toss, his theatre closed and his guest actors dismissed. Old Mr Porter, never one for words, unless learned painfully from a script, wrung the Otways' hands and dashed off to the workshop, where he was heard sawing frenziedly at nothing in particular, for there was no more scenery to be built. His wife rocked her thin body to and fro in her chair by the low-burning fire. 'That it should come to this!' she repeated over and over. It was a line she had spoken so often in tragedy that it sprang naturally to her lips.

Psyche, restraining the crawling Clio, was dumbly miserable. She had liked being an actress, all the school had envied her, and now it was at an end, another infant on the way to keep her a house-slave.

Matilda had left the party in the sitting-room, the Otways dressed for their coach-journey. Now she lumbered heavily down the steep stairs and put something into Sara's hands.

'Please take it. It's a little gaudy for every day, but I daresay you may find a use for it. And – to remember us by.'

It was a delicate India silk shawl, patterned in a Paisley design of many colours. Sara kissed and thanked her, knowing that the sale of it to an honest dealer would have kept the family for a week; knowing, too, that it could not stay long in her own keeping.

At last they were gone, off to the coach-office, climbing up to the top of the coach, for they could afford only outside places, Miranda wailing in her prison on Sara's lap, and braced themselves for the bitterly cold, bone-shaking, precarious journey to London.

And after all there was no work for them. At each theatre it was the same: 'Fully cast for Christmas – too late to apply now.'

At the stage-door of the Royalty Sara asked for Mrs Sorrel. The crippled woman who had always been very civil to her might find her some work in the wardrobe. But the sharp answer was that Mrs Sorrel had gone into retirement.

As they walked away Sara said, 'She must have gone to Jannie – Mrs FitzNeil. We could find her address . . .'

Tried beyond his patience, Raymond snapped at her. 'For what? To ask for work as bootboy and scullery-maid? No, my dear, you may have come to beg charity of a dancing-girl gone up in the world, but I ain't. As for the address, it was Hanover Square, she told us, and if you care to ring all the area bells I dare say you'll find her. Only leave me out of it.'

Sara said nothing, only walked on at his side, her shoulder aching cruelly from the weight of the cat-basket. There was no use in weeping. She must keep her strength, if they were not all three to die. The London atmosphere was acrid, stifling, after the clear air of the country, its cold of a different kind, a cold that seeped into the bones. The pavements glistened with London's peculiar muddy slime, biting through the shoes they had fortunately ordered from the cobbler at Hallsfield when times were better. Thank God for the shoes at least, Sara thought.

By the light of one of the rare gas-lamps that shone like stars of hope through the foggy gloom she saw a pawn-shop sign. Without a word to Raymond she hurried in; it would not close till after midnight, when anybody with anything to sell would have gone home. In the narrow booth she unfolded the India silk shawl before the lacklustre eyes of a pimply youth.

'Five shillin',' he said.

'Six. It's hardly worn. Only feel the silk . . .'

Trade had been poor, and his master would be too drunk to care what bargains he made. 'Orl right, six.' She had something else to offer: her mirror. Everything else had been sold to keep them in food.

Before she came out she put the money out of sight. There were always rat-eyes in the shadows, beggars and marauders waiting to pounce. To Raymond she said quietly, 'Now we can get something to eat.'

They were glad to find themselves in the stuffy bar-parlour of a haunt known to theatricals down on their luck, the P.S. and O.P., Russell Court. Its name, abbreviated from Prompt Side and Opposite Prompt, was most apt, most of its patrons looking as though they had seldom got nearer to a stage than the wings. Raymond ate greedily of bread and cheese, the best food they could afford, and emptied his mug of porter almost at a swallow. Sara sighed as he took it to be refilled. Best let him have it, if it would bring him any cheer.

It was she who saw the roughly-printed bill nailed to the wall, among other theatrical advertisements. It stood out by being slightly cleaner and less dog-eared than the rest.

WANTED
At the Theatre, Hertford,
Walking Lady and Gentleman,
with possibility of appearance
in
LEADING ROLES
if suited.
Season begins Boxing Day,
December 26th.
Apply in person to the Management.

Unscrupulously she tugged it away from the wall and took it to the bar-counter, where the landlord was reading a paper and consuming a pint of his best Old and Mild. She tapped his arm.

'This bill. Is it new?'

He raised his large head slowly.

'Wot, my dear?'

Impatiently she repeated the question, projecting her voice over the roar of conversation round the bar. At last he comprehended.

'Oh, that. Yerse, thass new. Only come in yes'day. Carrier from those parts brought it in.'

Sara was thinking quickly. 'Can you remember his name, please?'

The landlord scratched his head. 'Blest if I can, right off. Red-faced young feller. Nicely painted-up cart. Grows vegetables up Barnet way. Wilkes, thass it. Ben Wilkes. Why d'you want him, my dear? He ain't nothing in your line, I should think.'

'Just some information about the bill.'

'Oh, ah. Should be at the market tomorrer, maybe even ter-night.'

'Thank you. I'll find him in the moning.' She smiled dazzlingly. 'If you could very kindly let us have a bed for the night – me and my husband.'

He pondered. 'There's a little room under the slates you could 'ave. It's not much, but then I wouldn't charge you much. Shillin' each?'

Inwardly sighing, Sara agreed. It was, in fact, quite a lot for an attic at this particular address, but they had no choice. Leaving a shilling with him on account she led Raymond, slightly staggering, up the twisting stairs.

As St Paul's clock struck noon the next day they were sitting on an empty barrow under the comparative shelter of the pillared Piazza, out of the worst of the cold rain. They had located Ben Wilkes and his handsome wagon painted in gilt scrollwork on scarlet, a fine pair of farm-horses in the shafts, and a mono-tonously barking guard-dog on the box. He was surprised to be approached by such a fancy pair of townies, but perfectly agreeable to convey them to Hertfordshire when he went back later that day.

'Couldn't say what time, exact. Tell you what, though, I only goes as far as Hadley – that's north o' Barnet, see. If you want to get to Hertford, you got to walk.'

He agreed that he should come and find them when he was ready to leave. But Raymond said urgently to Sara: 'This is mad-ness. For all we know someone else has been engaged by now. That fellow knew nothing about it, only that a "flash chap" gave it to him. What if we find ourselves out there in the country, with no work?'

'Better there than here,' Sara said calmly. 'I have never much wanted to be found dead in the street and shovelled into a pauper's grave.'

He shook his head despairingly. 'Oh, Sara, Sara! Why not stay? Why not leave me? I'm only a drag on you, a damned heavy burden. Without me . . .'

'Without you I should be nothing. Please say no more. My mind is quite firm. Now wait here for me – I shall be only a little time.'

'But where are you going?'

'I'll tell you later.'

She was going to Brassey's, the chop-house. It was so early that the door was locked. She rang the bell, to be confronted a few moments later by Miss Brassey in a cotton bed-gown and curl-papers beneath a formidable cap. A delicious smell of cooking preparations enveloped Sara as she stepped inside.

'Miss Dell! Well, you're an early caller, and no mistake.'

'I'm very sorry – I hoped not to have disturbed you, Miss Brassey. But I have a favour to ask – a very great favour.'

'Yes?' The only favours that were usually asked of Miss Brassey were connected with credit, and were smartly refused. But Miss Dell was not that sort, she would swear. Proud to pay her way, she'd be.

Sara put down the basket she carried on a table. 'I am going into the country this morning, for a time. Miss Brassey, will you keep my cat for me? Oh, please say you will! She's travelled so far with me, and another journey in this weather will be too much for her – I know it. She does so need a warm house and some comfort, my poor Miranda.'

'Cat?' Miss Brassey was still not quite awake. 'What cat? Is that it, in the basket?'

'Yes.' Sara was undoing the hasps, faint cries coming from within. 'I've taken her everywhere with me since she was a kitten, but it's all at an end now, things are too bad.'

Miss Brassey watched in fascination as Miranda crawled out. Her seal-like sleekness had gone; her fur looked rusty-brown, the bones of her shoulders stood out, and her small face seemed as sharp as a weasel's. As Sara caressed her, she shivered and looked nervously round the room.

'Well,' said Miss Brassey, 'I don't know, I'm sure. We haven't got a cat, that's true. Jack loads the mouse-traps every night and that seems to take care of the little wretches. Looks a bit peaky, don't she.' With increased wakefulness her memory returned. 'That's right, first time Mr Otway brought you, he come back to ask for some scraps for your cat. That was her, then?'

'Yes, and you made her up such a beautiful supper.' Sara's eyes were pleading, as they had pleaded to many a stage tyrant, reducing the pit to tears. It was not in Miss Brassey's heart to resist.

'Well, I'd say, now, as you've made a great favourite out of this cat, more than most folks do that keeps 'em just for the mice. I'd have no time for all that, you know, ma'am, not with our business, up and down to the kitchen and the till to look after and I don't know what else. She'd have to take her chance.'

'I've treated her as a child,' Sara said desperately. 'She was all I had. Perhaps I shouldn't have done it – indeed, I know I shouldn't. It's her one chance, to stay with you. I could think of nobody else – nobody kinder.'

Miranda jumped down from the table, by way of a chair, for there was not much strength in her legs. Weakly she went over to the fire already burning cheerfully, a thick rug before it. She sat down and gazed at the flames, feeling the warmth stealing through her thin fur. The two voices went on behind her; instinct told her what they were saying. Her Mamma was leaving her, and that was regrettable. But the fire was warm here, and the smells delightful, and it was very pleasant to turn towards life again. For Miranda, with a cat's prescience, had already looked into the eyes of death.

'I can't promise to keep her in, o' course,' Miss Brassey was saying. 'But there's a good yard at the back and a pear-tree in it. She'll get plenty to eat, that I *can* promise. Looks like she needs it.' Kneeling, she stroked Miranda's bony spine. 'My mother used to have a cat something like this, I recall now. Yes,' said Miss Brassy meditatively, 'I think I could get quite partial to a cat.'

*

In the back of the wagon Sara and Raymond sat on a pile of sacks, a crate behind them so that sitting was not too uncomfortable. They had passed the top of Highgate Hill; the fog and reek of London was left behind, open prospects of winter landscape expanding before them, dormant fields and lonely cottages, country churches and quiet farms. Raymond's spirits rose, and he turned to Sara to share his pleasure with her. But she sat stony-faced and still, hardly seeming to breathe, unresponsive to the carrier's cheerful shouted tales of highwaymen on Finchley Common and a recent execution at Barnet which had been much enjoyed by all. Raymond sensed that something of her had gone away from him, leaving a blankness colder than the December air.

'No, no, no,' Ivor said. 'Terrible, that was. *Glissade* and *relève en arabesque*, is what you should be doing, not *pas de chat*.'

He was sitting astride a chair, his arms folded along its back, in the coachmaker Daniels' workshop, watching Jannie at her ballet practice. Because there was no room to move freely in the small rooms upstairs, Mr Daniels had kindly allowed them the use of the workshop in the evenings, when his men had gone home. It was cold, badly lighted, the floor littered with coach-parts, and smelt strongly of leather, paint and polish, but it was better than nothing. And they both needed to practise a great deal. Jannie was woefully out of condition after her long absence from dancing, and Ivor had only just summoned the strength to dance again, after his near-fatal illness. Jannie had charmed Tayleur and Fasoli into taking them both back for the Christmas pantomime, for which they rehearsed most of the day, then rested, and spent their evenings in private rehearsal.

'You're as bad as Fasoli,' Jannie said. 'I wonder you don't go and be a ballet-master yourself. Look, there's a nice little whip on the wall – like to cut me round the ankles with it?'

She paused for breath and stood, hands on hips, relaxing, and contemplated Ivor fondly. Youth and good nursing had pulled him through the perilous weeks after his rescue, but he was still thin to the point of emaciation, his face fine-drawn, arrowy, his waist slenderer than Jannie's; the mere ghost of Harlequin. But for all his wraith-like appearance he was now eating and drinking as heartily as a dancer does after a day's hard work. Lucy Sorrel often watched her daughter, at the supper-table, knife and fork suspended, gazing at Ivor demolishing a plate of beef and boiled onions with the look of a nun rapt in a holy vision. Love-struck, thought Lucy, a proper young mooncalf. She was glad she had insisted on his staying with them even after he was well enough to leave. Better to have him in the spare room and Jannie back in the turn-up bedstead, both under her gimlet eye, than him in lodgings and Jannie out at all hours. Not that she was not very fond of the young man herself by this time; there was something about nursing a boy who might have been her son that brought out her softer side. She no longer regarded him as a dangerous Lothario, though she had been deeply shocked by the affair of Mrs Thurloe.

Ivor had been perfectly frank about his intentions towards Jannie. To her parents he said, 'I want to marry her, and I mean to. There's no other girl for me, and no other man for her – at least I hope not. But I must win my own place first – at the top, where I was when . . . before all this trouble. I was brought up poor, and I don't intend to die poor. Now, you know stage folk and their ways – not a penny put by when they're earning, gifts right and left, and before they know it they're old and singing in the streets for money. I want to earn well while I'm young, and save, and live a proper life.'

The Captain nodded, though regretfully. 'Jannie has a little money of her own – could you not both manage on that?'

'I could never live off my wife,' Ivor said proudly. The Captain had no reply ready. He though privately that he himself would have found it rather a pleasant arrangement. Now that Lucy was too crippled to work in the wardrobe, and made only a scanty living from the work they sent her, he had regretfully resigned himself to picking up a few shillings by working, when his chosen race-horses refused to oblige him. For instance, he sometimes acted as a kind of superior potman at the Shades, near London Bridge: a highly respectable tavern housed in a large cellar, under whose vaulted arches patrons could enjoy wines from the wood, unadulterated spirits, and good ales. Officers from merchant ships frequented it, and merchants from the Borough, at first surprised to find themselves served by an affable gentleman of military mien and cultured speech, but drawn gradually into free conversation with him, and occasionally into a game of cards, which he generally won.

It was not a bad line to follow; but it would never have done near home. A man must keep his pride. He respected his future son-in-law's principles.

As for Jannie, she was totally happy for the first time in her life. It was wonderful to dance again, even though she was so rusty and her feet burned and her joints ached, wonderful to live under the same roof as Ivor, knowing them both to be free. There was a kind of pleasurable pain in it, too, though she knew that he was right, and they must wait. She knew his stubborn pride, knew that it hurt to be only a dancer, one of the crowd, after his triumph at the Wells. But it was the only way back. She had worked to get him there, even when he still lay ill. She had used all her powers on Tayleur and Fasoli, even allowing the ballet-master a few freedoms for which she would normally have slapped his face. When they hummed and ha'd about it, she went to Grimaldi and begged him to use his influence.

'What, me?' said Joey. 'I got no influence, darling, I'm only a poor old clown.' He was in one of his despondent moods, 'Grim all dye,' as he punningly expressed it.

She touched his hand. 'If I hadn't gone running to the poor old clown I wouldn't have found Ivor in time, and he'd be dead now. As it is, he's very weak still. If I could give him a promise that they'd have him and me back at the Royalty it would do him so much good!' Her eyes were shining, her hands clasped, and she looked very pretty. Joey gave her a melancholy smile.

'Can't refuse, can I, when you put it like that? All right, then. Gee-who, Neddy.' He clicked to an imaginary horse, the spectral

Neddy he rode on stage, a stool with a broomstick for tail and a horse's skull on a pole-neck. Jannie felt more hopeful. So long as he could joke he could reach other people, and be reached. If his lightened mood kept up he would speak to Tayleur, she knew it.

Even with such a persuader the manager was dubious. 'What guarantee is there that Mr Bryn will be fit to dance in time for rehearsals? If he an't, I shall have all the trouble of engaging another dancer at the last minute.' He knew, and Joey and Jannie knew, that this would present no trouble at all: he could engage a dozen from the hopeful queues of out-of-works that hung round the stage-door at audition time.

'Besides,' he added, 'there's the bad publicity. There've been a few queer stories going round.' He eyed them. 'May be true, may be not. We don't want Talk about the company, do we. In a case like this there's always Talk, after the papers get hold of it.'

Jannie exchanged a look with Grimaldi. Too true, the vultures of the Strand would fall ravenously on the case of Clara Thurloe.

'Oh,' she said airily, 'there won't be any talk. We'll see to that.' Just how was a different matter.

They had never intended anything to come out about the wretched business in Colebrooke Row. Where Tayleur's 'queer stories' had come from was a mystery. In the first horror at seeing Ivor's condition, Jannie had blurted the truth out to the doctor the Captain had fetched from round the corner. Mr Downe was an abrupt Scot who had attended the Sorrels for years, and whom Lucy liked because, she said, there was no nonsense about him. He had no difficulty in diagnosing the cause of his patient's state. Practising as he did in the Covent Garden area, with its teeming population of actors, scribblers, prostitutes, and other professions well-known for their irregular lives, he had come across poisoning cases before.

'Arsenic, the characteristic garlic exhalation,' he pronounced. 'No doubt of it. It's that or mercury, mostly. Would it be self-administered, maybe?'

'No!' Jannie exclaimed indignantly. She told him what had

happened in a tirade to which the Captain added grave confirmations.

'Weel,' said Downe, 'the laddie's been lucky. The doses stopped some time ago, or he'd be dead now. What's brought him to this is extreme malnutrition and exposure to cold.'

'It was deliberate! She starved him because she wanted to get rid of him in case he talked about what she'd done. Then, when she'd killed him, she'd have put him – put his body out in the street to be taken for a beggar.'

'Aye. And where did all this take place?' He wrote down the address and Clara's name, then, closing his notebook, said, 'The woman's a dangerous murderess by intent, of course. She must be reported to the magistrates.'

The Sorrels stared at each other; they had never thought of this. Jannie declared that the doctor was right, that the woman deserved to hang. Her parents argued, horrified at the idea of involvement in such a business.

'It wouldn't do at all to bring the law into it,' said the Captain. 'We got to him in time – now let's make the best of it and get him well again. Eh, doctor? An't that the wisest plan?'

Lucy agreed. 'Once you get into *their* hands there's no knowing what they'll make of it. Twist anything, they can. If that woman lied well enough they'd be saying we tried to do away with him ourselves, or some such rubbish. And then where'd we all be, I ask you?'

The doctor set his lips grimly. 'We'll see. He's not out of the wood yet.'

When Ivor was conscious, and able to speak, Downe told him, in spite of Lucy's protests that he was not well enough, what he proposed to do. Ivor shook his head weakly and murmured something they could not catch.

'What's that?' barked Downe. 'A foreigner, is he?'

'He goes back to Welsh sometimes,' Jannie exclaimed, and to Ivor: 'What did you say, *cariad*?'

'*Gorau doethineb, tewi*,' he repeated, his eyes closed. Then, stirring, 'I . . . forget. Sometimes.'

'Yes, darling, yes. Don't fret about it,' Jannie said, smoothing his damp hair. 'What did you say just now, when the doctor spoke to you?'

'The least . . . said, the better. All my fault. Forget. Let it be.'

The doctor had little patience with ramblings. 'Will you or will you not testify against this woman?'

'No,' said Ivor, and fell asleep.

That same day Downe reported the case to a magistrate. The snowballing processes of the law followed. Constables were sent to arrest Clara, who was conveyed to a magistrate's court, where she made a statement denying everything but that one Bryn had for a time lodged at her house. He was a young man of loose habits. He may very well have taken drugs or poison, she knew nothing of it. A man and woman unknown to her had made a forceful entry to her house, and taken the young man away. She had never knowingly administered poison to any person.

The magistrate was not known for his tender-heartedness or gullibility. His informer, the doctor, had submitted a very detailed account of the affair, including the reason, confided in him by the Sorrel family, why the poison might have been given. Without hesitation he committed the very angry and frightened Clara to Bridewell Prison to await trial at the next Westminster Sessions, which were due to be held in three weeks. The Sorrels, Jannie and Ivor, together with Downe, were subpoenaed as witnesses.

Which was why Jannie and Grimaldi held conference at Long Acre before the trial came on.

'We *have* to keep it as quiet as we can,' Jannie impressed on her parents. 'If it gets into the Press Tayleur will read it, and Dibdin, and they'll never have Ivor back at the Royalty or the Wells.'

'You say,' Joey put in, 'as the constables never asked what he did for a living?'

'No. Only his name and his age. And for some reason he said his name was David – or something like that. He was rambling a bit when they came here, and he always goes back to childhood when he wanders.' She touched wood. 'Though he's over that now, thank God. But that's what they wrote down, David Bryn. I was going to tell them different, but they were in such a hurry.'

'Lucky for you they were. Well, don't you tell 'em different in court, and never mind this here perjury they talks about.'

'Suppose they ask him again?'

'They won't – 'cause he won't be there. He's too ill, incapable, see?'

'But he's much better!'

Joey shrugged. 'Then he'll ha' to be taken bad again. It's the only dodge to get round a subpoena. He won't swear against her, will he?'

'No.'

'Then let him make a statement saying there was nothing in it, and look as pale as ashes while he says so, and if he can't do that natural I'll send round some pomatum. When it comes to the hearing, you know nothing only that this lady had a fancy for him. That'll be all to the good, mark me. They'll know what it means.' Joey, like Mr Downe, had a wide experience of poisons and the curious effects they produced. 'And don't none of you say anything but what you're asked, and not a word about the Royalty or the Wells or dancers, or me, come to that. If it an't presuming too far, I think my name's known a little. And anything that slips out you must talk away later, young lady, which if I'm not mistaken you can do.'

On a murky November day Clara was taken from the grim prison of Bridewell, in Tothill Fields behind Westminster Abbey, to Westminster Hall, the dignified survivor of the old Palace, where nobles and kings had been tried from mediaeval times onwards. She was confused, dirty, underfed, terrified by exposure to the miseries of prison life, only slightly alleviated by the extra comforts she had been able to buy. She hardly remembered what it was all about, what she was supposed to have done. White-faced, bedraggled, she listened, while one piece of evidence after another was produced against her. Mr Downe testified to his patient's desperate state when first seen, the effects of arsenic and starvation, the story the Sorrels had told him. The Captain gave his evidence with a straight back and a fixed eye, an impressive figure in his best coat and a clean stock. Yes, his daughter was the young man's betrothed, and his absence had caused them all some alarm. On information received they had gone to Mrs Thurloe's house and found the young man in the state described.

His wife corroborated this. She admitted that she was late of the Royalty Theatre, which caused a brief stir in the large crowd present, but her age and infirmity were no stimulus to their interest. Jannie, when summoned, described herself as 'widow', and wore the mousiest clothes and the plainest hair-style she could devise, together with a suspicion of make-up which gave her nose-to-mouth lines and a faintly furrowed brow. Nobody thought of her as a dangerous rival to the handsome, haggard woman in the dock.

Mrs Meakins, cook to the prisoner, was called. Yes, she had noticed the mistress visiting the kitchen frequently during the period described. Items may have been added to the food, she really could not say. She admitted that a scullery-maid and the kitchen boy had eaten the remains of several meals sent down from upstairs ('it's common practice, sir') and had complained of pains and sickness. Yes, the young man mentioned had stayed in the house, and Mistress had seemed uncommon sweet on him (laughter in court). As to the attic room and the key she knew nothing, it was not her department.

An officer was brought forward to testify to the old dispensary and its contents. A jar was produced, the contents of which Mr Downe pronounced to be powdered arsenic. Cross-questioned, on the Judge's instructions, he admitted that it was sometimes re-sorted to as an aphrodisiac, though he pooh-poohed the reality of such a claim. At this point the prisoner asked to be allowed to write down another statement, which after a brief adjournment was read out in court. In it she admitted that she had used the powder for just such a reason, hoping to inflame the young man's passion for herself.

The public benches stirred and whispered. Here was an interest-ing element coming into the case. Poison and passion were a delightful pair of reasons for murder, and for a female to be found guilty was an additional excitement. The accused might well turn out to be another Eliza Fenning, who two years earlier had violently denied the crime of poisoning, even on the very scaffold, and had been escorted to her grave by thousands who had cheered for her at the gallows. Would Clara Thurloe provide equal entertainment at Newgate? They wondered, among themselves, who was the swain that had driven her to such measures, and whether he would die during the proceedings, in which case the charge would be murder instead of attempted murder, and they would surely get their money's worth.

The Judge, making notes for his directions to the jury, gazed at the characters concerned over the top of his narrow oval spectacles. As to the prisoner's guilt, he was not certain: women were capable of anything, in his experience, this one no less, with her thick dark eyebrows and desperate look. There was something just a little odd about some of the witnesses. The Sorrel family (for Jannie had suppressed her married name) seemed rather well-drilled for such people, though the father was cut from rather better cloth than the women. They said very little, instead of going off into flights of irrelevance from which they had to be fetched back, as such types usually did. The young woman in particular looked unnatural in a way he could not define; or was it that his spectacles needed changing?

It was time for the prisoner to make her defence. Two officers at her side, she said in a barely-audible voice:

'I plead not guilty, Your Lordship. I did give him the powder, but it was only to make him more affectionate towards me, as my late husband said it would. I lead – led a very lonely life. As to . . . the rest, I was about to call a doctor when these people came and took him away. I . . . I have nothing else to say.'

The Judge cleared his throat, took a sip of water, shifted his wig and polished his spectacles. Then he embarked upon his favourite exercise of addressing the jury.

O woman! lovely woman! Nature made thee
To temper man: we had been brutes without you.

'So said the poet, gentlemen; but let us not be dazzled by such brilliant examples, though there can be no doubt that Nature has endowed the sex with every amiable quality. Yet, in justice be it said, when through temptation of the influence of bad example, the passions of women take on a wrong bias, their effects have been known to be as opposite and malign; for their passions generally go to excess upon emergencies, or trying occasions, by ruining the welfare of the object of their hatred, or disappointment, or by venting their spleen in revengeful acts – these passions, I say, are indiscriminately excited. In the case before us, it may be that . . .'

Twenty-five minutes later he was still talking to a court now mazed with verbiage. The accused was chalk-white and trembling, three of the witnesses almost as nervous. Please God, Jannie was praying, let them not bring her in Guilty. If there's a hanging it will all come out, and Ivor will never get his chance, and it will make him ill again . . . Her father was holding tightly to her hand, his own face nobly expressionless. Lucy was nervously twisting her handkerchief in her gloved fingers.

At last it was ended. He was telling the jury that if they did not think the evidence conclusive of intent to murder, they would in that case find the prisoner not guilty.

A few minutes' conference, heads together, whispering, and the Foreman spoke up.

'Not Guilty, my Lord.'

'Lucky for her,' Jannie said grimly, at home. 'She deserved to be transported, the murdering wretch.'

'I think, my dear,' said the Captain, 'a few weeks in Bridewell will have given the lady a sharp lesson as to what the laws of England allow in the way of administering medicines. She won't do it again.'

In fact, Clara's notoriety made her further residence in Colebrooke Row impossible. Within a few weeks she had left for Barbados, and was never heard of in England more.

Mr Downe was not pleased with the result of the trial. On subsequent visits he spoke very curtly to the Sorrels, believing them to have deliberately obstructed the course of justice for no good reason. It was months before he exchanged a civil word with Jannie, when, meeting her in the street, he remarked, 'A friend of yours has just become the patient of a friend of mine. Ah weel, it's a small world.'

'Oh – who is that?'

When he told her, and described the patient's circumstances, Jannie exclaimed, 'But I must go there, as soon as I can. Oh, poor thing, poor thing!'

CHAPTER FOURTEEN

Crazy Jane

From the hamlet of Hadley, where the carter set them down, Raymond and Sara set out to walk the dozen or so miles that lay between there and Hertford. The day was mild for December, the air damp; grey skies promised rain. At first Raymond took Sara's arm, but before long she shook him off.

'I can walk better alone.'

She hardly spoke, though he longed for her to talk to him, to repeat lines, anything to pass the weary miles. They had walked far in Sussex, but then it had been for pleasure or a change of scene, not, as now, a harsh necessity. When, some time in the afternoon, they reached the village of Essendon, he begged her to stop.

'It will be dark soon. Shall we stop here and travel the rest of the way tomorrow, my dear? You must be as worn as I am, and there are cottages, and an inn . . .'

'No. The engagement may be gone.'

The lanes were pretty enough, but unpaved, cruel to the feet. Raymond hoped constantly for a carrier to catch up with them and offer a lift, but none came, only the solitary rider or a farm-hand on foot. After Essendon the signposts ceased. Sara broke her silence to say that in her opinion they were lost, and Raymond was inclined to agree, but they had no choice: either go on or go back, which was unthinkable.

It was dark when they made out the shape of a church on a hill, and a few lights piercing the gloom. Raymond heard Sara give a deep sigh of relief.

'Hertford at last!' he said. But they soon saw it was no town, only a village, and a passing cottager told them it was Herting-fordbury, and that Hertford itself lay farther on.

When they came at last to the sprawling, ancient town, nestling by its river, they were weary beyond speech. The first inn they reached looked uninviting, but to Raymond it shone like the lights of a great ship to the eyes of a shipwrecked mariner in an open boat. He pushed Sara, unprotesting, through its door, into the blessed warmth and light and sat her down on a bench, where she slumped, her eyes closed. Then he ordered mulled ale for them both, and asked the barman for directions to the Theatre.

'What theatre would that be?'

'Why – I was given no name for it. Only the Theatre, Hertford. I thought it would be well-known.'

The man stared, then laughed. ' 'Tis well known, all right – if theatre you like to call it. Some has other names . . . Turn left when you goes out and you'll see the Swan a few yards up.'

'The Swan? But I understood . . .'

'That's where the theatre is – only one we've got.'

Half-carrying Sara, Raymond stared up at the half-timbered front of the Swan, its sign suspended from the overhanging upper storey.

'This is the place. But a strange one to find a theatre.'

The taproom they entered was busier than the one they had just left. Here the landlord himself was serving, and came forward at the sight of strangers.

'Good evening, sir. The lady not well?'

'A little faint. We have had a long journey.'

'Some refreshment, then, sir. What's your fancy?'

Raymond glanced longingly at the bottles and casks, but answered, 'Later, we shall be very glad. But we are looking for the

manager of the theatre, which I was told I should find here, though
I see no sign . . .'

'The theatre? Oh, that's at the back, sir, through that door, but
there's no play given tonight.'

'No, no – we came only to see the manager, if you could tell me
where he can be found.'

'Mr Sneyd? In the snug, sir, where he usually sits. I'll call him
for you.' He tapped the shoulder of an elderly rustic seated by the
fire. 'Out of that chair, George, and let the lady sit down.'

Mr Sneyd proved to be shortish, plump and pale, and to be
suffering from a permanent bad cold. Hurriedly Raymond unfolded to him their hopes, the bill glimpsed in London, the bad
health which had kept them from an engagement in town (it was
an acceptable excuse), their long experience and anxiety to play in
Hertford.

'If the engagement for a walking lady and gentleman is not
filled, we, my dear wife and I, would be most obliged to be considered . . .'

Mr Sneyd blew his nose. 'Oh, by all beads. Glad to have you.
Dot buch talent id this area. Cobe and see de theatre.'

Immensely relieved, Raymond helped Sara to her feet. They
followed Sneyd through the bar, through a door and a passage to
another door with a sign over it. He threw it open. 'There,' he
said, 'dice, isn't it.'

They were in a room which would perhaps hold fifty people,
packed pretty tight. A candle burned in a tin socket on the wall.
Sneyd eyed it reprovingly. 'Shouldn't have left that, might burd
the place dowd. But it will do to show you.'

Round the room there were candles (they were the smallest
size, costing a penny), and from the centre to the end wall plain
benches provided pit, boxes and gallery all in one. The stage was
a low deal platform, its curtain an old piece of sailcloth sewn on to
rings and evidently meant to be pulled aside by one person's hand,
as Sneyd now demonstrated. Two rough flats represented the
front wings, the back ones being completely absent, and a screen
masked the exit from one side to a door at the back.

'That leads to the dressing-rooms, I suppose,' said Sara faintly, pointing to the door.

'Oh do, badab, dose *are* de dressig-roobs. For the gentlebed. Fine of sixpence for ady gentlebad taking adother's small-clothes. Ladies dress behind de curtaid. All perfectly proper.'

'The orchestra?' Sara asked faintly.

'At de side, od de floor. Plenty of roob.' Here Mr Sneyd gave a fearful sneeze, at which the penny candles wavered visibly.

The forlorn visitors stood gazing at the prospect before them. It was all too clear that they had come to one of those ultra-cheap fit-up theatres still to be found in remote places, and not very far removed in resources from the inn-yard stages of mediaeval days. They had heard of, but never played in one.

Sneyd, even through his handkerchief, sensed their dismay.

'It don't signify being in an ale-house. Dey like it, draws custob, you see. De audience, when it cobes id, is cheerful and lively frob having stopped id de bar. Makes everybody happy that way. Good people, very fond of de draba.'

Raymond mustered courage to ask the important question. 'What salary are you offering, sir?'

Sneyd gave a long, painful sniff. 'Ted shillings. Each. With a bedifit, of course.'

The Otways turned to each other, exchanged looks, then words. 'Less than Hallsfield,' Raymond said quietly. 'And we had help there.'

'We must take it.'

He turned to Sneyd. 'Would there be any kind of arrangement for our lodging? Someone who might take us in, not too expensively? The salary is not quite what we expected. Anything respectable, but *not* expensive . . .'

The manager shrugged. 'The landlord bight know.'

Raymond was aware of Sara's nails biting into his wrist as she willed him to clinch the deal; he knew that she was terrified of the roads and the dark night.

'In that case,' he said graciously, 'we shall be pleased to close with you, sir. What piece are you presenting at present?'

'Oh, adything,' Sneyd replied airily. 'Up to you. Guest stars take their choice. We go up toborrow at seved.'

'But . . .' Sara said, and stopped. Stars? What had become of 'walking lady and gentlemen'? 'But if we chose a piece your company don't know? How would there be time to rehearse?'

'Oh, we don't rehearse, de company an't free. Other lides, lides of business, that is. Just pick what you like.'

Before Raymond could make a suggestion, Sara said, '*Antony and Cleopatra*. We played it with great effect in Dublin, if you recall, my dear? I've always fancied returning to it, and now comes the opportunity – and the perfect setting. Royal Egypt! Empress! The crown o' the earth doth melt!' She gave a wild laugh.

Raymond pulled at her sleeve. 'Hush!' But Mr Sneyd's face was again buried in his handkerchief, and he was oblivious to any strangeness in his guest artist's manner. When he emerged he agreed, to Raymond's surprise, that *Antony* would do very well.

The landlord of the Swan found them a room for the night, with a promise of something more permanent later on; five shillings of their precious savings gone, but they were weary beyond bearing and must sleep.

Whatever they may have feared proved all too true when they gathered to prepare for the play. The ragged bunch of assorted players dressing on the narrow stage resembled nothing either had seen during a long career. The 'other lines of business' mentioned by Sneyd were all too obvious. A tall, gangling, red-haired Irishman had Tinker written all over him, a plump painted woman with dirty hair clearly came from whatever stews Hertford might contain; a rheumy old man, trembling with age, being helped into his costume by a boy, proved to be Mr Sneyd's grandfather. A few men of assorted shapes and sizes, with strong local accents, were shop assistants and clerks who sought the excitement of the drama at night.

'Falstaff's ragged army was nothing to this,' Raymond murmured to Sara, who was holding up a costume made from sacking with tinfoil sewn all over it, which had been handed to her as

233

suitable apparel for the Queen of Egypt.

'This thing is filthy,' she said flatly.

Raymond pointed to the old sheet which was to do duty for Antony's toga. 'Mine has seen better days – but not much soap and water.' Ruefully he regarded his cloak, which had started life as somebody's red flannel petticoat. One or two of the other men had sheet-togas as well, but the rest of the company preferred the simple dignity of their own clothes, from pantaloons to dirty neck-cloths. The London pair saw, with horrified realization, that each one held a battered copy of Shakespeare. Rehearsals were unnecessary because the so-called performances were in fact readings.

A few people had straggled in and were huddled in the front seats, bottles in their pockets and food-stuffs in their hands. At least audiences could be relied on to run true to type.

The overture was beginning: a jig played by a man with a three-stringed fiddle. Sara and Raymond, lurking behind their respective wings, exchanged a long look of misery. Not resignation: they would never be resigned to this.

When they had staggered through the nightmare evening, to scanty applause, they were more exhausted than either had ever been before. Even holding the book, their colleagues had done everything wrong that could be done wrong. The part-time prostitute who played both Charmian and Iras had taken a jealous dislike to Sara's fine voice and grand manner, and had upstaged her royal mistress wherever possible or thrown her on her lines. Raymond had fared little better, his Enobarbus, Grandfather Sneyd, proving to be hopelessly deaf, while the boy who played Caesar and Messenger was going through that phase of boyhood when the voice is alternately a squeak and a growl. Now that the rough curtain had been drawn, and those who had worn costumes were scrabbling back into their own clothes, a fight had broken out between two apprentices, Mr Sneyd, between sneezes, was haranguing Pompey, the butcher's corpulent son, and the Irishman was sitting on the floor waving a bottle of which he had already drunk most of the contents, and singing:

Bould Robert Emmet, the darleeng av Oireland,
Bould Robert Emmet, he doied weeth a smoile . . .

In the cold little room over a stable, which was all the landlord
could offer by way of lodgings, Sara was scrubbing frantically at
her skin, stripped to the waist, with the cold water in a basin they
had to ask for.

'I am *dirty*,' she said, over and over. 'The smell of that filthy
cloth is on me. I shall never be clean again, never.'

Raymond looked on helplessly. He too felt dirty and degraded,
and afraid, for Sara, the calm and motherly and strong, was turning into someone for whose fortunes he must now be responsible,
and he dreaded his own weakness. When they were at last in the
cold, narrow bed, he asked her, 'Do you want to go back?'

She was staring up at the raftered ceiling.

'No.'

'We could just afford it – the coach journey – with what we have
left. This place is hell. Why should we not go back?'

'Because there's nothing left . . .' Conversationally she added,
'I wanted my mirror tonight. It was the first time without it.'

'Your mirror? But you always travel with it. What became . . .?'

'I pawned it. The morning we left.'

He tightened his arm around her. 'My dear, my dear. I didn't
know. But we can redeem it, when we get some money, and – you
can have Miranda back, once we're in town. Everything will be
better then.'

'I shall never see Miranda again,' she said. 'How can she live
without me, or I without her?'

The next day Raymond caught and brought to her a young cat
from the stables, a rough-haired little tabby, the only one of several that had responded to his blandishments. 'You could train
this,' he said hopefully. 'It's a pretty little creature, and it needs
someone to care for it.' But she looked at the cat as if she hardly
saw it, gave it a perfunctory stroke, and turned away.

The week went on, and another, and another. The Swan company attempted no more heavy drama, presenting such hack pieces as *The Provok'd Husband*, *The Day after the Wedding*, *The Castle Spectre*, and *The Miller and his Men*. If Sara did not already know the part she learned it, with professional speed and skill; otherwise she remained silent and withdrawn from Raymond. He walked by himself in and around the town, by the river Lea, in the grounds of the Castle ruins, past Christ's Hospital school with its figures of bluecoat boys and girls, his mind never quiet. Should he shake Sara, speak to her roughly? He had no experience of managing women – they had always managed him. Perhaps if he were to book places on a coach, and rush her forcibly away from the accursed Swan . . . But when they got to London, what then?

In the third week of their engagement he returned to their stable lodging from one of his long, puzzled walks, to find her lying on the bed, looking at nothing. When he spoke to her and touched her shoulder she jerked away from him. He turned her over, feeling her stiff resistance. Her face was blank, the face of a stranger; no smile, no light in her eyes.

'Time to dress, Sara,' he said gently.

She got up without a word and followed him. On the stage the cast were gathered, in their various tatters of finery, and the fiddler was playing his jig for the third time. From the audience came mutters and whistles.

'Cobe od, cobe od!' Sneyd said impatiently, hustling Raymond on and thrusting a cloak and hat at him. 'You too, Missus. Devilish late, an't you?'

Sara was to open the comedy, 'discovered, reading a Letter'. Seeing her make no move to put on the old-fashioned sacque dress worn by the character, Mrs Sneyd snatched it up and thrust her into it, hastily fastening enough buttons to hold it together.

'Now then, wake up, dear, wake up! In a doze, were you? There, take your prop.' Sara's fingers closed round it, but she remained up-stage, seeming not to know her next move, until Mrs Sneyd pushed her forward and gave the signal for the curtain to be drawn. A ragged clap went up from the audience of ten or a dozen people.

Instead of speaking her opening lines, Sara bowed and smiled to them, assumed an attitude, and glanced towards the fiddler, who was packing up his instrument.

'Get *on*!' Mrs Sneyd urged from the wings. ' "What is here? A letter from my cousin in the country?" '

Sara ignored the prompt. With clasped hands and her gaze fixed on the back of the room she began to sing.

> Why, fair Maid, in every feature
> Are such signs of fear express'd?
> Can a wandering wretched creature
> With such terror fill thy breast?

'Come off!' Mrs Sneyd's desperate whisper went unheeded. Raymond, listening behind the screen, was cold with horror as the singing went on.

> Do my frenzied looks alarm thee?
> Trust me, Sweet, thy fears are vain;
> Not for kingdoms would I harm thee –
> Shun not then poor Crazy Jane.

Both Sneyds were at her side, urging her off, amid catcalls, boos and missiles from the audience. Sara looked in bewilderment from one to the other.

'But there must be a song, you know! They always expect it, always . . .'

A May breeze tore at the ribbons of Jannie's gipsy bonnet, threatening the little wreath of red and white flowers that perched on the crown of it, and whisked up the short skirt of her blue gown to show a vista of shapely calves in white cotton stockings. Her cheeks were like the roses on the flower-stall where she and Mr

Downe had met; the doctor, misogynist though he was, felt a little sorry that his news had brought dismay to such a pretty face.

'Mad?' Jannie repeated. 'Miss Dell? Oh no, it can't be true.'

'I assure you it is, ma'am. A colleague of mine, an Edinburgh man like myself, has her in the care of friends who look after such cases. It seems she suffered a brainstorm while performing in some country theatre, and was taken by him from Hertford to Highgate, where she could be cared for in private. Just as well for her she was not stricken in London, or it would have been Bedlam for her.'

'*Bedlam*? That shocking place?' She thought of Sir Patrick. 'But they don't put respectable people there, surely, doctor?'

Downe shrugged. 'What else is to be done with the insane? If the King himself can't be cured . . . To my thinking your friend's been uncommonly lucky. It was her husband, it seems, who pressed to get her into a private place, and pays for her keep there.'

'Her . . .?' Jannie thought quickly. Mr Otway, of course. 'But . . . is he still acting?'

'I couldn't tell you, ma'am. I know very little about the case, only what McAndrew told me, knowing I'd many players and such on my books.'

'Poor thing, poor thing. I must go to her as soon as I can. If you could give me the direction, doctor.'

He gave it, slightly unwilling to have been drawn into discussing a patient, even though someone else's, with this young woman of whom he could not approve. 'I can't say what ye'll find, or whether the lady can be seen at all.'

Jannie, dismounting from the gig the Captain had hired to take them to Highgate, was troubled by doubt and uncertainty. What if Sara were a raving maniac? She had never seen a truly mad person, only the poor creatures who wandered about talking to themselves, or made parcels of their persons with newspaper and sat rocking to and fro on public benches. Standing at the green-painted door of the large four-square house, bow-windowed and ancient, just off the main street of the almost rustic village, she felt a very strong disposition to get back into the gig and drive down Highgate Hill again. Then she told herself not to be such a coward. In any case she had her father's company, and he appeared perfectly cheerful. She drew a deep breath and pulled the brass bell.

A small, exceedingly neat and clean maid opened the door. She was dressed all in grey, with a wide white collar and a white winged cap.

'Good day to thee, friend,' she said, without a curtsey, but smiling pleasantly. 'Thee is to come in.'

Somewhat startled, Jannie obeyed, stealing a glance at her father, who had swept off his hat and made a fine military bow. The girl led them into a room handsomely furnished in the most severe of taste, where at a writing-desk sat a woman dressed exactly in the same fashion as the maid, but that her gown was of grey corded silk. By a window stood another, so like her that they must be sisters, high-nosed and strong-featured, with dark eyes under heavy dark brows, softened by a kindliness of expression and a smiling look to the mouth. The seated woman rose.

'Friend Janetta, is it not?'

Jannie stammered that it was, and introduced her father.

'Thee is very welcome, friend, and thy parent. Sister Dorcas and I rejoice to see thee.' Taking pity on Jannie's puzzled face, she added, 'We are of the Quaker persuasion, thee must know.'

'Indeed, ma'am.' She had wondered for a moment if they might be nuns, and was relieved to find it was not so, for confused notions of the fires of Smithfield and walled-up bodies had been impressed on her by her mother at an early age. Seated between Miss Bridget and Miss Dorcas Hewitt she felt like a very gaudy, even vulgar bird of bright plumage between two doves, but soon found herself chattering away naturally enough, with the Captain putting in the odd word now and then – to reassure her, she knew, for the two ladies said very little, but sat faintly smiling, calmly listening. Jannie remembered that people said the Society of Friends was opposed to war, to the dictates of the Established Church, and, oh heavens, to playhouses. What must they think of her? But then they had taken in Sara.

Miss Bridget was asking her, 'Thee would like to see friend Sara, would thee not?'

'Oh, if you please.'

'Thy father may remain and talk with Sister Dorcas.'

'Charmed, enchanted, ma'am.' The Captain leapt to his feet and stood to attention as Miss Bridget led Jannie out. She wondered what they could possibly talk about, but decided that her father's tact and élan were equal to anything.

On the way upstairs she asked timidly, 'Is she . . . very troubled in her mind?'

'Thee need not fear. There is no violence in her.'

Miss Bridget opened a door on the first landing. A pretty, bright room met Jannie's eyes, soft-coloured and feminine; a copper vase of mixed flowers caught the sunshine on the broad window-sill, more flowers filled the fire-grate. The room smelt of roses and lavender. Evidently the sisters did not apply their own ascetic rules to their charges.

Sara sat by the window in a rocking-chair. As she turned her head Jannie saw that under the lace cap the once-fair hair was quite grey. The face was just as she remembered, but now wore a childish sweet blankness. Jannie hesitated. 'Go to her,' Miss Bridget said.

Approaching Sara, Jannie took up one of the small pale hands; it was quite limp and cool in hers. 'Dear Miss Dell – Mrs Otway,' she said. 'I am so happy to see you again.' She thought that a puzzled look came into Sara's eyes for a moment, then it was gone.

'She will not know thee, I fear. We had hoped she might. She hears us and does what we say very meekly, but that is all. Others can find no way to her.'

'Even Mr Otway?'

Miss Bridget shook her head. How it must hurt him, Jannie thought.

'Does he lodge here?' she asked.

'No, that would not be fitting, in a house of females. He has a room nearby, with good people.'

'And does he . . .' Jannie steered round any mention of play-acting. 'Has he found work?'

'Happily, yes. He is employed as clerk in a counting-house, in Finsbury. A firm of India merchants, Friends, like ourselves.'

Jannie gasped. That conspicuous, dramatic figure, 'Actor' written all over him, stooped over a ledger scratching away with a pen?

'Is he – contented with that work?' she asked.

'I believe he is,' replied Miss Bridget placidly. 'It is not his chosen calling, we know as well as thee, but he should do well at it, being honest, sober and industrious.'

Jannie noticed a slight emphasis on 'sober', and Miss Bridget saw that she had noticed it. 'Friend Otway was given to strong drink, he has told us, but that is now past. Sometimes it is hard to see how an affliction such as this,' nodding towards Sara, 'can work in some way for good. It may even be so for her. The things that troubled her are gone; she remembers nothing, and that is a blessing. Think of her ailment not as madness, but as a kind of sleep sent to give rest to her mind.'

'Yes. Yes, that's a beautiful way of looking at it.' Jannie bent and kissed Sara's brow, getting a glimmer of a smile in return. Then Miss Bridget led her from the room.

She visited Sara every week thereafter, always alone. She asked Ivor to go with her, after the first few times, but with a man's distaste for illness he refused.

'What good would it do? If she don't recognize you, how would she know me? I doubt she's seen me out of costume more than three times.'

'No. But the sisters say any pleasing reminders of her past days can only be good for her. At least she'd see in you a friendly face. *Won't* you?'

'*Cariad*, I would do almost anything for you. If I must, I will.' He heaved a theatrical sigh.

'No, of course there's no must about it. I'll think of something else, never fear. Besides, you have rehearsals.'

He brightened. 'So I have. You, too. Why do we talk of going visiting?'

Indeed, it was all to him, and much to her, that Sadler's Wells was reopening with a pantomime in July. Encouraged by the success of pantomimes with an Eastern setting, showing Grimaldi in fantastic Chinese or Egyptian transformations, they had settled upon a theme from the *Arabian Nights' Entertainments*, exotic tales known to Europe only in French, but translated recently by an enterprising librettist. The stories were full of romantic situations, sometimes more than a little daring, full of possibilities for conjuring, transformations and spectacular sets and costumes. The new pantomime was to be *Harlequin Prince Camaralzaman*, the fable of a king's son from the Isles of the Children of Khaledan, and the Princess Badoura of China. There was a novelty to the production: Harlequin and Columbine were to represent the persons of the front-piece, acting and speaking, with a long Transformation Scene to enable them to change into their pantomime characters. A trusting management, hoping to build on Ivor's past successes, had engaged him as Harlequin. And Jannie, on the strength of her dancing in the Royalty's Christmas *Mother Goose*, was to be Columbine to Ivor's Harlequin. It had been the dream of her life; now she was to realize it and her joy was great.

'Not,' said Ivor, studying the costume sketches, 'that we shall need all that time for changing. It seems to me we shall be wearing very little, look you.' He passed over to her a drawing of the Prince in a brief robe belted by a cummerbund, the Princess in an even sketchier gown of gauze with a couple of jewelled breastplates. Jannie studied it.

'If they're expecting me to dance barefoot they'll be disappointed,' she said. 'The idea! It would be the ruin of one's feet for ever. And I don't know what Ma will say to the costume, I'm sure.'

They exchanged rueful glances. Lucy Sorrel's chaperonage of her daughter became fiercer as time went on. If they spent a moment alone together in the Long Acre rooms it was an accident, and Jannie had had to quarrel with Lucy to prevent the maid Susan being sent to and from the theatre with her.

'If I'm going to go wrong, Ma, I'll do it my own way! Ivor and

I are promised, and there's not the least need to watch me like you do. I've been a married woman, haven't I, for what it was worth? Well, then, let me alone.'

'Promised you may be, but there's such a thing as piecrusts. And there's many a slip, let me remind you. I've heard of other young women that one's had his eye on. Oh, he's a good boy as they go, by all appearances, but you never can tell, and there was that shocking affair of the widow. Now, how did he get into that business? Oh, you may scowl at me, my girl, but it's only for your good, and sitting here day and night as I do, I can't help but think.'

'Yes, well, you'd do better to get on with your sewing, Ma, and let the Devil look after his own. After all, what have you to grumble about? The Captain married you, didn't he, and stood by you?' Then she was ashamed of herself for speaking so. But her mother answered quietly, 'I hope your intended may do the same, I'm sure.'

Jannie knelt at her side and embraced her. 'I'm sorry, Ma! I don't know what's come over me. It must be the worry of learning lines.'

She knew it was more than that. The young ladies of the ballet were a remarkably attractive lot, chosen by a manager with an eye for beauty. The Benevolent Agent was not, as so often, played by an older female, but by a young lady calling herself Dorinda St Clair (in fact she had started life as Dora Clegg), an English rose of blond blue-eyed prettiness, perfectly cast as the Fairy Maimoune, whose admiration for Prince Camaralzaman set off the complicated pattern of the plot. It was natural enough that the Fairy and the Prince should rehearse together whenever they could; but need she cast so many sidelong glances at him from those china-blue orbs, or throw quite such enthusiasm into discovering him asleep and rhapsodizing over his beauty? Ivor certainly enjoyed it: few men would not. Jannie thought of the unsatisfactory life they led in her parents' rooms, so near and yet so far, the snatched embraces, moments of desperate temptation, and, in between, the longing and the wakeful nights. It was so cruel that they should not possess each other. Once or twice she had tried to insist, when the house was empty but for them. But Ivor had gently pushed her out of his arms.

'It will be, in its own time. Don't force Fate, *cariad*.'

She was mutinous. 'You don't want me, that's clear.'

He said almost angrily, 'If anything's clear it is that I *do* want you. But don't you see that we must work now, not spend ourselves making love – charming though it would be. Once we let our thoughts wander we shall dance badly. Oh, Jannie, don't torment me . . .'

She knew he was right. But she could not help being unreasonable; wondering, sometimes, whether her charms were perhaps growing thin with familiarity. She began to fancy coldnesses on Ivor's part, neglect of her, Princess Badoura in the front-piece, for the tiresome Fairy who popped up with a reassuring speech whenever Fate turned too sharply against the Prince and Princess.

Grimaldi, the evil genie Dauhasch, saw her jealous concern.

'Don't you fret yourself,' he told her. 'Never you mind about fairies. Just you think about Columbine. She's what matters, she is.'

CHAPTER FIFTEEN
The Isles of Ebony

In spite of the heat of the July night, Sadler's Wells Theatre was full to capacity. Seventy-two large candles burned in twelve chandeliers, more heat streamed from the floats, even more exuded from the close-packed spectators, smart bonnet jostling milkmaid's cap, waving feathers brushing against the greasy locks of artisans, old-fashioned scratch wigs removed for comfort and placed on their owners' knees. The whole house was a-flutter with fans, conversation buzzed and bottles popped. It might have been a social gathering that had chosen a theatre for its arena, but for the brave efforts of the orchestra, almost drowned by rival noises.

Then, as the last notes of the overture died away, the crimson curtain began to rise, and the uproar of the audience subsided into oohs and ahs. For they were looking on a triumph of the scene-painter's art, the Gorgeous East captured and parcelled and unwrapped for them in the north of London. Against a painted sky of burning blue, palm-trees arched their graceful fronds, distant brown mountains reared, snow-white minarets and towers loomed, tiny Arabian dwellings crouched beneath them; and far, far off, so clever was this scene-painter, a shining river encircled the whole landscape; one might without too much difficulty see crocodiles basking in it.

And the ladies of the ballet, ranged so alluringly in Eastern attitudes, their muslin dresses enriched with bright scarves, little head-dresses of gauze weighted with gilt coins, wide bands of embroidery confining their slender waists, bracelets on their wrists, metal rings hung with tiny bells on their ankles – what could be more deliciously foreign? It was fortunate that the audience could not have heard the remarks of the young ladies at being expected to dance thus fettered. But dance they did, with much arm-waving and undulating, only pausing to sing of their ruler, King Schahzaman of the Islands, and his only son Prince Camaralzaman, as yet unmarried, to his father's disappointment. After some pensive reflections on this situation, the ladies danced off, anklets tinkling. No sooner were they gone than, centre-stage, a sudden explosion of pink smoke caused the audience to start and gasp, and from it appeared Miss Dorinda St Clair, with her blonde hair down and tin stars in it, a vision of fairy loveliness, even to her little rainbow wings and uncommonly short skirt. To trembling violin music she informed them:

> The Fairy Maimoune you behold in me,
> The goddess of these islands, fair and free.
> Free when the moon shines, that is: truth to tell,
> By day I must reside – well, in a well,
> (*Well* in.) But when the night falls, out I skip,
> And round the King's great palace make a trip.

First must I to that lonely ancient tower,
Where, in soft slumber, lies the very flower
Of manly beauty – vie with him who can?
I mean, of course, Prince Camaralzaman.
Come shades, come shadows, come, Arabian moon:
Look on this sight, young ladies, and then – swoon.

Behind her, the backcloth of mountains, towers, and river had vanished. In its place was the ornate interior of a Moorish tower, high pointed windows outlined against a now darkened sky in which a huge moon shone. And within it, on a couch piled with many-coloured cushions, lay Ivor.

The ladies in the house, young and older, did not go so far as to swoon, which would have been a sad waste of their time and money, but peered closely and admiringly at the figure disposed on the couch. His costume was not as scanty as he had expected – was, indeed, quite decent, a loose sashed tunic over brown fleshings. It was the colour of beetles' wings, dark green shading to lighter green and mid-blue, as the light took it, and made of taffeta, or shot silk. A turban of paler shades was twisted round his head; on his feet were gold Persian slippers. His face and hands were tinted a light brown, and his brows darkened. He was the complete young Prince from that French translation of *The Thousand and One Nights* which the librettist of the pantomime had carefully studied before throwing it away and writing his own doggerel.

Maimoune had scarcely begun to eulogize his attractions before a flash of green fire caused shrieks from the audience. As it died down a grotesque figure something between an Arabian eunuch, a negro slave, and a knife-grinder girded with his own wares materialized from the smoke. Its face was black, its hair was brilliant green striped with purple, its mouth was enormous and red: it was Grimaldi.

Fairy, avaunt! Your claims I'll smash and dash.
Behold the powerful genie, black Dauhasch!

At this green lights flickered on and off, and there were general boos.

> This callow youth's a dishcloth to the girl
> *I've* just beheld – now, Madam, there's a pearl!

> In far-off China is she domiciled,
> Reared by her parent, from a very child
> To wed, forsooth, a whiskered Mandarin.
> But that she won't. So now, a tower she's in
> Much like to this. 'Tis true, I'll not deceive you.

Maimoune bridled.

> Dauhasch, foul fiend, I'm hanged if I believe you!
> My Prince in grace and beauty sure doth shine a
> Far brighter star than any seen in China.

Dauhasch regarded first the fairy, then the audience, with a countenance which gradually assumed an inexpressible look moving through phases of incredulity, wrath, stupidity, dawning cunning, and final triumph.

> If so you think, then let me tell you, you're a
> Liar, false Fay! Behold – Princess Badoura!

With a skip and a bound he was at the wings, leading on someone by the hand. She moved slowly, driftingly, her eyes half-closed, her face languid; it was easy to see she was sleep-walking. If Badoura were indeed a Princess of China, there was nothing particular to show for it, but for the tiny silver bells on her tunic and slippers. White flowers were scattered in her loose ringlets, and the twin breastplates glittered with points of many-coloured light. An irrepressible cheer broke from some gallant male members of the audience; Dauhasch bowed to them, with a smirk, and disposed his fair charge on cushions beside the Prince.

To and fro the fairy and the genie argued about the respective beauties of their claimants, until Maimoune exclaimed:

> Since we can't judge, thus let it be decided.
> You waken one, I t'other; we'll be guided
> By which most praises which. Is that not fair?

> Fair enough, for a Fairy, I declare.

Saying which, Dauhasch waved his large hands over the Prince's head. Slowly, sleepily, Camaralzaman sat up, rubbing his eyes; appeared not to see the supernaturals hovering near, but fixed his eyes on the sleeping lady. He said nothing, but hovered over her, wonderingly touched her hair, her eyelids; stood back and admired her face, while a gentle tune was played on the flute. Now tired of doggerel, the house watched raptly the grace of his movements, the long eloquent hands, the fine-boned face; surely this was an Arabian Prince indeed. At last he took a sparkling ring from his finger, and put it on hers, sketched the lightest of kisses on her lips, and, as if dazed, returned to his couch and once more fell asleep.

Now Maimoune awakened Badoura. In contrast to the boy's languor, the girl was all excited joy. She knelt at his side, clasped her hands in admiration: he was a fallen star, she the lucky finder. He was Ulysses on the seashore, she Nausicaa; all happy discoveries of love were in her looks and gestures. She saw his ring, kissed it, and placed one of hers on his finger; then bending tenderly over him, folded him in a close embrace and laid on his mouth a long, heartfelt kiss – so long that there were murmurs of surprise and some disapproval from spectators. 'La – the bold thing!' They were not used to seeing such frank expressions of passion on their stage, particularly in pantomime. But it was done with such innocence and sweetness that nobody hissed, any more than they would have hissed Juliet.

Charles Dibdin, who had wandered from his managerial box to the back of the theatre, looking at the show from all angles, began to feel slightly confused. Miss Sorrel had certainly not given this performance before – it was a shade outrageous, but very effective, certainly – and it brought back to his memory a pert, anxious young woman who had come pestering him last year about Ivor Bryn's whereabouts. He scratched his head, elaborately curled à la Brutus. Surely it was the same; but *she* had been called Mrs Fitz-Something. *Could* the two persons be the same? If so, Mrs Fitz-Something had found Bryn all right, and was uncommonly pleased about it, judging by the enthusiastic way she was cuddling him. Dibdin abandoned speculation. The scene was changing to the Court of the King of China, and he was anxious to see what the Procession of Mandarins looked like from the front.

Ivor leant against a batten in the gloom of the back wings. Prince Camaralzaman was temporarily out of action during a twist of plot in which a magic talisman had been lost, and was at that moment being energetically sought by a number of dancers in a stage forest, through which brilliantly-coloured birds flitted, operated on sticks by unseen hands, while a soprano warbled, 'Come, pretty bird, and sing to me, Here no danger shall you see.'

He was glad to be off, briefly relieved of the strain of acting without dancing, and especially of speaking on stage for the first time. Jannie had worked on him without ceasing, remembering points from her own voice-training, and he had profited, helped by the good acoustics of the Wells and the fact that his lines had been kept to a minimum. His Welsh accent worried him most, for he still had it, even after years in England, but it came out far more strongly in conversation than in stage speeches. True, there had been a titter or two at first, and he had heard 'Taffy!' and 'Shenkin!' called, but after that they had accepted him; perhaps it helped to emphasize Camaralzaman's foreignness.

He flexed his muscles, and wished he could go away and practise. Above all he wanted to be fit for the Harlequinade. Mentally he went over the arrangements. Before the last scene of the front-piece he was to be off long enough to change into his Harlequin's dress, then covered completely in an enveloping golden cloak with a jewelled headdress, for the final scene in which Camaralzaman is reunited with Badoura, only to find that she has confusingly assumed his own identity and is ruling the Isles of Ebony as king, even more confusingly 'married' to another Princess. In the Transformation Scene, under cover of the 'Midnight in Arabia' effect which was the management's pride and joy, his dresser Pratt would whisk off the cloak and headdress and hand him bat, cap and mask, while Jannie's was removing her royal robe to reveal herself as Columbine. Then there was a *pas de deux*, before Clown (who had been Dauhasch) . . .

He was distracted by a presence beside him, an arm gently linked through his own. No light was needed to tell him who it was. Dorinda's perfume, a strong blend of musk and violet, challenged the combined forces of gas-floats, audience odours, size, carpentry and sweat, and won hands down.

'All right then, Ivor?'

'Yes,' he said shortly.

'Don't sound it. Anything I can do to help?'

'I said, I'm all right. Run away, Dora, there's a good girl. I must be quiet, see.'

He knew she was pouting in the darkness. 'You're always wanting to be quiet. I thought you Harlequins was the same off stage, all larks.'

'Funny lot we'd be if we were, wouldn't we?' Silently he cursed, for she haunted him like this, a pretty, dollish, powerfully-scented shadow, always trying to be alone with him, and just at the moment she had that advantage. She was whispering something which he could not hear because of the gauze turban. Sighing, he pushed it aside, and her breath was warm on his ear.

'I said what a waste, alone like this, and another ten minutes to go.' She pressed closely against him, soft, insinuating. A second later, and he felt her lips against his neck, just below his ear; a spot in which he was particularly vulnerable to caresses, but this was of all moments the one when they were not welcome. She sensed his response, unwilling though it was, and before he could resist she had taken his hand and placed it in a warm, soft, seductive place. For young male flesh and blood it was almost too much; instinct pulled at him to yield, but sheer anger at the unfairness of the attack came to his help and forced the hand back into his possession.

'*Diawl!*' he said savagely under his breath. 'Do you want to ruin me, then?' He glanced down into the orchestra pit, and toyed longingly with the thought of tossing her down among the bent powdered heads and the fiddle-strings. She was clinging like a leech. If he threw her off there might be some awful crash which would attract attention. Then, out of the corner of his eye, he was thankful to see someone behind them, a black figure with its half-mask pulled up above the great red painted mouth. With an effort he pushed Dorinda off, sending her lurching against a flat, and turned.

'Joey!' he whispered. 'For God's sake, stay with me.'

'Got the rats?' Grimaldi enquired. 'So've I. Rum stuff, this piece, ain't it; I don't think it'll take. Ah, I see you've company – no friend like a fairy.' So saying, he gave Dorinda's small plump bottom a fearsome pinch, at which she turned and slapped his cheek soundly – a slap which missed fire because it caught the half-mask and merely hurt her fingers. With a gasp of anger, she darted away into the shadows, where a knot of other dancers were gathering. Joey laid a fatherly hand on Ivor's shoulder.

'Red pepper to the ladies, an't you, boyo. What we going to do with you?' Gently musing, he embarked in an undertone on a reminiscence about a tomcat, which made Ivor shake with silent laughter so much that he too was forced to move further from the stage.

The action had by now moved to the Isles of Ebony, and the audience was being treated to a last burst of song before the true business of the evening began. A comic sailor regaled the company with the ballad 'When last in the *Dreadful* your Honour set sail,' and a blacked-up attendant at Badoura's court rendered one of the ever-popular negro laments, also by Dibdin the Elder. The management liked to include as many of its own products as it could. Ivor wished they would hurry and get on with it. He could see Jannie's tenseness, perched on her jewelled throne, waiting for the moment when the stage lights would go down. He began to break into a light sweat, wondering if he would be able to repeat his glories of the previous summer; if some blundering stage-hand would fail to catch him when he jumped through the leap-trap; if J.S. would take it into his head to play one of the stupid jokes he sometimes indulged in, to his father's distress. Sometimes he had thought the boy smelt of gin . . .

Then it was his last entrance, to confront his lost Badoura and find their problem still unsolved and their union as far off as ever. Regally he swept on and with thankfulness uttered the last lines he was called upon to speak. The moment came at last. The stage darkened, wheels turned, scenery was noisily shifted under cover of the orchestra's playing, men rushed from one side to the other while dancers scurried off. Pratt was there, taking his cloak and headdress, handing him Harlequin's bat, cap and mask, and he could half-see Jannie's white Columbine dress glimmering out, as a glow came up on an eminence top right, and Maimoune stood graciously brandishing her wand.

> Poor Camaralzaman! A parlous thing
> It is, to find your Queen become a King.
> The marriage knot's a hard one to untie,
> E'en in the pagan Isle of Ebony.
> Yet stay! My magic sceptre I'll enforce
> To bring about a rare – Royal Divorce!

(Uproarious laughter and applause at this topical allusion.)

> Sad Prince, forsake the state of life you're in –
> Be metamorphosed into – Harlequin!
> And you, fair Princess, for his love who pine,
> I herewith change you into Columbine.
> My foe Dauhasch I banish in disgrace:
> And Joey, your own Clown, shall take his place!

A clash of cymbals, a roll on the drum: lights up, the Eastern scene vanished like a mirage, in its place an extremely English fishmonger's shop-front bearing the name GUDGEON, Joey peering through the door with a string of fish round his neck, other little shops grouped around. Down stage, brilliant in the glow of the floats, Harlequin posed in his first attitude, one arm curved above the black-capped head, the other across his breast, ready to grasp the baton from his belt. His silk fleshings blazed with sequins, his patches glowed with Harlequin's symbolical colours – red for jealousy, blue for love, scarlet for anger, lilac for faith, black for invisibility. Lucy Sorrel had sat up till her eyes failed in the candlelight to sew on the pounds of sequins. A more glittering Harlequin had never appeared at the Wells, the dazzled audience were whispering. Beside him Columbine was a slender white wind-flower, a nymph in gauze and ribbons, immortal to his immortal, his fond and faithful mate, like him a child of air.

A swift sinuous movement and he had drawn his bat and pointed it to the triangle of blue over his heart. Blue for love, Harlequin's first move. She blew him a kiss and danced away, as Clown emerged from the fishmonger's and made gestures of violent affection towards her. A flash of silver from Harlequin's eyes behind the mask, a tap of his bat, and a gigantic lobster appeared behind Clown and seized him. Clown ran, lobster pursued, Harlequin and Columbine paused to embrace, the fishmonger's shop and its neighbours suddenly vanished and a great paper moon sailed down to take place. Both Clown and lobster turned to beset Harlequin – but with a fantastic leap he dived straight through the middle of the moon, to ecstatic gasps and squeals from the house. Jannie held her breath as the paper burst, swallowing him – but no cry or crash came from behind it. They had caught him safely.

The moon disappeared up to the flies as suddenly as it had arrived, and a rustic scene materialized, peasant maidens dancing in a ring to the music of a beribboned fiddler. Clown appeared beating a drum, with a junior Clown, J.S. in a monkey's head, playing a fife behind him. A shadowy tree turned into Harlequin, who struck the monkey with his bat. It vanished, to reappear chattering in a cage, Clown dancing round it in an ecstasy of frustration.

A rose-tree up stage left burst into pink flower; a touch from the bat, and it became Columbine, who rushed into Harlequin's arms only to be torn from him by Clown, who bore her away on a grotesque hobby-horse. So chase and rescue, knockabout combat and bewildering transformation followed each other through seventeen scenes, delighting the hot, noisy audience more and more until the climax, a ruined temple entwined with greenery and flanked by living statues of gods and goddesses, and soaring fountains all bathed in the soft bright silver light from the now restored moon, which hung low above the temple bestowing a benevolent smile on the two lovers, gracefully poised in a formal rapturous embrace. Nobody noticed how they panted, or how runnels of sweat coursed down Harlequin's white-painted face.

It was over. In the Green Room everybody agreed noisily and with much back-slapping that it had been an uproariously successful evening. Dibdin was a happy man. He was already jotting down yet more tricks and transformations to be added during the run – for run there would be, judging by the response. Not a thing had gone wrong, and so much might have done. His music had never sounded better, his new Harlequin would be the rage of London after having, so to speak, risen from his own ashes in the previous year. As for little Sorrel, his doubts about her were all banished; she was no amateur, she had Style, and she was ravishingly pretty.

Lucy, who had watched with silent pride, was in Ivor's dressing-room going over Harlequin's costume under the disapproving eyes of Pratt. It was her creation, hers to maintain in all its gorgeousness. But the Captain was drinking wine in the Green Room, his arm round his daughter's shoulders.

'Capital, capital, capital. Never saw anything better. And you, my boy, words can't express . . . so proud to have you in the family. That is, to, er, know you so well, feel almost, as it were . . .' He cleared his throat and took another swig of claret. Ivor smiled, understanding. The good Captain loved happy endings. His dearest wish was for Ivor to go down romantically on one knee, swathed as he was in a woollen cloak against the danger of chill, and ask him formally for his daughter's hand. But Ivor was going to do no such thing. His aims were as clear and businesslike as though a lawyer had drawn them up. He had fought his way back to the stage and made a good beginning. Now he would work to become better and better, to surpass Bologna and get the maximum salary out of the management, until he could pay the Sorrels back every penny he had cost them in lodging and care. Jannie would understand. Across the table he met her look, fond and sweet as ever. Half an hour ago they had been two professional dancers, oblivious of everything except their moves and timing. Now they were themselves again; but like the stage lovers, they must wait for their happiness.

Dorinda paused by their table, attended by a slavish young dandy.

'Angel!' she addressed Jannie. 'You were quite, quite ravishing. But there, I don't need to tell you.' As a proof of her admiration, she bestowed a fulsome kiss on Jannie's cheek, leaving behind a smear of lip-rouge.

'As for you, sir,' she laid a hand on Ivor's shoulder, 'I declare sometimes I thought you were the Devil himself.'

'Oh, no,' Ivor said gravely. 'But I believe there is a slight relationship.' If she expected him to kiss her, she was disappointed. Some young men never missed an opportunity; pity he wasn't one of them, for she knew him to be as hot-blooded as any, if only he were not so apron-tied to that Sorrel. It was so unfair. Sorrel had caught a young sprig of nobility, and been careless enough to lose him and crazy enough to drop his name. Wasn't that enough, without having Bryn for her fancy man, as he clearly was? Dorinda had no real hopes of netting a lord or even a Sir. Her father kept a rag-and-bone establishment, and her mother supplemented the family income by picking lavender at Mitcham and selling it in the streets. So a dancer would be the best she could aspire to; and Bryn would go far, if he didn't break his neck. Besides, he had such eyes, and such a look . . .

The dandy at her side pressed her arm; she gave him a false bright smile.

Camaralzaman was in its second week when Jannie, taking up her position on a divan in the second scene of the front-piece, as Badoura languishing for her dream-prince, was conscious of a new and unpleasant sensation. Her skin, where it touched the fabric of the divan, was itching. She reclined, her head on a pile of cushions, her arms flung wide, the very picture of a lovesick maiden. The itching spread, growing more fierce, and she shifted position sharply, conscious that the scene had begun and the public's eyes were on her.

'What ails thee, mistress? Restless dost thou seem,' enquired her handmaiden, only too appropriately. Jannie, longing desperately to scratch, managed to keep still long enough to reply.

' 'Tis nought, Fatima, but a troublesome dream.'

If only it were! The whole scene to get through, and this fearful irritation spreading all over her back and neck, where it touched the cushions, as though armies of ants were crawling over her, biting. She longed to scream and run off, to tear off her clothes and plunge into water, but it was out of the question. No improvisation could cover such an exit. The only action she could take was to get up with alacrity, to the hand-maiden's surprise, and speak her lines walking up and down as if distracted – which she was. For twelve minutes she endured the torment, hardly aware of what she was saying. At one point she managed to glance down at the divan. It was upholstered in purple cloth, on which, here and there, were visible tiny patches of fine greyish dust. In the wings she stopped a stage-hand. 'Get on there at the next change,' she hissed at him, 'and cover that divan with something. I don't care what – a dust-sheet or a cloak, anything you can find.'

He stared. 'But why, miss?'

'Because it's got itching-powder on it, that's why.'

Dorinda, wiping off her make-up at her mirror, and humming happily, felt her head violently jerked back by its long hair, and spun round to confront a blazing-eyed Columbine, who continued to twist the hair round and round her hand until her fist was against the other girl's neck.

'Ere, 'oo the 'ell d'you think you're maulin' about?' cried the rag-and-bone merchant's daughter, with a sudden reversion to her father's vocabulary. 'You gone stark mad? Let go o' me!'

Jannie tightened her grip, aware that two or three of the other dancers had come in and were staring transfixed at the scene.

'I'll let go of you,' she said, 'when I've got your word that you won't try any more tricks like tonight. Oh yes, Miss Innocence, you may make big eyes, but there's no doubt in my mind who put that nasty stuff on that couch and tried to spoil my scene. Not to mention the whole piece! Oh, very nice for you, Dibdin seeing his leading lady wriggling about like a dog with fleas. I suppose you thought the house'd give me the goose, did you, and you'd get rid of me that way? And we both know why you want rid of me, don't we? Well, let me tell you this, and you girls can witness it. If you do anything like that again, I'll come in here and grab your hair like this, and I'll cut it off – right up to *here*.' She gave it a vicious twist, drawing a shriek from her victim. 'So be warned.' And with a swirl of her delicate skirt and a toss of her garlanded head she swept out.

Dorinda looked after her, tenderly feeling her sore scalp, as her friends gathered round, twittering.

'Pity,' she said. 'Next time it was to have been a frog.'

CHAPTER SIXTEEN

Harlequin Performs A Transformation

Summer was over, September bland and golden, and still *Camaralzaman* ran. More and more splendid effects had been added until the Eastern scenes were a veritable glimpse into Paradise, and the pantomime had gained in fun and ingenuity. True, those who watched with professional eyes began to see a faint but perceptible change in Grimaldi. Lucy Sorrel, her own face now permanently etched with lines of pain, noticed the slight stiffness with which he rose from a prat-fall, and the swelling joints of the big hands that had stolen so many property sausages and ducks.

'It comes to all acrobats in time,' she told her family. 'Look at my father. The smartest rope-dancer you ever did see, and finished up a cripple. Look at me, no more use than a wooden Dutch doll.'

'Nonsense, Ma,' Jannie said. 'Your hands are as nimble as ever they were. And I've never heard Joey utter a word of complaint.'

'You wouldn't. Nobody will, till it's gone too far for them not to notice. And speaking of which, that young man of yours is going to fade away one of these days if he don't eat better.'

'Ivor? Oh, really, Ma! You don't expect him to stuff like a prize pig and play every night?'

'I remember what he looked like this time last year,' said Lucy darkly. 'There isn't so much of him that he can go starving himself.'

'He don't starve.' But Jannie knew that Ivor lived as cheaply as it was possible to live, saving every penny of the now substantial salary he was earning, yet seemed to flourish on a fraction of the fare the average man was consuming. Eating was in fashion. Grimaldi's appetite was prodigious, as a Clown's should be. But Ivor, that prudent Welshman, ate frugally and remained apparently ethereal yet strong as a horse. He had now removed himself to a room in Grimaldi's neighbourhood, feeling himself freer there to come and go as he wished, and nearer to the Wells. Better, too, for him to live separate from Jannie and out of temptation's way. Sometimes he walked home with Joey after the pantomime, and noticed increasingly his friend's exhaustion and painful gait. One night he ventured to offer his arm for support, and got a warm grateful smile.

'There's kind of you, boyo.' Joey liked to mock him gently. 'Getting an old man, that's me.'

'Rubbish. But you're not suffering, are you, Joey?'

'Ah, well. Broke every bone in me body, one time or another, so it's bound to tell one day. In a delicate condition, I am, like the ladies say. Take no notice. But thanks for the arm.'

Young J.S. was walking many yards ahead of them, whistling and slashing the hedges with his cane. Ivor reflected that he might have been better employed in helping his father instead of leaving it to an outsider.

Every Sunday Jannie drove out to Highgate to visit Sara. The quiet house in the square was unchanged, the Quaker sisters, those twin doves, gently watchful over their patient and pleased with her progress from silence to a little conversation. She would answer simple questions, utter thanks for a present of flowers or sweets, express mild pleasure at a new dress Lucy had made up for her from material supplied by the sisters. But she knew nobody, and when Jannie entered her room looked at her as a complete stranger.

More than Sara's passivity, the change in Raymond shocked her. All trace of the once-great Thespian had left him, but for the eagle features and the mellow voice, though now its resonance was gone. His stooping shoulders took inches away from his height, and his hair-line was receding rapidly; he looked many years older than when she had last seen him.

He liked to talk to her, somebody from the world that had once been his. After she had been to Sara's room she would join him in the severe parlour, one of the sisters remaining as chaperone, sedulously employed at her needlework and just as sedulously in not listening to their conversation.

'I miss it so much, my dear,' he said, 'the company, the talk one used to have about old days. Not the past year or two, that brought my poor Sara to this – God knows, they were times to forget. But we actors – well, you know how it is. We like to recall when we were young, and thought ourselves Garricks and Kembles . . . There's no one to listen to my tales now.'

Jannie's eyes filled. 'You can talk to me. I'll listen as long as you like. I expect I'll be just the same one day – we all will. I'm so – sorry for you.'

'Don't cry, my child. I assure you, I'm perfectly content. My work is really quite congenial, you know. I write quite a pretty hand, and take a pride in it, and it keeps me from . . . bad company. The Friends are good people, like these dear ladies. It's only that they don't speak one's language. Quotes, and the like. Sara used to recognize the least snippet from the Bard. Now she merely looks at me. It makes one feel not quite a person; more a silly old shadow, which I suppose I am.'

Jannie mopped her eyes and made herself speak sensibly. 'Do you think she'll ever come to herself again? What do the doctors say?'

He shrugged. 'Doctors. Even Quaker ones, they have nothing to say to the brain. Starvation, leeches, blooding, darkness . . . all the terrible old remedies. Or they sit staring at the patient waiting for the spirit to move them. Either way it makes no difference. She was like this once before.' He stirred his cup of tea slowly, seeing in its swirling brown depths the young distraught Sara, the boy-child's unmarked grave, the country lunatic asylum. 'It was after a severe shock to the nerves. She recovered then, but now . . . I suppose age makes a difference.' He looked up, meeting Jannie's damp gaze. 'My wife died two months ago.'

She had not known anything of his wife, but said, 'I'm sorry.'

'Pray don't be. There's no need for sorrow. We hadn't lived together for many years. Now my daughter's married and gone to America, and I have the income from the Surrey house. I would never have known, but the lawyers at Kingston wrote to me care of the Royalty, and I happened to call in one day. How strangely things fall out. Now I would be able to marry and live comfortably, if my poor girl . . .' He trailed away into silence, staring at the fire.

To Ivor, at the theatre, Jannie wept and stormed as she had not been able to in front of Raymond. 'She can *speak*, she smiles and talks about the ducks on the ponds and know it's autumn because of the red berries on the trees, but she don't know me, or him, or the Miss Hewitts! Oh, it's a crying shame. There must be *something* we can do.'

Ivor caught hold of the small fists which he guessed were about to start battering his chest, and put their owner firmly into a chair.

'She was like this before. What brought her round then?'

Jannie shook her head.

'This is only a bow drawn at a venture. There she sits, in a dull house with quiet people. Why should it remind her of anything? If she were to see the things she was used to seeing . . .'

'She sees me.'

'And it does no good.'

'Very well, come and let her see you.'

'No. And don't tell me again I'm a weak cowardly man that can't bear to look on someone not right in the head. If she saw me now, what would it do for her?' He gestured towards his neat blue cutaway jacket, dark pantaloons and high boots. 'The very image of a respectable young man. Do I look like a Harlequin, or you like a Columbine – a mere member of the corps, even? And if you're about to suggest, as I see you are, that we put on our full stage gear and drive up Highgate Hill in a hackney bowing to the populace, then you may think again. It may have suited Joey to gallop through the streets from the Wells to the Garden in Clowny's rig, but I have my feelings.' He expressed them by performing a dazzling series of *fouettés* which made her stare and clap.

'Then what shall we do?' she asked. Ivor told her.

Miss Bridget Hewitt was as nearly displeased as Jannie had ever seen her.

'Neither my sister nor I could possibly accompany friend Sara to the Playhouse. We have never been near such a place. We had *hoped* that her sojourn with us might persuade her mind from such worldly thoughts and temptations.'

'But her mind is not awake,' Jannie pointed out. 'How can she do what you think is right, when she's like a child of five? Don't you see, ma'am, we can but try whether old associations will recall her memory? Oh, pray do bring yourself to see it as we do. If she could only see our performance, the costumes, the lights, the audience . . .'

Miss Bridget shuddered faintly and Miss Dorcas closed her eyes in sympathy. 'Dr McAndrew would not advise it. Strict seclusion and peace of mind were his directions. Such vanities as thee would drag her back to would only do great harm.'

'Very well,' Jannie said calmly, 'then I'll see to it myself, and you need have nothing to do with any of it.'

'Thee must do as thee thinks best, friend Janetta.'

Raymond was eager to try the experiment. But he was never back from the counting-house before eight at night, too late to accompany Sara. Jannie and Ivor would already be at the theatre. Only one possible escort remained: the Captain.

With the greatest willingness and alacrity, that born squire of dames looked out his smartest clothes, the lace neckcloth, the hunter's-green inexpressibles. His moustache was curled, his hair shining and redolent of bear's grease, an elegant fob dangled from his waistcoat. Like a Court emissary he appeared at Sara's door, his wife's best shawl over his arm.

She half-started from her chair at the sight of him, aware in the dimness of her mind that he was a most unusual visitor. He bowed sweepingly.

'Mrs Otway, dear lady. Your servant.'

'My servant?' Poor thing, did she think him some new kind of attendant on her? Smiling, he advanced and put the shawl round her shoulders. It was nothing very grand, a cheerful cotton in reds and yellows, but she picked up a corner of it and gazed at it wonderingly, so much brighter than the greys and dark blues she and the sisters wore. The Captain arranged it for her with a gallant flourish.

'Charming. Now the bonnet.' But there seemed to be no bonnet. When she was taken out for a walk they put a stiff white cap on her head. She looked at him blankly. But he had a remedy for every emergency.

'And why a bonnet, indeed? Quite unnecessary.' From his pocket he whipped a scrap of pretty lace with a hairpin at each end. He had seen it in Lucy's workbox, and abstracted it with no very clear idea of its mission. He laid it across Sara's head and pinned it deftly in place, cap-wise. Then, from his waistcoat pocket, he produced a pair of long earrings, pinchbeck set with coloured stones. They had been Jannie's choice, borrowed from Wardrobe. Very gently, like a mother dressing her child, he fastened them to Sara's ears, tightening the tiny screws until they clung close. There was no mirror in the room, but he stood back and let his face serve as one.

'Charming. Enchanting.' He flipped one of the earrings with his finger, making it swing. 'Quite ready for a delightful evening at the play. Madam.' He offered his arm, and, with a wondering look, she took it.

A special, secluded place had been kept for them at the Wells, near the tip of the horseshoe circle where it joined the wings, but not too near, so that illusion could prevail and distance lend enchantment. The house was fullish, but well-behaved; he was glad there was no unseemliness or racketing to alarm his charge. So tense was he that the overture had ended before he realized he had not taken a drink from his pocket-flask, as he intended. Never mind. Better to stay clear-headed.

He had seen the front-piece so often that he was barely aware of his daughter and his intended son-in-law going through their opening scenes. Appearing to look at the stage, he was only conscious of the woman at his side. She had not spoken since their arrival except to ask 'Here?' when he motioned her to her seat. He had watched her look round the theatre, with wide, blank eyes; up at the glistening chandeliers, down to the seething people in the pit. Then, when the curtains parted and Maimoune appeared from her pink cloud, Sara's face seemed like a face of marble, utterly still; intent, he realized. What was she making of it? He began to have awful fears that it might send her hysterical and cause an interruption to the performance. Why in Hades had Lucy not agreed to come with him? Squire of dames he might be, but this sort of occasion needed a woman's touch . . .

He thanked Heaven when the Cat Scene came and the stage was dark. Furtively he wiped his brow and felt the comforting shape of the flask in his coat-pocket. Perhaps a quick nip would not be noticed.

'. . . And Joey, your own Clown, shall take his place!'

Maimoune stepped back, vanishing with the Eastern temples, as plaice, haddock, whiting and mackerel appeared laid out on a slab in neat cardboard piles, in front of Mr Gudgeon's shop. But Sara was leaning forward over the red plush balcony, her eyes riveted on shining, sparkling Harlequin. And his eyes were fixed on her, glittering behind their mask, just as Columbine's graceful head was turned in her direction, so that the audience stared and craned to see what important personage sat in the box. Then, with a swift dazzling smile, he pointed his bat – and nobody but Columbine saw that it was towards the colour of Faith over his heart.

The Captain had never seen magic before, but he saw it now. As the opening sequence began, Sara turned to him in the most natural and ordinary way possible, and said chattily, 'How remarkably that young man has come on. We saw him in Dublin, you know, at the Smock Alley theatre, or was it Crow Street, and even then I thought he had a kind of genius.'

'Yes,' replied the Captain in stunned tones. 'Yes, quite.'

'And your daughter, dear little Janetta, what a beauty she's become. She reminds me so much . . . now where have I seen a face very like hers – quite lately?'

The Captain extracted his flask and took a long swig of brandy. He had heard that Roman Catholics crossed themselves at such moments, and he wished the Established Church permitted such a gesture. As it was, he could do nothing but sit quietly to the end, beside a lady who appeared to be in every way normal, indeed, extremely well-informed and observant, even to noticing Grimaldi's slight lameness. She talked, indeed, rather more than was usual in the best seats, but at a pantomime nobody minded, for there were no words to miss. When, after the curtain, she asked to be taken round to the Green Room, he was beginning to recover and to look forward greatly to seeing Jannie's face.

It surpassed his expectations, flushing like dawn, then paling, as he presented the restored Sara to her.

'Don't say anything,' he muttered in her ear. 'She don't know anything's been wrong. Just behave naturally.'

'What do you take me for?' she returned in a whisper, then turned to Sara and embraced her. Somebody, bidden by the Captain, fetched wine, and they sat down and chattered as old friends do, and Sara began to giggle because wine had not passed her lips for so long; and then Ivor appeared, and stood transfixed,

264

hardly daring to believe what he saw. Jannie knew that the bright-ness of his eyes was the shine of tears, and ached to get him to her-self, but the moment was not yet. In a hurried conference, while Sara's attention was distracted, she said to her father, 'She mustn't go back to that place tonight. It would remind her – undo all the good. Take her home with you – wait, we'll go together.'

'But the ladies . . .'

'Damn the ladies, and don't look so shocked, Pa, because I think they've been turning her into a cabbage whatever their intentions might be. She can have the spare room and we'll make up some sort of story.'

Sara agreed placidly to returning with them to Long Acre. She seemed to remember nothing of her immediate past, and when they told her she had left her lodgings that day because they were unsatisfactory, she believed them. 'How kind. Just until I can find another place.' Then she looked round. 'Where is Raymond? I thought . . . was he not with us tonight?'

'No,' improvised the Captain. 'He – he had some other business. You'll see him tomorrow. I assure you he'll know you're in good hands,' he added, praying that this was true, and that a distracted Raymond would not spend the night combing Hampstead Heath for his lost lady.

Leaving Sara in her father's charge, to await a cab, Jannie flew down the stairs to the dressing-rooms; Ivor had only stayed in the Green Room a few minutes. He was sitting at his dressing-table, turning Harlequin's bat over and over in his hands. She flung herself on him.

'Oh, my darling, my dearest own love! Was there anyone ever as clever and wonderful as you? Poor thing, as mad as a hatter one minute and the next . . . well, you saw her. And all your doing, all thanks to you.'

'No,' he said. 'Not me. Him.' He glanced from the slender bat to the costume on its hanger, flinging back sparkles from the candle-flames, and the mask, blank-eyed, hanging above his mirror. 'Very strange people, Harlequins.'

*

265

Raymond's joy at the restoration of Sara was wonderful to behold. He had appeared in Long Acre almost before the Market was stirring, while the Sorrels were still in bed. Lucy heard the frantic knocking, and hobbled to the door, night-capped and curl-papered.

'I knew it'd be you – come in,' she said with admirable good-humour for that hour of the morning to the haggard, grey-faced caller.

'Is she here?'

'Of course, where else? You'd better sit down before you fall down.' She saw his glance at the bed in the corner of the sitting-room. 'Never mind Jannie, she can sleep through a thunderstorm. I'll make some tea, the kettle's been on the hob all night.' Stumbling about, she produced a cup of scalding liquid which he drank without noticing its fierce heat.

'I'm sorry to call so early,' he said. 'Wretchedly uncivil of me. But I haven't slept all night, you see, and the Misses Hewitt are so anxious . . .'

'Very proper. Now you just sit there and listen to me, though I warn you, you won't believe it.' And she proceeded to tell him in the most matter-of-fact way of the extraordinary metamorphosis of the previous night.

'No explaining it, is there, really, we must just be thankful.'

'"More things in Heaven and Earth . . ."' murmured Raymond.

'Yes, that's right. What a lovely Hamlet Mr Kemble made, to be sure; pity he's had to retire. Have another cup, and I expect you wouldn't say no to a little something in it.' The little something proved to be gin from a black bottle on the mantelpiece. Revived, Raymond asked her, 'But do you think she will remember . . . I mean, when she wakes, will she be herself?'

'How do I know who she'll be? My guess is she's wakened up for good and all and you won't have any more trouble. Nobody ever heard tell of the Sleeping Beauty going off again, did they? And if you'll take my advice, *and* the Captain's, *and* Jannie's, you won't take her back to that place where I've no doubt they took care of her and fed her up nicely, for she's in very handsome looks, but good-living people though I'm sure they are it don't do for professionals to be fish out of water.'

The door opened, and Sara stood there, enveloped in one of the Captain's nightshirts with her hair tumbling from a blue ribbon. She looked fresh, rested, and completely in her right mind. Smiling from one to the other, she said, 'Raymond, how delightful. I didn't know you were coming to breakfast.' She kissed him, then Lucy. 'I've been such a trouble to Jannie's mamma, and she hasn't said one scolding word to me. So I shall make the toast if you'll tell me where the bread is.'

In such cheerfully mundane circumstances did the long drama of Sara's madness end. Lucy Sorrel helped everybody by behaving as though nothing odd had happened at all; but from then onwards her manner towards Ivor was tinged with respectful awe.

As things befell, the Otways were to return to Highgate, though to Raymond's relief Sara showed not the slightest recognition of the place. Now that he had the income from the substantial house in Surrey, which he should have been receiving for years, he was in a position to rent a house of his own. The one he chose stood in a terrace of modest dwellings some thirty years old, built about the time of the American War on Highgate Ridge, high above London, with a fine view to the south-east, as far as woody Epping and the faint gleam of the Thames Estuary. Between lay Highgate Common, where cattle grazed and children played, and little market-gardens provided vegetables free from the taint of town. It was, as Sara said, exactly like living in the country, except that their small house was really quite elegant, with its double drawing-room boasting twin marble fireplaces, its bedrooms with deep cupboards and room for handsome beds, and a 'secret' staircase behind a little door to the attic where their servant, Mary, slept.

Mary was far from being the put-upon slavey found in so many households. She was no orphan, but the youngest daughter of the local baker, and of a romantic nature that delighted in waiting upon two such grand people as the Otways. A seat for the play sent her into transports of delight, and Raymond had never had a better captive audience. As he perched on the kitchen table, his rendering of 'Now is the winter of our discontent Made glorious summer by this son of York' would bring a livelier scarlet into the poppies of her cheeks as she stood, transfixed with pleasure, by the hearth. She was a good little cook, but there was never any guarantee that one of Mr Otway's recitals would not cause the odd onion to turn up in an apple pie.

There was another inhabitant of the house in the Terrace. Sara remembered with perfect clarity everything leading up to their departure for Hertford, though the year that followed was completely wiped from her mind. On the morning of her reunion with Raymond in Long Acre she demanded that they go to Brassey's to enquire after Miranda.

'Poor creature, how she will have missed me. It must be weeks . . . that is, days . . . I really can't recall. How could I have left her? But it was the only thing to do. We were going . . . where were we going?'

'To look for an engagement,' Raymond said truthfully.

'Yes, that was it,' Sara said, thoughtful, but fortunately did not pursue the subject. 'I expect she will have pined. Oh dear!'

Oh dear indeed, Raymond echoed to himself. Only he realized that the separation from her cherished cat had been the final blow that had turned Sara's mind into a blank, echoing the loss of her baby son, when the same thing had happened, and coming as it did in a train of misfortunes.

She imagined that it had been only a little time since she had left Miranda at Brassey's. Raymond knew how many months had passed. The cat had looked ill then. They should never have subjected it to the life they had had to lead themselves, but he had not dared to suggest that she leave it in some comfortable home. If they were to find that it had died, what would the effect be on Sara? He dreaded to think of the possibilities.

He put his arm round Sara's shoulders, still draped in Lucy's shawl. 'If she has she'll soon mend, my dear, when she sees you. Now you must promise me not to upset yourself, whatever we find. These separations happen, you know, and Miss Brassey is the kindest of women.' He had sent a message to the counting-house to say that he was prevented from coming in that day; he steeled himself to discovering what had happened to Miranda.

Miss Brassey herself opened the door. 'Oh, my gracious, what a surprise! Mr Otway and Miss Dell, well now. It's been so long, I thought as you'd gone to the Colonies or somewhere.'

Out of Sara's view, Raymond laid his finger to his lips and made exaggerated signs to her not to go on. 'Yes,' he said easily, 'quite a few weeks. Country engagements, things cropping up, you know how it is. We thought perhaps it was time we looked in to see how Miss Dell's cat was faring.'

Miss Brassey was not slow-witted. 'Ah,' she said. 'Yes, well, come in, do. There's only a few customers in yet and Jack can see to them. Down the stairs, and mind your head on the beam, sir. Delivery boy caught himself a nasty crack the other day.'

They were in the big kitchen, surprisingly light for a basement and rich with savoury smells. A huge dresser filled one wall, barrels of oysters were stacked in a corner, hams and sides of pork were suspended from ceiling-hooks. A large Rumford range, U-shaped, of the most modern design, dominated the room; not one, but four coal-fires fuelled it, each one serving the oven above it.

On the tiled floor in the precise centre of the U, where the maximum of heat collected, reposed a cat. It was black and long-legged, and slightly pointed about the face, but elsewhere as plump and sleek as a bag of black velvet stuffed with butter. Its eyes were not visible, being closed in bliss produced by the energetic sucking of four kittens, two blacks, a ginger and a tortoiseshell.

'There,' said Miss Brassey. 'She's done all right for herself, you see. I couldn't keep the toms away, you know what they're like, but she seems to have got a steady one, old Budge from the Blue Lion. I reckon he's quite proud of them kits – he comes in of an evening and licks 'em. The ginger's the very image of him.'

'Miranda,' Sara said wonderingly. 'Miranda.'

'That's right, I remember now that was what you said. It slipped my memory, I'm sorry to say, so we called her Sooty and she answered all right.'

Raymond watched in trepidation as Sara went down on her knees beside the group. She stretched out a hand and touched the cat's head.

'Miranda?'

Miranda opened first one eye, then both, but made no other move.

'They're beautiful kittens, Miranda,' Sara told her softly. 'You're a clever girl, to have such lovely kittens, aren't you? And happy. Yes, I can see you're happy. It wasn't a very comfortable life, was it, travelling with your Mamma. I was very selfish to make you do it. So it was a good thing, after all, that we . . . what did we do, Raymond?'

'Went to look for an engagement,' he said hastily.

'Yes, of course. I was very sad at the time, but I see now it was for the best.' She stroked the shining black head again; a pink tongue came out and gave her hand a cursory lick before the gold eyes closed again in rapture at the urgent kneadings of her children's claws.

'Thank you, Miss Brassey,' Sara said, getting up. 'How can I thank you enough?' And, suddenly tragic, 'You *won't* drown them, will you? I know people do. Oh, please, I beg you, don't!'

'As if I would, ma'am! Next door's asked for one, and the butcher wants another – that'll have a good home, I can tell you. As for the others, they'll help Sooty keep down the mice. Jack never did like emptying the traps.'

'Perhaps *we* could have one?' Sara looked imploringly up at Raymond.

And have one they did, as soon as they were settled in the house in the Terrace. Sara chose the black, because it was most like Miranda, and after much debate they called it Claribel. 'Because,' Sara pointed out, 'she was Alonso's daughter, "the king's fair daughter Claribel" who married the King of Tunis, and so being Ferdinand's sister she was Miranda's sister-in-law. By the end of the play, of course.'

'Of course, love,' Raymond agreed. The only reminder of Sara's lost year was her tendency to ramble back to her youthful days and the parts she had played, for which her memory was quite remarkable.

'To be truly accurate, we ought to call her after Miranda's daughter,' Sara reflected. 'Prospero's Miranda, I mean. But we don't know that she had any daughters, because she and Ferdinand were only just married . . . Still I expect the Bard *meant* her to have, don't you? "Long continuance and increasing." And she'd certainly have called one of them Claribel, being a family name. So it fits beautifully, you see.'

'Beautifully,' Raymond said, though privately he thought that Claribel was a quite awful name to inflict on an innocent cat, and that Sara would have to get used to people calling it Clarry; which, indeed, they did.

However, it was only fitting that any pet of theirs should be named from Shakespeare, for Raymond, by the good agency of the Headmaster of Highgate School, that ancient establishment for the education of boys which occupied a handsome old house at the end of their Lane, established himself as a lecturer in the Works of Shakespeare, and was a great deal more happy and comfortable in that capacity than he had been as a strolling player. Mr Otway the Tragedian and his impressive lectures, with dramatic illustrations, came to be known at Eton, Harrow, even as far away as Rugby.

And it was Mrs Otway in truth that he left behind when he went on his travels from the beloved house; for they had been married, very quietly, with only Ivor, Jannie and her parents present, at the old chapel that stood in its pretty graveyard beside the School.

When she died, after years of quiet happiness, Raymond put up a beautiful tombstone to her, guarded by two angels, bearing the inscription:

'She was Meekness, Charity, and Love, uncomplaining and true.'

CHAPTER SEVENTEEN

Harlequin In His Element

'Whatever are you about, Ivor?' enquired Lucy, from her seat by the fire, where she was stirring the last brew of toddy. Supper was over, a supper which followed a markedly alcoholic party in the Green Room for the last night of the pantomime. None of the Sorrels was seeing any too clearly, but Ivor, who modestly described himself as having a head like teak, was meticulously clearing the littered supper-table and transferring its contents to a tray, which would next day be taken down to the kitchen by the maid.

'Just tidying,' he replied, disappearing into the passage with a pile of plates.

'But it's two o'clock in the morning, my boy,' the Captain said, enunciating slowly and carefully. 'Oughtn't you to be off home? Streets very dangerous, this time of night.'

'Ah. Now that's just why,' he replied mysteriously.

'Oh, Ivor, do leave it,' Jannie said. 'You've no call to be doing such work, especially after this evening. I mean it *was* your Benefit and you were so wonderful . . .' She gave a tremendous yawn. '*Now* what are you doing?'

'Warming up some coffee,' replied the hero of the evening. 'I want you to stay awake just a little longer.'

'But what for?'

He surveyed the round, plush-clothed table top. 'There's nice and clear. Now watch.' He picked up a largish canvas bag obviously of some weight, gathered at the neck by a string, poised it above the table, untied the string, and before three pairs of sleepy, incredulous eyes poured out slowly and carefully a seemingly unending stream of sovereigns.

'My benefit money. You see, it wouldn't have done at all for me to be carrying this to Islington, now would it. There's plenty of crime about without encouraging more.'

'But,' said Jannie, and stopped. Her parents were speechless. It

272

seemed that the entire surface of the table was now hidden by the golden coins.

At last the Captain managed to ask, 'You want us to keep them for you?'

'Just to keep them.'

'Why?'

'For saving my life. For nursing me back to health. For Jannie.'

He was gone as swiftly as Harlequin through the moon, leaving them staring at the table, then at each other, before they fell into bed, leaving the humble cloth still bearing its rich load.

In the cold light of day the Captain said, 'A noble gesture, dear boy. But you must see that it would be quite impossible for us to take them. What we did for you – and it was very little – was out of Christian charity, and for Jannie's sake – not to mention your own. Money don't come into it.'

'Not as such, no, sir. But I would like you to have it. There will be plenty more, and I have some put away in Coutts's – for my old age. You know what we folk are – what we have, we spend. Three hundred guineas in all you'll find – you can do some good with it, I know.' He looked at the Captain, through whose mental vision strings of fleet racehorses were romping. 'I have a friend, a man named Jenkins, with a great feeling for the Stock Exchange. He would give you good advice, I know.'

The Captain nodded, as the racehorses galloped away into the distance and over the horizon. He had lost so often lately; something told him his luck was out. And Lucy's ailment was worse. Mary Grimaldi had sent round a generous flask of the Elixir, but it had done little good, and one day the sewing would be at an end, and the payments from the theatres.

'Well,' he said at last, 'it goes against the grain, but from one of the family, as I take it you will be . . .' He held out his hand.

Ivor took it and held it warmly in his own strong grasp.

'I intend to be, sir, very soon, with your permission and Mrs Sorrel's. But first, I want to take Jannie away.'

It was Jannie's turn to start with surprise. 'Away? Why? Where?'

He smiled enigmatically. 'Call it a wedding trip.'

'But we thought . . .' Lucy's disappointment was obvious. 'We thought she'd be married from here. I was looking forward to it all – we'd thought of Christmas . . .'

Jannie had been watching Ivor's face, reading his mind, and now she understood. 'Oh, Ma, don't you see it wouldn't do? I was married from home once before. It would bring it all back, and I don't want to remember it. This time it must be quite different – just ourselves, no fuss or feathers. And – it would be nice to go away, and rest, and see different places . . . isn't that what you mean, love?'

She saw by his eyes and his smile that it was. 'I want to take you home. To Wales, where I come from. It will be beautiful there now – how beautiful, you don't know.'

'No. I've never been anywhere – only London. And Bath. And . . . Sussex.'

'I shall take you to my Mam and Tad, to my family. They are very simple people, but you will like them, I think. I write to Mam quite often; she knows what has happened to me, to us.'

Immensely reassured by this, Lucy exclaimed, 'Oh, then it will be a family wedding after all. That makes everything quite different. We'll miss not being there, won't we, Captain, but I shan't fret about it, not a bit.'

The time had been when she would have nagged and scolded and put obstacles in the way of her daughter being carried off to what might as well have been foreign parts, with the possibility of coming home ruined and ringless. But she was going with Ivor, that mysterious, magical young man who inspired her with the nearest approach to reverence she had ever felt. There was a tale that one night at the Wells Grimaldi's performance had cured a deaf and dumb sailor, so convulsing it was. 'What a damned funny fellow!' the Tar was said to have exclaimed to his neighbour. 'What, Jack, can you speak?' 'Aye, and hear too!' Well, that was as it might be, Lucy thought – everybody knew what sailors were like. But the miracle of Sara's cure – now *that* she had witnessed with her own senses. After all, Harlequins transcended the laws of nature, gravity, life and death – what limit was there to their powers?

The night before the two were to set out for Wales Jannie said, 'Could we go and see Joey? Just because . . . I don't know, but I think he'd want to wish us well.'

They arrived, uninvited, at the house in Baynes Row, from which came sounds of music. A party was in progress, the cluttered parlour crowded with people. At the pianoforte Louisa Bologna, Mary's sister, was singing, 'Will you come to the Bower?' in the penetrating soprano which had once rung round Covent Garden, while Mary played for her and another sister, Maria, plied the company with refreshments from the kitchen. Jack Bologna, smoking his pipe in the corner, watched his wife admiringly. He had courted her, the prettiest of the Bristow sisters, so long before they had been able to marry. Joey's Pantaloon, Jim Barnes, was there, demolishing a mug of porter, and, chattering in Italian, a young rope-dancer who was becoming popular at the Wells. Also present, Jannie saw with annoyance, was Dorinda St Clair, perched on a gentleman's knee. She saw them enter and tossed her blonde head. Ivor smiled secretly. He had no intention of going anywhere near her.

And Joey, the one they had come to see, not expecting such a large company, lay on the chaise-longue; not from indolence, but from weakness. While the pantomime had been running he had kept up his energies and given of his best, like a horse that knows it must run the race even though its heart bursts when the winning-post is reached. Now, though he smiled, laughed and quipped, his face had fallen into lines of suffering which would never be wiped out again, and when he moved an arm or leg he winced. Jannie recognized the symptoms. She had seen them take over her mother's body and reduce it to the likeness of a gnarled tree. There was premature age on Joey's face, and pain in the great round eyes that had twinkled and winked so brightly. On a table beside him was a glass; it held not spirits, but a mild tincture of laudanum.

'Let's not stay,' she whispered to Ivor. 'He's not well. These people ought not to be here. I can't think why Mary allows it.'

'She knows best, *cariad*. Would he want to be alone with such pain? No, we must stay and have a word – and not show that we see any change in him.'

They moved to his side, at last, through the people who thronged round him, and his face lit up at the sight of them.

'Bless me, the two folk I most wanted to see and clean forgot to invite! But I'd some notion or other that you were out of town or,' he winked, 'otherwise engaged.'

'We *are* engaged,' said Ivor, on one knee beside him, 'to be married, Joey, and tomorrow we go out of town. We wanted to see you before we left, and get your blessing.'

Joey reached out stiffly and pressed Jannie to the floor beside Ivor, pushed their heads together and, laying his hand over them, began to intone a wild parody of a parsonical blessing which made them laugh helplessly and set the rest of the party roaring too. Impossible to remember what he said, or even if it was funny in itself; his face, his voice, his gestures were all so irresistibly comical that the words were meaningless, and indeed were largely gibberish.

'Arise, my children,' he concluded, 'but lastly and fourteenthly the bride shall bestow upon me a smacking kiss.'

Jannie hugged and kissed him, though feeling him wince at her touch. Then she was being passed round the company and kissed by everybody, while Ivor was receiving the same attention from the ladies. When he came to Dorinda she enfolded him in a passionate embrace and imprisoned his lips much longer than propriety dictated.

'All right,' she whispered as she let him go, 'you marry your intended, and I hope it keeps fine for you. But if ever you wants a change, there's a certain young lady as would be your girl to-morrow, ring or no ring, so just you remember that.'

'Thank you, I will,' Ivor replied politely. He could never bring himself to be rude enough to women; it had got him into trouble before, and he hoped, how fervently, that Jannie would help him to keep out of it in future.

They said goodbye to Mary, Louisa, and the others, then to

Joey; and this time he only took their hands and said quietly, 'Be happy. Don't fret about me. You'll see me back on the boards, never fear.'

As the front door shut behind them they heard a roar of encouragement, a piano prelude, then Joey's upraised voice, slyly innocent as ever:

> A little old woman her living got
> By selling codlins, hot, hot, hot;
> And this little old woman, who codlins sold,
> Though her codlins were hot, she felt herself cold.
> So to keep herself warm, she thought it no sin
> To fetch for herself a quartern of . . .

Arm in arm they walked down Baynes Row, the chorus floating after them.

'Ri tol iddy iddy, Ri tol iddy iddy, Ri tol iddy iddy, Ri tol lay!'

The coach journey to Hereford would remain a blur in Jannie's memory. There were emotional farewells to her parents in the coach-yard behind Fleet Street, and the excitement of setting off westward, with the consolation that they and two other passengers occupied the only inside places. The 'galloping ground' beyond Hounslow seemed to pass in a flash, they were out of London, country superseded town; it was all thrilling. Then, as they began to catch and hold glimpses of the Thames, to see the bridges of Maidenhead and Henley, Jannie became increasingly aware that she was very tired indeed, and that Ivor was no less so. Three months of daytime rehearsal and energetic evening dancing, and suddenly an end to it. They had left London at four o'clock in the afternoon. By dusk, at half-past seven, they were fast asleep, Jannie's head on his shoulder and his coat round her. Somewhere or other they were called to get out and take refreshments, coffee and cold meats which they barely tasted. After that, when the coach stopped for the horses to be changed, they surfaced, dazed, aching, and cold, before sheer tiredness put them to sleep again.

It was too dark when they reached Oxford to see anything; even the romantic spires hidden in the gloom. There, and at Cheltenham, other passengers embarked, and watched with curiosity, by the fitful light of other passing vehicles, the young sleeping pair, their faces and limbs of a delicacy not usual among ordinary travellers, an odd likeness between them in a sort of flyaway or other-worldly look. Their faces were pale, their eyelids heavy, the girl's ankles slender yet strongly-developed, the boy graceful as a child in relaxation. Runaways, disguised gentlefolk? Who could guess? Their fellow-passengers fell asleep.

'Hereford! Hereford! Alight, if you please!' It was just on noon, a bright September morning in a busy old town with a strange look about it, to London eyes; the clear river Wye winding through it, a sturdy bridge, rosy-faced people. Jannie had an impression of ancient black and white houses, a looming castle and old churches, fresh cold air with a scent of hay, orchards bright with red apples; and then they were in the dining-room of an inn, eating as though they had not eaten for a week. They were completely awake, rested, restored, ready to wander about the town stretching their legs and exploring, until Ivor said, 'We must be on our way while the light lasts.'

In a yard behind a saddler's he hired a curious little vehicle, the sort of trap used by farmers to take small produce to market. It carried them with comfort, and their two bundles of luggage, and was drawn by a stout brown horse with a tendency to pause and nibble any hedge or ditch-growth it fancied. Jannie was puzzled and charmed by Ivor's reaction. A London driver, she knew, would have whipped it on with curses. He watched it eat, waited until it was ready to move, then clicked at it to start. They moved through country ever more wild and lovely, in changing light, the first orange blush of sunset, the dark pearl of early evening cloud, all glowing above dark forest, mountain slopes clad in rosy bilberry and bracken. It was not at all like Sussex; it was not like anything she had ever seen or imagined.

Ivor began to sing, one song after another in Welsh. His voice was light and untrained, naturally sweet.

'I never heard you sing before,' she said.

'Don't get much chance, do I?'

She leant against him, listening, asking sometimes, 'What does that mean?'

'It's a song about sheep-shearing; the young lambs dancing for joy of being free of their wool.'

'And that?'

'A girl going with a boy to Towyn fair.'

Dusk was falling, a dark high shape rising to the right of them.

'What's that?'

'The Black Mountain. Beyond is Clun Forest. Now we're almost at Beguildy, and Felindre lies beyond.'

'Beguildy, Felindre. Strange names.'

'Stranger than the Arabian Nights. What are the Isles of Ebony to these? Are you tired?'

'No. I could drive all night.'

He began to sing again, a compulsive, alluring tune with a gentle refrain, and looked down at her glimmering upturned face.

'Don't you want to know what *that* means?'

She pressed close against his shoulder. 'Yes.'

Very softly he sang, translating as he went, pausing here and there for a word.

> Through Cymru rings your fame,
>   Whitest Gwen, brightest Gwen,
> The mountains sing your name,
>   Whitest Gwen;
> The lamps ahead invite you
> With comforts to delight you;
> Then homeward let them light you –
>   Venture, venture, venture, Gwen.

' "*Mentra, Gwen,*" ' he repeated. 'For now we are in Wales.'

There were indeed lamps ahead, just down the valley, and in a few minutes they had reached the little inn from which they shone.

Ivor jumped down from the driving-seat and helped her to descend.

'I know this place. It's comfortable and clean. We can't get home tonight.'

They were standing in the porch, the lamp above it shining down on them. The horse had wandered away without waiting to be released from the shafts, and someone had appeared from a stable-yard to deal with it. Ivor put his hands on her shoulders and looked down into her eyes, his own brilliant in the dusk as though they shone through Harlequin's mask.

'Will you stay here with me tonight? "Mentra, Gwen?"'

Her arms went round his neck. 'I will, and gladly,' she said. 'Whatever that may be in Welsh.'

Ivor might have written to his mother of the things that had been happening to him and of his intended marriage, but she had not, it seemed, taken much of it in. Jannie recalled his saying, when they first knew each other, that she herself was like one of the Tylwyth Teg, the fairy folk, and it was clear that his whole family shared this opinion; not only of her but of him, their own kinsman. From far and wide they came, the Bryns and their cousins the Joneses and the Llwyds, to stare at these two strange creatures, so elegant, so graceful, so utterly unlike themselves. Were all the people in Llundain like this, they whispered among themselves? And could the young man really be that Dafydd Ifor who had run away so many years ago, and sent a letter to Mam every now and then saying that his life was now of the *theatr*, that abode of Belial which the preacher had told them was worse, far worse, than the Cities of the Plain?

Surrounded by these small, dark, brown-faced people with their puzzled curious eyes, Jannie felt at first like a sheep being inspected by farmers, and was almost overcome by an impulse to kick up her legs and give them the most abandoned dance she knew. If they thought she was as wicked as all that (and they knew nothing of the inn on the Welsh Border) she would let them have a taste of it.

But Ivor sensed her mood and said, 'Don't. Behave yourself. They'll soon be used to you.'

She, in fact, soon got used to them, as, here and there in a glance or a bone-structure or a laugh, she was reminded of Ivor. He talked to them in rapid Welsh and to her in English, introducing the bewildering numbers who came and went in the long rambling farm-house perched high above the river Dovey, where salmon played in clear pools and among limestone rocks, and on the slopes between its strand and the farm Dafydd Bryn's small, sturdy sheep grazed.

'My sister Marged, my brother Emrys. My brother Trevor. My brother Vaughan. And this is my cousin Owain Jones and the little Prys, who wasn't born when I left home . . .' Gradually she came to know one from another, and to shake off the shyness which had come over her in the presence of Ivor's mother and father, those two small, wizened people who had looked at her more oddly than any of the others. Both spoke enough English to communicate, and her ear was quick to pick up Welsh key-words, so that before long she was chattering away as freely as she did at home, and aware, with relief, that they had accepted her.

'But they think it very strange of us not to be married,' Ivor said. 'I think we should be, as soon as we can.'

'Yes, if only to be on the safe side,' Jannie said. 'They won't want any more little Pryses or Owains on their hands as soon as this. I suppose it takes months to get licences and banns and things?'

'No, not in the *capel*. My father will arrange it with the Minister.'

The Reverend Huw Evans was pleased to welcome what he hoped would be an addition to his flock, but sad to hear the couple he was to marry were returning to London. 'There's a pity, Ifor. I baptized you, I remember as though it were yesterday; I should like to have done the same for your children.'

'Perhaps you will – who knows?'

The Bryn ladies were astonished to find that Jannie had not brought any kind of wedding-dress with her. It had not even occurred to her, indeed, so anxious was she to forget the empty trappings of that other wedding. It was Marged, about Jannie's height but stouter, who suggested timidly: 'I have my own put away. I was not so fat when I married Twm. If you would like to try it, Sioned . . .' This was the nearest they could get to her name. She agreed happily; it was a plain, high-waisted, slightly old-fashioned gown of white sarsnet, the best material Mrs Bryn had been able to buy in Machynlleth. It made Jannie look demure, countrified, more like one of themselves, they agreed, admiring.

But Ivor was not allowed to see it until the morning when they stood together before the Reverend Evans in the austere little chapel in whose graveyard Ivor had once kept rendezvous with bold young girls. He looked solemn and dignified now, in respectable black lent by Emrys, and very pale indeed. The ceremony was conducted in English, out of consideration for the bride, but the two hymns were in Welsh, set to tunes of a wild melancholy beauty. Jannie was not sure whether she was more inclined to laugh or cry, but it would have been most unsuitable to do either, and she only smiled as she walked on her husband's arm down the aisle to the door, and along the path between the old grey graves.

There was a feast at the farmhouse; a great deal of good food, home-killed meat, bread from the stone ovens in the bakehouse and beautiful yellow butter, and *cwrw*, the potent local ale. A lot of serious eating, some pious toasts, and of course a prayer beforehand; what would Joey and the Bristow clan have made of such a solemn bridal? Yet afterwards, when the candles were lit and the *cwrw* began to take effect, it was amazing how old Dafydd's normally severe expression began to mellow, and how the rather stiff young men became loquacious and much fonder of their wives and sweethearts than they normally appeared to be. Ivor sat on a stool at his mother's feet, while she stroked his hair, remarking that the characteristic crest of it above his brow was exactly like her own father's, and that his son would probably have it, too.

Then Owain's wife Dilys went to the harp that stood hooded in the corner, the family *telyn*, and began to play ravishing, rippling melodies on it, singing *penillion* to them in a high sweet voice, like a veritable nymph of the Dovey that sang in the valley below; and Ivor asked her to play and sing *Mentra, Gwen*, which she did, while Jannie studied the ground and only when the song was over met Ivor's eyes with a burning blush, which everybody noticed and thought most fitting.

And at last, decorously early, the company went to their homes, leaving Mrs Bryn to show the bridal couple to the room that she herself had come to as a bride: because it had rough-cast walls and was cold, a fire burnt tonight in the hearth where fires had burnt in the times of the Tudors. In the large solid bed with its rust-coloured hangings many generations had mated, borne children, and died. A branch of bright rowan berries had been jammed into a stone jug in honour of the occasion. Ivor's mother kissed her son and his wife solemnly upon their brows, and left them.

Jannie went to the mullioned window and looked out at the lovely prospect; the river, half-hidden by September mist, the crags of Dinas Mawddy, the high green walls of the Ddolgoed mountains, the little white specks below that were late-cropping sheep. A shepherd's dog barked, and a bird flying overhead gave a long, shrilling call, again and again, on its way towards the sea.

Ivor touched her cheek gently. 'Don't cry. Why are you crying?'

She sniffed. 'I don't know . . . Yes, I do. Because I want this to be real. It's the most beautiful place . . . time . . . I've ever known. Everything else seems like a dream – dirty London, the mud and the smoke. Yes, and the stage, too. The flats and the lights and the paint. All false. I never, never, want to go back there.'

He tilted up her chin and scanned her eyes. 'They are real too, *cariad*. They have their place in our lives. Wasn't that how we came together? I am real, aren't I?'

She pinched his wrist, half-smiling. 'Yes.'

'But I am your Harlequin too. Do you never want to see him again?'

'Of course! I love him . . . you. Both of you.'

'And I love my Columbine, and my Sioned, and my Jannie, my wife. So you see everything is real, and we must take it as it comes. This is our dancing-time, while we're young. We have a living to make. After that, who knows? When London has finished with us the valley will still be here, and the farm and the acres. Perhaps we'll come back then.'

The tilted mirror on the dressing-chest caught their reflection in the dim light from the old green glass of the window and the flicker of the single candle at the bed's head; the grave-faced young Welshman in Sunday black, the wet-cheeked bride in her staid high-necked frock. For this short, idyllic time they would be no one but themselves, until the Benevolent Agent who rules Pantomime would transform them again into Harlequin and Columbine.